Seduced by a Sultan

Passion in the desert…

Seduced by a Sultan

CLIMAX OF PASSION
by
Emma Darcy

MISTRESS OF THE SHEIKH
by
Sandra Marton

HIS DESERT ROSE
by
Liz Fielding

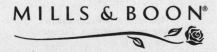

MILLS & BOON®

*All the characters in this book have no existence outside the imagination
of the author, and have no relation whatsoever to anyone bearing the
same name or names. They are not even distantly inspired by any
individual known or unknown to the author, and all the incidents are
pure invention.*

*MILLS & BOON and MILLS & BOON with the Rose Device
are registered trademarks of the publisher.
Harlequin Mills & Boon Limited,
Eton House, 18-24 Paradise Road, Richmond, Surrey, TW9 1SR*

SEDUCED BY A SULTAN
© by Harlequin Enterprises II B.V., 2004

Climax of Passion, Mistress of the Sheikh and *His Desert Rose*
were first published in Great Britain by Harlequin Mills & Boon
Limited in separate, single volumes.

Climax of Passion © Emma Darcy 1995
Mistress of the Sheikh © Sandra Myles 2000
His Desert Rose © Liz Fielding 2000

ISBN 0 263 84071 9

05-0604

*Printed and bound in Spain
by Litografia Rosés S.A., Barcelona*

Initially a French/English teacher, **Emma Darcy** changed careers to computer programming before marriage, motherhood, and the happy demands of keeping up with three lively sons and the very social life of her businessman husband, Frank. Very much a people person, and always interested in relationships, she finds the world of romance fiction a thrilling one and the challenge of creating her own cast of characters very addictive.

Don't miss Emma Darcy's latest sizzling story:
THE OUTBACK WEDDING TAKEOVER
Out now, in Modern Romance™!

CLIMAX OF PASSION
by
Emma Darcy

To Linda McQueen,
for her love of words
and getting it right

CHAPTER ONE

XA SHIRAQ was notable for many things.

The impression that most people took away with them was of a penetrating gaze that seemed to strip souls bare.

His eyes were stygian black and deeply socketed. It was said they could see through any duplicity. They could burn with the heat of the desert or be as cold and cutting as the wind from the topmost peaks of the Atlas Mountains in the freezing heart of winter. They revealed nothing, yet they knew everything.

He had not inherited the Shelkhdom of Xabia. He had won the right to rule through the sheer force of his will and character. He retained and increased his power by not letting anything escape his notice. His vigilance over matters that others might regard as of little consequence, was legendary. Its effect was that Xa Shiraq was never surprised. He had no intention of ever being surprised.

'Tell me about the geologist's daughter,' he commanded of Kozim, his closest aide.

'No...o...o, ah...problem,' came the habitual sing-song reply.

A slicing flash of black eyes was enough for Kozim to clear his throat and bring forth a flurry of detail.

'She is still at the hotel in Fisa, working front of house. She is in charge of reservations. There is a complaint lodged against her. She will not last.'

Xa Shiraq's long, supple fingers tapped a thoughtful rhythm on the armrest of his chair. 'Why did she take the position? Why has she stayed? With her qualifications she could have done better. It makes no sense unless my suspicion has substance. Each step... one step closer.'

'She has applied for a transfer to Bejos,' Kozim added as a possible point of interest.

'Ah!' It was the sound of satisfaction. 'So the purpose reveals itself beyond all reasonable doubt. She is a woman of remarkable determination.' He looked sharply at Kozim. 'If application is made for entry to Xabia, it is to be refused.'

'I will see to it immediately,' Kozim said with fervour, hiding his surprise at such a leap in anticipation.

'Never believe in coincidence, Kozim. Has the transfer to Bejos been granted?'

'No, Your Excellency. It was blocked by the assistant manager at Fisa.'

'For what reason?'

'He claims unsuitability on the grounds that she is a striking blonde and may draw troublesome attention at the Bejos hotel.' Kozim shrugged. 'That is what he says officially.'

'And unofficially?' the sheikh prompted.

'It is inferred that there are more personal reasons.'

The sheikh sat back, hooding his eyes. 'Correct me

if I'm wrong, but isn't the Fisa hotel one of the poorest performers in the Oasis chain?'

'You are not wrong, Your Excellency,' Kozim quickly assured him. 'It has one of the lowest occupancy rates.'

'There have been a number of complaints about the hotel,' the sheikh said broodingly.

Kozim didn't know of any. His ignorance did not disturb him. It was not unusual for him not to know what the sheikh knew. Xa Shiraq had many sources of information.

The fingers tapped again. 'I will act. I can kill two birds with one arrow.'

Kozim had no idea what the sheikh meant, but he was glad he was not going to be on the receiving end of the arrow that would undoubtedly reach its targets with deadly accuracy. He was glad he had no connection whatsoever to the running of the Oasis Hotel at Fisa. He was glad he was not the geologist's daughter.

CHAPTER TWO

AMANDA Buchanan thought she had developed a thick enough skin to withstand most of the put-down jokes that came her way. Normally, she let them flow past her like water off a duck's back. After all, she had been born with three strikes against her. Her mother had been Polish, her father Irish, and she was a natural blonde.

The latest rash of 'dumb blonde' jokes was the most belittling she had so far encountered. It was almost enough to drive her into dying her hair black. Her stubborn sense of self-worth, however, would not countenance any backing off from who and what she was. Apart from which, it would give her snide detractors the satisfaction of knowing they had got to her.

One day, she vowed, she would make a lot of people eat their words. Not only on her own account, but on her father's. Amanda wasn't quite sure how she was going to achieve that end, but working for the Oasis chain of hotels had seemed a likely step in the right direction. What she needed to do was get into a high level management position which might...just might...open the door to where she wanted to go.

In the meantime, she had to grit her teeth and suffer

the assistant manager's malicious manner and spite in putting her down in every possible way he could conceive.

She knew why he did it. It was a payback for her lack of interest in him as a man. Charles Arnold combined a huge ego with small performance. His principal aim in life was to downgrade everybody to his own level so that he could feel superior. He had no idea how badly it reflected on himself and on his job.

If Amanda had been willing to accommodate him, his attitude and that of the male staff would have been very different. A shudder of revulsion ran through her at the mere thought of submitting to Charles Arnold's touch. That was never going to happen, no matter what subtle or unsubtle pressure he brought to bear. As it was, the other staff took their lead from him, having their bit of 'fun' with her, knowing they were completely safe from any complaint of harassment.

There was only one person who could have fixed the situation for Amanda, and that was the vague, shadowy figure of Xa Shiraq, the owner of the Oasis chain. It was said that he held all the key decisions regarding personnel in his own hands. He was never around. He was never seen. There were doubts he really existed.

Amanda knew better. When her father lay dying in her arms, revealing what had happened in halting, stumbling words...it left no doubt in Amanda's mind that Xa Shiraq existed.

This was the third Oasis Hotel Amanda had worked

in. The mysterious owner had not once made an appearance at any of them. Promotions and sackings were done by impersonal faxes, never in person. Despite this lack of any substantial evidence of his actual presence, her father's assurance and certainty had convinced Amanda that Xa Shiraq was indeed flesh and blood reality.

Her belief, however, was of no help to her in her present situation. It was difficult to keep her cool while she burned with the injustice of what was happening to her, but Amanda was determined not to put a foot wrong.

Soon, very soon, she hoped, her transfer to the Oasis Hotel in Bejos would come through. Then she would be one step closer to her real goal, one more step removed from her persecutors. Charles Arnold and his minions would then become so much flotsam that she could jettison from her life.

A telephone call claimed her attention. She lifted the receiver and projected a pleasant, welcoming note into her voice. 'Good morning. The Oasis Hotel. Reservations.'

'Is the Presidential Suite available tonight?' a male voice inquired without preamble.

'Just a moment, sir, I'll check it on the computer.'

Amanda knew perfectly well that the most expensive suite in the hotel was vacant. In the five months she had worked here, it had been occupied only seven times. On every one of these occasions it had been given to bridal couples on a one-night complimentary basis as an inducement for the booking of the wedding reception. No-one had paid good money for it. This was not something the hotel management wanted broadcast to the rest of the world.

'Yes, sir, it is available,' she said after a suitable pause. 'For how long would you like to make a reservation?'

'For how long will it be available?'

Amanda chose an encouraging reply. 'We would do our very best to ensure you have undisturbed occupancy for as long as you require.'

There was no response. The click of a receiver being quietly replaced sent a highly disquieting tingle down Amanda's spine. Had someone been testing her, checking that she was not too free with information about bookings? There had been one fabricated complaint lodged against her, engineered by Charles Arnold to demonstrate the cost of his displeasure.

She assured herself there had been nothing to criticise in her handling of the call. If anyone had been playing funny games she'd given them no rope to hang her with. Nevertheless, the incident nagged at her mind long after she should have dismissed it.

It was the voice that had made her think the caller was genuine in his inquiry about the Presidential Suite. A hard, distinctive voice with a ring of arrogance about it. The kind of voice one instinctively associated with a position of power or wealth. A voice that expected requests to be automatically carried out to the letter, yet lacking any trace of the spoilt petulance that came from people born to riches.

It had been rude of him, though, to leave her hanging like that on the telephone. The courtesy of a 'Thank you' would have cost him nothing. Amanda decided if she ever met the man behind that voice, she would know him immediately. She knew how she would treat him, too.

While giving him all the courtesy and attention demanded by her job, she would maintain considerable reserve, aplomb, dignity and aloofness. A rueful smile flitted over her lips. More likely than not, he wouldn't notice her manner. He was probably the type of person who didn't acknowledge anyone who was not his peer.

A busload of tourists trailed in en masse for a three-night stopover. Charles Arnold put in an officious appearance, extolling the facilities of the hotel to the tour leader. Amanda helped with the process of checking everyone in and dispensing room keys.

She saw the man come in.

He emerged from the huge revolving door that gave entrance to the foyer and paused, taking in the melee around the front desk. There was something about him that arrested Amanda's attention. Not his clothes. They were unremarkable; a white open-necked shirt, beige linen jacket, brown trousers. Not his looks. She had seen more handsome men. He was tall and lean, like an athlete honed to perfection. Amanda had seen that before with the Olympic Games team.

It was his stillness, his ability to concentrate and focus his full attention that was unusual. He observed the crowd of tourists and the piles of luggage strewn around the foyer in careless disarray. Amanda knew immediately that if he had been tour leader there would have been no carelessness and no disarray.

The signs of contempt in his eyes and on his face were marginal, but they were there. He was a man born to organise—people, places, things. He absorbed everything down to the minutest detail.

Amanda found his intensity disquieting. Making judgements, she thought, and not favorable ones.

'Have any messages come in for me? My name is...'

Amanda smiled at the woman who had addressed her and obligingly checked for messages. When she darted another glance at the man, she found he had moved to the lounge setting beside the fountain. He was seated in an armchair that faced the reception desk. He had not picked up a newspaper or magazine to idle away the time. He was watching Charles Arnold's effusive performance with the tour leader in the same way as a hawk watched a sparrow.

Again Amanda was struck by his stillness. Very few people could control and maintain immobility for more than a few seconds. It took the kind of discipline and training of both mind and body that Amanda associated with the ceremonial guards outside Windsor Castle in England. Yet she felt intuitively that this was not a man who took orders. He gave them. He was waiting…waiting for the right moment to take command.

It was difficult to guess his age. He had taut, smooth, dark olive skin stretched over strongly delineated bones; skin unmarked, unblemished, like polished wood—an ageless face.

There was no grey in his black hair. It was thick and straight and shiny, as shiny as his deeply set black eyes. He had certainly reached the age of maturity but whether he was as young as thirty or a decade or more older, Amanda found it impossible to decide.

Handsome was not the right word for him. He was distinctive. Her mind kept coming back to *commanding* as she dealt with other requests and inquiries from the party of tourists. He was also disturbing. Very disturbing. So disturbing that Amanda had a serious difficulty in tearing her eyes away from him.

Briefly he caught her glance, held it, and dismissed it.

Amanda's heart skipped a beat. By the intense application of willpower she managed to wrest her attention back to what she was supposed to be doing. What had happened was more than disturbing. She had never reacted like this before in her life.

The worst part of the situation was that Amanda was convinced that this man, this outsider, this stranger had read every thought that had flashed through her mind. He knew, and understood, and did not care. He had come across similar situations many times in his life.

She was nothing new to him. No-one to hold his interest. Amanda was used to put-downs. It was silly to let it hurt, yet for some unfathomable reason, coming from him, it did.

His attention had switched back to Charles Arnold. His stillness was minimally broken. The fingers of his right hand began to tap across the end of the armrest in a steadily paced rhythm as though he was counting.

The tour leader called for attention and gave schedule details, stipulating the time for the next group meeting in the foyer. The crowd dispersed, picking up luggage, heading for the elevators and the rooms allotted to them.

Amanda automatically tensed as Charles Arnold chose to join her behind the front desk, a look of smug satisfaction centered on his face. 'Well, that should put the numbers up. What's the intake for today, Mandy?'

Amanda gritted her teeth and pressed the keys to bring up the total on the computer. She hated the way he drawled his version of her name, making her sound like some brainless kewpie doll. She also hated the way he crowded her as he looked over her shoulder at the monitor screen, not exactly touching, but only a breath away. A hot breath. A breath that made her skin crawl.

'Not bad,' he commented. 'I've done well. A pity everyone else can't do as well. Now do a breakdown on singles, doubles and suites.'

Her fingers faltered and stopped as she had the

strangest feeling of being gripped by some alien force. She looked up. The man from the armchair was walking towards the desk, his black eyes focused directly on her, giving her more concentrated attention, seeming to absorb all that she was.

Amanda's heart skittered into a faster beat. He hadn't dismissed her, after all. She could not help wondering what he saw, how she was adding up in his mind, how he would attempt to organise her.

He probably thought her a soft pale creature compared to himself. Although her fair complexion had acquired a light golden tan in the tropical sunshine at Fisa, this only tended to accentuate the bright clarity of her aquamarine eyes, and made her long ash-blonde hair look whiter than it was, especially against the black suit that was the standard hotel uniform for her position.

Amanda was no fragile flower, but her facial features did have a delicate femininity, and she was slender and softly curved. Her physical appearance gave many men, men like Charles Arnold, the impression that she would be malleable and easy to manage. Amanda was quite happy for them to think so. Until such time as they crossed her mental line of what she considered wrong for her, anyone could think what they liked.

'I have not been attended to.'

The sharp, demanding edge to the stranger's voice made the statement sound like the most culpable crime against responsibility since the captain of the *Titanic* ordered full steam ahead.

Amanda's fanciful speculations came to a dead halt. Her mind did an abrupt about-turn. She knew that voice. She had already heard it once today. *This man owed her an apology for his rudeness on the telephone.*

Charles Arnold gave the gentleman a perfunctory glance. 'Everyone has to take their turn here, sir,' he said brightly. 'We'll be with you in just a moment.'

In typically arrogant dismissal of anyone who impinged on his personal priorities, Charles turned back to Amanda. 'Well, get on with it. The figures, please, Mandy,' he urged. Then in an insultingly condescending tone, he instructed, 'Put your finger on the Enter key and...'

'No! You will not touch the Enter key.'

The tone of absolute authority shivered through the air-conditioned atmosphere. Amanda had been right about one thing. The owner of the voice did not like having his orders disobeyed. He probably had an intense dislike for the word 'no', as well. Unless it was he who was using it.

She did her best to retrieve the situation. 'We have a new arrival, Mr Arnold,' she stated quietly. 'Perhaps we could attend to him first.'

She flashed the stranger a quick glance, all ideas of aloofness, reserve, dignity and aplomb forgotten for the moment. She could not afford to have another complaint lodged against her. Her look carried a simple message. It said, please be aware that you are placing me in a difficult situation.

The man's eyelids lowered fractionally for the briefest of moments, as if he had received her message, understood it completely, but nothing would divert him from the course of action he had chosen.

'Don't give me your dizzy blonde act, Mandy,' Charles Arnold said, having missed the byplay between Amanda and the newly arrived guest. 'These figures are important to me. My next promotion depends on them.'

'I will have the Presidential Suite.'

That arrested Charles Arnold's attention. Amanda hadn't told him about the earlier inquiry. A paying customer in the Presidential Suite was a feather in any management cap. The dangling prize effected a complete reversal of attitude in Charles Arnold.

'You are very welcome, sir.'

Pure smarmy syrup, Amanda thought, barely hiding her disgust as the sucking up act began.

'We will attend to your every need immediately. Most regrettable that you've been kept waiting. If you'd alerted us earlier... However, we shall make generous amends. A porter for your luggage, sir? Any special refreshment you'd like in your suite? I'll have your butler rung so it can be delivered while we... uh...take reservation details. Your name, sir?'

'It is not necessary for you to know my name.' It was a cold rebuff. The stranger, who was apparently intent on remaining a stranger, withdrew a folded sheet of paper from the inner pocket of his sports jacket and tossed it onto the desk. 'This is all you need to know.'

Amanda watched Charles Arnold unfold the paper. It was thick, creamy, expensive. Her breath caught in her throat as she saw the emblem at the top of the page. She was not in a position to read the typed lines underneath, but that notepaper, that emblem, represented the man she most wanted to reach.

She had seen it before amongst her father's papers...the personal insignia of the Sheikh of Xabia...a gyrfalcon at full wing, its talons poised ready to strike.

Her stomach seemed to turn over. Despite a sudden and debilitating feeling of weakness in her bones, Amanda forced herself to look once more at the commanding, ageless face in front of her. Was he...could he possibly be...Xa Shiraq himself?

CHAPTER THREE

No sooner had the electric thought gripped Amanda's mind, than a wash of common sense defused it. No way would Xa Shiraq arrive at any hotel as casually as this man had, or dressed as this man was. The Sheikh of Xabia would have a retinue, bodyguard. He wouldn't wait for anything. He'd be waited on hand and foot!

'This isn't signed,' Charles Arnold said huffily. 'Anyone could have typed those words. I do not consider it an authorisation to give you complimentary use of our Presidential Suite. Unless you can produce more than that, sir...' he tossed the page back onto the desk in contemptuous rejection '...you are wasting our time.'

It gave Amanda the opportunity to read what was written on the page. The message was short and succinct.

By order of Xa Shiraq, the bearer of this note is entitled to have any request within my jurisdiction fulfilled.

Her mind dizzied again with the enormity of what was happening in front of her. This man was certainly not Xa Shiraq but he had to be important to have such

a note. He could be one of Xa Shiraq's three great
supporters, all military men who by their loyalty and
skill had helped Xa Shiraq win the sheikhdom in the
first place. There was Jebel Haffa and…

Amanda took a deep breath. She pulled her mind
into order. This man could lead her to one of her
primary goals, the secretive and elusive Xa Shiraq
himself.

'You question its authenticity?' The icy sting in his
voice was not propitious to any pact of friendship.

'Naturally a man in my position of authority has to
do so,' Charles Arnold observed coldly.

On the surface, it was a reasonable statement. It
was true, Amanda reflected, that anyone with access
to that particular notepaper could have written the letter. The hotel had discreet procedures for checking
authenticity and credit ratings for guests. These procedures should now be followed.

'Perhaps…' she began.

Charles Arnold cut her short. 'The figures please,
Mandy.'

He turned back to the stranger, intent on cutting
this arrogant foreigner down to his own level.
Amanda had seen it all before. 'As I've already said,
anyone could have typed this order…'

'Who would dare?'

The challenge sent a quiver through Amanda. Her
gaze flew up to the hard commanding face. This man
had to be close to Xa Shiraq. Very close. And his
eyes missed nothing. How could she possibly get

close to him? Yet if she could... must...her pulse quickened. Given half an opportunity...and she would leap at it.

'I will not fall prey to a cheap confidence trick,' Charles Arnold scoffed, losing control of the situation but reasserting his sense of superiority.

To reinforce it even further, he picked up the type-written authorisation, held it gingerly by one corner as though it were contaminated, slowly drifted it to a position above the disposal bin, then released his grip. The letter floated down to join the rest of the garbage paper in the bin.

'That,' said Charles Arnold with satisfaction, 'is what I think of that.' As far as he was concerned, he had just won his encounter with the stranger.

The stranger said nothing. The black blaze of his eyes would have incinerated most people but his tar-get was cocooned in self-importance. He lifted a hand. Amanda prayed for more time. The hand moved up to shoulder height as though he intended to slap it onto the counter. But it did not descend.

A man loitering near the fountain moved abruptly into a brisk walk towards the desk. He wore a black suit and carried a black leather attaché case. Amanda recognised him as a guest who had booked in two days ago, a Mr Kozim from Bejos, a rather portly, middle-aged man, darker in skin tone than the stranger in front of her and more obviously of Middle Eastern origins.

He came to a halt beside the stranger who then

lowered his hand but did not so much as glance at the man who had responded to his signal. Mr Kozim placed his attaché case on the desk, opened it, removed a typed page with the letterhead of the Oasis chain, and passed it to Charles Arnold.

'For legal purposes you will find that document is signed by Jebel Haffa,' the stranger stated bitingly. 'I hope you will recognise his signature.'

Charles Arnold began sputtering. 'What is the meaning of this? It can't be...'

'It means that as of this moment you are relieved of your duties as assistant manager of this hotel,' came the hard, relentless reply. 'You are no longer employed here. You have no further involvement with the Oasis chain.'

'We'll see about that,' Charles Arnold blustered. 'I'm calling the general manager.'

'That would be expedient.'

Amanda reached for the phone. Charles Arnold beat her to it. This call was too important to be entrusted to a menial like Amanda.

Charles Arnold protested his fate in acrimonious terms.

Amanda's mind whirled.

Charles Arnold had given her hell. He had fabricated a complaint against her. He had harassed and hounded her, belittled and demeaned her, persecuted her to the limits of endurance.

The stranger had told her not to do it.

She ignored the order.

Amanda's need to even the score between herself and Charles Arnold was a stronger force.

She pressed the Enter key.

She turned to face Charles Arnold directly, her gaze level, her voice level, her manner civil and courteous, her bearing reserved, dignified and aloof.

'You wanted these figures, sir,' she said evenly. 'For your promotion, sir.'

'You dumb stupid blonde bitch!' Charles Arnold snorted like a chained killer dog deprived of its prey.

'I'm sorry I'm a dumb stupid blonde bitch, sir,' she said, taking intense pride in appearing totally unruffled. There was no way Charles Arnold could ever hurt her again. She had given him the *coup de grâce*. There would be no festering wounds left over from this encounter. She would not spend any more nights blistering over her resentments at his petty tyranny.

She turned slowly towards the stranger and caught the look in his eyes. It took her breath away. She had seen desire before in men's eyes. Occasionally she had seen lust. She had never before confronted a message of such blazing conviction. *I want you*, his eyes said. *I'll have you. And what I have I keep*.

She saw it, felt it, yet it was over in an instant. A shutter snapped closed. The blaze was gone, replaced by impenetrable darkness.

The muscles of her stomach clenched. Her thighs tightened in response. Her eyelids dropped fractionally as his own had done previously, but her facade of cool composure did not falter.

The stranger and Mr Kozim ignored every word uttered by Charles Arnold. Like water off a duck's back, Amanda thought. Xa Shiraq's hatchet man and his secretary had probably arranged this scene long before it was enacted.

She felt no sympathy for Charles Arnold. After his persecution of her, he deserved none. She was relieved at his removal from the staff.

The general manager made his entrance, coming in behind the front desk to line up beside his chief assistant and lend authoritative support. 'What is the problem?' he demanded in frowning inquiry.

'Did you employ this man?' Mr Kozim asked, pointing at Charles Arnold.

'I most certainly did,' the manager replied happily.

'Here is an official letter, relieving you of your position and responsibilities within the Oasis chain,' Mr Kozim said affably. He reached inside his briefcase, scanned the contents of a letter, and passed it to the general manager. 'You will note it is signed by Jebel Haffa,' Mr Kozim added idly.

'You...you can't do this...' The words stuttered out.

'It's done,' the voice of the stranger cut in peremptorily.

'But you have no senior management left...you'll need us.'

'It has been taken care of. Miss Buchanan...' His gaze swung to her.

Amanda was astonished. 'You know my name.'

'I know *everything*,' he said with becoming modesty, 'that is important to me.'

Amanda pulled herself together. 'Yes, sir,' she said with becoming deference. 'I'm sure you do.'

'Miss Buchanan, there is a letter for you.' The stranger nodded to Mr Kozim whose hand dived into the attaché case.

Amanda's heart sank. The fabricated complaint had served its purpose. Her future plans were shattered, her goals more unattainable than ever.

She noted the triumphant smirk on Charles Arnold's face. Despite his immense chagrin at his own predicament, nothing diluted his pleasure in bringing someone else down.

She forced herself to take the letter. Her hands felt nerveless, divorced from her body. The words printed on the page were scrambled and incomprehensible. She concentrated her attention, and deciphered what was written.

By the order of Xa Shiraq, Miss Amanda Buchanan is appointed general manager of the Oasis Hotel at Fisa, commencing at 3 o'clock on...

The date followed, and beneath the date was the signature of Jebel Haffa.

Her hand trembled at the import of that briefly stated command. Her eyes flew to the wall clock. It was exactly three o'clock. Clockwork precision. A little masterpiece of organisation and planning, everything accounted for.

'Your new assistants will arrive within the hour.'

Her gaze swung back to the man who served Xa Shiraq with such unswerving commitment to his orders. He did not ask her whether she would take the job. He knew she would.

'Kozim, you will accompany these two gentlemen to their respective offices in order to clear their desks,' was his next command.

Amanda watched them go, their numb disbelief equalled only by her own.

'You have two minutes to effect a temporary reorganisation.' This command was directed at her, galvanising her attention. The black eyes glinted with unyielding purpose. 'Then you will escort me to the Presidential Suite.'

'Very well, sir,' Amanda said with all the aplomb she could muster. She had to think quickly. The front desk had to be restaffed. The rest could wait.

She dialled the office secretary. 'Please come and fill in at the front desk,' she commanded. The man in front of her, listening to what was going on, was ruthless.

She met resistance. 'That's not in my job description.'

'If you're not here in one minute you won't have a job.'

'Mr Arnold said...'

'Mr Arnold has been relieved of all duties.'

Amanda put the receiver down. Next was house-keeping. She organised butler service for the Presidential Suite. She commandeered an affable young waiter for the front desk in case the secretary didn't turn up.

There was something else she had to do. She had to find out the name of the man in front of her, and what his connection was to Xa Shiraq.

Amanda headed for the computer. 'What name will I use for your reservation, sir?' she asked sweetly.

'Complimentary Upgrade,' he replied laconically.

Amanda could play word games too. Some boldness was called for if she was to get what she wanted. 'Very good, sir. That's no trouble, sir. First name is Complimentary, surname is Upgrade.' She typed the letters out on the keyboard, glanced up at him to see how he took that.

A quirk at the corner of his mouth told her he found it rather droll.

'Your reservation is complete, sir. I'm now ready to escort you to the Presidential Suite.'

He looked at his wristwatch. 'That's very good, Miss Buchanan. You had ten seconds to spare.'

'In that case, sir, I'll use the time to assemble the paperwork relating to this afternoon's activities.'

Amanda hurriedly assembled all the letters lying around. The men had not bothered to take their dismissal notices with them. She deposited them in the bottom of the cashier's register. They would be safe there until she could find time to get back to them.

'Time's up.'

There was no demand in his voice, nothing peremptory. Amanda knew as well as he did she had satisfied every demand he had placed upon her. So far. How long that would last...

'Do you have any luggage?'

'None that is of concern to the hotel.'

'Thank you, Mr Upgrade,' she challenged him. 'It's my pleasure to escort you to your suite.'

He looked at her in reassessment, decided to let the challenge go unremarked.

'I hope it will be a pleasure, Miss Buchanan,' he said mildly. 'A great pleasure.'

Amanda looked at him again. A prickle of danger ran down her spine. She was quite certain that the pleasure Upgrade had in his mind was not identical to the pleasure she had in hers. She needed to get close to this man, but not *that* close!

CHAPTER FOUR

HE HAD stipulated nine o'clock.

Amanda paced her room, waiting for the last few minutes to tick by before she had to face the man in the Presidential Suite again. She felt too on edge to sit down. Impossible to relax. So much depended upon what happened in the next hour.

He was a reasonable man, she assured herself. He hadn't tried to detain her this afternoon. He had not said anything suggestive, nor made any move that could be interpreted as taking a liberty. He had agreed she had many pressing duties as the new general manager…and in the same breath, made this appointment for a discussion on her future.

Nine o'clock was not an unreasonable time. It had given her six hours to deal with whatever problems arose from the shock departure of the senior management and her startling promotion to the top rank. Implicit in that choice of hour, however, was the understanding that Amanda's time was his, free of all interruptions. Amanda could not fool herself that he only wanted to talk business with her.

She couldn't forget that brief blaze of searing desire this afternoon. She couldn't deny the fascination

30

he exerted on her. She was going to be in deep trouble if he rejected the schedule she had set in place.

Surely, as a reasonable man, he would accept what she had arranged. All the preparations had been made. She had covered every contingency. He couldn't take offence at what she had done for him and it gave her a smooth getaway.

The only problem was…she had never met anyone like this man before. He affected her in ways…but there was no future in dwelling on that. If she gave in to this…attraction…compulsion…she would end up in his power, and where would that lead?

Amanda shook her head. It was too dangerous. However tempting it was to have the experience, to know all that *he* was, she had no doubt it would mean ceding control to him. And that she would not do.

Her decisions were made. She could not afford to waver from her chosen course. She had to seize the authority she now had and use it while time was still on her side. It was daring, so daring her heart had been pumping overtime ever since she had thought of it. Once she started there could be no stopping, no turning back. Her actions would be irreversible.

But first she had to face *him*.

She checked her watch. It was time to move. Punctuality was mandatory. She left her room and headed for the elevators. Her legs felt shaky. She steeled her mind to cope with the situation. She only had to get through one hour with him. She could keep her wits about her for one short hour.

She took deep, calming breaths as she rode up to the top floor. Her legs were much steadier on her walk to the door of the Presidential Suite. It was precisely nine o'clock as she pressed the buzzer to announce her arrival.

The door clicked open. 'Good evening,' she said to the butler.

'I'm just leaving, Miss Buchanan. I've served the champagne.'

'Thank you,' she said on a note of resignation. The butler had obviously been given his orders. Mr Complimentary Upgrade meant to have her to himself, no third party around to inhibit whatever he wanted to happen between them.

The butler stood aside to let her through, and then, empty tray in hand, made his departure.

Amanda was immediately aware that the rooms beyond the vestibule were dimly lit. Champagne...soft lights...but the Presidential Suite was very large. Like a penthouse really. She had plenty of space to move around in.

Besides, this man was not the type to rush anything. Not something he wanted. He would wait patiently, wanting it all precisely as he planned it. Step by step. Relentless and ruthless in his execution.

Amanda shivered, then took firm control of herself. Nothing was going to happen that she didn't want to happen. Determined to hold her own against this disturbing man, she set forth into the living room, back straight, chin up, a brave smile of confidence hovering on her lips. She felt rather foolish when he wasn't there to greet her.

The table lamps on either side of the white leather lounge setting were switched on. Spotlit by one was a silver ice bucket containing a bottle of champagne. The cork had been removed and the sparkling fluid poured into two crystal flute glasses.

Amanda's hands clenched. If he was about to appear in something *more comfortable*...

'The stars are brightly shining tonight.'

Amanda almost jumped. His voice was enough of a magnet to draw her gaze instantly to where he stood at the far end of the room, a darker shadow amongst the shadows beyond the long expanse of glass that faced the balcony.

It made Amanda acutely conscious of being in a pool of light, of having been observed without her knowledge. He would have noted she was still in her black suit, noted the body language that revealed her inner tension, and had probably already decided how best to deal with the situation. She felt at a distinct disadvantage.

'It's a good omen,' he said softly. 'I like watching the stars.'

'Do you? I find a great deal of pleasure...' Amanda began, rushing into speech to cover her disquiet, then wishing she'd held her tongue. Pleasure was a word she did not wish to use tonight. 'There is a grandeur and sweep to it,' she acknowledged, trying to put the conversation on an impersonal level.

He left the shadows and strolled towards her, projecting a totally relaxed manner. Amanda was relieved to see he was fully dressed although he had changed his clothes. He wore black. Easier to merge with the night, Amanda thought. Then she saw the sheen of silk in his shirt and knew that his choice had more to do with sensuality than darkness. It was an invitation to touch, to feel, to lose herself in a night with him.

He paused at the table where the drinks were laid out. 'I have taken the liberty of ordering some Dom Perignon to celebrate your promotion,' he said with a smile that was both whimsical and seductive. 'Will you partake of a glass with me?'

He was already having an intoxicating effect on her...a man of mystery, of immense fascination. She couldn't risk heightening it by any relaxation of her defences. 'I don't drink when I'm on duty,' she said quickly.

'And I don't drink at all,' he said slowly. 'Nevertheless, these are challenging times in which we live, Miss Buchanan.'

He picked up the two glasses and brought them to her, standing close, making her extremely conscious of her vulnerable femininity. Something primitive pulsed from this man. It was muted by the civilised clothes, the civilised manner, yet her every instinct recognised the barbarian in him, the hunter, the conqueror, the possessor.

Amanda had the sense, the feeling of potent danger.

He was so vibrant, so intensely alive, as though he thrived on challenge, as though it was meat and drink to him, the very essence of life.

'Let us dare to break our own rules,' he tempted softly, his eyes engaging hers with mesmerising directness.

She had to speak, to keep him talking. Only words could battle the effect he was having on her and keep him at a distance. 'Wouldn't that be flirting with chaos? You struck me as a man who appreciates and demands order, Mr Upgrade.'

'Chaos can be brought into order, if the will is strong enough.'

'Do as you will, but I shall not put my sense of order at risk. I prefer to keep my promotion than lose it on a glass of champagne.'

One black eyebrow arched quizzically. 'Surely you make something out of nothing.'

'I find it somewhat surprising that I was chosen for the position of general manager. That was something out of nothing.'

'Call it impulse.'

'With an already signed letter from Jebel Haffa?'

'Xa Shiraq provides for all contingencies.'

'Was it your... impulse...or that of Xa Shiraq?'

He smiled as if at some secret irony. 'All was provided for. You need to know nothing more.'

'What does Xa Shiraq know of me?' she asked boldly.

'Everything and nothing.'

'Can you stop speaking in paradoxes and talk directly?'

He laughed softly, completely in control of the situation. 'Yes and no,' he replied.

Amanda realised he was toying with her, deliberately provoking her, inciting her to some rash step. She was equally determined not to be provoked, not to be played or toyed with, not to take some hasty, rash step.

'An admirable response,' she retorted dryly, 'which answers all my questions.'

He hadn't expected that. He eyed her again, let his gaze slide down her body, then turned aside to set the glasses back on the table, having abandoned any further thought of pressing the champagne on her and apparently not inclined to drink by himself. 'I believe what I see and feel. I believe in myself, Miss Buchanan,' he said quietly.

The light from the table lamp played over his chin and cheekbones and she thought he had the kind of profile that had once been struck on ancient coins, a noble, immortal face. Then he straightened up and the illusion was lost in the vital furnace of his eyes, desire that curled around her, encompassed her, and tugged on something basic inside her that made Amanda feel alarmingly out of control.

'As deeply and with as much conviction as you believe in yourself, and in what you see and feel,' he said, his voice a low velvet throb.

How did he know that? Could he see into her mind and heart?

'You judge character quickly, Mr Upgrade,' she remarked, knowing she must keep him talking, keep him at a safe distance.

His hands were free now, free to touch…and if he touched… She felt her skin yearning for it, her palms itching for it. Never before had her body reacted like this to a man, and she didn't even know who he was. Didn't want to know. If he gave her his name, his identity, she suspected that would make him a more powerful memory. Unforgettable.

'One look at a person and much is revealed. You were described to me as a striking blonde. That suggests certain images. None of them was accurate.'

'How do you judge me?' she asked, too intrigued not to satisfy her curiosity.

'To you, purpose outweighs feminine vanity. You have no desire to heighten sexual attraction. You are sensual. Your hair is long, beautifully fair, and uncompromisingly straight. That strengthens your charisma. Frequent visits to a hairdressing salon do not interest you. The fringe is neat and tidy. From that I conclude it is an easy solution to keeping the long fall from intruding on your face. There is no artifice or disguise. Your vision is not obscured. Practical. Efficient. You think of yourself as a person first, a woman second. Your inner needs are more important to you than drawing attention from men. An admirable quality indeed.'

Amanda was stunned by the truths he had so easily perceived. She had gone past the point of wanting to attract men. She had concluded years ago, after a number of disillusioning disappointments, that if a Mr Right did come along, it would happen quite naturally without any need for her to do anything except be herself.

She was not desperate for a man. She had other things to do that were important to her. And she was not about to let *this* man stand in her way, no matter how fascinating she found him. He could not be right for her even though…no, it was impossible.

'Are you a hairdresser by trade, Mr Upgrade?' she mocked at him, trying to restore her equilibrium.

'I have shorn many sheep,' he mocked back, 'but none as fair as you.'

'If you see so much in hair, what do you make of my eyes?'

'When they look upon me and shine as brightly as the stars do tonight, I will tell you. In the meantime, let us concentrate upon the draping of your hair down to the soft, supple swell of your breasts…'

His gaze followed his words and Amanda had the prickling sensation of her nipples pushing against the lace fabric of her bra. The lace felt tight, constrictive, abrasive. She wondered what it would be like having his hands cupping her swelling breasts and was shocked at the vividness of the image that leapt into her mind, the darker tone of his skin against hers, those long lean fingers closing over her soft flesh, caressing her, sensitising her.

She gave herself a mental shake and was grateful that the black suit was not so form-fitting that he could see the effect he was having on her. 'You judge much from my appearance, Mr Upgrade,' she said dismissively, needing the distraction of some other subject, yet failing to bring her mind to focus on anything other than what he was making her feel.

His eyes simmered up to hers. 'Salome used seven veils to seduce a king's mind. I think you would only need one.'

'I'm not a dancer,' she stated firmly. Nor was she going to try.

He ignored her interjection, pressing the image in his mind into hers. 'A veil in shimmering shades of blue and green and silver...translucent. To match your eyes.'

'My eyes aren't silver,' she said pettishly.

'They are like crystal over water, reflecting many facets, tantalising glimpses of what lies behind them.'

Instinctively Amanda lowered her lashes, afraid of revealing too much, not realising how provocative the action was.

'Ah, yes...the strength of mind is greater,' he said with satisfaction, walking towards her again, diminishing the space between them. 'But it is encased in a woman's body. A body I could bend to my will.'

She stiffened as he reached touching distance. Every nerve in her body twanged with tension, whether from anticipation, excitement or fear, she did not know.

He stopped. 'You have nothing to fear from me, Miss Buchanan.'

She wasn't at all sure of that. She could feel his power draining what strength she had. Her impulses were going haywire.

'I give freely, generously—to the right people,' he said persuasively.

By what standard did he judge the *right* people? Her father had not been considered a *right* person by Xa Shiraq, and since this man carried out Xa Shiraq's orders, perhaps he had been the one who ensured her father's unique discovery went discredited in the eyes of the rest of the world.

'Measure yourself against me,' he invited. 'You are smaller, softer, more slender. Women were made to be partnered by men. They need a man to stand by them, protect them, look after them.'

'An old-fashioned idea,' Amanda protested. 'No longer appropriate.'

'A physical reality. Never dismiss the physical strength of a man and the pleasure it can give, Miss Buchanan. However steely your will, it is not proof against it.'

'Why do you feel it is necessary to tell me what I know?' Amanda asked, holding her ground with increasing difficulty.

'Because you are denying what is self-evident. Mind over matter. But I know what you are feeling,

Miss Buchanan. Whether you choose to indulge yourself or not.' His black eyes burned into hers. 'I know what you are feeling. I feel it, too. I think we both will always feel it. And remember it.'

'How can you be so sure?' Her voice was a bare husky whisper.

'Because I have never felt it before,' he murmured.

Her eyes warred with his, fighting the link of intimacy he was forging with her. Amanda was certain of one thing. If she succumbed to this man she would never be herself again. He would dominate. She knew he would. He was that kind of person.

He suddenly laughed and turned aside. 'It is a joke, is it not? A man of my age and experience...to be touched...by you...of all women. Yet touched I am... and there will be a resolution to it, Miss Amanda Buchanan. We have met...as perhaps we were always destined to meet.'

Amanda found her breath whooshing out of her lungs as she watched him stroll to the floor-length windows. Her knees were jelly. She wanted to sag onto the nearest lounge. Only a desperate determination to show no weakness kept her upright. Her dazed mind broke out of its enthralment and groped towards a need to understand this man who touched her in ways she had not thought possible.

'How old are you?'

He did not answer immediately. He stared out at the night sky. 'Sometimes I feel as old as the stars...'

slowly he turned to look at her again '…but you stir my youth.'

'So you are both young and old.'

'Yes.'

'I am not of your race or culture,' she reminded him.

His words…*you, of all women*…were still ringing in her ears. He knew as well as she did that a liaison between them would give rise to many problems. Yet she could not deny a thrill of pleasure that she had stirred the youth of this man, more particularly as it was against his will.

'Does that matter? Are we not beyond race and culture?'

'There have been other men in my life.'

He shrugged. 'None that you will remember.'

'I'm not a virgin.'

'How unusual!' His lips curled in a humourless smile. 'Nor am I.'

'You're evading the point,' she insisted accusingly, her face flushing at having to be so direct.

'That you could be no more than one light-of-love in my life?'

'Yes.'

He shook his head. 'That is not worth having. It is not what we're about. It's too easy.'

He moved closer. 'Anything worth having exacts a price. I shall pursue you. I shall try to make you submit to my will. You will do everything in your power to make me submit to yours. It becomes an interesting contest, does it not? Who will win, Miss Buchanan?'

For the first time he touched her, his fingers stroking lightly down her cheek, his eyes illuminated with an invigorated lust for life, lust for her, lust for the contest he envisaged.

'Who will win?' he repeated, his voice a low murmur that pulsed through her veins.

Somehow Amanda dredged up the strength to step back from him. 'I have taken the liberty of ordering you a sumptuous supper, Mr Upgrade.' Her voice sounded thin but she plunged on, defiantly ignoring the gauntlet he had thrown at her feet. 'The finest delicacies the hotel has to offer will be brought to you. For your pleasure. Your great pleasure, I hope. And afterwards a dancer to entertain you. The best dancer in Fisa. I believe she does something with veils. If you'll excuse me, I'll go and ensure that your night here is one of entertainment. A night to remember.'

For the merest fraction of time she saw the flash in his eyes. Not admiration. Respect. It was enough. It sent a thrill of elation surging through Amanda. He had not anticipated such a move from her. Please God, he did not anticipate the next one.

'How thoughtful of you!' he said. 'By all means go, Miss Buchanan. There will be another time for us.'

With the thrill of victory thrumming through her,

she turned aside. His next words were quietly spoken, but as a counter-stroke, they were chilling.

'The daughter is more impressive than the father.'

She could not stop herself from looking at him again. The black eyes gleamed their victory. He knew who she was, knew far, far, far too much.

'Goodnight, Mr Upgrade,' she said quickly, and spun on her heel away from him, hoping he had not seen or scented her fear.

Her father had died a broken man.

But she would see justice done to him.

The man in the Presidential Suite did not know it yet, but he had opened the door to Xabia for her. He had opened the door to Xa Shiraq. Let him answer for that, Amanda thought fiercely. Then let him see who would win!

CHAPTER FIVE

XA SHIRAQ spoke to Kozim.

'If you wish to see a horse gallop, one must loosen the bridle,' he mused as his fingers tapped out a rhythmic beat on the edge of his chair.

'True. Very true,' Kozim agreed.

'I have loosened the bridle.'

'Wise. Very wise,' Kozim assented. He had no idea what Xa Shiraq was talking about, but as this was usually the case, no great harm was ever done by admiring the sheikh's wisdom.

'Two details were overlooked in the operation at the Fisa Oasis Hotel, Kozim,' the sheikh continued.

This was alarming news indeed. Kozim did not know of any operation where any detail was overlooked. Not only that, but his report to Jebel Haffa had affirmed that the operation was entirely successful. What had gone wrong? Was the fault his?

'I have attended to both details,' Xa Shiraq said. His fingers stopped drumming.

'Then there's no o o, ah...problem,' Kozim said in relief.

'Kozim, where would you look if you wanted to find a jewel, a jewel almost beyond all price?'

Xa Shiraq was always asking difficult questions. It

posed a problem to Kozim. He shrugged. 'Perhaps, in the mountains…' he suggested tentatively.

'Don't be a fool, Kozim.' It was an impatient interruption, not a cutting one. The sheikh's black eyes held a glint of amusement as he enlightened Kozim. 'You only find rare jewels of that quality in trash cans, Kozim.'

Kozim struggled to accept that revelation. It had to be true because Xa Shiraq knew everything. Kozim made a mental note that tomorrow he would have all the trash cans in the sheikhdom searched for jewels.

CHAPTER SIX

THE *cachet blanc* that Amanda had so carefully recovered from the trash can in the reception area at
the Oasis Hotel, was better than Aladdin's lamp. All
she had to do was produce the magical piece of notepaper bearing the gyrfalcon crest of the Sheikh of
Xabia, and not only did doors open, the red carpet
was laid out for her.

What wonderful words they were!

By order of Xa Shiraq, the bearer of this note is
entitled to have any request within my jurindiction
fulfilled.

A visa for Xabia from the embassy at Bejos had
been produced in a flash. She was even given a complimentary first class ticket on the first available flight
to Alcabab, the capital of Xabia. No customs check
for her at the terminal. She was waved through, or
rather bowed through, as though she were royalty.

Mocca had claimed her. He was an enterprising
youth who scouted the airport terminal for foreign
pigeons waiting to be plucked. In the guise of offering
his services to provide any service—any service at
all—he had offered himself to Amanda.

The clear-eyed limpid innocence, the fresh vitality

of his olive skin, helped Amanda to come to a quick decision.

'I need help,' she declared.

'There is no one better than I with help,' he had replied with deep fervour to press his claim. Amanda had shown him the sheikh's note of authority.

His eyes were larger than saucers and brighter than a Christmas tree when he read it. He treated Amanda with something akin to reverence. She figured she had turned out to be the plumpest, fattest, most succulent pigeon Mocca had ever plucked.

Amanda thought she needed one truck. Mocca opted for three four-wheeled drives, nineteen heavy-duty trucks and a desert cruiser.

Amanda thought she might need a little mining equipment. Seven of the trucks were now loaded with enough TNT, plastic explosive and dynamite to make a sizable hole in any mountain.

'What about the cost?' Amanda had asked cautiously.

'No…o…o problem,' Mocca assured her.

Mocca had an incredibly extensive family. It didn't matter what Amanda requested, Mocca had an uncle or a brother or a cousin who could provide it for her.

Mocca had brought up the subject of her bodyguard. He eyed her up and down in dispassionate assessment. 'You will need two, three men,' he declared. 'Maybe four.'

The number turned out to be fifteen, all Mocca's blood relations. When she accosted him on the subject, Mocca had replied with complete confidence that it was no more than what Xa Shiraq wanted. Mocca displayed an uncanny ability to read Xa Shiraq's mind.

Amanda had to put a stop to it. Her secret foray into the Atlas Mountains was taking on the proportions of a Cecil B. deMille Hollywood extravaganza.

'Where is the money coming from?' she demanded of Mocca.

'It's simple,' he explained. 'I invoice everything to the palace.'

The invoices to the palace must have been flying thick and fast, a veritable flood of invoices which surely had to be brought to the sheikh's attention sooner or later.

Amanda's blood ran cold. She hoped it would not be sooner. She had to get evidence of what her father had found before anyone was aware of what was happening. That not only applied to people in the palace. Amanda was acutely aware that her trail to Alcabab could be easily picked up by the man she had left behind in the Presidential Suite at Fisa.

She had caught the last flight to Bejos on the night he had stated his intention to pursue her. That put her at least twelve hours ahead of him since there had not been another flight until the next day. If the entertainment she had organised for him had gone well, he might not have realised she had slipped the coop for twenty-four hours.

Two days had passed since then. By now he would

have discovered at Bejos that she had used the authority that was rightfully his. She didn't know if he would confess what had happened to Xa Shiraq or try to find her first, but she suspected the latter. He had said himself he was a man who made his own rules. Amanda did not doubt that. The strength of his personality still haunted her.

As did his challenge to her.

It went far deeper than a contest of wills.

It forced Amanda to examine what it meant to her to be a woman, and what part a man should play in her life. Was she short-changing herself with mind over matter, repressing basic needs that she had found easier not to dwell on? Perhaps she was blocking off something more wonderful than she had ever dreamed of.

When he had touched her...and before that...the way his presence had somehow infiltrated her, tugging on feelings that both excited and frightened her...was she being a coward to deny what might happen with him?

It was not only the heat in Alcabab that kept her awake and restless at night, yet in the end common sense always re-asserted itself. It would be all too easy to slip into a dangerous, exhilarating affair, but the letdown would inevitably come and it would probably take years to get over the emotional scarring. Or was she too frightened, too cautious? Perhaps if the opportunity came again, she should seize it.

As for his pursuit of her, he would have a difficult

job finding her in Alcabab, Amanda assured herself. At her request, Mocca had found her an apartment. If Mr Complimentary Upgrade was scouring hotel registers for her name and a person of her description, he would meet with nothing but frustration.

In the meantime, her purchases were so outrageous they could not be overlooked by the palace accountants for long. Xa Shiraq would inevitably demand to know who was using his money and authority to buy such things. Once her identity was known, he would have Patrick Buchanan's daughter brought to him. She would then have the opportunity to demand that he rectify the damage done to her father's reputation. But not before she had the evidence.

Amanda decided she must get out of Alcabab as soon as possible. The longer she stayed in the capital the higher the risk that she would be found by the man pursuing her. He knew whose daughter she was. Her purchases were all aimed at a geology expedition. He was quite capable of putting two and two together and then making inquiries that could lead to the apartment she had rented.

The crisis arose late in the afternoon of the second day.

'Inquiries are being made for a person of your description,' Mocca had informed her gravely.

Amanda's heart rose to her mouth.

'Who is making the inquiries?'

'His name is Charles Arnold.'

That staggered Amanda. 'What?... How?'

'Does it worry you?'

'It's vaguely disturbing.'

It made no sense to her. Charles Arnold had no reason to pursue her. Surely petty malice didn't extend that far. Was Mr Complimentary Upgrade making use of that name to confuse her?

'The bodyguard can dispose of him,' Mocca said with satisfaction. 'We will throw him in the well from which no-one ever returns.'

'No, no, no,' Amanda said hastily. 'That's going too far. But it does mean we must leave Alcabab immediately.'

'All is not yet ready.'

'Then make it ready. We will leave tomorrow morning at three o'clock.'

'But everyone is asleep at that hour.'

'That's precisely why we're leaving at that time. Those who are too sleepy need not come.'

Mocca showed disapproval at such impetuosity, but did as he was bid.

They left the city only an hour and a half late. None was too sleepy to come. Mocca accompanied her. So did most of his uncles, brothers, cousins and others who laid claim to some more complicated relationship. As occasion necessitated, they were skilled truck drivers, mining engineers, explosive experts, camping specialists or generally useful for such a safari into the Atlas Mountains. What they did in real life, Amanda had no idea.

Wives came, as well. To do the cooking, Mocca

explained. All their wages, of course, had already been invoiced to the palace. Mocca was riding on a sea of riches, the like of which had never come his way before. He clearly believed in making hay while the sun shone. Every night he prayed to Allah for more. The palace was as good as a money-machine, as good as owning the printing press itself. He seemed to have a permanent smile on his young face.

Amanda eyed him curiously as they began their long trek to the location marked on her father's map. 'How old are you, Mocca?'

'Seventeen, but nearly eighteen.'

'How is it that the older members of your family are happy to defer to you and take orders from you?'

His grin flashed very wide. With his mass of black curly hair, his unlined skin, his dancing dark eyes, he looked like a precocious, mischievous child who was far too knowing for the years that he had lived.

'It has always been recognised that I am the intelligent one in the family,' he boasted. 'Much has been expected. Now I have proved myself. I am no longer the boy. I am the man. I bring in the business. Ever since I was a little boy, I make more money than anyone else. This brings me much respect.'

It did everywhere in the world, Amanda reflected, yet she preferred the respect given to her by the one man who had all-seeing black eyes. He respected the person she was inside. She wished she could stop thinking about him. He disturbed her equanimity, her peace of mind, her composure…even the sense of

duty which had driven her to resign her position as
general manager of a first-class hotel.

She concentrated on watching the land unfold as
they travelled on. Her father had passed this way
many years before. He had headed towards the high
plateaus. They were his undoing.

The Atlas mountain range traversed several north
African countries, Morocco, Algeria, Tunisia...but
here in Xabia, the geological formations were especially rich in minerals. Amanda imagined her father's
excitement at being granted the chance to discover
whatever he could find. With his intelligence, knowledge and endurance it would have been the highlight
of his career.

He had found what he had been looking for in the
ancient crystalline rock, but Xa Shiraq had turned on
him, smashed his triumph, obliterated its existence
from any known map.

One way or another, Amanda intended to redress
that injustice. She was brooding over how it could be
most effectively done when she saw a band of horsemen wearing black burnooses moving onto the road
to block their route.

'Trouble?' she asked Mocca.

He shrugged. 'Members of the Chugah, the Berber
tribe that inhabit this region. They are part of Jebel
Haffa's personal troops. But we have the sheikh's permission to pass. There will be no trouble.'

Amanda hoped that was the case. The unsigned *chit*
had worked like a dream so far. Yet the powerful

name of Jebel Haffa sent a chill down her spine. He
was Xa Shiraq's right-hand man. What if his troops
had received orders to intercept the convoy and escort
it back to Alcabab under guard?

The truck ground to a halt. The rows of horsemen
parted to let through one lone rider on a magnificent
white Arabian horse. He looked both majestic and
intimidating in the black hooded cloak. Was it the
Berber chieftain or Jebel Haffa himself? Amanda
wondered anxiously. Another horseman broke ranks
to follow him, holding his pace to the rear of his
leader.

Mocca seemed to have no concern in confronting
them. He alighted from the cabin, as brightly cheerful
as ever, and waited beside the truck to greet the two
men. The man on the white Arabian stallion did not
dismount, nor did he make any acknowledgement of
Mocca's greeting. He remained in his saddle, main-
taining a haughty dignity as the second rider dismounted and conversed with Mocca in rapid Arabic.

Mocca broke away to come around the truck to
where Amanda sat on the passenger side. She had the
sheikh's note in her hand, ready to pass it to him but
he did not ask for it.

'We are being honoured with a guide to take us
through the mountain passes. He is to ride with us,'
Mocca informed her.

'But we don't need a guide,' Amanda argued. 'I
have precise maps of where I want to go.'

'It is not a matter of choice,' Mocca explained with

an expressive shrug. 'It is a matter of honour. They will be insulted if we refuse the offer. It is not wise to insult the Chugah. The guide is to ride with us.'

Amanda sighed, resigning herself to the customs of the country. 'Very well. If we must.'

There was a rustle of cloth, the squeak of the seat beside her. Amanda swung her head around from the passenger window to find their Berber guide already taking up the space between her and where Mocca would sit behind the driving wheel. She instinctively shrank away from the intruder, not because there was anything offensive about him but because she was suddenly assailed by the sense of some powerful alien force in his presence. It had happened to her once before quite recently.

Her nerve-ends jangled, even as she quickly reasoned that she was being absurdly fanciful. A guide was no more than a guide. She simply wasn't used to a hooded stranger in close proximity to herself, a big, hooded stranger whose face was obscured by the cowl and a masking cloth. Both were totally superfluous in the cabin of the truck where no dust was kicked up by horses' hooves.

The guide did not remove them. His arms were folded beneath his cloak, and his attention remained rigidly directed to the road ahead. He was totally immobile.

Most probably he was offended by her, Amanda assured herself. A bare-headed, bare-faced, foreign woman in jeans and shirt might be shaking his sense of propriety. They were a long way from the civilising influences of a capital city now, and the Berbers were born and bred mountain men.

Mocca swung into the driver's seat and closed his door, trapping the three of them into an awkward intimacy. Amanda steeled herself to get used to it and turned her gaze firmly forward. She was stunned to see the Berber spokesman leading the white Arabian stallion away, a riderless white Arabian stallion!

The back of her neck prickled.

Who was the man beside her? Why would the leader of these fighting troops belonging to Jebel Haffa appoint himself her guide? It was a lowly task that could have been undertaken by any of his men. How could any guide give directions to where she wanted to go if the guide did not know where she was going?

It only made sense if he was charged with more than guiding her. Amanda had told no-one exactly where they were heading. She had given Mocca only the most general instructions.

Mocca switched on the engine and the truck started to rumble forward again. The rest of the convoy followed suit. If everything went to plan they would be at their first camping site in the next hour or so.

Amanda concentrated on acting naturally as she put away Xa Shiraq's note and spread out her map of the area. Any deviation from the route marked by her father and she'd know for certain she had a problem.

A big problem.

CHAPTER SEVEN

THEY came to the wine village of Tirham in the Ozimi valley without further incident. Only then did their self-appointed guide break his stillness. He waved his hand and pointed to a junction side road.

'What does he want?' Amanda asked tersely. She was tired after travelling for twelve hours. Tirham was their destination for today and she certainly did not want to go any further.

'We must go where the guide points,' Mocca answered, resignation in his voice, and turning the truck onto a narrow road that led away from the village.

Amanda would have liked to argue the point, gave the inscrutable stranger next to her a quick glance, and decided against it.

'The villagers will be disappointed,' she reflected in courteous disapproval.

'True,' said Mocca, but he did not turn back.

Amanda was not so trusting. On the other hand, Mocca believed he had good reason to trust whereas she knew she was on borrowed time.

The man beside her was a disturbing enigma. Was he a deaf-mute? There had been absolutely no response from him to the spasmodic conversation between Mocca and herself. His presence had blighted the last hour.

As much as Amanda had tried to ignore the Berber leader, she had been unable to lessen her tense awareness of him, waiting for a movement, waiting for a word that might confirm her worst fears. She hoped Mocca was right and this detour was insignificant and meant nothing more than the end of today's journey.

They passed through a forest of magnificent cedar. At the dawn of civilisation cedar trees like these had flourished throughout the fertile crescent. They came to a cleared area beside a quickly flowing stream of sparkling water. A large, ornate tent and another group of silent, unmoving Berbers filled a small portion of the area.

Their guide tapped Mocca's shoulder and pointed to where Mocca should park the truck and those that followed. It was some fifty metres from the tent, the furthest possible distance away within the clearing. Some of the Berbers moved forward to direct the rest of the convoy to their corresponding places.

Amanda had the sinking feeling she had seen clockwork precision planning like this before. Who, she wondered, was in the tent?

Mocca hopped out to assert his position in this matter.

For the first time the enigmatic Berber guide turned his face towards Amanda. All was still hidden, but Amanda had the impression of the darkest sable eyes, deeply socketed, radiating energy and light. He waved his hand and the gesture was unmistakable. He wanted her to alight.

'I'm staying right here,' Amanda said, hoping the stranger understood English.

There was a shrug of the shoulders and the guide turned to the other side of the cabin and stepped out, Mocca deferentially holding the driver's door open for him. Without another sound or gesture, the Berber leader headed for the tent, his cloak billowing out behind his tall and imperious figure as his long strides ate up the short distance.

He paused at the entrance to the tent, turning slightly to one of the two men who seemed to be standing guard there. The man nodded as though he had been spoken to. Not a mute, Amanda deduced, her fears and suspicions growing stronger by the second.

She couldn't drive away. That would be admitting defeat. To run away would be to jeopardise her quest. Besides, if this was, indeed, the long arm of Xa Shiraq reaching out to gather her in, she doubted there would be any way to escape. Better to sit tight and wait to see what happened next. Tomorrow she would insist on having her own way and see if that produced any result.

The black cloaked figure moved inside the tent and disappeared from her view. The man who had received his instructions moved to meet up with Mocca and converse with him. Both men then turned and came to the truck where Amanda still waited.

'You are invited to take refreshments while the camp is being set up. There are more comforts for you inside the tent,' Mocca informed her. He smiled infectiously. 'It is also necessary. There is no other way.'

Neatly arranged, Amanda thought, certain now she was dealing with Jebel Haffa himself, the most loyal of Xa Shiraq's lieutenants. Her business in Xabia would be discussed privately in his tent. The decision of how to deal with her might have already been made. She might never get to Xa Shiraq. Nor to the crystal caves in the mountains.

'Get my bodyguard,' Amanda directed Mocca.

'There is no need. We are under protection,' he excused.

'Some bodyguards they turned out to be,' Amanda scoffed. 'The first time I need them, they evaporate like water under the midday sun. You can reimburse the palace for them, Mocca.'

He gestured an eloquent appeal for forbearance. 'They will be at your service, if service is required. But this is a matter of hospitality, not hostility.'

Amanda knew all about complimentary hospitality, as masterminded by Jebel Haffa. With a sense of fatalism, she picked up her bag and stepped down from the truck. The least she could do was conduct herself with dignity. Her heart was pounding painfully but she would show no hesitation, no fear, no faltering. She had come to right an injustice. She would be heard, if nothing else.

The Berber guard escorted her to the tent and gestured for her to enter. She felt the trap closing around her as she stepped inside and the door flap behind her was lowered into place, ensuring complete seclusion from Mocca and his extended family.

Richly patterned carpets had been laid on the ground. The aroma of freshly brewed coffee wafted on the air. But there was a stronger scent permeating the interior of the tent, a fresh, beautiful scent she had never smelled the exact likeness of before. It was tantalising, making it difficult to concentrate on the proceedings that were about to take place.

It was intensely discomfiting to find only one man waiting for her, the man in the black burnoose who had sat beside her in the truck. For the past hour he had known this moment was coming, ignoring whatever transpired between Mocca and herself because he knew all he had to do was ensure they took the road to this tent. When had he laid his plans...this morning after she had left the city?

He stood beside the table where the coffee and plates of sweet biscuits and fruit were waiting. He waved an invitation to the chair that had been set for her...opposite his. It was not a camp chair, any more than the table was a camp table, set as it was with an embroidered linen cloth. The backs of the chairs were ornately carved, the seats cushioned and upholstered in burgundy brocade. This tent and its contents marked his status as a very important person.

Amanda decided not to speak until she was spoken

to. There was no profit in saying anything until the situation was clarified. She moved to the chair indicated and sat down. He walked to the other end of the tent where there was a large divan bed covered with the same burgundy silk as on the chairs. A group of plump, decorative cushions were piled on top of it. Her host obviously didn't believe in sleeping rough.

Outside the tent music began to play. Amanda wondered if this was to be the entertainment. She identified a violin, flute, tambourine, and possibly a guitar.

What was the scent teasing her nose? It seemed to be sharpening all her senses...or was she confusing it with the very real sense of danger that was making her feel more acutely aware of herself and everything else? Especially the man who was now discarding his burnoose, tossing it negligently on the bed.

He swung around to face her and Amanda's stomach contracted as though absorbing a physical blow. She stared at him, her mind cartwheeling through a dizzying series of logical steps that brought home the realisation she could never achieve what she had set out to achieve. Not in the way she had planned it. Xa Shiraq and his men had been one step ahead of her, all the way.

And this man...who would have been her lover if she had allowed it...this man who had pursued her from Fisa...this man who could command the Chugah, Jebel Haffa's personal troops...could she still *touch* him...sway him from his loyalty to the sheikh?

He stood absolutely motionless, watching her re-action to him with those all-knowing, all-seeing black eyes. She should have known, in the truck, who he was. Her instincts had told her. Neither cloak nor cowl could smother the innate power of the man. She had never met his like before their encounter at Fisa. It had been blindly stupid of her not to link the same force with the same source.

Not that it would have changed anything, Amanda assured herself. He would have engineered this result regardless of any effort she might have made to change it. This was his territory. Without an army to fight his troops, Amanda could not have evaded him. Tirham was the gateway to the mountains that held the crystal caves.

'You knew I would be coming here,' she stated flatly.

'Yes.'

'The promotion at Fisa was to see if I would be content with a career in hotel management.'

Again that flash of respect in his eyes. 'Yes.'

'The *cachet blanc* from Xa Shiraq...that also was a deliberate test of my purpose. To see how quickly I could think.'

'Yes.'

'Why was I allowed to come this far?'

'There is a saying in your country—''Give a person

enough rope so they can hang themselves.'' You were given sufficient rope, Miss Buchanan.'

He paused to let her feel the noose tightening around her neck. Both ruthless and relentless, Amanda thought, with a little shiver of apprehension. As he had been with Charles Arnold, after giving him enough rope to damn himself.

They both knew he could have had her arrested at the embassy in Bejos for false representation of the sheikh's authority, but it would have been dealt with by officialdom in Bejos. Perhaps the fraudulent act might have been dismissed as a misdemeanour at that point. Not any longer.

'You wanted me in Xabia,' Amanda reasoned.

'It had a certain piquancy. Yes!'

'Revealing my intentions.'

'Beyond all reasonable doubt,' he affirmed.

'Putting myself in your power.' Would he use it to condemn her or rescue her? Did he still want her, or had she put herself beyond the pale as far as he was concerned?

'I arranged it that way,' he acknowledged.

'Under the jurisdiction of Xa Shiraq,' she mocked, reminding him he wasn't entirely his own man, hoping it might prick some deep core of pride that she could reach and use to her advantage.

There was a hard, unyielding look to his face. His black eyes bored into hers with merciless judgement. 'You cannot dispute you have broken the law. You made an illegal entry into this country. To that of-

fence you have added the illegal acquisition of per-
mits and goods that would be considered criminal acts
in any country. You are guilty of so many counts of
fraud and grand larceny, there is no international body
you could appeal to that would interest itself in fighting your cause.'

'I have justice on my side,' Amanda bit out determinedly, refusing to accept the defeat he was pressing
upon her.

His lips curled in contempt. *'Fiat justitia, ruat coe-
lum,'* he said. 'Let justice be done though the heavens
fall.'

'As you sow, so will you reap,' Amanda retorted.

He dismissed her words with a wave of his hand.
'You have discredited yourself in the eyes of the
world.'

'The same ploy was used on my father.' She stood
up in disdain of his indictment of her. Her eyes
flashed their contempt back at him. 'Do you feel
proud of your petty schemes and plotting?'

'It was efficient,' he stated coldly. 'And served its
purpose. You are here in Xabia, Miss Buchanan.
There is no avenue of escape.'

Was there no chink in his armour? Did he belong
body and soul to his sheikh?

'That doesn't mean you win,' Amanda fired at him,
trying to stir the sense of contest he had seemed interested in before.

It provoked him. The black eyes blazed, their chill
obliterated by a heat that seared her skin. 'Time is on

my side. As much time as I need. As much time as I want. You can hardly say I have lost, Miss Buchanan.'

Amanda was left in no doubt of what he meant. The arrogant confidence with which his eyes roved over her made her burn with furious resentment. It also triggered a flood of responses that shamed her.

Chemical reactions were uncontrollable, she reasoned wildly. There probably wasn't a woman in the world who wouldn't think he was overwhelmingly attractive in those form-fitting trousers and riding boots, outlining the strong muscularity of his legs and drawing attention to his virility. It was only natural that she should feel...a tingle of interest.

Though, if she was honest with herself, it was more than that. Much more. She had the strong sensation of desire licking over her skin, sending curls of excitement through her stomach, down her legs. She found herself staring at his mouth, wanting it to ravish hers. She dragged her gaze down to his throat. The smooth polish of his bare skin in the V of his open-necked shirt incited a compelling urge to touch. She wanted to feel the power of the man enveloping her in physical intimacy, surging inside her, loving her for what she was.

Amanda struggled to come to terms with the strength of these feelings. It wasn't like her to have erotic thoughts. There was something else bothering her, as well. The scent...it seemed heavier, richer now. But that was irrelevant to the problems she faced.

'I have had this tent prepared for you. For your comfort and pleasure.' His voice was suddenly a low velvet purr, a caress that squeezed her heart.

'What *is* that scent?' she blurted out. It was a stupid question, yet she somehow needed to have it settled and out of her mind.

'It is the scent of the jasmine that was banned by the Sultan of Zanzibar.' He walked towards her with the slow, threatening grace of a panther on the prowl, his black eyes gleaming with satisfaction. 'The Arabs complained that it unduly excited the women when they were having sexual relations. Personally, I don't mind that happening.'

Resentment welled over the strange excitement that had gripped her. 'Does having me as your prisoner give you the right to do anything you like with me? Is that what you think?'

'I will use whatever means I have to make you face the truth of your feelings as a woman. And your response to me as a man.'

'Does that include taking me whenever you want to?'

He laughed derisively. 'I want more than that.'

He was close now, so close that the compelling demand in his eyes made her feel intensely vulnerable. 'Do you have Xa Shiraq's approval for what you are doing?' she fired at him, desperate to find some weakness she could play on.

'If I risk that disapproval, it is for you.' His arms came around her waist, drawing her to him. His eyes burned into hers. 'What would you risk for me, Amanda?'

It was the first time he had taken the familiarity of using her name. It was seductive. It was also revealing. For all his steely control he was not immune to her. She still *touched* him…and troubled him…as no other woman had. That was what he had told her in Fisa. The critical question was how far would he go to have the complete conquest he wanted.

She pushed her hands up his chest to retain some distance between them. She barely resisted the impulse to explore further. She had to think, act, win!

'What do you want me to risk?' she asked.

'Yourself. Open yourself to me—your mind, your heart—in ways you never have before.'

'And you?' she whispered, spreading her fingers over the firmly delineated muscles of his chest, feeling them tighten under her touch. The primitive urge to claw, to hold the beat of his heart in her hands was incredibly strong. 'Would you do the same for me?'

'Yes,' he rasped.

But would he pay the price?

'Even if it means being disloyal to Xa Shiraq?'

CHAPTER EIGHT

AMANDA felt the brief suspension of his heartbeat beneath her palm. It stopped completely then resumed at a slower rate. Shock, followed by a clamp of control that amazed her with its swift and steady application. A shutter came down on his eyes, as well.

Mentally regrouping himself, Amanda surmised, and doubted this man would ever entirely lose himself in passion, no matter how deep or urgent or compelling the physical desire.

'Do I take a viper to my heart?' he mused. His hold on her slackened.

'You said you would open your mind to me,' she pressed, sliding her hands up to his shoulders, moving closer in desperate supplication, her eyes begging his for a stay in judgement. 'Have you never questioned Xa Shiraq's decisions? Might they not sometimes be wrong? Wrong about my father?'

She saw his eyes harden.

'You said you wanted to know my heart,' she argued. 'Well, I have loyalties, too, and they go as deeply as yours. How can I commit myself to you if you deny what I am?'

'You are mistaken,' he said flatly.

'How do you know? Does the sheikh tell you everything? Or do you carry out his orders with blind faith in his judgement?'

He stiffened, his pride stung. His eyes flared a warning. 'It is well that I had the musicians play to drown out all sound. You talk of disloyalty and treason...'

'I need a few days of freedom. That's all. You've let me come this far. Please...' her hand moved instinctively to touch the pulse at the base of his throat '...it means so much to me.'

His head jerked back. He pulled her hand away from him and stepped out of her reach, his eyes slashing her with fresh contempt. 'You seek to corrupt me with your body. I will not take it. Your price is too high.'

He swung on his heel and strode towards the bed, tall, straight-backed, bearing a supreme dignity in his incorruptibility. It struck a deep chord of respect in Amanda. How Xa Shiraq must value this man!

If only she could have him at her side...his strength of mind, his sense of integrity, the power of his spirit. Her heart clenched. She could not let him go, thinking so badly of her. It wasn't true. She had to make him see it wasn't true. Somehow that was far more important than proving her father right.

'How can it be anything more than bodies...when you deny me understanding?' she said quietly.

He stopped in the act of bending to retrieve the black burnoose. Slowly he straightened, his back still rigidly turned to her as he considered her words.

'I loved my father,' she pressed on, wanting him to realise it was a statement of fact, unshakable, enduring, an intrinsic part of her that he could not cut out.

'He is at rest now. It is best that you leave him there,' he said just as quietly, not without sympathy.

Relief poured through Amanda. She had *touched* him again. Encouraged, she asked, 'Would you, if it was your father?'

She saw his shoulders lift and fall as he breathed deeply and released some of his tension. He swung around to face her, an implacable look in his eyes.

'If there was good reason, yes,' he said with steely resolution.

'And I suppose Xa Shiraq gave you good reason for my father to be discredited,' she said with an acid bite. 'Making him out to be a liar when all the time he was a victim of your sheikh's chicanery.'

He grimaced. 'Xa Shiraq does not expect you to see the matter in the same way he does.'

'For years I lived with the need to clear my father's name. Do you expect me to forget it all in a minute on your word that it is best that I do?'

He made no reply.

'Tell me the good reason!' she demanded.

He shook his head.

'Why not?'

'You know not what you ask.'

'So you decide for me,' she mocked. 'Where is the sharing of minds and hearts in that?'

'There are matters of far greater consequence than you,' he snapped.

She ignored that and advanced on him, adrenaline running high, determined on *touching* him again. 'All the time in the world will not win my trust if you won't give me yours. Or is it your plan simply to dominate me, and keep yourself apart?'

For the first time she saw conflict in his eyes, a dark raging turbulence that coalesced into one searing need. 'I am tired of being without a true companion.'

'So am I,' she whispered, her heart turning over at the vulnerability he revealed.

He stepped forward and scooped her hard against him. She felt a tremor run through him at the full impact of their bodies coming together. There was a quiver inside herself, as though of something momentous being recognised.

'You,' he murmured, his eyes burning into hers, probing her mind and heart and soul with an intensity that pierced any possible deception. 'You could be the price that cost a sheikhdom.'

He lifted a hand to her cheek, his fingers stroking her skin as though needing to draw absolute truth from her. 'Show me what you promise,' he commanded.

Then his fingers raked through her hair to grasp her head and hold it to his as he kissed her.

If that was what it could be called.

Certainly his mouth claimed hers and ravished it with an invasion so passionately intense, Amanda was totally lost in the bombardment of sensation, drowning, yet connected to a source of vibrant energy that thrummed through her body, a surging river of it, stirring an overwhelming compulsion to stay linked to him.

Yet it was not a subjugation. While she had the sense of falling into him, she felt him falling into her. Her arms curled around his neck, her hands cupped his head, holding him to her, and she felt strong and invigorated, and soft and melting all at the same time.

There was no remaining aloof from what was happening. It was captivating, enthralling, touching deep hidden places that rejoiced and savoured being drawn from isolation, suppressed no longer, released and winging free from the cage of loneliness, soaring and swooping from one to the other in jubilant recognition of finding at last there was somewhere else to belong…welcomed…wanted.

She was barely aware of his mouth leaving hers, of her head dropping onto his shoulder, cradled there against the warm strength of his neck. Her mind was intoxicated with dreams of what could be possible, her body safe in the warm haven of his arms. She felt him breathe and her own lungs filled. He sighed and she knew it was the wind of change.

She felt the ripple of new energy through his body, the stirring of purpose, control firming, but she did not believe he could retreat from her now. Physically yes, but not mentally, not emotionally, not spiritually.

If he did, it would be a violation of something so precious it would be akin to homicide.

'Amanda...' There was both awe and pain in his voice.

So strange, she mused. He had not even given her his name. She tried *Jebel* in her mind. It didn't quite fit the deep dark strains of power in him...the elemental primitive man that called to all that was untamed in her.

'You would come to me...of your own free will?' he asked.

The strained note in his voice told her he wanted to believe it, but his intelligence questioned it. She wanted him to let her go free. She wanted her father exonerated. The stakes were high.

'Yes,' she said, not knowing where this would end, no longer caring.

However it had happened, an act of destiny or pure accident, Amanda was sure in her own mind that there would be no other man for her. Why it should be, she didn't know. The perversity of fate was imponderable. A collision course had been set, and once effected, there was no going back.

She felt the quickening of his pulse. He eased back from her, lifting his hands to cup her face, draw her gaze to his. He looked into her eyes and she didn't mind him seeing the desire for him openly reflected there. She was sorry to see the torment of uncertainties in his.

'I will put an end to this matter. You are tired after

your long journey. Perhaps distraught. I should let you rest. I should not have pressed so hard. For all your inner strength…you remain a woman.'

It was a strange, tortured mixture of concern and tenderness and self-criticism. It was as though, having hunted, he was struck by an empathy with his prey, and he could not bring himself to move in for the kill.

'Was *more* too much?' she asked with rueful irony.

'No. You both humble and exalt me.' His hands glided slowly, gently, down her throat to her shoulders. 'I will leave you now. I will send you a serving woman who will see to your needs. I will not have you sleeping in the company of herdsmen and goat keepers. There is no reason for you not to accept the comforts I can provide. It is all for you.'

He stepped back, picked up his burnoose. With a whirl of black cloth it settled around his shoulders and he strode away from her, heading for the door.

'Where are you going?' she called after him.

He paused, looked back. 'To contemplate the oddity of human foolishness. Including my own.'

'Where will you sleep?'

'Under the stars.' His lips quirked into a self-mocking smile. 'They have been my companions for a long time.'

'What about tomorrow?'

'It will come.'

'Will you be here?'

'Yes. Whatever happens…whatever is decided…you are now under my protection. We are linked...you and I. Though much can come between us, and probably will, the link is irreversible, is it not?'

'Yes.'

'Are we damned by that knowledge...or blessed with it?' he mused.

'I don't know,' she murmured, aching to go to him, yet accepting that he must work through his own quandary of spirit. 'Are you Jebel Haffa?' she asked, wanting to put a name to him.

He seemed to consider the question far longer than was necessary. 'Jebel Haffa is loyal beyond all price,' he answered enigmatically. 'His loyalty is legendary and goes beyond that of any figure who has lived through history.'

He reflected for a moment and continued. 'He is part of me. The part that is rational and far-seeing. The part that executes what needs to be done for the good of the people of Xabia. But there is another part of me that is not Jebel Haffa.'

The part I touch, Amanda thought. The personal side.

'It is the part of me that has journeyed through the long years alone, in a void of emptiness that was never filled no matter what I did or how much was achieved.' His eyes glittered derisively at her. 'Was it worth it?'

'Of course,' she protested.

'When you have all the answers to the questions about your father, what will be the worth of it,

Amanda? Will you end up holding an empty goblet in your hand, with nothing left in it to drink?'

A chill ran down her spine. Was she chasing a rainbow that had no substance to it?

'I've been there before you,' he said quietly, sadly. 'One strives for the goal, but when it is reached, the satisfaction never lasts. It is so brief. Ephemeral. And afterwards, one looks back…and counts the cost. It is all too easy not to think about the cost…until afterwards.'

'You're saying that my quest is futile and I should give it up now?'

He shook his head. 'I know it is futile but until you are aware of it, you will not give it up. Cannot. Therefore I must set my course accordingly.'

He lifted the black cowl over his head and turned to leave.

'Wait!' she cried. 'I don't want you to pay a price for me. I take back what I asked of you. It wasn't fair. I had no right.'

His head swung back towards her. His black eyes burned like live coals in the shadow of the cowl. 'Don't you know, Amanda?' he said softly. 'There is always a price to pay for everything. There is a price you and I will both pay. It is written in the stars. It is inescapable.'

He left her with that remorseless thought.

The scent of the Xabian jasmine drifted back into her nostrils, reminding her of all the needs of a woman. She didn't know why tears came to her eyes,

why they kept welling up and trickling down her
cheeks. Human foolishness.

She had won something, hadn't she?

Yet there was no sense of triumph. Not even satisfaction.

She was alone. And cold. And the memory of her
father had somehow lost the power to spark the fire
in her belly. Another man did that. The man, almost
certainly, used by Xa Shiraq to shame, damage and
humiliate her father.

CHAPTER NINE

HE WAS outside the tent when Amanda emerged the next morning. He was alone. Clearly no one else was allowed within the vicinity.

His face was rendered indistinguishable by the cowl of his burnoose, but now Amanda would have known him anywhere. In any clothing.

She felt his eyes snap over her in quick appraisal. Amazingly she had slept well. Perhaps the jasmine scent also had soporific qualities. The early morning air was crisp, engendering a sense of vitality, but *he* added dynamism to it. Amanda waited for him to speak, aware that her fate lay in his hands.

'You are ready to depart now?' he asked without preamble.

It was the authoritative part of him that spoke. No desire. No intimacy. Cool, decisive, distant. His night under the stars seemed to have brushed aside the part of him he had revealed the previous evening. Perhaps disloyalty to Xa Shiraq sat uncomfortably on his shoulders. Perhaps much depended on her attitude this morning.

Was he waiting to discover which way she would turn? Was he watching like a cat to see how the mouse would try to avoid the danger and traps which abounded?

Amanda had decided last night he was not Jebel Haffa. The roundabout way he had answered her question about his identity inclined her to believe he was a far more complex man than the faithful follower Jebel Haffa was purported to be, probably someone higher in authority who worked behind the scenes. That fitted the anonymity he was intent on keeping. It also fitted what had happened at the hotel in Fisa.

'I'm ready for any new challenges,' she answered calmly. In her mind she added, *Mr Complimentary Upgrade*.

'You will instruct Mocca to lead your convoy on to the location marked on your father's map.'

Amanda could not hide her surprise. 'You know about that?' For years she had considered the maps her secret weapon.

'Your father was hardly discreet. You are not the first to come looking for Patrick Buchanan's great discovery,' he said dryly. 'It is as well to have another failure, particularly by his daughter's expedition.'

He was so confident it would fail. Had her father been mistaken? Amanda couldn't believe it. Even in the delirium preceding his death by pneumonia, her father had still been lucid about the crystal caves. They had to exist.

'You're allowing me to continue?' she asked, wary of misunderstanding his intentions.

'Your convoy will follow your exact instructions in everything. They will go, they will search, they will not find what you are looking for.'

'Where will I be in the meantime?'

'With me.'

It was a flat statement of fact, not allowing her any choice in the matter. It gave her no indication of what they would be doing together.

He nodded towards the camp where Mocca and his extended family were bustling around, packing up, ready to depart. There seemed to be far more efficient organisation in their activities this morning. 'Go and give your orders. Then you will return here to me.'

It was clear she was to appear to be a free agent, although she wasn't. If she deviated in any way from his instructions, Amanda had the sinking sensation that her fall into disgrace and oblivion was virtually certain. She resigned herself to doing what was requested and set off to speak to Mocca, determined that both her manner and words be above criticism.

She had no idea if Upgrade's reference to being partly Jebel Haffa was significant or merely symbolic. Whatever and whoever he was, he was still acting under orders from Xa Shiraq. It seemed highly unlikely that these arrangements were his own. Although he probably had some latitude in carrying out the sheikh's will.

She hoped his manner would be different once they were alone. *If they were to be alone*. How she had got herself into this situation, and how she was going to get herself out of it, Amanda did not precisely know.

She might be about to be whisked off to Alcabab to face justice according to Xa Shiraq. She might be accused of treason against the State.

On the other hand, if she were to rejoin Mocca at the site to be explored, and that exploration did prove to be an exercise in futility, the sheikh could consider her failure as the definitive means to bury the question of Patrick Buchanan's discovery once and for all. In which case, why wasn't she being allowed to go to the site and confirm the failure?

If he wanted her expedition to fail in a blaze of publicity she would be accompanying it. As neither of these situations seemed feasible, it meant one thing with certainty. There was a deeper purpose behind what was happening.

Excitement tripped her heart into a faster beat. If Upgrade had wanted her simply for his pleasure, he could have had her last night. He had chosen differently. Perhaps his words revealed not so much desire and wanting and vulnerability, but instead constituted an excuse to withdraw.

Amanda had the disturbing feeling that she was nothing but a pawn. If that was the case, Amanda knew enough about chess to know that pawns could become queens. She hoped to show Upgrade how it was done.

'Good morning, Miss Buchanan,' Mocca greeted her in singsong triumph. His grin was very wide.

'You see? There was no…o…o problem. Your body-guard would have been an insult to your great patron.'

'Who is my great patron, Mocca? What is his name?'

Mocca shrugged. 'Many words are whispered, but none can tell. Some things it is better not to know.'

'Well, my great patron has invited me to stay with him while you get on with my business, Mocca. I guess it wouldn't be wise of me to make a daring escape.'

Mocca shuddered. 'Forbid the thought. To so blatantly refuse hospitality could cost us all our lives.' He rolled his eyes for emphasis. 'You are highly honoured, Miss Buchanan.'

The honour was highly questionable as far as Amanda was concerned.

Mocca pondered a moment. 'The camping equipment I bought for you was not good enough.' He gestured towards the tent. 'My eyes have been opened. I did not foresee the will of Xa Shiraq to the proper degree.' He smiled infectiously. 'Trust me, Miss Buchanan. I am the brains of the family. Next time I do better. My third cousin twice removed is an importer of camping equipment.'

'I'm sure he is,' Amanda said dryly. 'Now this is what I want you to do…'

Mocca listened attentively to her instructions. He repeated them back to her word for word. He volubly assured her that all would be ready for her, when she was ready.

In the meantime they would do a preliminary search for the caves, although they were not to enter them without her.

Maybe he would collect more supplies. He would purchase a special tent for her. For someone who held a *cachet blanc* from the Sheikh of Xabia, nothing was too much trouble.

Amanda thought of her list of crimes as outlined by Upgrade. She firmly instructed Mocca to spend nothing more. He was simply to do what he had been told.

She handed the map to the Berber who was to accompany Mocca. He was the spokesman of yesterday. She suspected he would keep Mocca's natural bent towards excession under direct and strict control.

The far more important map remained in her bag. She had not been asked for it and she wasn't about to hand it over. Other people might have scouted the general area where her father had made his discovery. Amanda refused to believe they could have had a duplicate of the precious map that marked the exact location of the caves. She might yet be able to turn the tables on Xa Shiraq. All she needed was the opportunity. Then seize it.

She had promised her father on his deathbed she would do her best to remedy the injury he had sustained. She had not considered the possibility that there could be good reason not to. Did that invalidate a deathbed promise?

Amanda felt less certain than she had for years. Her

sense of purpose was being eroded. She was deeply troubled as she walked back to where Upgrade was waiting for her. He had said yesterday there was much that could come between them. It was probably already in place. He would have put it there.

Horses had been brought into the clearing. He stood beside his white Arabian stallion. Next to it was a beautiful black mare. Her luggage, which had been brought into the tent by the serving woman, was now loaded onto a packhorse. The mounted troops formed a guard of honour by the road back to the village.

Her serving woman was standing by, a black burnoose draped over her arm and a pair of riding boots in her hands. Amanda had no trouble in deducing she was going on a journey which would begin on horseback. She exchanged her Reeboks for the boots without a murmur of disagreement.

'How did you know I could ride?' she asked, turning to the man who had the power to change her life.

'It was a recreation you partook in at the Fisa hotel,' he replied, moving to help her mount the black mare.

'Where are we going?'

'To do my will.'

That was the very information she needed. Not Xa Shiraq's will. *His* will! It didn't precisely tell her where they were going but she now definitely knew whose *will* was taking her there.

'I don't like not being consulted,' she said, trying out a small challenge.

'You will see for yourself that it was far better that you were not consulted,' he replied with frustrating equanimity.

She shot him a brooding look. 'I don't like you one bit when you get into this all-knowing mood.'

He ignored the contentious comment.

Amanda wondered if there was anything he didn't know about her. She knew nothing of him. His life was a complete mystery to her. What of his family? Where had he come from? When had he first become allied to Xa Shiraq? What was their connection to each other? Surely this journey must provide her with some answers.

Once she was in the saddle, he set about adjusting her stirrups so she would ride more comfortably. It seemed wrong to her, this leader of men, carrying out such a task while his troops watched and waited.

'Should you be doing this?' she asked, acutely aware of the interest and attention being directed at them.

He paused and looked up, the black eyes burning from the shadow of his cowl. 'That which is precious must be pampered. I would not allow any other man to touch you.'

Heat raced through Amanda's veins. It was virtu ally a claim of possession in this country. *His* woman. Was that why he had sat between her and Mocca in the truck yesterday, isolated her in the tent last night? As sternly as he was standing back from her this morning, she was most certainly under his personal protection.

He took the black burnoose from the serving woman and handed it up to Amanda. 'Put this on,' he commanded, 'so that idle eyes will not note our progress once we leave.'

He didn't explain why idle eyes could be a problem. Amanda wondered if it was to hide her from other men's vision. On second thoughts, she realised the burnoose was purely practical if Mr Complimentary Upgrade was going against Xa Shiraq's will.

Amanda watched him swing himself into the saddle on the white stallion. He was so lithe, supple, strong, graceful. A little quiver of anticipation fluttered through her stomach. He was a man worth having. It might be incredibly primitive, but she secretly revelled in the idea of being claimed by him. Claimed and possessed.

He nudged his horse forward with his knees. Amanda's black mare needed no urging. The moment the white stallion moved, the mare followed, ready to fall into place beside it.

That was natural, Amanda thought. It had always been so.

The Berber horsemen formed a cavalcade, some riding ahead of them, most behind, both groups far enough away to allow private conversation between herself and the man beside her.

They did not stay on the road to the village. They struck out on a trail through the cedar forest, bypassing the village altogether. She heard the drone of the convoy's engines fall further and further behind them. At a signal from her companion, the Berber troops departed. The white stallion was reined in to a prancing halt. The black mare simply stopped.

'What happens now?' Amanda asked.

'We strike off into the mountains on our own. We will ride hard and fast. I will not spare you.'

He paused to reflect a moment. 'You asked for my trust. I give it.' He looked at her with hard unyielding eyes. 'I hope you are worthy of it. The price of betrayal is death.'

It sent a quiver of fear down Amanda's spine. Was he speaking of his betrayal in not following the sheikh's orders, or the vengeance he would wreak on her if she betrayed his trust?

Amanda quickly gave him her assurance. 'I will not betray you.'

'And the cock crowed three times,' he said sardonically.

It was a wretched feeling, being torn two ways, Amanda reflected. She wondered if she would end up betraying the promise she'd made to her father. 'I'm sorry you feel that,' she said quietly.

The soft words seemed to spur him on. 'We are now set on the path that leads to either heaven or hell. There is no in-between. There is no going back. Unless you do so now. You can say goodbye and we will never meet again. You can link up with the con-

voy as it passes through the village of Tirham. Make
your choice.'

His inner tension reached across to her, squeezing
her heart. She knew intuitively he was playing the
biggest gamble of his life. What that gamble was she
could only guess at. She had no doubt he wanted her
with him, wanted her to prove her mettle, yet there
was this hesitation within him, perhaps because she
was a woman and he considered any woman softer,
weaker than himself.

She remembered the way he had withdrawn from
her in the tent, observing that she was *a woman*. And
this morning he had remained aloof, pressing nothing
except organisational commands. Had he deliberately
refrained from applying any emotional influence so
that she could freely make the decision he now offered her?

It affronted Amanda.

'How could any woman resist your entreaties when
they are put in such endearing terms?' she mocked at
him. 'Of course my decision must be to go with you.'

Once again there was a flash of compelling respect
in his eyes. It was a look Amanda would have gone
to the grave for. All her miserable existence as the
butt of jokes dissolved into a nonentity of the past.
To earn the respect of such a man as this squashed
every cruel malicious word spoken by Charles Arnold
and others of that ilk.

She looked at the strong ageless face, saw the loneliness behind it, and knew she was not alone. The

yearning for a true companion was sufficient to take any risk.

'I'll go on with you,' she repeated simply.

'So be it,' he answered.

She caught a brief raw blaze of desire before he turned his head forward. Amanda's heart began a wild pumping. She had taken the plunge. It should be fear she was feeling, she thought, but it wasn't. It was excitement.

She wondered what manner of man she was dealing with, who could offer her heaven or hell—whatever one or the other or both would be like—then ride on towards it with a bold hand on the rein of her horse.

If she wanted to let her mare gallop, she had to loosen the bridle. That was the thought uppermost in her mind.

Then she wondered about herself. That she could make the choice so easily...and ride with him... wherever he cared to take her.

CHAPTER TEN

AMANDA was determined not to wilt. By late afternoon it was sheer willpower that kept her in the saddle.

They had ridden hard and fast. She was certainly not spared. The mountain trails were rough and became narrower and narrower. There was no such thing as an easy walk, let alone a canter. Galloping, thank heaven, was too dangerous to attempt on this terrain.

Every bone in her body was jolted. Every muscle screamed in protest. It was just as well that the black mare followed the white stallion without any urging. Amanda was reduced to hanging on. How much further? she longed to ask, but pride would not allow her any confession of weakness.

When they'd stopped for lunch, hours ago, she had still felt fine. The morning ride had been a lot faster but not nearly so arduous. They had emerged from the forest to slopes that were terraced for agriculture. There were apricot and apple orchards, fig and olive trees. It had been quite pleasant, climbing to the high pastures which were dotted with flocks of sheep.

That was all behind them now. Scattered stands of green oak and juniper trees grew between outcrops of bare rock, but vegetation was sparse this far up amongst crumbling gullies and limestone ledges. Amanda was in no state to appreciate the scenery anyway. She figured she was going through the hell part of the path they were set upon, and the heaven part had better make up for it.

At last they came to a resting place. It was like an oasis in a mountain desert. For a few moments, Amanda wondered if she was hallucinating. She blinked several times but the natural rock-pool was still there. So was a glade of pine trees and grazing grass for the horses.

'We'll camp here for the night.'

It was a welcome announcement. The only problem was, Amanda didn't think she had strength enough to get off her horse. She watched Upgrade dismount with an easy fluid action. His legs weren't seized up. His arms weren't limp.

Mind over matter, she sternly advised herself.

It didn't help. The messages from her brain simply didn't penetrate to her booted feet. They remained stuck in the stirrups. She did manage to unclench her fingers from the reins and grab hold of the pommel of her saddle.

'I'm afraid I'm incapable of moving,' she declared ruefully. 'I've never been riding this long. It's not that I'm weak,' she argued. 'I'm simply all used up.'

She didn't realise the words came out slurred. She thought they were very precise and her logic was perfectly reasonable.

Amanda wasn't quite sure how he got her off the

horse but his arm around her waist certainly assisted. She was glad he didn't try to set her on her feet because she had the feeling her knees would buckle. It felt extremely comforting to be cradled securely in his arms. He carried her some distance and laid her gently on the grass.

'I'll be back in a minute,' he said.

'Mmmh,' she answered, overwhelmed with fatigue.

She closed her eyes and let herself float above the aches and pains. She felt her riding boots being eased off her feet and vaguely thought that was a good idea. Loosen up her toes. Her jeans were another matter. When he unfastened them and started pulling them down, Amanda jolted out of her daze of exhaustion. Undressing her to that extent was distinctly inappropriate. She was in no condition to feel or respond to anything.

'Not yet,' she mumbled.

'I'm going to massage your legs with liniment.'

'Sensible,' she agreed, relieved that nothing was expected of her.

He had wonderful hands. Wonderful liniment. It spread tingling heat deep into her muscles. Or so it seemed. Amanda thought she could take a lot of what he was doing to her. Her legs were beginning to feel as though they belonged to her again.

When he started working on her toes, there were definitely messages working up through her body to her brain. Squirmy, exciting, little messages. She had read somewhere that women could have orgasms

from having their toes fondled. She thought it would
be interesting to check it out.

'I'll do your back now.'

With that assurance, Amanda saw no reason to resist being further undressed. He unfastened the burnoose, unbuttoned her shirt, lifted her a little to draw
the sleeves from her arms, then gently rolled her onto
a rug that he must have fetched from one of the pack-
horses.

He covered her legs, keeping them warm, then removed her bra and swept her hair aside. She still had
her panties on and she had lain on many a beach like
this, so there was really nothing to feel self-conscious
about. The fact that she was alone with a man halfway
up the Atlas Mountains didn't change anything. He
was the right man.

Besides, he was being very professional, like a
nurse, and it was undoubtedly for her own good. His
slow, deep, controlled breathing indicated nothing.
Nevertheless, she couldn't help wondering how much
he liked what he saw, how really physically appealing
she was to him, whether touching her was pleasur-
able, exciting…and where it would stop. If it did.

He moved to kneel astride her, his knees pinning
the rug on either side of her thighs. Amanda's eyes
were closed but the image of him poised directly over
her supine body burned into her mind, stirring an exquisite sensitivity to his touch. It wasn't until he had
worked over her back and shoulder muscles for some

time that Amanda could relax completely and simply let the soothing motion flow through her.

She drifted off into a sensual dream where she was floating on a gentle sea and delicious waves rolled around her bottom, making her feel especially soft, buoyant and feminine. Then utter oblivion swallowed the dream and she was aware of nothing until she awoke to a range of little noises; horses snuffling, the crackle and spit of a camp fire burning, the soft crunch of footsteps.

She became conscious of other things. She was warmly and softly cocooned in a sleeping bag, a makeshift pillow under her head. It was dark. The sky was ablaze with stars. There was the smell of coffee with a touch of cloves. Her body, when she moved it, was slightly stiff in the joints, but no longer aching. She turned herself slowly towards the sounds and the smell.

He was crouched beside the fire, his body still cloaked in the burnoose, but with the hood thrown back. The flickering light threw his profile into sharp relief. Again she thought he had the kind of strong, noble face that was struck on ancient coins. Its ageless quality suggested an endurance that could suffer and rise above any adversity. Indomitable.

She wondered about his origins. He didn't look Arabic. The Berbers were a Caucasian race, but he didn't look like one of them, either. Perhaps, he was simply unique to himself and that set him apart, contributing to his loneliness.

He was still holding himself apart from her despite the need he had revealed, despite her willingness to embrace the man he was and go with him wherever he led. Was he having second thoughts? Did her collapse after the long ride diminish her in his eyes?

She wished she could tell what he was thinking...feeling. She wished she had woken up in his arms. She was sure that the physical contact would have reduced everything to simpler, more basic terms. Her body tingled with the memory of his hands moving over her bared flesh. He already knew her far more intimately than she knew him. If she called to him now...

'Have I slept long?' she asked.

He wasn't startled by her voice. He turned his head to look at her, his face gathering shadows that made his expression indecipherable. 'It is almost dawn. We must leave soon.'

His voice was quiet, calm, decisive. So much for any thought of making love! This man was not about to be tempted from the course set in his mind. His air of relentless, ruthless purpose was not softened or mitigated in any way.

Amanda felt decidedly frustrated. She was both surprised and chagrined to find she had slept a good eight hours, the night was virtually over, and she was none the wiser about Mr Complimentary Upgrade apart from the fact of him being a superb masseur.

She suddenly realised her stomach felt very empty. 'I need food,' she said bluntly, wary of the pace he had set yesterday and the need to restore a high energy level.

'We will eat as soon as you have washed and dressed. You will find fresh clothes beside you.'

The thought of another day's riding made Amanda quail inside. 'Aren't the horses tired?' It was the only excuse she could think of that might allow her more rest.

'They are. They are also mountain bred. They will not let fatigue hold us up.'

Amanda sighed. A petulant stand was out of the question. She would lose his respect. She had made her choice, accepted his conditions, and it ill behove her not to continue with as good a grace as she could muster. Particularly since he was looking after her aches and pains and feeding her as best he could.

He was organised and efficient. By the time Amanda had finished breakfast, the camp fire was doused and scattered into non-existence, everything was packed up, the horses were saddled, and there was no trace left behind of their night's sojourn here. Amanda wondered if he was still concerned about idle eyes. Or was he expecting Xa Shiraq to have them tracked once it was realised they were no longer with the convoy?

The sky was lightening as he helped her mount the black mare. Her bottom settled gingerly on the contours of the saddle. Amanda decided, on behalf of the torture her muscles were anticipating, that one small challenge was in order.

'I think it's only fair you should tell me how far we're going today so I can get myself mentally prepared for it. After all, a marathon runner knows he only has to pace himself through twenty-six miles, three hundred and eighty-five yards. How many yards do I need to pace myself through?' she added dryly.

'Many,' he said.

'Thanks for the precision,' Amanda rejoined.

He pointed to the highest point of the mountain range they were traversing. 'That is our destination. If you can steel yourself to the journey, we should make it there in good time.'

In good time for what? she wondered. 'Does it have a name?'

'In Arabic it is called the Gemini Peak.'

'Does it have a twin?'

'To the north. Where your convoy is going to. We cannot view it from here,' he said dismissively.

Amanda's grey cells hit turbo assist as they went into overdrive. Pieces of the puzzle left by her father slotted neatly into place with those few words from Mr Complimentary Upgrade. A twin peak to the one her father had described!

No wonder her father's discovery had been discredited. No wonder that no one else had been able to refind the caves her father had spoken of. They were being directed to the wrong mountain top!

Every map, including the precious one she had so carefully kept to herself, positioned the crystal caves on the peak to the north of the wine village of Tirham.

Its *twin* peak, to the south, was not entered on any map Amanda had seen. The omission had to be deliberate and her father somehow misled about direction. That was why Xa Shiraq's duplicity had lain unrevealed for so long.

Upgrade knew the answer to it all. He was betraying his sheikh to show her the secret. It explained the restraint he had forced upon himself, no matter how pressing or urgent the desire he felt for her. First, he would give her what she wanted, what she had come to achieve. Only after that was accomplished would he come to her as her lover. Only when he had given all he had to give.

It touched Amanda deeply. When the time came, she would repay this man with all the love and affection and tenderness in her heart. What he was doing for her was a sacrifice of heroic proportions. Her instinctive reactions to him had been so right.

He had already mounted. She urged the black mare up beside the white stallion before he set off. 'Come what may,' she said with renewed determination, 'I will ride with you this day. I will not fail you. I will not falter. I'll be with you at the end.'

His stygian black eyes gleamed their approval. 'That is how it should be,' he said simply. He turned his horse's head, and led off into the blaze of glory as the sun crested the mountain ridges with its mantle of fire.

Amanda found it impossible to estimate the distance they had to cover. It was reassuring to know where the termination point was. Bubbles of adrenaline spurred her on. What had once appeared so unattainable was now within reach.

The thrill of knowing that her father, now dead, could figuratively hold his head high in pride diminished the jolting, bruising ride. There was a sense of purpose in the gruelling journey, although she still didn't know what the end result would be.

She pondered further on the problem as they rode steadily upwards. Perhaps the Gemini Peak marked the border between Xabia and another country. Furthermore, it might be a safe route for her out of Xa Shiraq's grasp.

Considering the crimes listed against her, Amanda realised that Upgrade could be rescuing her from a lengthy term of highly unpleasant imprisonment, as well as saving his own skin from retribution. It made sense of the speed he pressed on her, and the need to avoid any possible witnesses to their passage into these mountains.

Amanda was not keen on running away. Not if she actually found the crystal caves. It nagged at her mind. Would Upgrade be happy as an exile to a country he had served with great personal commitment? Would she be happy knowing her mission to establish the truth of her father's discovery was aborted without full restitution being made? Could anyone ever scuttle all that had made up their past lives?

Amanda felt as rootless as her father had been. She had a conviction that some things were worth fighting for. Like justice. And fair play. Her instincts told her it would be better for both her and Upgrade if they faced up to Xa Shiraq.

The problem lay in whether Upgrade would agree to it or not. Could she rescue him from Xa Shiraq's wrath by playing her cards right, forcing a stand-off so that Upgrade didn't have to face exile? Power could be challenged with power. Firstly, she would have to re-establish contact with Mocca, then get to her embassy. Amanda had a lot of faith in Mocca's resourcefulness.

Once that had been done, and she had her own government's support, she would beard Xa Shiraq in his den. There were ways and means of establishing a truce once she had her bargaining tool.

As plans revolved around Amanda's mind, she started taking more notice of landmarks along the trail they travelled. She might have to go back alone if Upgrade rejected her ideas. He would follow her. She had no doubt of that. However, she might very well need a head start to accomplish what she wanted.

The day wore on. They didn't stop. A water canteen and a bag of dried fruit and biscuits were attached to Amanda's saddle. She didn't starve and she didn't die of thirst but the long exhausting ride took its toll. She was almost reeling with fatigue when a halt was finally called beside a small rocky mountain stream that trickled down from the peak.

'This is far enough. We leave the horses here.'

The black mare came to a stop next to the white stallion.

'Why?' Amanda asked. The peak looked so close now. Enticingly close. 'Surely an hour or two more....'

'The horses cannot go where we will go. This is the best place for them to rest.'

'You mean we are to continue on foot?'

'Exactly.'

'So we save the horses and kill ourselves,' she said with an attempt at ironic humour.

'You cannot go on?' he asked, his dark eyes scanning hers in concern.

'Where you go, so, too, will I,' she said loftily.

'Good,' he approved, taking her at her word.

Nevertheless, he helped her off the mare and gave her some time to wash her hands and splash her face with the cold water from the stream while he saw to the horses, unsaddling and tethering them. She did her best to collect a second wind as she watched him swing a pack on his shoulders, ready to trek forward.

He didn't say anything. Neither did she. He took her hand in his, and strode off without a backward glance.

They climbed.

He assisted her, supported her, pushed her. Amanda went on like an automaton, beyond fatigue, holding on, moving one foot after the other. They came to a ledge which was blocked by a monstrous stone.

'It's no good,' Amanda said. 'We can't go past it or get around it.'

Upgrade took no notice of her. He dropped the pack from his shoulders, unbuckled it and took out two hydraulic jacks.

'I will lift the rock sufficiently for us to bypass it.'

He suited his actions to his words. Curiosity drew Amanda forward to observe. The rock had been cut at the base on either side, but one side much higher than the other in order to take the jacks.

Upgrade manoeuvred them into place, then started the lifting process. One side was kept at the same level to form a fulcrum on which to lever the other.

Amanda watched in fascination as millimeter by millimeter the great block began to tilt. It revealed a small crevice set into the rock wall.

'You will crawl through that.'

Amanda looked incredulously at Upgrade. He had to be joking.

He waved her forward. He wasn't joking.

Amanda did as she was told with deep trepidation. What if the great block slipped off the jacks? The thought of entombment sent spears of horror through her. She tried to calm herself with the assurance that at least she wouldn't be alone. He followed her into the narrow space, pushing her towards an impenetrable darkness.

She could feel her throat choking up. She thought of *Aida*. How the two lovers had sung together after their entombment was beyond belief. That was opera. This was real life.

Then there was no rock constricting her passage. She swept her arm around to make sure. There was nothing in touching distance. Very cautiously she rose to her feet and stepped forward into a sense of time-less, eerie space.

She heard Upgrade straighten up behind her. Then there was a click and in the glow of torchlight she saw for the first time what her father had discovered.

Only then did she understand why it had haunted him for the rest of his life!

CHAPTER ELEVEN

THE illumination refracted from thousands of millions of facets of the crystal lining the cave, protruding from the walls in flower-like shapes, feathering down from the roof. It was like a magical fairyland, sparkling with ancient mystery and the promise of riches beyond belief.

It was entrancing, enthralling, and as the torch swung in an arc, it magnified the effect of being encased in a fantastic prism that bathed them in glittering rainbows. It was all her father had described. More. The memory of it must have been burned into his mind...an inescapable torment, impossible to forget.

Tears welled into Amanda's eyes. To have the enormity of this discovery suppressed and disbelieved when he knew all along he had seen what she was seeing now... 'It's true,' she whispered in an agony of apology for the doubts that had sometimes clouded her faith in his claims about the neodymite crystal caves. 'All true.'

She turned blindly to the man who had brought her here, instinctively reaching out to him in the darkness behind the torch. 'I can't tell you how much it means...'

Her heart was so full she could not find the words to express all she felt. She stumbled forward and half fell against him. His arms swept around her, holding her to the strong, warm solidity of his body. She couldn't help it. She wept, overwhelmed by this resolution to years of striving…trying to console her father, trying to bolster his cause with her belief, trying to work her way to proving the truth, once and for all.

'Thank you,' she choked out. 'Thank you for doing this for me.'

'No man could have asked more of a daughter,' he said softly. 'Your father has a right to be justly proud of you.'

'But I'd never have found it without you.'

'You had an unquenchable belief. Such beliefs move mountains. You would have found it, or lost your life striving for the unattainable. I merely took it into my head to save yours.'

'You've been here before. You must have been.'

'Once.'

'Before the entrance was sealed?'

'Yes.'

'Why did you decide to share it with me?'

The hand on her hair moved to her face, feather-light fingertips caressing her cheek. 'Would I be a true companion to you if I let you suffer the pain of never knowing what you wanted and needed to know?'

His lips brushed her fringe aside and pressed a kiss on her forehead. 'I want your mind to be at rest.'

His hand dropped to the soft swell of her breasts. 'I want your heart to be content.'

His body moved more intimately against hers. 'I want you to be at peace with yourself, and with me.'

Amanda was transfixed by the beautiful simplicity of his words, the sweet transmission of giving implicit in his touch. It rippled through her body, washing away the lassitude of deep fatigue, stirring anew the deep womanly needs that called out to be mated with this man.

She felt his physical response, the hardening thrust of his flesh against hers, the sense and urgency of his youth pulsing from him, reaching out to her, wanting. Her mind danced with a wild singing of yes…oh, yes, I want you…yes…and her heart took up the refrain with a rapid tattoo of affirmation.

He expelled a deep sigh and turned away from the tempting contact, his arm curling around her shoulders to hold her close to his side as he moved forward. 'I will show you all there is to see,' he murmured, his voice strained with the necessity to complete the task.

He was right, Amanda thought with a heartfelt rush of gratitude. This place belonged to her father. They were walking now where he had been before them, their feet crunching on orbs of crystal that had broken away and shattered on the rock floor. This was one of the great natural mineral repositories of the world…and the justification of her father's belief in himself.

'It's magic,' she whispered, as strange shapes loomed up ahead, some fluorescing under the light of the torch, others taking on the appearance of transfigured images. 'How far does it go?'

'There are many caves.'

'All like this?'

'Some smaller, some larger.'

She thought it strange that the air did not smell musty. Perhaps she was intoxicated by the sheer splendour of light reflected into myriad fascinating fantasies by the crystals. Perhaps the crystals freshened the air.

Or maybe she was light-headed from the excitement coursing through her at the continual brushing of her body against his, thighs, hips, the nestling of her shoulder under his arm. It made her feel small, feminine, protected. He hugged her more firmly whenever she stumbled.

The caves were interlinked, apparently honeycombing a considerable part of the peak. She knew they were looking at untold wealth and could well imagine her father's elation at having found one of the greatest treasures in the world. As a geologist he would have been in seventh heaven. Yet he had ended up in a personal hell.

Her feet faltered to a halt. 'I've seen enough for today.'

'As you will,' came the quiet rejoinder. 'There is always tomorrow.'

Amanda felt drained of the energy that had kept

her going. All this had brought her father long-lasting misery. What had been done to him was unforgivably wrong. Her sense of injustice swelled as they started retracing their steps.

'Why was my father's discovery discredited?' It was a painful cry of protest. 'Why was the existence of the neodymite crystals suppressed?'

'You realise it's used as a catalyst in the manufacture of rocket fuel and other chemical processes?'

'Yes.'

'Your father refused to comprehend the consequences of what he had found,' came the quiet and unemotional reply.

'I don't understand,' she pleaded. 'There is a vast wealth for your country here.'

'I see death and destruction.'

'It could be used for good...'

'Don't be naive, Amanda.' His voice hardened.

'Whoever controls the source of neodymite controls the future,' she expostulated.

'Do you imagine any of the world's great powers would care what happened to Xabia and its people while they fought for their share of what is here?'

'Mining the crystals could be managed for the benefit of the people,' she insisted, not wanting to accept his dark view of inevitable consequences.

'Xabia will not become another Kuwait,' he went on remorselessly. 'Neodymite crystals are more valuable than the black gold that motivates war. There would also be the price of corruption.'

The cold certainty in his voice dampened her ardour for argument. 'Yet it cannot forever remain a secret.'

'No geologist will ever be allowed to venture into this area again. Every trace of this discovery has been expunged from the records. It will remain so.'

It stirred a fierce resentment in Amanda. 'You have no idea what that did to my father.'

'Your father was blindly obsessed. He would not see the danger.'

'He was an orphan. A homeless, Irish orphan. The butt of cruel jokes. You wouldn't know what it's like to be put down,' she said heatedly, smarting from the memory of all her recent treatment from Charles Arnold.

'We must all rise above such things.'

'Dad wanted recognition. Nothing more. It would have made him worth something to himself,' she defended. 'Xa Shiraq killed that in him.'

'Xa Shiraq was right, Amanda,' came the remorseless reply. 'Your father was wrong.'

'Not in my view,' Amanda said fiercely. 'Not by my standards. Xa Shiraq wasn't prepared to reach for the stars.'

She was stepping forward as she spoke. He stopped. His arm dropped from her shoulders. Amanda hesitated, glanced back. He stood absolutely still, a dark and suddenly menacing figure. The atmosphere in the cave seemed to thicken. She sensed turbulent emotion coursing through him, emotion that focused on her with frightening force.

Before she could do or say anything to appease it, he stepped forward, and played the torch once more over the cavern of crystal about them.

'What do you see, Amanda?' he demanded harshly. 'Fame and fortune? Is that what you crave?'

'No,' she cried in protest.

'Does your father's greed run in your blood, too?'

'It wasn't greed!'

'Power is very seductive…'

'It's not so,' she denied vehemently.

'Look at them. Millions of neodymite crystals twinkling their temptation. Beautiful and deadly. For thousands of years they have glittered unseen, storing up energy, waiting to shower it upon the world. Do they whisper to you to release it?'

It was strange. What she had initially seen as a magical fairyland now seemed to glint coldly, malignantly. She shivered. He pulled her against him, her shoulder blades meeting the firm masculinity of his broad chest, her bottom crushed to rocklike thighs.

'Xabia is prosperous,' he stated bitingly. 'There are no beggars in the streets of Alcabab. We have schools. We have hospitals. The people are not in want. Of what benefit are more riches, Amanda?'

She didn't know the facts well enough to dispute what he claimed. To speak out of ignorance could only earn his contempt. It was true what he said about the capital city. It had been surprisingly clean and orderly compared to other cities she had visited in the Middle East. Even the enterprising Mocca and his extended family had no complaint about their lot in life.

'As for the stars,' he continued mockingly. 'Isn't the space above our planet already filling with the debris of our rocketships? Why should mankind interfere with the stars? They have been more constant companions to me than anyone else. Leave them alone, I say.'

Amanda's heart sank. She had failed him. He had gambled on her seeing things his way, gambled she would give up her quest in favour of a greater wisdom. He had opened his mind to her and instead of sharing his perceptions, she had clung to her father's cause.

Amanda closed her eyes to her father's lost treasure and felt the pained thump of the heart behind her. 'I'm sorry,' she whispered. 'I've lived with this secret…for so long…to put everything right…'

'The decision is now yours, Amanda. To reveal or not to reveal. That is the choice I have given you.'

Her father was dead. He was beyond hurting any more. It tore at her heart. To admit he had been wrong in pursuing what had been forbidden him was unthinkable. Yet…

'Success and failure,' she whispered, 'both at the same time.'

'I have known it often.'

She believed this enigma of a man. The crystal

caves belonged to the people of Xabia. Yet they could not use them. It was the paradox of life.

She would not take it upon herself to change anything for them. To right the injustice to her father was to wrong others. Let justice be done though the heavens fall, he had said with grim irony.

She would not let the heavens fall.

'Amanda...' It was both a demand and a growl of need, dispensing with choice as he turned her in his arms and tilted her face to his.

His mouth claimed hers before she could utter a word.

The swift infusion of his passionate energy dispelled the limp feeling of defeat. It smashed the tormenting spectre of a promise that would not now be fulfilled. It stamped another promise into her mind that seduced all reason, then into her heart, allowing room for nothing else but the stampeding pulse of togetherness.

Take me, his kiss said. *There is no fame or fortune or power in the world that could compensate for what would be lost if you choose another path.*

He reforged the link between them with tempestuous fire, welding the softness of her body to the burning rigidity of his, his hands sliding over her in pressure patterns that secured a fierce and intimate contact. He was rampant male, compelling submission to his will, yet inducing a yielding that exulted in his forcefulness, and the yielding brought its own harvest of response from him.

She felt the straining of his muscles, the tremor of need that rippled through him, the pounding of his heart, the endless thirst for her giving of herself to him. He had waited, restrained himself to breaking point, but now the floodgates of wanting were cast open and a torrent of desire swept all before it.

'Does this make up your mind?' he demanded hoarsely, his breathing as tortured as hers between kisses. 'Tell me it does. Give yourself to me.'

'Not here,' she pleaded, her voice raw with her need for him, yet the thought of the crystals surrounding them—her father's crystals—was abhorrent to her at a moment which should be clean of the past.

'This is not the place for us,' he agreed.

He swept her along with him, Amanda's feet barely touching the ground. He virtually carried her through the shimmering kaleidoscope of caves, back the way they had come, unerring in his sense of direction, urgency driving his every step.

Amanda was riven by her desire to go with him wherever he led. The knowledge she was leaving her father's dreams forever behind her was submerged. It had to be so, she told herself. She had her own life to live. The choice was made. There *was* good reason for letting things be as they had been for time immemorial. Her father had been the disturbing influence. This was her final farewell to him. She hoped he would understand.

They reached the entrance to the tunnel that led out to the pure mountain air, to a clear vista of the country so loved by the man who would be her lover, to a future she couldn't yet envisage, but it was waiting out there for her.

'Go ahead,' he urged as she knelt to crawl through to the crevice in the rock-face. 'I will follow in a minute. There is something I must do for you first.'

She couldn't imagine what it might be, but she didn't protest or linger. She hated the claustrophobic feeling of the narrow passageway and manoeuvred herself through it with driven haste, emerging on the open cliff ledge with an intense sense of relief.

She didn't touch the hydraulic jack near her feet. She was certain afterwards she did not. The weight it was supporting must have caused an overload in its mechanism. There was a loud crunch. The huge block of stone started to tilt towards her.

The shock of it robbed her of any wits at all. The instinct for survival must have taken over, forcing her feet to scramble out of harm's way. It was only when the massive stone rocked into its resting place, sealing the exit from the crystal caves that she began to scream, the horror of it bursting through her mind, clawing at her heart.

If he had not been crushed to death, he was sealed inside the caves...entombed with no way out. In irrational panic she rushed at the monstrous rock, tried to free the crushed hydraulic jack, tried to push the massive weight aside. She wept, she sobbed, she called out to him again and again.

There was no answer. Not a sound issued from the

mountain to assure her she was heard, that all was well with him.

Dead, she thought numbly.

Finally it dawned on her that she had to go for help. She had to leave him and find people who could rescue him if he was alive to be rescued. If an arm had been pinioned under that great weight... Amanda shuddered in horror at the mental image. She had to get help before it was too late.

The secret of the crystal caves could not be allowed to be a secret any longer. She couldn't let him die in there. She wouldn't let him die in there. Whatever it cost, she would get him out.

CHAPTER TWELVE

AMANDA slid, fell, stumbled, scrambled and hurtled down the narrow paths and slopes on the way back to where they had left the horses. Scratches, scrapes, grazes and bruises meant nothing to her. Heedless of any damage she might sustain, her mind was set on one goal and one goal only. Despair and desperation drove her on.

Wearied beyond belief, she made it back to their base camp before sunset. She could not afford the luxury of sleep. Once she closed her eyes it might be a day before she opened them again. There was only one thing she could do. She had to go on.

At least coming down the paths and trails had been far easier and faster than going up. She hoped that would hold true for the journey she had to make on horseback.

She tried to saddle the white Arabian stallion, reasoning he could go faster than the black mare. He wouldn't let her near him. She fell back on the mare, frantic to keep moving.

She hauled her battered body into the saddle. She tried knees, hands, reins, everything she could think of, but the mare only circled around, refusing to go anywhere without its mate.

Amanda cursed like an Arab caravan overseer. She cursed as she had never cursed before. Finally she managed to untether the white stallion and slapped it hard on its rump. It reared high on its back legs. Finally, and by good luck only, it took off along the trail by which they had come.

The black mare quickly raced onto its heels. Amanda knew she had no control over where they went, how they went, and the speed at which it was accomplished. She could only pray the white stallion would lead them to the nearest habitation so she could beg for a rescue party. If she could make herself understood.

They descended helter-skelter and Amanda felt sorry for her horse, obsessively intent on keeping up with the riderless stallion in front of them. It wasn't fair on the mare, but the mare didn't seem to care that she was carrying Amanda's weight.

Amanda understood the instinct that wouldn't let the female be parted from her male. Wasn't that why she was pushing herself beyond any rational limits of endurance to keep going?

She could hardly bear to think of what it must be like to be imprisoned in those caves. Was there a fresh supply of air creeping in from a crack somewhere? Was it enough to last for…however long it took to bring help?

How powerful were the batteries in the torch? If he was plunged into utter darkness… Amanda shuddered.

Hold on…hold on…hold on…

She did so herself.

I'll come back for you, her heart said, forever and always.

The mindless refrains of holding on, forever and always, helped to detach herself from the exhaustion enveloping her. She was no longer in control. The sheer mechanics of riding kept her in the saddle. She was oblivious to where she was, how far she had come.

The light was fading. She didn't know what she would do once night fell. Would the horses keep going? Was it wise to risk it? She had to!

Had to…had to…

She was numb, numb all over when she heard the helicopter. She had to concentrate hard on focusing her eyes, turning her gaze to the sky. It was too high, too far away for any occupant to spot her. She doubted she could find the energy to lift her arms to wave anyway. Futile effort. The helicopter went out of her line of vision without deviating from its course.

Despair dragged at her heart. She tried to pick out the landmarks she had taken note of earlier in the day. She thought she recognised a couple but had no real idea what they meant in relation to how far she had travelled from the Gemini Peak. The light was going fast now. She had no choice but to trust the horses to take her where she needed to go.

She remembered that in the days of Genghis Khan messengers had been tied to the saddle. She wished she had taken the same precautions. If she stopped, dismounted, she suspected the black mare would take off with the white stallion and leave her alone.

Impossible to contemplate such an outcome.

She caught herself reeling and forced herself to sit upright again. Darkness nearly on her. Have to stay awake, she told herself. She twisted the reins around her wrists, a warning tug if she should start to fall off. Sound of the helicopter again. No use to her. She didn't bother looking for it this time. No energy for that. It couldn't land here.

Darkness. At least she had the stars as her companions. She had to ensure he would see them again. The link between them couldn't be broken. Their togetherness was written in the stars. He had told her so. She believed him.

Body sagging. Rolling in the saddle. If she could rest for a moment. Close her eyes. So hard to keep them open. Just for one moment. Mustn't fall off...

A shout snapped her awake. She had slumped across the horse's mane. She dragged herself up. The mare slowed to a tired walk. Amanda couldn't see the white stallion. There was the drumming sound of hooves clattering towards her. Someone coming. Voices. She had found help. At last!

That thought was enough to sustain her wretched body, stirring it to an awareness of pain. None of it mattered. Only the message she had to deliver mattered.

Other horses steamed and stamped around her. Berbers talking across her in Arabic, taking the reins from her hands. She didn't have the strength to resist. She grabbed the pommel of the saddle to steady herself.

'Stop! Listen!' she cried. 'Does anyone speak English?'

'You will come with us,' one of them replied.

'No.' Amanda shook her head dizzily. 'I need help. We have to go back. To the Gemini Peak. Up there a man is trapped in one of the caves.'

'There is no order but the order of Xa Shiraq. You will come with us,' came the inflexible reply.

'But the man will die.'

'Undoubtedly. In the meantime, you will come with us.'

'No, I won't,' Amanda yelled hysterically.

Her plea fell on deaf ears. 'It is not a matter of choice,' she was told. 'You will go to the helicopter.'

Through the dizzying waves of fatigue, Amanda grasped one thing clearly. Using a helicopter to transport her bespoke power. 'By whose order?' she asked.

'It is the order of Jebel Haffa, who fulfils the will of Xa Shiraq.'

'These are the men I must see,' Amanda said, trying to drive conviction into her voice. 'I will use their power to have my way. Take me to the helicopter.' She hoped the words sounded as brave as the ideas behind them were.

Her horse was urged forward. The Berber riders were beside her, behind her, in front of her. She no longer had the reins. There was no room to dismount even if she mustered the strength to do so. She was comprehensively trapped by the escort.

'How long will this take?' she begged in utter desperation.

'Our orders are that we are not to be swayed by anything you say,' came the flat, relentless reply. 'We must not listen to any words you speak.'

'Oh, that's really great,' Amanda grumbled, frustration eating into her courageous facade.

She closed her eyes, silently and bitterly cursing Xa Shiraq. He must have found out she was no longer with Mocca and the convoy. He must realise he had been betrayed by the man now entombed inside the Gemini Peak. Xa Shiraq had entrusted that man with the task of seeing she never confirmed her father's discovery. Now her impossible task was to convince Xa Shiraq to go to the help of his betrayer.

The helicopter had probably been searching for them when she had seen it pass overhead. It was certainly no coincidence that it had been sent to this area. Xa Shiraq had been checking out the worst scenario he could think of and he'd come up trumps.

'Where is the helicopter going to take me?' she asked, hoping for some enlightenment.

'To the sheikh's palace at Alcabab.'

The vision of Mocca's invoices to the palace rose in Amanda's mind.

'Will I see Xa Shiraq himself?' she asked, keeping her tone light to hide the despair she felt.

The Berber shrugged. 'It will be as he wills.'

It was hardly a conclusive reply. Nevertheless, it did make sense that Xa Shiraq would want to question her. She wondered if he would order a public trial for her crimes. Unlikely, she decided. He wouldn't want her blabbing about the crystal caves to all and sundry in an open court. Amanda was only too well aware of how much trouble he had taken to hide their existence. She would be spirited away, never to be seen again.

Yet she would surely get the chance to talk to him face-to-face. She would tell him all, plead with him, appeal to his finer senses of humanity. She would convince him to rescue the man who had served him loyally and faithfully for so many years.

Or would Xa Shiraq leave the man to die miserably of thirst and starvation in the deep black vaults of the crystal caves?

'Help me off this horse,' she demanded when the troup of cavalry halted at the helicopter. Bravado seemed to be her best recourse in this situation.

'No.' It was the Berber captain who spoke.

'How am I to get off it then?' she asked.

'Fall off it,' he prompted unsympathetically.

'Why won't you help?'

'It is forbidden to all men to touch you,' he said.

Amanda swore again in the most unladylike manner. In her present condition there was no way she could maintain any dignity without assistance. If this was a deliberate act of humiliation...

'Let me get this straight,' she said in biting anger. 'You are not to listen to any words I speak, you are to say as little as possible to me, and you're not to touch me.'

'That is correct,' came the unemotional reply. 'That is the order of Jebel Haffa to the will of Xa Shiraq.'

Amanda gritted her teeth. Words were useless weapons. She was faced with brick wall adherence to orders. If she was to get to Xa Shiraq, she had to make it to the helicopter by herself.

Somehow she managed to slide herself around the neck of the horse. It galled her that she presented anything but a dainty picture. The Berber men looked on expressionlessly as she eventually staggered onto her feet at ground level.

Amanda was more riled than she had ever been in her whole life. She was being treated as an outcast. A pariah. Purdah in its cruellest form! She felt the steam level of her boiler rising.

'Take me to Xa Shiraq,' she demanded. 'I'm going to give him a fair whopping piece of my mind!'

CHAPTER THIRTEEN

KOZIM found it very stressful when Xa Shiraq maintained silence for longer than five minutes. Kozim found it so stressful that he timed Xa Shiraq's silences so he could be quite sure whether to feel stressed or not stressed.

What was even more stressful was when Xa Shiraq accompanied the lack of speech with the tapping of his fingers. It meant the sheikh's mind was working in mysterious ways that would inevitably confuse him. Kozim could then lose respect by giving the wrong answers.

Xa Shiraq's respect meant a great deal to Kozim. Indeed, it was imperative he keep it. To Kozim, it was the most important thing in his life.

He decided a safe comment was in order to prompt the sheikh into talking again. This would almost certainly diminish the build-up of stress.

'I had all the trash cans in the sheikhdom intimately examined and scrutinised,' he said.

The black eyes focused on him with nerve-tingling intensity. 'Why did you do that?' The voice gave no indication of approval or criticism.

The question spread uncertainty through Kozim's mind. 'I wondered if a rare jewel might be found.'

The fingers tapped again. 'Did you find any jewels, Kozim?'

'No, Your Excellency.'

'Don't bother doing that again.'

'Of course not,' Kozim said miserably. 'Most unfortunate.'

'The geologist's daughter requires attention, Kozim.'

'I thought it would come to this,' Kozim said quickly. 'Will I block payment of the bills?'

Xa Shiraq's mouth curled sardonically. 'No. Mocca has an extensive family. It behoves us to give an occasional boon to such people. From such matters, legends are born.'

Kozim blinked. It was extraordinary how Xa Shiraq knew everything. Even the least significant of his people in Alcabab did not escape his attention.

'Fire must be fought with fire,' came the grim announcement.

'That's so wise,' Kozim hurried to agree.

'The woman has gone too far.'

'Women always do.'

'Entombing people goes beyond good-natured fun.'

'Absolutely.'

'It calls for the most severe retribution.'

Kozim had some expertise in the field of retribution. 'Beheading was a favorite device of the British monarchy for many centuries. Henry the Eighth had a certain natural flair...'

'I need worse,' Xa Shiraq growled. His fingers tapped a particularly strong rhythm.

'The unspeakable or the unmentionable?' Kozim asked. 'Which do you prefer?'

'Both!' Xa Shiraq said decisively. 'She should suffer both!'

'Wise,' said Kozim. 'You are not only esteemed, respected and loved for the qualities of mercy and justice, but, oh, so very wise.'

Kozim glanced quickly at Xa Shiraq. The deadly resolve in those all-knowing black eyes made him shudder. Once more he reflected how glad he was that he was not the geologist's daughter.

CHAPTER FOURTEEN

As SOON as the helicopter landed in the palace grounds a swarm of women came forward to help Amanda. They lifted her into a richly ornate sedan chair that could have been commissioned by an empress of Rome. Although she welcomed the softly piled comfort of silk and satin cushions after the rigours she had been through, it was a painful reminder that the man she had left behind had nothing but cold, hard stone to lie on.

No-one would listen to anything she said. The women were as deaf as the Berber men to her pleas, to logical argument, to any compassionate understanding of the situation. They were unswervingly persistent in following their own schedule and Amanda simply didn't have the strength to resist the ministrations that followed her arrival in what had to be the sheikh's harem.

She was stripped with gentle but firm efficiency, pushed and pressured into a spa pool and thoroughly lathered and washed as though she were a baby. In truth, she felt as helpless as one. Her hair was shampooed and brushed dry. Her thoroughly cleansed body was massaged with some wonderfully soothing body lotion.

Her guilt at accepting such treatment was appeased by the thought that it had to be against all protocol to be presented to the sheikh looking the way she had. Fighting this process would only cause more delay in getting to Xa Shiraq. But it was agony thinking of what might be happening up in the crystal caves.

She was clothed in a simple gown of white silk. She was urged into eating a thick creamy soup. It seemed sensible to comply since she couldn't afford to be weak from hunger. The soup was delicious and filling. Her tastebuds told her it was a mixture of seafood. As she ate, the drowsier she became.

She awoke in a luxurious bedchamber, lying between satin sheets, and it was broad daylight. A woman attendant smiled benevolently at her. Amanda wanted to scream and rant and rave at the appalling passage of time that represented untold suffering for the man she had to save.

'How do I get to Xa Shiraq from here?' she demanded, with little hope the woman would understand.

She didn't. Or pretended not to. She made a swift exit from the bedchamber and before Amanda could swing her feet to the lushly carpeted floor, a whole team of twittering servants poured into the room to start the pampering all over again.

Amanda kept repeating the name of Xa Shiraq to no effect whatsoever. The women insisted she dress in a long-sleeved caftan-style gown. It was black and reminded her of the burnoose that she hoped was providing some warmth for Upgrade if he was still alive.

She went into rebellion. She couldn't, wouldn't eat anything from the platter of exotic fruits provided for her breakfast. She wouldn't drink her coffee. She searched for a way out of the harem. There was none that she could find quickly.

In anguished frustration she cried again, 'I must get to Xa Shiraq. I have to see him. Please...can somebody help?'

A reply came from the oldest woman in attendance. 'A messenger was sent that you are rested and well, Princess.'

'How long will it be before I'm granted an audience?' Amanda demanded, ignoring the odd form of address to her.

The woman shrugged. 'It may be a day, perhaps a week, a month or two...who can tell the will of Xa Shiraq?'

'I can't wait that long!' Amanda protested. 'I have to talk to Xa Shiraq within the hour.'

A gong resounded from somewhere close. The women burst into excited twittering. The older one who had answered Amanda in English moved to the locked door at the far end of the room and opened a peephole. There was a quick exchange of Arabic. The woman turned to address Amanda.

'The time has come. An escort awaits to lead you to the sheikh.'

Amanda barely stopped herself from running to the

door. It was unlocked and opened for her before she reached it, but a few more seconds weren't about to make any difference. She knew she had to control her seething impatience. It was paramount that she impress Xa Shiraq with reasonable behaviour or he would undoubtedly scorn anything she had to say.

The escort of four men was in ceremonial military dress. They marched along on either side of her. It looked like a guard of honour, but Amanda had no delusions about that. She wondered if it was supposed to lull her into a false sense of confidence before the axe dropped on her neck. Xa Shiraq certainly had no reason to welcome her presence in his country, let alone his palace.

She fretted over how best to beg his mercy, whether any approach at all would soften his heart or appeal to some generosity of spirit. She was totally blind to the beautiful works of art she passed in the corridors on her way to him; splendid mosaic murals, exquisite urns, ancient carvings, all testaments to a cultural heritage that was proudly displayed and cared for. She thought only of what she had to accomplish and the ways and means to accomplish it.

Her mind flitted over many explanations that would justify Upgrade's betrayal to his sheikh. None satisfied her. She doubted Xa Shiraq would comprehend an emotional link that went beyond rationality.

The paired escort in front of her came to a halt at a double set of huge doors. With well-trained timing they opened them and stood back for Amanda to enter

the room ahead of her by herself. As she had anticipated, it was no open court filled with people. It
looked like a private library, the walls lined with
books, the furniture comprising highly polished desks,
leather armchairs, reading lamps.

Her gaze quickly swept the room as she stepped
inside. She tried desperately to quell the nervousness
and apprehension that threatened to reduce her to a
jittery and hopelessly inadequate advocate for her
cause. She was determined that none of what she really felt would show on her face or in her body language. If anything, she wanted to project defiance.

There were two men present, only two to confront
and convince, she told herself in an attempt to min-
imise the mountainous problem facing her. While
they looked intimidating in their official Arab robes
and headdresses, Amanda steeled herself to think of
them as ordinary human minds she could bend her
way.

The one rising from the chair behind his desk was
short and stout. The other, apparently perusing the
book in his hands, was turned away from her but
Amanda instantly identified him as the sheikh by the
gold and black twisted 'iqal that held his headdress
in place.

He was a tall, formidable figure, and Amanda felt
her stomach knot with apprehension as she heard the
doors close behind her. An overwhelming sense of
force and power emanated from him, holding her captive, yet he made no movement, gave no sign of ac-

knowledgement that she had intruded on his consciousness.

She'd experieced this before.

Twice before.

Her heart clenched in painful yearning for the man who had made her feel so much. He had to be alive. If only he were here, Amanda was sure he could meet Xa Shiraq's power with an equal strength that would have commanded respect. She had to act in a manner worthy of him.

The sheikh read on, ignoring her presence, or pretending to, perhaps waiting to see if she would crack, perhaps silently expressing contempt for her.

There was a waiting stillness about him that accelerated her heartbeat to a painful tempo. It reminded her of the stillness of the man who might at this moment be still for a more deadly reason.

She darted a glance at Xa Shiraq's associate and was startled to find she recognised him. It was Mr Kozim, the man who had handed her the page telling of her promotion to general manager of the Fisa hotel.

A spark of hope kindled in Amanda's heart. Surely he would be sympathetic to an appeal for the life of a man he had worked closely with, even though his first allegiance was to Xa Shiraq. Mr Kozim definitely had an air of stress about him. He cleared his throat with a nervous little cough.

'Your Excellency, the…uh…geologist's daughter is here.'

Amanda had no doubt the Sheikh of Xabia was

aware of that. He was letting her stew, wanting to unnerve her. What was more, he was succeeding. She could feel his wish to torture her with his silence, to keep her on tenterhooks until she snapped into an outburst that he would use against her.

She grasped at the straw that Mr Kozim represented and did her best to turn the situation to her advantage.

'Mr Kozim, you are a man of great understanding and humanity,' she appealed, not knowing if he was or not, but a little flattery could not go astray. 'I appeal to you on behalf of the man who carried the orders of Jebel Haffa at the Oasis Hotel at Fisa. I ask you to intervene on his behalf to Xa Shiraq himself.'

Mr Kozim's face went pale. His hands fluttered nervously along the desk. He coughed. 'You do not know what you ask,' he said in a strangulated voice.

Not much help there, Amanda thought, and her eyes swung away from him so they would not reveal her despair.

She said no more. She grimly held her tongue, determined to outplay the sheikh in this contest of wills. She knew instinctively she would win nothing by grovelling. She had to convince him that the crystal caves meant nothing to her. Only then might he listen to her appeal to free the man who had gone against his will.

Amanda had the sinking feeling that few people went against Xa Shiraq's will without suffering horrendous consequences. She had to quickly decide on her course of action.

Any lack of control on her part would raise suspicions about the reliability of the promises she would give him. A man such as he would only respect strength. She must show that strength and let nothing daunt her.

She straightened her shoulders more rigidly than they had even been set before. She turned to face him square on. She took one step forward to draw his attention, then stopped. She would go no further until he gave his response.

The book in his hands was slowly clapped shut. It was replaced in the empty slot on the shelf behind him. Amanda felt her chest constricting as he started to turn towards her. Her mind jammed with desperate prayers.

His profile came into view and shock hit her like a sledgehammer, completely smashing all her fiercely held resolutions.

'You!'

The cry burst from her lips in a released avalanche of pent-up tension and frustration, combined with all the pain and bitter suffering that had tormented her waking hours since she had last been with him.

Blazing black eyes scorched over her with scathing contempt. 'I trusted you…and you betrayed my trust.'

The condemnation in his voice lashed deeply into Amanda's soul. It stung, yet shock anaesthetised the sting momentarily. Shock demanded explanations that would make sense of the unbelievable.

'You're supposed to be entombed in the crystal

caves.' That was the reality that had tortured her. Questions tumbled from her lips. 'How did you get out? How did you escape? How did you get here?'

'How much satisfaction it must have given you to leave me to die as you thought...'

'I did everything I could to try and save you,' she defended hotly, aghast that he had interpreted her actions so wrongly.

'How clever you are, Amanda,' he said sardonically. 'Twisting the truth of your flight down the mountain to give yourself another chance to justify your father's behaviour.'

His offensive manner riled her into pointing out a few little truths to be taken into account. 'You set out to deceive me from our first meeting and you've obviously deceived me about no-one knowing where we were. You were never really in trouble, were you?'

His silence goaded her on. 'And I almost killed myself trying to save you, worrying myself sick over whether you were dead or alive, while all the time... all the time...'

She was rendered speechless by the base calculations of the man who was now revealed as Xa Shiraq himself! There must have been another way out of the caves and he'd had some means of communicating with his people. That was why the helicopter had flown towards the peak...to collect him! He had been flown home in comfort, perhaps even seeing her manic ride on the way.

'Do you think I can still be seduced by your lies?'

he demanded. 'You knew I would stop you from doing what you wanted and you sacrificed me for the secret of the crystal caves.'

It focused Amanda's mind on refuting the abominable idea of base treachery. 'I did not! The hydraulic jack broke. I rode for help but you ordered people not to listen to me,' she flung at him, outraged that he could accuse her of such dreadful things—premeditated murder, no less—when he was so palpably at fault for reacting in a totally extreme and unjustified manner, making her suffer agonies for a crime she hadn't committed.

'Nor will I listen to you now,' he bit out in icy, arrogant pride.

'Examine the jack,' she challenged in similar biting tone, glaring her scorn for his unreasonable stance.

'I disdain to prove more clearly what is already proved.'

'How can you call yourself just if you will not look at the evidence?' Amanda retaliated, smarting over the fact that he had always been in control, never once risking anything while he tested her to the limit!

'Be thankful I choose not to.' His eyes seared her with a blistering indictment. 'I prefer mercy to justice. If your perfidy were proved beyond all doubt I could show you no mercy at all.'

Amanda felt a quiver of fear. She suppressed it, and took another pace forward. 'Are you too proud to face the truth?' she hurled at him. 'Is it your will to believe the worst of me? I thought more of you as a man than that.'

His lips compressed into a thin, bloodless line. His facial muscles tightened grimly. 'You cannot hurt me with your words,' he said, his black eyes boring into her with hard and unrelenting intensity. 'I admired and respected your cleverness, the quick facility of your mind at seeing through to the end of what was possible. But you have used it against me.'

He *was* hurt. Deeply hurt. The realisation slammed into Amanda's heart and pumped a different perception through her mind. This was why he was so unyielding. He had let himself be vulnerable to her and he hated her for supposedly fooling him, and himself for being fooled.

'All my thoughts and energies were directed to finding and bringing back a rescue team to get you out,' she said quietly, hoping to reach into him again. 'I couldn't move that huge rock. I had no choice but to leave you there until…'

'You had a choice, Amanda. I gave it to you in the caves…whether to reveal the existence of the neodymite crystals as your father wanted…or whether to leave Xabia the way it is,' he reminded her savagely. 'You did not give a reply.'

'I needed time to think.'

It must have seemed to him…afterwards…that she had fobbed off giving a reply, but Amanda knew it wasn't true. When he had kissed her and asked her to give herself to him, that had seemed more important than bringing up something she had already decided and was no longer an issue between them.

'I had made up my mind to keep the secret and let my father's dream die with him,' she pleaded. 'I would have told you so once we were outside.'

Even as she spoke the words she realised it was too late to say them. The wrong time and the wrong place. There would never be a right time now. For years she had worked towards the goal of clearing her father's name and proving him right. That single-minded purpose was burned into Xa Shiraq's memory, reinforced by what she had done and all she had poured out to him in the intimacy of their togetherness.

'I showed you the crystal caves,' he said simply. 'And you betrayed my trust and left me to die in darkness.'

Amanda cracked. She lifted her hands to her face in despair. 'That's so untrue,' she cried brokenly. 'So untrue.'

'You've had a taste of the choice you could have made *with* me. Now you can have a taste of the choice you made *for* me.'

'You've got it all wrong.' It was a desperate bid for understanding. She pulled her hands down, spreading them out to him in appeal. 'Surely what we felt together meant as much to you as it did to me. How can you imagine I would sacrifice that for…?'

She faltered under the terrible look in his eyes…the pain…the dull, black emptiness that followed it.

'You will be placed in the deepest cellar of the lowest basement within the granary that supplies the palace,' he intoned, as though he had pulled a hood of judgement over any last twinge of feeling he had for her. 'There are no windows. There is no light. You will be in darkness…as I was in darkness…when you left me.'

Amanda shivered, remembering the claustrophobic feeling in the tunnel. 'I don't like being alone.'

'You will not be alone,' he said with dark derision.

'Who…?' She swallowed hard and tried to correct the quaver in her voice. 'Who will be with me?'

'The cellar has another name. A sobriquet. It is more commonly known as…the rat-hole. The rats are huge. They are voracious. I hope you will enjoy your new friends and acquaintances.'

CHAPTER FIFTEEN

AMANDA stared at Xa Shiraq in glazed horror. Her skin prickled in revulsion. Her stomach turned queazy. Beads of sweat broke out on her forehead. Her hands went clammy. Her whole body shuddered.

'You can't do that to me,' she whispered. It was the only defence her mind could construct against the terrifying picture he had drawn of the rat-hole. She would go insane in such a place.

The black eyes glittered with vengeful satisfaction. 'Call the escort, Kozim,' came the merciless command.

'No...no!' Amanda cried, turning a frantic look of appeal to Xa Shiraq's personal aide. 'I'm innocent of this charge. I swear it!'

Mr Kozim's gaze determinedly evaded hers. He picked up a bell from his desk and rang it loudly. He obviously didn't want to hear any more from her.

Amanda swung back to Xa Shiraq, her heart pounding in sheer panic. 'You're supposed to know everything. That's what they say of you. Why don't you know I couldn't do what you accuse me of?' she argued, hoping against hope he meant to relent.

He pointedly shunned her, walking off to a leather armchair on the far side of the library. He flung himself listlessly and dispiritedly into it without so much as a glance at her. His eyes focused on some empty spot on the ceiling.

Amanda heard the doors opening behind her, the tramp of military feet coming to take her away to the rat hole. She couldn't bear it.

Xa Shiraq waved a gesture of dismissal towards her.

He should know better, Amanda thought, her mind racing to find some solution. He would never do this if his emotions weren't involved. But they were... they were!

'Wait!' Amanda cried imperiously, raising her extended arm above her shoulders.

It stopped nothing. The military feet kept advancing. Xa Shiraq ignored her. Mr Kozim found another empty spot on the ceiling for himself and gazed steadfastly at that.

Amanda was thinking more furiously than she had ever needed to before. Xa Shiraq might have submerged the link he felt with her but it had been a powerful, compelling link. Somehow she had to find that link again.

'I have a better plan,' she announced.

Boldness be my friend, she prayed wildly. If there was any substance in the form of address used by the old serving woman, she had to have some chance of changing what was happening.

The guards halted around her in escort position, ready to about-turn and take her out as soon as the order was given. Amanda swiftly forestalled the order.

'Will you not allow me one last word?' she demanded of Xa Shiraq.

His black eyes slashed at her. His fingers pressed savagely into the armrest, indenting the cushioned leather one by one, back and forth. He said nothing. The guards remained at attention. Amanda seized on the tacit permission to advance on Mr Kozim.

'Is it constitutionally correct that a princess can be sent to the rat-hole?' she asked, pulling his gaze down from the ceiling.

Mr Kozim not only looked sheepish but very, very unhappy at being chosen to interpret the sheikh's will.

'Over the centuries,' he said ponderously, 'more princesses ended up in the rat-hole, per capita of population, than any other category of our people. It was…uh…standard procedure in cases of…' he coughed '…rebellious intransigence.'

That certainly fitted, Amanda thought, but did the rest follow? 'Am I a princess?' she pressed.

'A proclamation was signed that you were to be treated as such,' Mr Kozim mumbled, shooting a worried glance at the sheikh.

Uh-huh! Amanda thought with satisfaction. A chink in the armour. Xa Shiraq was in two minds about her. Or rather, his heart was warring with his head. He wanted his people to honour her even as he condemned her as unworthy of being his true companion.

His mind was set on punishment to fit the crime he believed she had committed against him, but it wasn't what he really wanted. Not deep down. He wanted the fulfilment of the promise that had shimmered through both of them in the crystal caves. And so did she.

Clutching that conviction to her heart, Amanda walked across the room to where Xa Shiraq indolently lounged, her clear aquamarine eyes reflecting strong and unwavering purpose.

'There has to be a better way of resolving what is between us,' she said.

'Name one,' he invited, his face stonily closed to her, his eyes watchful but giving nothing away.

She knelt beside the armrest of his chair, close enough so that only he could hear her words. 'Tell me of your secret desires and passions,' she said softly, caringly, her eyes openly promising an answer to them.

'I do not desire you,' he replied curtly, contemptuously. 'You could not provoke it in me.'

Amanda refused to be deterred. 'Let me try to change your mind,' she persisted, trying to bore past his wounded pride to the primitive mating instinct that yearned for fulfilment.

His hand curved over the end of the armrest, his long, restless fingers lying still. She lifted her hand and stroked her fingers over the bare skin of his. She saw the sudden tightening of his neck muscles, the leap of his pulse at the base of his throat. He sprang to his feet, whipping his hand out from under hers. He towered over her, his black eyes ablaze with fierce turbulence.

'You do have the capacity to gall me,' he grated. 'No more of this talk. You know nothing of men nor of their pleasure.'

'How can you pass such judgements?' Amanda immediately replied, whirling up off her knees to confront him head-on.

'At the Fisa hotel you inflicted on me a fat cow from the bazaar whose dancing was supposed to entertain me,' he mocked savagely. 'She bored me more thoroughly than I've ever been bored in my life.'

'I can do much better than the fat cow from the bazaar,' Amanda promised quickly, thinking any promise was better than the rat-hole.

His eyes derided her claim. 'Are you suggesting you are not culturally inept?'

'I chose the fat cow from the bazaar for other reasons than entertaining you,' Amanda excused.

'You have the temerity to remind me of your duplicity?'

'I have no trouble remembering yours,' she retorted. 'I also remember the link that crossed those barriers. I doubt that even you can crush that memory.'

His eyes burned into hers, seeking truth, doubting her integrity. 'You want another way to resolve things between us,' he said softly, a dangerous glitter leaping into the black blaze. 'Something other than the justice of the rat-hole.'

'Your justice is blind.'

'Then open my eyes, Amanda...by dancing for me.'

He was calling her bluff. If she didn't do better than the dancer she had chosen for him in Fisa, she would end up in the rat-hole. Amanda figured she had one advantage. However bad her dancing might be, he would not be bored if she could stir the desire he was so determinedly repressing.

'How many veils would you allow me?' she asked.

He raised one finger.

It didn't give her much to use in the way of teasing or tantalising. Not that she was particularly adept at that. In fact, she wasn't adept at all in the ancient art of seduction. But she would try.

This was more a mental challenge than a physical one, she assured herself. If she was to prolong her time with him while she danced, what she needed was the longest veil in the world. She also needed time to learn what had to be done.

'Agreed,' she said. Already she was quickly plotting a few more moves she could make to break down his present resistance to her.

His eyes narrowed into slits. He obviously didn't trust her one bit. 'Do not think my admiration for your cleverness will cloud my vision, Amanda. You have much to prove to me. As a woman.'

The rat-hole wouldn't have proved anything,

Amanda thought petulantly, but she wisely held her tongue on that matter. She had won a stay in judgement. Better to leave him now while the going was good.

'I'll need time to prepare,' she said.

'Undoubtedly,' he dryly agreed, stepping back and waving her to join her escort again. 'Send a messenger to me when you are ready. Remember I await the outcome of your...plan...with some disbelief.'

'Thank you for the reprieve,' Amanda said with every air of confidence, and gave Mr Kozim a friendly nod as she resumed her place in the middle of her elite squad of soldiers.

The command was given to return her to her quarters.

Amanda found her legs were quite wobbly once they had left the library but she managed to keep them moving, one after the other, until they had traversed the necessary distance.

After all, a princess didn't collapse in a heap when the going got rough. A princess was supposed to be tough. A princess held her head high and sailed through the storm to a safe port.

If she was to be a princess she had to find precisely the right sail to get her there.

Amanda's practical mind descended from the clouds.

It wasn't the right sail she needed.

It was the right veil!

CHAPTER SIXTEEN

KNOWING she had been officially proclaimed a princess gave Amanda the confidence to issue a few orders.

For a start, she was not going to be pushed around by a pack of women who thought they knew more about her body than she did. She took a leaf out of Xa Shiraq's book. They could carry out *her* will instead.

Once she was back in the royal quarters, she ordered a good solid brunch; sausage, fried tomatoes and a piece of buttered toast. After the episode with the sheikh she was not hungry but she forced herself to eat some fruit to stiffen up her wobbly knees. If she was to deliver the performance of her life, energy was a necessary requirement.

The matter of the veil was more complex. Amanda ordered bolts of filmy cloth in shades of blue and green and silver to be brought to her. They were the colours *he* had suggested at Fisa.

Amanda intended to please. She had a vested interest in pleasing him. If she could, she would make him eat his words about her not knowing anything about a man's pleasure.

In a way, Xa Shiraq was right. Amanda had received no advice on such matters from her mother who had died before Amanda had reached the age of puberty.

At the school she had attended during her teenage years, the list of attainments thought desirable for a modern woman did not include any knowledge on how to please a man. The general attitude was that if it did happen, it would occur naturally all by itself.

The natural occurrences that had come Amanda's way in later years had not taught her much. She hadn't been particularly pleased herself, and it seemed that all that was required of her was her consent. Being kissed by Xa Shiraq had been totally different to anything she had experienced before.

Amanda had the feeling that Xa Shiraq would be much more demanding in his pleasure than anyone she had met before, both in giving it and receiving it. If she kept thinking of the feelings he had aroused while kissing her, it might help her to stop worrying about what response she was drawing from him while she did whatever was going to be done.

By the time her tiny appetite was fully satisfied, an extraordinary number of bolts of cloth had been lined up for her to view. With the fear of the rat-hole ever present in the background, and her poor, sick, empty stomach nicely filled, Amanda considered this matter of dancing her way out of trouble and into the heart of Xa Shiraq where she rightfully belonged.

The reflection that she shouldn't be in this trouble at all pricked a little resentment. The manner in which

Xa Shiraq had dismissed her sufferings as though they were nothing pricked quite a lot more. To balance that, her crimes of illegal entry into the country, and the charges of grand larceny seemed to have been forgotten. She hoped the unfortunate experiences on the Gemini Peak would also soon be forgotten.

What she could not forget was all the hours he had kept her in a waiting torment of ignorance as to his fate. It seemed absolutely fair to her that he do his share of waiting for her. Besides, being trapped in the caves like that—she shuddered—had obviously tormented his mind about her.

He needed time to consider all she had said in her defence this morning. He needed time to come to the conclusion he must have the hydraulic jack examined, and then more time to adjust to the fact that he was wrong, and she truly loved him.

That might assist him to be more receptive to her, and stop this terrible misunderstanding between them. She wanted to be his lover, not his murderer.

She cast her eyes over the bolts of cloth, then sent for a messenger.

'Please inform Xa Shiraq that there is no cloth in the sheikhdom in shimmering shades of blue and green that meet my requirements. Mindful of his pleasure, I request permission to order that some be dyed to the desired colouring I need. The process will only take several days.'

Then, of course, the veil would have to be made. Amanda's agile mind thought up several more delays, as well. The looms would break. The woof and warp would be wrong. The series of delays she could invent would know no bounds.

She was tempted to add a rider to the message that he should use the time to have the broken hydraulic jack examined, but decided not to raise that sore point yet again. Perhaps, tomorrow. Or the day after.

Amanda was humming happily to herself when the messenger returned with a reply from Xa Shiraq.

'''Permission granted. Be prepared to leave with your escort within the hour. Enjoy your stay in the rat-hole until the dyeing process is completed.'''

Amanda's delightful little bubble of hopes and plans burst into droplets of despair.

But Amanda was a fighter. She would not go down without making a stand. If she was going to be submerged for the third time, she was determined to take someone down with her. That person was Xa Shiraq.

'Please inform Xa Shiraq that a suitable cloth has now been procured. The women who will do the silver thread-work require me for fittings to ensure their design will be pleasing to his discriminating eye. Since there is no light in the rat-hole, I request permission to remain in these quarters until such time as the veil is ready to be worn to its best effect for his pleasure.'

Let him argue against that, Amanda thought with satisfaction. She could spin out the silver embroidery for a good few days. Perhaps a week. Clearly his vengeful mood was still in full force. The longer she held out, the more likely he might have second thoughts about what had happened.

His reply did not exactly demonstrate that a softening process had begun.

'"Thread or no thread, you will dance for me at midnight tonight."'

Midnight!

Amanda checked the current time. Almost three o'clock. He had given her nine hours. If she didn't deliver what she had promised to his satisfaction at his deadline, Amanda had little doubt she would endure the same fate as many illustrious princesses before her. Xa Shiraq was not a man to be crossed lightly.

Amanda gave her reply much deep thought. Xa Shiraq had to be forcibly reminded of what they had shared together before they met tonight. Amanda's understanding of his grievances only stretched so far. If he didn't open his mind and heart to her again, they would both end up very lonely people.

The prospect of that inner darkness weighed more heavily on Amanda's heart than the prospect of future darkness.

She addressed the messenger one last time.

'Tell Xa Shiraq that the women's fingers grow more nimble by the minute. His will shall be done.

'Then you are to advance upon him. You are to tell him the words you utter cannot be said aloud, and they are for him alone.

'When permission is given, you will whisper to him in tones of love—*May the stars shine brightly for us tonight.*'

CHAPTER SEVENTEEN

KOZIM shifted uncomfortably in his chair as the messenger returned for the third time.

Xa Shiraq was being highly unpredictable today. Many silences had lasted longer than five minutes. Kozim was deeply stressed.

It was clear to him that the geologist's daughter was having a very strange effect on the sheikh. What had seemed an absolutely firm decision about the rathole had not turned out a firm decision at all.

How was he to understand anything if everything kept changing? It had been alarming enough when the geologist's daughter had turned to him for succour, although Kozim assured himself he had acted creditably. It was even more alarming to witness Xa Shiraq's reaction to her messages.

The first one had evoked a burst of derisive laughter. Kozim had not thought it a laughing matter. The message had sounded quite impertinent to him. However, the sheikh's reply had certainly put the geologist's daughter in her rightful place. Kozim had heartily approved of that.

To Kozim's mind, the second message should have earned the same result. Xa Shiraq had mused over it, a knowing smile lurking on his lips, his black eyes glittering with calculations. He did not share them with Kozim. His reply, when it came, seemed an extraordinary concession.

Kozim had found it extremely difficult not to expose his surprise. He reflected that the sheikh's mind often worked in mysterious ways. Yet there was a lack of consistency over this business with the geologist's daughter that Kozim found disturbing.

The messenger had barely finished bowing when the sheikh commanded her to speak, not waiting for the usual form of salutations and address.

Xa Shiraq's obvious impatience, indeed, his air of anticipation to hear what the geologist's daughter had to say, was unlike any manner Kozim had witnessed in his long years of service with the sheikh.

The messenger intoned the words.

'Go on. Go on,' Xa Shiraq urged, waving his arms in encouragement. 'There must be more. She would not leave it there.'

The messenger advanced. 'These words are for your ears only.' They were whispered in his ear.

For some reason Kozim could not fathom, Xa Shiraq was so struck by this private communication, his unusual burst of mobility was instantly cut dead. He went absolutely still. Kozim recognised the quality of stillness. It was always thus when the sheikh was absorbing every shade, every minute detail, every nuance of an important problem.

He remained in this state of intense introspection for several minutes, revealing nothing of his thoughts.

'Did the princess say anything else?'

The question ended the long, tense silence.

'No, Your Excellency,' the messenger smartly replied.

'Then you may go.'

The messenger's departure did not end Kozim's growing sense of insecurity. Several more minutes passed before the sheikh deigned to notice him.

'Is there a full moon tonight?' he asked in a voice that rang with decision.

'No, Your Excellency. What moon there is will set before midnight.'

Kozim had already checked his calendar. It was said that a full moon could induce a temporary madness in a man who was under the spell of a woman. Kozim had thought it worth checking if such a dangerous phase was looming on the horizon.

'Order the freshest and finest samples of Xabian jasmine, Kozim. I want it placed in every room.'

'I will see to it,' Kozim said, wondering if partial moons could have the same ill effect.

There was a gleam in the sheikh's black eyes that confirmed Kozim's suspicions. However, if what followed after midnight did not live up to the sheikh's expectations... Kozim thanked his lucky stars he was not the geologist's daughter!

CHAPTER EIGHTEEN

FRUSTRATION edged into desperation as Amanda tried one experiment after another with the veil. She had done a course in pareu tying as practised by the Polynesians. The only difference between a pareu and a veil was that the latter was more diaphanous. She had thought one style or another would produce a desirable effect but none of them did.

What was fine on a tropical beach simply did not have the seductive elegance she was searching for. She needed to entrance, to enthrall. She didn't think she could achieve that by looking...obvious.

The harem women followed her activities with amused interest and much chatter. Amanda felt she was in centre ring of a circus. Irritation added to her edginess and despair. 'Do any of you have a better idea?' she demanded, discarding her last effort as utterly hopeless for her purpose.

The old woman who spoke English rose from a settee. 'Gaia,' she said with a confident air of authority.

The other women clapped with enthusiastic excitement.

Amanda had no idea what it meant. 'I want help,' she said.

The old woman nodded approval and sent off a messenger.

Amanda pulled a robe over her nakedness and sat down to wait for whatever was going to eventuate. She felt totally dispirited. The one-veil idea was a disaster and she was only too aware that her ability to outdance the woman from the Fisa bazaar was pure fantasy. She closed her eyes and imagined the blistering scorn in Xa Shiraq's. She prayed for mercy.

A hubbub from the harem women aroused her attention. A small, sharp-nosed woman was being ushered into the salon of the royal quarters. She was brought to Amanda and introduced by the old woman who had sent for her.

'This is Gaia. She is the best one-veil designer in Alcabab. She has a national and international reputation.'

Gaia's eyes were as sharp as her nose. She made a shrewd appraisal of Amanda as she bowed. Then she stepped back and clapped her hands. It was the signal for an entourage of models to parade in a dazzling variety of single veils, long flowing designs that hid all and revealed everything.

Amanda ruefully realised how amateurish her own efforts must have seemed compared to the sophisticated creations that were being displayed for her benefit. She should have asked for help sooner.

As the last of twenty models filed past, Gaia came forward to inquire, 'Which design would the princess prefer?'

Amanda shook her head, too dazed to make a decisive selection. They were all superb, far beyond anything she could conceive.

'You are right,' Gaia declared, bewildering Amanda with this interpretation of her silence. 'If you are to win the sheikh's heart forever, Princess, only the best will do.'

Like a grand impresario she snapped her fingers and the door to the salon opened once more. A solitary figure entered. All the women gasped in awe and admiration.

'This model,' Gaia said, 'is based upon the exact replica of the one worn by the Queen of Sheba when she arrived at the court of King Solomon.'

It was a brilliant scarlet, looped gracefully over one shoulder where it was fastened by an elaborate gold brooch. From the brooch there fell a rainburst of gold thread, running in cunning diagonals around the model's body, emphasising and highlighting every feminine curve.

'For you, Princess, it can be copied in shimmering shades of blues and greens with a silver accent,' Gaia assured her. 'May I respectfully suggest that it is not only appropriate for you to be so dressed, but also essential?'

Palace gossip must have been running hot, Amanda thought. Probably everyone was more aware of what was really going on than she was. But the outfit was absolutely stunning. Amanda felt a stirring of excitement. And hope.

'We use a little artifice,' Gaia explained. 'An invisible stitch here. An invisible stitch there. Men are so transported by what they see, they never notice.'

'I believe it,' Amanda agreed. A man wouldn't be human if he paused to deliberate on the engineering skills that had put this little number together.

'We have little time, and much to do,' Gaia prompted. 'A design such as this has to be fitted. I have brought my best invisible stitcher with me. The art is to get the best result with the minimum of interference to the natural flowing of the drapery.

'Legend has it that Solomon was so taken by the Queen of Sheba, he granted her all she desired,' Gaia continued. 'Your entrance to the sheikh's quarters must effect the same result so that legend can repeat itself.'

'I hope so,' Amanda said fervently.

'Come with me,' Gaia demanded, leading Amanda into the next room where her assistants waited with the necessary materials for Amanda's requirements. 'My art must remain a secret,' Gaia explained, closing the door on the harem women.

Amanda's robe was quickly removed. She was draped in shimmering blues and greens, the material measured for the length needed for the design. Busy hands fluttered around her, tucking, adjusting, smoothing.

Gaia pointed to a bolt of midnight blue silk taffeta. 'You will require a cloak. This will be most suitable.

We shall attach a hood so that your initial presentation will be one of hidden mystery.'

Amanda eagerly agreed to the idea. 'Who pays for all of this?' she asked a little nervously.

'No...o...o problem. I will invoice the palace.'

More crimes, Amanda thought, but she had no choice but to put herself completely into Gaia's hands. She needed all the help she could get.

Under Gaia's private ministrations, Amanda found the time flying all too rapidly. In between fittings of the veil and the cloak she attended to the rest of her appearance. She bathed and had her hair washed and dried and brushed until it shone and felt like silk. The harem women persuaded her to have her body rubbed with a lotion that made her skin glow. Her nails were manicured and varnished an opalescent pink. She eschewed exotic make-up in favour of a subtle high-lighting of her eyes and a lip gloss that matched the colour of her nails.

'What of the dance?' Gaia asked. 'Do you need instruction?'

It was clearly in Gaia's interests that Amanda did not let the designer down by failing in other areas.

'I have a plan,' Amanda answered, projecting a confidence she didn't really feel. She knew there simply weren't enough hours to turn her into a skilled dancer, no matter how masterly the instruction. What happened between her and Xa Shiraq would depend on a dance of the mind and heart.

Midnight approached.

The veil was a triumph of erotica by the time Gaia finished arranging it to emphasise and enhance Amanda's curves. Amanda had never thought of herself as a *femme fatale* but she certainly began to see what had induced King Solomon to dally with the Queen of Sheba. There was a definite art to looking and feeling sensual and seductive.

The midnight blue cloak was carefully lowered over her shoulders so as not to disarrange the effect of the veil. Her hair was gathered back and hidden by the hood which formed a shadowy frame for her face. Amanda practised undoing the fastening at her throat so she could open it in one fluid movement.

I'm ready, she told herself. *As ready as I'll ever be*.

She took several deep breaths.

Her nerves were playing havoc with her stomach. Her nipples had tightened into hard little buds. Her thighs were aquiver. She was sure her blood had turned to water.

The clock ticked on.

Near midnight her escort arrived to take her to the sheikh. Her attendants' well wishes rang hollowly in her ears. Gaia accompanied her to the door that led out of the harem. 'My princess…my queen…' she whispered, a last benediction that Amanda desperately hoped was prophetic.

With her heart pounding a painful yearning for everything to turn out right, Amanda stepped out of the harem and moved towards her fateful encounter with Xa Shiraq.

CHAPTER NINETEEN

THE doors softly closed behind her. Amanda stood in a circle of light cast by two wall-lamps. The rest of the room receded into darkness. She was spotlit as she had been in their original meeting at the Oasis Hotel in Fisa. It made her feel like a rabbit trapped in the headlights of a car with nowhere to escape.

Where was he?

Music was playing. Soft, romantic music.

In front of her was a magnificent room thickly carpeted in royal blue, with rich furnishings in the same colour combined with white and gold...deeply cushioned sofas in velvet and silk brocade, beautifully grained marble tables, exotic lamps, gold urns holding luxurious plants, exquisite vases from which trailed arrangements of tiny white flowers.

Xabian jasmine.

The scent was unmistakable, stirring Amanda's senses, arousing a tingle of anticipation, soothing her fears. Her pulse quickened. Surely it meant he wanted her to be excited. Or was he teasing her with what could have been?

At the far end of the room was a row of high, graceful arches. Beyond them was total darkness.

'Do you call that a veil?'

The mocking question had a cutting edge to it that sliced into Amanda's assurance in her appearance. So much for an air of mystery!

Her trembling hands went to the fastening at her throat. With the one fluid motion she had practised, the cloak parted. She pushed back the hood then tossed the long coverall from her shoulders. Her hair dropped like a waterfall of spun silk, caressing the bare skin around her collarbones. She held her hands apart as if in supplication.

'Do you want other men to see me like this?' she asked softly.

She heard the voluble intake of his breath.

Her gaze swung to the source of the sound. His tall, lithe body was framed in the last arch on the right-hand side of the room. He was clothed in a pure white robe and headdress, the black and gold coiled *'iqal* circling his head like a crown. He looked every inch the formidable ruler of Xabia.

Amanda took a few steps away from the circlet of light to merge with her own shadows. It suddenly seemed important to meet him on equal terms, person to person, regardless of dress and position.

His black eyes were hidden but Amanda could feel them riveted on her, burning with intensity.

'If the beauty of your mind reflected the beauty of your body I would love you for an eternity.' There was a curl of contempt in his voice as he tried to vanquish the feelings she was arousing in him.

Amanda knew he was affected, deeply affected by

her. But he didn't believe in her, she thought despairingly. Not in her words, her love, her need for him.

He gave a derisive laugh. 'Perhaps it was appropriate that you came wrapped in darkness…a phantom of the night. It hides what is best not seen.'

He was trying to negate what he felt, wish it into nonexistence. Amanda knew she had to reach out to him before he set himself irrevocably on a path that would turn him away from her forever.

'I'm as human as you are,' she said quietly. 'You know it. You've felt it. I didn't come here because you ordered me to. I came because I wanted to. I wanted to be with a man who has aroused passions in me that can never be forgotten. I wanted to…'

'Enough!' The tortured command was driven from his throat by forces he could no longer master.

He said nothing more. He stood utterly still.

Amanda bravely held his gaze, willing him to remember she had chosen to go with him and be with him wherever he led, not knowing he meant to reveal the crystal caves to her.

It seemed that the very air between them thickened and thinned with the sheer force of feeling that flowed and swirled in turbulent currents from one to the other. Amanda sensed a mental shift in him, a decision made or a barrier moved aside.

His gaze dropped from hers, gathering a different intensity as it ran slowly over her body, touching every part, heating her blood, sensitising her skin, making her breasts ache with a swollen heaviness, brushing her nipples into taut peaks, circling her stomach with an erotic sensation that arrowed down to the centre of her womanhood, stirring the warm moistness of desire.

He moved. It was as though he drifted along high-tension wires that were strung between them, each step a tug on her heart, a tremor quaking through her body, a wild exhilaration thrilling her mind. His eyes feasted on her, drawing on her innermost being, *wanting her to be all he desired.*

'Dance for me,' he commanded.

Amanda thrust her breasts forward against the flimsy silk chiffon, wanting to feel the imprint of his hands upon them. She swayed her hips in rhythm with the chords of the Eastern music, conscious of the veil sliding and shimmering with every slow, undulating movement. She felt sensual. She was sensual.

'Dance *with* me,' she invited, holding out her arms to him, her voice throbbing with intense emotion and the deeply felt need to be once more taken into his embrace.

'Never!' he said, halting several paces away from her. 'You twist and turn as it suits you. Prove to me you can keep your word. Dance as you said you would.'

Amanda fought against letting this further evidence of his mistrust hurt her. He didn't want it to be this way. She was sure he didn't. 'I thought it would give you more pleasure,' she appealed, swaying to the music in seductive invitation.

He looked at her with hard, scornful pride. 'Do you know nothing of our culture? For centuries, milleniums, women have danced for the pleasure of men.'

Amanda did not have the skill or knowledge to match his Xabian dancers. To try would only invite derision. She needed to reach him, touch him.

She advanced towards him, uninhibitedly provocative in the way she moved as she pleaded her cause. 'That may be true in Xabia. Where I come from, men dance with their women. It has always been so, not only because it is more equal, but because it gives greater pleasure to both.'

'You are in *my* country,' he reminded her.

Amanda opened her hands in a gesture of giving. '*Are we not beyond race and culture?*' she whispered, repeating the very words he had spoken to her in the Presidential Suite in Fisa, the words that had tapped so powerfully at her resistance to him.

He stiffened. His chin lifted fractionally, tightening as though she had hit him. She sensed the conflict raging within him, the strong impulse to accept what she was offering, against his rigid sense of what was owed to him.

'You said you would dance for me,' he bit out, still holding her to her word.

'For you...with you...so you can feel the dance that is only for you.'

'I would not be able to see you,' he said, dismissing her argument, turning aside in disdainful rejection of it.

She quickly reached out and touched his shoulder, arresting his movement away from her. He did not pull away but he did not turn back to her, either.

'You will see all you need to see,' she promised huskily. 'You will see my eyes.'

Amanda trailed her hand down his arm. She sensed his struggle to exert control over the desire she stirred in him. Slowly he turned, the swing of his body dislodging her hand so that it dropped away from him. It didn't matter because his eyes told her she had touched him in far more than a physical sense. The violence of his feelings was reflected in their dark turbulence. His chest rose and fell several times before he spoke.

'Your eyes have the depths of oceans, and hold the mystery of the skies. They hold the promise of unknown delights; they would tempt any man…beyond endurance.'

She moved closer to him. 'Take what I can give and give to you alone. Feel my body pulsing in harmony with yours.'

His fingertips bridged the distance between them, barely brushing her waist, yet his touch was magnified by the fineness of the material that barely separated his flesh from hers. An electrifying tingle raced over Amanda's skin. It was as though the shimmering veil transmitted the compelling power of his desire for her, making her body more responsive, more aware than if she'd been naked.

Amanda knew she had to show this man she loved

him. He had to know it beyond all doubt. Only by giving him the absolute assurance that she held nothing back from him, now or ever, would he come to a true appreciation of what she felt for him.

She let the music seep into her body, breathed deeply of the intoxicating jasmine scent and moved forward, undulating against him, provoking, prompting, her thighs sliding over his, the tips of her breasts rolling across his chest, and not for one second did her eyes leave his, challenging him to see, to know, to believe.

His loins hardened into rigidity.

The fingertips at her waist drifted down, tracing the curve of her hip, then slowly tempted to move over the soft mound of her buttocks. His other hand joined the voyage of discovery, caressing her back, following the sensual curve of her spine. She shivered in his arms and saw the leap of exultant pleasure in his eyes, the knowledge that her response was beyond any design or control.

Amanda slid her own hands over his shoulders, under the flowing headdress, finding and stroking the bare nape of his neck. A muffled cry was torn from his lips. He gripped her body more firmly, moving it to the rhythm she had incited in his, crushing her breasts against the hard masculinity of his chest.

Amanda felt the heat suffusing her body, becoming concentrated between her thighs, the sharpening awareness and piercing sensitivity growing, strengthening, spiralling towards involuntary orgasm, and her eyes clung to his, mirroring the sweet drowning inside her, her lips parting on a gasp of wonder, a breath of life that she offered to him as a gift of utter abandonment to the feelings he evoked in her.

If he could see her heart, he must know it pounded for him.

If he could see her mind, he must know he obliterated everything else.

If he could see her soul, he must know he resided there.

'Amanda…'

It was a whisper of seeing and knowing and believing. He carried it to her parted lips, his mouth closing over hers, warm, sensual, the breath of his life mingling with hers, so softly, caringly, nurturing her gift of love with infinite tenderness, tasting it as though it was the most exquisite wine in the world, incredibly, wonderfully, uniquely intoxicating.

His fingers found the brooch that fastened the veil. With a single movement he unclipped it. He parted the flowing panels, baring her shoulder, and his mouth moved from hers, trailing soft burning kisses down her throat. Instinctively, Amanda arched her neck to the beat of his pleasure. Her hands moved restlessly, throwing off his headdress in her need to touch more of him, her fingers revelling in the silky thickness of his hair.

He eased the chiffon over her breasts with his tongue, absorbing the texture of her skin, sensitising it to his taste, leaving her with hot, licking imprints of himself that burned into a deeper possession of her consciousness. As the veil undraped and slid from her hips he followed it, adoring her body, the revelation of her nakedness, her satin-smooth flesh, all the way down until what the Queen of Sheba had once worn lay as a pool of formless cloth about her feet.

Agile fingers, never still in their ceaseless roaming, sent ripples of pleasure down her thighs. His mouth began its relentless march up her body towards the object of his pleasure. Amanda felt herself going limp, overwhelmed by the almost unendurable sensations he was evoking. She had to restrain herself from crying out in case it made him cease his exquisite ministrations.

Her breasts heaved. Her legs trembled. In a flowing motion he picked her up into the warmth of his arms, cradling her across the strong wall of his chest. Amanda was beyond caring where he took her. She clung to him, wanting him with a deep, desperate ache that yearned to be filled by this man and only this man.

He carried her through the archway to a terrace, and here the scent of the Xabian jasmine was stronger. The air was warmer, more sensual. Amanda could see the sky. The stars were brightly shining.

He lowered her on to an opulently cushioned dais, thickly strewn with the soft petals of wild mountain roses. Fronds of freshly cut jasmine leaves formed a semicircle around her upper body. The realisation that this had all been prepared for her was sweet confirmation of her faith in the feelings they had shared together. He had hoped...dreamed...wanted...and like a gently wafting summer breeze his fingers caressed her waiting breasts.

'Come to me,' she moaned. 'Love me!'

His clothes were tossed aside. Her eyes feasted on his physical beauty. He was perfectly proportioned, his body sleekly honed to tight flesh stretched over the curves of muscles that were strongly delineated. The smooth sheen of his skin looked like polished bronze in the starlight. She was enthralled by the power of his maleness, the visible pulsing of his need for her.

She was aflame with desire. She did not try to hide her willing receptivity and need for his embrace. She lay fully exposed, her back arched in anticipation, her arms outflung across the cushions in complete abandon.

He came to her like a man who had ceased to function for anything other than joining with her. He slid between her legs. With a hoarse cry he plunged deeply into her body. Amanda felt a fierce and triumphant satisfaction as at last their union was completed. She closed around him, squeezing, a wild, exultant joy pleasuring along his manhood.

A gasp of astonishment emitted from his lips. Amanda felt a sense of exaltation. She knew he had not experienced anything like this before in his life. She was putting her imprint on him, possessing him as no other woman had or would, making him as deeply hers as she was his...linked forever by this moment of mating.

He started a fierce stroking that super-heated her inflamed responses. Her thighs trembled. Her body tap-danced to the beat of his rhythm and her need for climactic release. She gasped involuntarily as a suffusion of moisture melted around his pulsing flesh.

Xa Shiraq appeared to take it as some kind of signal. His back was arched like a bow, his weight supported by his extended arms, as he drove faster and deeper and faster within her. His breathing came in short gasps, feral and unrestrained. Amanda convulsed around him again. Short, rapid, staccato thrusts preceded a guttural exclamation of appeasement and release as the innermost seeds of his passion spilled from his body into hers.

Instinctively Amanda's arms reached up to hug him and bring him closer to her. She had to be close to him now, closer than she had ever been. She had to prove her love and want and need for him. He had to know that he was the one.

He did not resist. His torso met hers and he cradled her in his arms. His lips brushed across her forehead, her temples, her cheeks, her mouth.

He rolled to one side, carrying her with him, then onto his back so that she lay on top of him. He rested her head upon his shoulder, their bodies still connected although the first rush of desire had been appeased.

'Be at peace with me,' he murmured.

His hands moved over her back and shoulders while applying a sweetly scented lotion to her tingling skin. His strokes were long and languorous and mesmerising, weaving another dimension of intimacy. Amanda felt herself relax under the spell of his hypnotic touch. He drew gentle, entrancing patterns over her body, down her arms, even to her fingers so that every part of her that was accessible to him was caressed into tranquillity.

Amanda was almost asleep from his gentle pleasure-giving when she felt him stir and quicken inside her. She did nothing. Curiosity as to what he would do and how he would behave towards her encouraged her to give no visible sign that she was aware of what was happening.

She felt him engorge to his full extent within her. She forced herself to remain limp and relaxed in his arms. She controlled her breathing so that no alteration could be detected.

He found the contours of her breasts and traced their soft fullness with the delicate touch of moonbeams upon a mountain mist.

He stirred within her, yet with the waft of a sigh, his hands moved away from her breasts and onto the cushions beside him. He moved no more, leaving her to her repose.

Amanda waited. His desire for her did not abate. But he did nothing that would awaken her. Slowly she shifted, as though aroused from sleep. She lifted her head close to his ear.

'I had a beautiful dream,' she whispered, 'in which you gave me great pleasure. More pleasure than I ever thought it possible for a woman to have. Now it is my turn to please you.'

She started moving on him until he could bear it no longer. When he had to take control, Amanda did nothing to restrain him. She gave of herself with all the ecstatic bliss of knowing the giving in his heart.

Afterwards, as the stars faded from the skies, they slept together in each other's arms.

CHAPTER TWENTY

KOZIM could barely conceal his bewilderment. Life is change, he told himself, but the changes were so sweeping it was difficult to adjust to them and the rate at which events were unfurling was truly staggering.

The wedding preparations were no problem. Kozim was used to organising huge ceremonial occasions. This, of course, would be the grandest of them all, but there was no set of ordered arrangements he could not handle with ease.

The proclamation that no future queen could be sent to the rat-hole was another matter entirely. It was a complete break from tradition. Not only that, it was to be imbedded in the constitution of the country, turning the proclamation into unbreakable law. Such tampering with history had no precedent. Kozim found it deeply disturbing.

The geologist's daughter, he reflected, had a way of getting things done that he himself had never possessed. Kozim pulled himself up on that thought. It was the princess, not the geologist's daughter. A slip of the tongue on such a point over the future queen could result in the most fateful consequences for himself. He needed to take care. Xa Shiraq was obviously besotted over his wife-to-be.

She certainly had the most voluptuous and exciting body…and the radiance of her hair was entrancing…

Kozim sternly suppressed such thoughts. They could lead to the permanent separation of the head from the body, a punishment he had once favoured, but upon more mature reflection, it seemed as extreme as the rat-hole. Perhaps the mellowing effect that this woman was having on Xa Shiraq was also having an effect upon himself.

Today had been very busy with the sheikh holding open court for his people. The *majlis* had extended into the afternoon and still there was one more deputation to deal with, yet Xa Shiraq appeared amazingly relaxed. His fingers were not tapping like a measured metronome. They seemed to be dancing on the armrest of his chair, in time to some light, frivolous melody.

Kozim shook his head. There was so much that was beyond his comprehension. How Xa Shiraq had changed his mind about the geologi—the princess—and obviously believed her, long before the hydraulic jack was examined, was a total mystery to Kozim. But it had proved right. The device had snapped under the load of that huge rock and the woman was not to blame at all.

Still, Xa Shiraq could very easily have lost his life. If he had not been able to leap the chasm and work his way up through the mountain to the eagle's eyrie, from where he could use the transmitter in his signet ring to summon the helicopter, Xabia could now be without a ruler. Kozim could be without a job. He shuddered at such a terrible prospect.

And all for the sake of gathering those strange crystals for his wife-to-be! It made no sense to Kozim. The crystals were quite pleasant to look at, and for some reason the air about them seemed sweeter and fresher, but obviously they were intrinsically worthless. Why Xa Shiraq had ordered them to be set in gold seemed...Kozim clamped down on the critical thought. The gold did increase their value. He still thought it a poor wedding gift for the future queen, but undoubtedly the sheikh had his reasons.

Kozim noticed, with alarm, that more than five minutes had passed and Xa Shiraq had not said a word. Kozim gave a nervous little cough. 'I did send a messenger to the princess, Your Excellency,' he said, anxious not to be found at fault.

Xa Shiraq bestowed a benevolent smile. 'It is of no consequence, Kozim. The princess will arrive when she is ready.'

That was another thing that disturbed Kozim. The rigid time-keeping to a planned schedule had suffered considerably since the night of the Queen of Sheba veil. It was totally incomprehensible to Kozim that Xa Shiraq apparently accepted that the princess exercised a will of her own. Kozim did not like to think where such a thing might lead. He consoled himself with the assurance that Xa Shiraq knew everything and it must therefore be a wise course.

The doors to the hall of government opened. Kozim and Xa Shiraq instantly sprang to their feet as the princess entered. She was a vision of rare beauty. She wore a misty lilac gown that flowed enticingly around her very feminine body as she walked forward.

Kozim struggled to pull his thoughts into appropriate order. Of course the gown was supremely modest, whispering down to her feet, and with long graceful sleeves that caressed her soft, shapely arms. The princess was certainly a credit to the sheikh. Kozim had thought the proposed marriage a mistake at first. It would not cement any alliances or extend profitable areas of trade but...no man could possibly look upon the princess for long and continue to think of her as a mistake.

Amanda flashed Mr Kozim a smile as she walked up to meet Xa Shiraq. The stout little man was such a sweet person once one got to know him, a trifle uncertain of himself at times, but she would help him find his feet. He was always so anxious to please, to get everything right. He also thought Xa Shiraq was the fount of all wisdom, which made him invaluable as a personal aide.

She extended a much brighter smile to the man she loved. His eyes were soft black velvet as he greeted her. A smile hovered on his lips, giving them a sensual curve. He took her hand to lead her to the chair that had been set beside his, and Amanda once again marvelled at the pleasure of his touch, the tingling warmth of his skin against hers, the strength and the tenderness of his long, supple fingers.

'Why did you want me here?' Amanda asked, surprised that he should ask her to join him at a *majlis* where he listened to the problems brought to him by his people.

His eyes twinkled wickedly. 'I want you everywhere.'

She laughed. 'Not in front of Mr Kozim. He would definitely be shocked.'

'You are right. I am not sure Kozim can sustain many more shocks. We shall consider his feelings. There is a matter that concerns you.'

He saw her seated, and raised a hand to Mr Kozim as he settled in the chair beside her.

Mr Kozim rang a bell.

The doors opened.

Amanda was mystified as to what the matter could be. Then Mocca came bouncing in, his boyish face beaming with what looked suspiciously like mischievous delight. He performed an elaborate bow, then followed it with a long flattering address, extolling the wisdom *and generosity* of Xa Shiraq.

'You may address the princess,' he was dryly told.

Mocca was not slow to pick up his cue. 'I have come with good news and bad news.'

'What is the bad news?' Amanda asked, wondering

if there was another mountainous pile of invoices about to be sent to the palace.

'We could not find the caves for which we were searching,' Mocca announced dolefully.

'Then it is proven that they do not exist,' Amanda declared. 'You have done well, Mocca. I thought it was a wild-goose chase but I wanted to know. Thank you. I am glad the matter is finally settled.'

Xa Shiraq squeezed her hand. She squeezed back. The secret would remain with them.

Mocca's face lit with pleasure. 'In that case,' he said cheerfully, 'there is only good news.'

'What is the good news?' Amanda inquired.

'Your bodyguard has performed an invaluable service for you.'

That was certainly news to Amanda, but she was not confident that it would be good.

'They have caught the man who has been saying the most ridiculous and offensive things about people who have the colour of hair that you have, oh, Princess,' Mocca continued.

Here, too? Amanda thought in exasperation.

'He has been saying you are stupid, you are dumb and you are a female dog.'

Amanda bristled.

Xa Shiraq leaned over and whispered, 'I rejected Charles Arnold's petition to appeal against his dismissal from the Oasis Hotel chain. Apparently he thought that gave him a license to be as offensive as he pleased.'

So that was why Charles Arnold had come to Alcabab. No doubt he was taking out his peevishness by insulting Xa Shiraq's choice of wife. Amanda felt a warm glow of approval for her bodyguard.

'What has my bodyguard done with him?' she asked Mocca.

'As you are aware, people of your hair colouring are much admired in Xabia,' he declared fervently.

'I knew this was a wonderful country,' Amanda declared with equal fervour.

'So we hung a sign of what he'd said around his neck and marched him through the streets. The populace showed their disapproval. They booed him. They pelted him with camel dung…and other evil-smelling refuse.'

'Oh, dear!' Amanda wasn't at all sure he deserved that much humiliation. 'He is a creep and a slime, but I'd better go and see the poor man in case he's damaged.'

'I wouldn't do that if I were you,' Xa Shiraq remarked very dryly.

Mocca flashed him his friendliest grin. 'We also carried out the unspeakable. It felt really good doing it to him.'

A vision of the rat-hole flew into Amanda's mind. She sprang to her feet. 'Take me to him at once!' she commanded.

'Princess!' Mr Kozim started up in alarm.

Xa Shiraq gave Kozim a knowing look as he rose to accompany Amanda. 'There's no stopping her once she gets the bit between her teeth, Kozim. The only thing to do is to satisfy her.'

'Wise. Very wise,' Mr Kozim mumbled, but could not hide his distress at this highly inappropriate turn of events.

Mocca led off through the corridors of the palace. As they approached a courtyard that opened out to one of the gardens, Amanda's nose was assaulted by a revolting smell. She refrained from comment but she privately decided the sewerage system urgently needed updating.

Mocca threw open the door to a room that over-looked the courtyard and stood back for Amanda to see the occupant. The stench was dreadful.

'We painted him with asafoetida,' Mocca proudly announced. 'He can't stand the smell of himself and no-one else can, either. It is the vilest-smelling naturally occurring substance on the planet. Wasn't that a great punishment?'

Charles Arnold was a pitiable sight. He fell to his knees in a grovelling plea for mercy. 'Mandy, for God's sake! Please do something! Help me!'

She fought for breath. 'Mocca...' she gasped, unable to share his boyish delight in the retribution taken, even though it certainly was a powerful deterrent to any human intercourse at all. Charles Arnold did deserve to know what it was like to have nastiness heaped upon him. Nevertheless, enough was enough! 'Take him away...and let him wash it off,' she choked out.

'Oh, thank you, Mandy. Thank you, thank you, thank you,' Charles Arnold raved, clearly at the end of his tether.

Amanda was sharply reminded of the abuse she had suffered from him. 'In future, Charles, please remember that my name is Amanda, not Mandy.'

'Princess Amanda,' Mocca corrected, 'and very soon to be Her Majesty,' he added for good measure. Then he clapped his hands and the bodyguards started streaming in from the courtyard. 'Okay, boys,' he said cheerfully. 'Take him away and throw him into the well from which no-one ever returns.'

'No, no, no!' Amanda cried. 'I meant take him away and give him a scrubbing brush and strong soaps and deodorants…' She gasped for breath again. The smell was suffocating. 'I'm sorry, Charles. You are the most offensive person it's ever been my displeasure to meet. Please learn from this experience and treat people decently in the future. I must go now.'

Xa Shiraq took her arm and gave a stern, finishing touch to her command. 'When he is deodorised, Mocca, he is to leave Xabia and never return.'

'Perhaps he need not wash until we see him over the border, Your Excellency,' Mocca suggested eagerly.

Xa Shiraq curbed his enthusiasm. 'Do as your princess commands, Mocca.'

'Yes, yes! Her will is my will. Your will is my will, oh, most gracious and generous…'

'How much did you pay him?' Amanda muttered as Xa Shiraq swept her away from the putrid area.

He chuckled. 'Such an enterprising young man deserves a reward. He turned a problem into a triumph for you, my love. The populace of Alcabab have taken you into their hearts. There is no greater joy than pelting camel dung at someone who richly deserves it. Perhaps Mocca has even given birth to a future legend. The filthy-tongued foreigner who denigrated the beauty of the Queen...'

Much later that evening Amanda was with Xa Shiraq in his private apartment. She was comfortably curled up on one of the blue velvet sofas as she questioned him about the guests who would be attending their wedding.

'Did you realise that Jebel Haffa is not on the list?' she asked, puzzled by the omission.

Xa Shiraq gave her a bemused little smile. 'I as good as told you, that night in the tent outside the village of Tirham, that Jebel Haffa does not exist.'

Amanda shook her head in astonishment. 'The second most important man in Xabia does not exist?' she repeated incredulously.

'It goes a long way back to the time of troubles. I needed someone who was absolutely loyal to me, whom I could always trust. There was no such person I could find. I invented Jebel Haffa.'

'You said he was part of you,' Amanda mused,

more to herself than to him. She realised now how truly he had expressed himself.

'It is why I have had to live a rather reclusive life,' he explained. 'So I could play both roles as necessary. It made a legend live. It made Xabians feel doubly secure.'

The man who was never seen, Amanda thought, except in a black cloak and hood that kept his face in shadow. 'And no-one knows of this?' she asked.

'Not even Kozim.'

'So how will you explain his absence from the wedding?'

'It will be Jebel Haffa's duty to look after the realm during the period of our marriage and honeymoon. When we return, Jebel Haffa will have to die. He has served his function, the role he had to play.'

'I don't want Jebel Haffa to die,' Amanda said. 'He was a wonderful person. He was part of you. Can't he be retired to his country estates?'

Xa Shiraq gave her a rueful smile. 'Enough,' he said. 'You shall have your way. When we return, we will mutually decide Jebel Haffa's fate.'

Xa Shiraq walked over to her, took her hands in his and gently urged her up from the sofa. His arms slid around her, drawing her close. His black eyes shone with a brilliance Amanda had never seen before.

'You are now my Jebel Haffa,' he said softly. 'Only more so, Amanda. Much more so. In you I have found the true companion and partner of my life. In you I place my absolute trust and know you will give me absolute loyalty. As I will give to you. For we are as one, as I was one with him. In mind, in heart, in soul.'

He was completely open to her. No shutters. No veils of mystery. The brilliance of his eyes were the stars of a universe she had yet to explore fully, but it was hers to travel with him, to share, to know and to love.

She curled her arms around his neck and drew his head down to hers. They kissed…tasting the future that was theirs…and the goblet was full.

Sandra Marton, a bestselling, award winning author for Modern Romance™, wrote her first novel while still in elementary school. Her doting parents told her she'd be a writer someday and Sandra believed them. In high school and college, she wrote dark poetry nobody but her boyfriend understood. As a wife and mother, she devoted the little free time she had to writing murky short stories. Not even her boyfriend-turned-husband understood those. At last, Sandra decided she wanted to write about real people. That didn't actually happen because the heroes she created—and still creates—are larger than life but both she and her readers around the world love them exactly that way. Sandra has written more than fifty novels for Harlequin Mills & Boon. She's won the Holt Medallion and has twice been a finalist for the RITA, the award given by Romance Writers of America. She's won three Reviewers Choice Awards from *Romantic Times* magazine, and a Career Achievement Award from *Romantic Times* as Series Storyteller of the Year. When she isn't at her computer, Sandra loves to bird watch, walk in the woods and the desert, and travel. She can be as happy people-watching from a sidewalk café in Paris as she can be animal-watching in the forest behind her home in northeastern Connecticut. Her love for both worlds, the urban and the natural, is often reflected in her books.

**Look out for Sandra Marton's latest sexy and compelling title:
CLAIMING HIS LOVE-CHILD
On sale in July 2004, in Modern Romance™!**

MISTRESS OF THE SHEIKH

by

Sandra Marton

CHAPTER ONE

SHEIKH Nicholas al Rashid, Lion of the Desert, Lord of the Realm and Sublime Heir to the Imperial Throne of Quidar, stepped out of his tent and onto the burning sands, holding a woman in his arms.

The sheikh was dressed in a gold-trimmed white burnoose; his silver-gray eyes stared straight ahead, blazing with savage passion. The woman, her arms looped around his neck, gazed up at him, her face alight with an unspoken plea.

What's the matter, Nick? she'd been saying.

There's a camera pointed straight at us, Nick had answered. *That's what's the matter.*

But nobody seeing this cover on *Gossip* magazine would believe anything so simple, Nick thought grimly.

His eyes dropped to the banner beneath the picture. If words could damn a man, these surely did.

Sheikh Nicholas al Rashid, the caption said, in letters that looked ten feet tall, *carrying off his latest conquest, the beautiful Deanna Burgess. Oh, to be abducted by this gorgeous, magnificent desert savage…*

"Son of a bitch," Nick muttered.

The little man standing on the opposite side of the sparely furnished, elegant room nodded. "Yes, my lord."

"No-good, lying, cheating, sneaky bastards!"

"Absolutely," the little man said, nodding again.

Nick looked up, his eyes narrowed.

"Calling me a 'desert savage,' as if I were some kind of beast. Is that what they think I am? An uncultured, vicious animal?"

"No, sire." The little man clasped his hands together. "Surely not."

5

"No one calls me that and gets away with it."

But someone had, once. Nick frowned. A woman or, more accurately, a girl. The memory surfaced, wavering like a mirage from the hot sand.

Nothing but a savage, she'd said....

The image faded, and Nick frowned. "That photo was taken at the festival. It was Id al Baranda, Quidar's national holiday, for God's sake!" He stepped out from behind his massive beechwood desk and paced to the wall of windows that gave way onto one of New York City's paved canyons. "That's why I was wearing a robe, because it is the custom."

Abdul bobbed his head in agreement.

"And the tent," Nick said through his teeth. "The damned tent belonged to the caterer."

"I know, my lord."

"It was where the food was set up, dammit!"

"Yes, sire."

Nick stalked back to his desk and snatched up the magazine. "Look at this. Just look at it!"

Abdul took a cautious step forward, rose up on the balls of his feet and peered at the photo. "Lord Rashid?"

"They've taken the ocean out of the picture. It looks as if the tent was pitched in the middle of the desert!"

"Yes, my lord. I see."

Nick dragged his hand through his hair. "Miss Burgess cut her foot." His voice tightened. "That was why I was carrying her."

"Lord Rashid." Abdul licked his lips. "There is no need to explain."

"I was carrying her *into* the tent, not out. So I could treat the—" Nick stopped in midsentence and drew a ragged breath deep into his lungs. "I will not let this anger me."

"I am so glad, my lord."

"I will not!"

"Excellent, sire."

"There's no point to it." Nick put the magazine on his desk, tucked his hands into the pockets of his trousers and threw his secretary a chilling smile. "Isn't that right, Abdul?"

The little man nodded. "Absolutely."

"If these idiots wish to poke their noses into my life, so be it."

"Yes, my lord."

"If people wish to read such drivel, let them."

Abdul nodded. "Exactly."

"After all, what does it matter to me if I am called an uncultured savage?" Nick's smile tightened until his face resembled a mask. "Never mind my law degree or my expertise in finance."

"Lord Rashid," Abdul said carefully, "sire—"

"Never mind that I represent an ancient and honorable and highly cultured people."

"Excellency, please. You're getting yourself upset. And, as you just said, there is no point in—"

"The fool who wrote this should be drawn and quartered."

Abdul nodded, his head bobbing up and down like a balloon on a string. "Yes, my lord."

"Better still, staked out, naked, in the heat of the desert sun, smeared with honey so as to draw the full attention of the fire ants."

Abdul bowed low as he backed toward the door. "I shall see to it at once."

"Abdul." Nick took a deep breath.

"My Lord?"

"You are to do nothing."

"Nothing? But, Excellency—"

"Trust me," the sheikh said with a faint smile. "The part of me that is American warns me that my fellow countrymen are probably squeamish about drawing and quartering."

"In that case, I shall ask for a retraction."

"You are not to call the magazine at all."

"No?"

"No. It would serve no purpose except to bring further unwanted attention to myself, and to Quidar."

Abdul inclined his head. "As you command, Lord Rashid."

Nick reached out, turned the copy of *Gossip* toward him, handling it as gingerly as he would a poisonous spider.

"Phone the florist. Have him send six dozen red roses to Miss Burgess."

"Yes, sire."

"I want the flowers delivered immediately."

"Of course."

"Along with a card. Say…" Nick frowned. "Say that she has my apologies that we made the cover of a national magazine."

"Oh, I'm sure Miss Burgess is most unhappy to find her photo on that cover," Abdul said smoothly, so smoothly that Nick looked at him. The little man flushed. "It is most unfortunate that either of you should have been placed in such a position, my lord. I am glad you are taking this so calmly."

"I am calm, aren't I?" Nick said. "Very calm. I have counted twice to ten, once in Quidaran and once in English, and—and…" His gaze fell to the cover again. "Very calm," he murmured, and then he grabbed the magazine from the desk and flung it against the wall. "Lying sons of camel traders," he roared, and kicked the thing across the room the second it slid to the floor. "Oh, what I'd like to do to the bastards who invade my life and print such lies."

"Excellency." Abdul's voice was barely a whisper. "Excellency, it is all my fault."

The sheikh gave a harsh laugh. "Did you point a camera at me, Abdul?"

"No. No, of course—"

"Did you sell the photo to the highest bidder?" Nick swung around, his eyes hot. "Did you write a caption that makes it sound as if I'm a bad reincarnation of Rudolph Valentino?"

Abdul gave a nervous laugh. "Certainly not."

"For all I know, it wasn't even a reporter. It could have been someone I think of as a friend." Nick shoved both hands through his black-as-midnight hair. "If I ever get my hands on one of the scum-sucking dung beetles who grow fat by invading the privacy of others—''

Abdul dropped to his knees on the silk carpet and knotted his hands imploringly beneath his chin. "It is my fault, nevertheless. I should not have permitted your eyes to see such an abomination. I should have hidden it from you."

"Get up," Nick said sharply.

"I should never have let you see it. Never!"

"Abdul," Nick said more gently, "stand up."

"Oh, my lord…"

Nick sighed, bent down and lifted the little man to his feet.

"You did the right thing. I needed to see this piece of filth before the party tonight. Someone is sure to spring it on me just to see my reaction."

"No one would have the courage, sire."

"Trust me, Abdul. Someone will." A smile softened Nick's hard mouth. "My sweet little sister, if no one else. We both know how she loves to tease."

Abdul smiled, too. "Ah. Yes, yes, she does."

"So, it's a good thing you showed me the cover. I'd much rather be prepared."

"That was my belief, sire. But perhaps I erred. Perhaps I should not—"

"What would you have done instead, hmm?" Nick grinned. "Bought up all the copies from all the newsstands in Manhattan?"

Abdul nodded vigorously. "Precisely. I should have purchased all the copies, burned them—"

"Abdul." Nick put his arm around the man's shoulders and walked him toward the door. "You took the proper action. And I am grateful."

"You are?"

"Just imagine the headlines if I'd had this temper tantrum in public." Nick lifted his hand and wrote an imaginary sentence in the air. "Savage Sheikh Shows Savage Side," he said dramatically.

The little man gave him a thin smile.

"Now imagine what would happen if somebody manages to get a picture of me slicing into the cake at the party tonight."

"The caterer will surely do the slicing, sire."

Nick sighed. "Yes, I'm sure he will. The point is, anything is possible. Can you just see what the sleaze sheets would do with a picture of me with a knife in my hand?"

"In the old days," Abdul said sternly, "you could have had their heads!"

The sheikh smiled. "These are not those days," he said gently. "We are in the twenty-first century, remember?"

"You still have that power, Lord Rashid."

"It is not a power I shall ever exercise, Abdul."

"So you have said, Excellency." The man paused at the door to Nick's office. "But your father can tell you that the power to spare a man his life, or take it from him, is the best way of assuring that all who deal with you will do so with honor and respect."

A quick, satisfying picture flashed through Nick's mind. He imagined all the media people, and especially all the so-called friends who'd ever made money by selling him out, crowded into the long-unused dungeon beneath the palace back home, every last one of them pleading for mercy as the royal executioner sharpened his ax.

"It's a sweet thought," he admitted after a minute. "But that is no longer our way."

"Perhaps it should be," Abdul said, and sighed. "At any rate, my lord, there will be no unwanted guests lying in wait for you this evening."

"No?"

"No. Only those with invitations will be admitted by your bodyguards. And I sent out the invitations myself."

Nick nodded. "Two hundred and fifty of my nearest and dearest friends," he said, and smiled wryly. "That's fine."

His secretary nodded. "Will that be all, Lord Rashid?"

"Yes, Abdul. Thank you."

"You are welcome, sire."

Nick watched as the old man bowed low and backed out of the room. Don't, he wanted to tell him. You're old enough to be my grandfather, but he knew what Abdul's reply would be.

"It is the custom," he would say.

And he was right.

Nick sighed, walked to his desk and sat down in the ornately carved chair behind it.

Everything was "the custom". The way he was addressed. The way Quidarans, and even many Americans, bowed in his presence. He didn't mind it so much from his countrymen; it made him uncomfortable, all that head-bobbing and curtseying, but he understood it. It was a sign of respect.

It was, he supposed, such a sign for some Americans, too.

But for others, he sensed, it was an acknowledgment that they saw him as a different species. Something exotic. An Arab, who dressed in flowing robes. A primitive creature, who lived in a tent.

An uncultured savage, who took his women when, where and how he wanted them.

He rose to his feet and walked across the room to the windows, his mouth set in a grim line, his eyes steely.

He had worn desert robes perhaps half a dozen times in his life, and then only to please his father. He'd slept in a tent more times than that, but only because he loved the sigh of the night wind and the sight of the stars against the blackness of a sky that can only be found in the vastness of the desert.

As for women... Custom permitted him to take any that pleased him to his bed. But he'd never taken a woman who hadn't wanted to be taken. Never forced one into his bed or held one captive in a harem.

A smile tilted across Nick's mouth.

Humility was a virtue, much lauded by his father's people, and he was properly modest about most things, but why lie to himself about women? For that matter, why would he need a harem?

The truth was that women had always been there. They tumbled into his bed without any effort at all on his part, even in his university days at Yale when his real identity hadn't been known to what seemed like half the civilized world.

They'd even been there in the years before that.

Nick's smile grew.

He thought back to that summer he'd spent in L.A. with his late mother. She was an actress; it had seemed as if half the women who lived in Beverly Hills were actresses, starting with the stunning brunette next door, who'd at first taken him for the pool boy—and taken him, too, for rides far wilder than any he'd ever experienced on the backs of his father's pure-bred Arabians.

There'd always been women.

Nick's smile dimmed.

It was true, though, that some of the ones who were drawn to him now were interested more in what they might gain from being seen with him than anything else.

He knew that there were women who wanted to bask in the spotlight so mercilessly trained on him, that there were others who thought a night in his arms might lead to a lifetime at his side. There were even women who hoped to enter his private world so they could sell their stories to the scandal sheets.

His eyes went flat and cold.

Only a foolish man would involve himself with such women, and he was not a—

The phone rang. Nick snatched it from the desk.

"Yes?"

"If you're going to be here in time to shower and shave and change into a tux," his half sister's voice said with teasing petulance, "you'd better get a move on, Your Gorgeousness."

Nick smiled and hitched a hip onto the edge of the desk.

"Watch what you say to me, little sister. Otherwise, I'll have your head on the chopping block. Abdul says it's an ideal punishment for those who don't show me the proper respect."

"The only thing that's going to be cut tonight is my birthday cake. It's not every day a girl turns twenty-five."

"You forget. It's my birthday, too."

"Oh, I know, I know. Isn't it lovely, sharing a father and a birthday? But you're not as excited as I am."

Nick laughed. "That's because I'm over the hill. After all, I'm thirty-four."

"Seriously, Nick, you will be here on time, won't you?"

"Absolutely."

"Not early, though." Dawn laughed softly. "Otherwise, you'll expect me to change what I'm wearing."

Nick's brows lifted. "Will I?"

"Uh-huh."

"Meaning what you have on is too short, too low, too tight—"

"This is the twenty-first century, Your Handsomeness."

"Not when you're on Quidaran turf, it isn't. And stop calling me stuff like that."

"A," Dawn said, ticking her answers off on her fingers, "this isn't Quidaran turf. It's a penthouse on Fifth Avenue."

"It's Quidaran turf," Nick said. Dawn smiled; she could hear the laughter in his voice. "The moment I step on it anyway. What's B?"

"B, if *Gossip* can call you 'Your Handsomeness', so can I." She giggled. "Have you seen the article yet?"

"I've seen the cover," Nick said tersely. "That was enough."

"Well, the article says that you and Deanna—"

"Never mind that. You just make sure you're decently dressed."

"I *am* decently dressed, for New York."

Nick sighed. "Behave yourself, or I'll have you sent home."

"Me? Behave myself?" Dawn snorted and switched the portable phone to her other ear as she strolled through her brother's massive living room and out the glass doors to the terrace. "I'm not the one dating Miss Hunter."

"Hunter? But Deanna's name is—"

"Hunter of a titled husband. Hunter of the spotlight. Hunter of wealth and glamour—"

"She's not like that," Nick said quickly.

"Why isn't she?"

"Dawn. I am not going to discuss this with you."

"You don't have to. I know the reason. You have this silly idea that because Deanna has her own money and an old family name, she's—what's the right word—trustworthy."

Nick sighed. "Sweetheart," he said gently, "I appreciate your concern. But—"

"But you want me to mind my own business."

"Something like that, yes."

His sister rolled her eyes at the blond woman who stood with her back against the terrace wall. "Men can be clueless," she hissed.

Amanda Benning did her best to smile. "Have you told him yet?"

"No. No, not—"

"Dawn?" Nick's voice came through the phone. "Who are you talking to?"

Dawn made a face at Amanda. "One of the caterer's assistants," she said briskly. "She wanted to know where to put the cold hors d'oeuvres. And speaking of knowing, aren't you curious about what I got you for your birthday?"

"Sure. But if you told me, it wouldn't be a surprise. And birthday presents are supposed to be surprises."

"Ah. Well, I already know what my gift is."

"You do?"

"Uh-huh." Dawn grinned. "That shiny new Jaguar in the garage downstairs."

Nick groaned. "There's no keeping anything from you."

"Nope, there isn't. Now, you want to take a stab at what I'm giving you?"

"Well, there was that time you gave me a doll," Nick said dryly, "the one you wanted for yourself."

"I was seven!" Dawn grinned at Amanda. "Definitely clueless," she whispered.

"What?"

"I said, you're clueless, Nicky. About how to decorate this mansion of yours."

"It's not a mansion. It's an apartment. And I told you, I don't have time for such things. That's why I bought the place furnished."

"Furnished?" Dawn made a face at Amanda, who smiled. "How somebody could take a ten-million-dollar penthouse and make it look like a high-priced bordello is beyond me."

"If you have any idea what a bordello looks like, high-priced or low, I'll definitely send you home," Nick said, trying to sound affronted but not succeeding.

"You don't, either, dearest brother, or you'd never have the time or energy to bed all the females the tabloids link you with."

"Dawn—"

"I know, I know. You're not going to discuss such things with me." Dawn plucked a bit of lint from her skirt. "You know, Nicky, I'm not the baby you think I am."

"Maybe not. But it won't hurt if you let me go on living with an illusion."

His sister laughed. "When you see what I've bought you, that illusion will be shattered forever."

"We'll see about that." Nick's voice hummed with amusement.

Dawn grinned, covered the mouthpiece of the phone and looked at Amanda. "My brother doesn't believe you're going to shatter his illusions."

Amanda thumbed a strand of pale golden hair behind her ear. "Well, I'll just have to prove him wrong," she said, and told herself it was just plain ridiculous for an intelligent, well-educated, twenty-five-year-old woman to stand there with her knees knocking together at the prospect of being the birthday gift for a sheikh.

CHAPTER TWO

AMANDA swallowed nervously as Dawn put down the phone.

"Well," Dawn said, "that's that." She smiled. "I've laid the groundwork."

"Uh-huh." Amanda smiled, too, although her lips felt as if they were sticking to her teeth. "For disaster."

"Don't be silly. Oh, Nicky will probably balk when he realizes I've asked you to redo the penthouse. He'll growl a little, threaten murder and mayhem…" Dawn's brows lifted when she saw the expression on Amanda's face. "I'm joking!"

"Yeah, well, I'm not so sure about that." Amanda clasped her arms and shivered despite the heat of the midsummer afternoon. "I've gone toe-to-toe with your brother before, remember?"

Dawn made a face. "That was completely different. You were, what, nineteen?"

"Eighteen."

"Well."

"Well, what?"

"Well, that's my point," Dawn said impatiently. "You *didn't* go toe-to-toe with him. He had the advantage from the start. You were just a kid."

"I was your college roommate." Amanda caught her bottom lip between her teeth. "Otherwise known as The American Female With No Morals."

Dawn grinned. "Did he really call you that?"

"It may sound funny now, but if you'd been there—"

"I know how you must have felt," Dawn said, her smile fading. "After he hauled me out of the Dean's office, I thought he was going to have me shipped home and locked in the women's quarters for the rest of my life.''

"If your brother remembers me from that night—"

"If he does, I'll tell him he's wrong. Oh, stop worrying. He *won't* remember. It was the middle of the night. You didn't have a drop of makeup on, your hair was long then and probably hanging in your face. Look, if it all goes bad and Nicky gets angry at anybody for this, it'll be me.''

"I know. But still…''

Still, Amanda thought uneasily, she'd never forgotten her first, her only, meeting with Nicholas al Rashid.

Dawn had talked about him. And Amanda had read about him. The tabloids loved the sheikh: his incredible looks, his money, his power…his women.

Back then, Amanda didn't usually read that kind of thing. Her literary aspirations were just that. Literary. She'd been an English major, writing and reading poetry nobody but other English majors understood, although she'd been starting to think about changing her major to architectural design.

Whichever, the tabloids were too smarmy to catch her interest. And yet she found herself reaching for those awful newspapers at the supermarket checkout whenever she saw a photo of Dawn's brother on the front page.

Well, why wouldn't she? The man was obviously full of himself. It was like driving past an automobile accident; you didn't want to look but you just couldn't keep from doing it.

Dawn thought he was wonderful. "Nicky's a sweetheart," she always said. "I can't wait until you meet him.''

And, without warning, Amanda did.

It was the week before finals of their freshman year. Dawn was going to a frat party. She'd tried to convince Amanda to go, too, but Amanda had an exam in Renaissance design the next morning so she begged off, stayed in the dorm room they shared while Dawn partied.

Unfortunately, Dawn had one beer too many. She ended up sneaking into the bell tower at two in the morning along with half a dozen of the frat brothers, and they'd all decided it would be cool to play the carillon.

The campus police didn't agree. They brought Dawn and the boys down, hustled them into the security office and phoned their respective families.

Amanda was blissfully unaware of any of it. She'd crawled into bed, pulled the blanket over her head and fallen into exhausted sleep just past midnight.

A few hours later, she awoke to the pounding of a fist on the door of her dorm room. She sprang up in bed, heart pounding as hard as the fist, switched on the bedside lamp and pushed the hair out of her eyes.

"Who's there?"

"Open this door," a male voice demanded.

Visions conjured up from every horror movie she'd ever seen raced through her head. Her eyes flashed to the door, and her heartbeat went from fast to supersonic. She hadn't locked it, not with Dawn out—

"Open the door!"

Amanda scrambled from the bed, prayed her quaking knees would hold up long enough for her to fly across the room and throw the bolt—

The door burst open.

A thin, high shriek burst from her throat. A man dressed in jeans and a white T-shirt stood in the doorway, filling the space with his size, his rage, his very presence.

"I am Nicholas al Rashid," he roared. "Where is my sister?"

It took a few seconds for the name to register. This broad-shouldered man in jeans, this guy with the silver eyes and the stubbled jaw, was Dawn's brother?

She started to smile. He wasn't a mad killer after all...but he might as well have been.

The sheikh strode across the room, grabbed her by the front of her oversize D is For Design T-shirt and hauled her toward him. "I asked you a question, woman," Nicholas al Rashid said. "Where is my sister?"

To this day, it bothered Amanda that fear had nearly paralyzed her. She'd only been able to cower and stammer instead of bunching up her fist and slugging the bastard. A good right to the midsection was exactly what the tyrannical fool deserved.

But she was just eighteen, a girl who'd grown up in the sheltered world of exclusive boarding schools and summer camps. And the man standing over her was big, furious and terrifying.

So she'd swallowed a couple of times, trying to work up enough saliva so she could talk, and then she'd said that she didn't know where Dawn was.

Obviously, that wasn't the answer the sheikh wanted.

"You don't know," he said, his voice mocking hers. His hand tightened on her shirt and he hauled her even closer, close enough so she was nose to chest with him. "You don't know?"

"Dawn is—she's out."

"She's out," he repeated with that same cold sarcasm that was meant, she knew, to reduce her to something with about as much size and power as a mouse.

It got to her then. That he'd broken into her room. That he was on her turf, not his. That he was behaving as if this little piece of America was, instead, his own desert kingdom.

"Yes," she'd answered, lifting her chin as best she could, considering that his fist was wrapped in her shirt, forcing herself to meet his narrowed, silver eyes. "Yes, she's out, and even if I knew where she was, I wouldn't tell you, you—you two-bit dictator!"

She knew instantly she'd made a mistake. His face paled; a muscle knotted in his jaw and his mouth twisted in a way that made her blood run cold.

"What did you call me?" His voice was soft with the promise of malice.

"A two-bit dictator," she said again, and waited for the world to end. When, instead, a thin smile curved his mouth, she went from angry to furious. "Does that amuse you, Mr. Rashid?"

"You will address me as Lord Rashid." His smile tilted, so she could see the cruelty behind it. "And what amuses me is the realization that if we were in my country, I would have your tongue cut out for such insolence."

A drop of sweat beaded on Amanda's forehead. She had no doubt that he meant it but by then, she was beyond worrying about saying, or doing, the right thing. Never, not in all her life, had she despised anyone as she despised Nicholas al Rashid.

"This isn't your country. It's America. And I am an American citizen."

"And you are a typical American female. You have no morals."

"Oh, and you'd certainly know all about American females and morals, wouldn't you?"

His eyes narrowed. "I take it that's supposed to have some deep meaning."

"Just let go of me," Amanda said, grunting as she twisted against the hand still clutching her shirt. "Dammit, let go!"

He did. His fist opened, so quickly and unexpectedly that she stumbled backward. She stood staring at the man who'd invaded her room, her breasts heaving under the thin cotton shirt.

For the first time, he looked at her. Really looked at her. She could almost feel the touch of those silver eyes as they swept her from head to toe. He took in her sleep-tousled hair, her cotton shirt, the long length of her naked legs...

Amanda felt her face, then her body, start to burn under that arrogant scrutiny. She wanted to cover herself, put her arms over her breasts, but she sensed that to do so would give him even more of an advantage than he already had.

"Get out of my room," she said, her voice trembling.

Instead, his eyes moved over her again, this time with almost agonizing slowness. "Just look at you," he said very softly.

The words were coated with derision—derision, and something else. Amanda could hear it in his voice. She could read it in the way his eyes darkened. There was more to the message than the disparagement of American women and their morality. Despite her lack of experience, she knew that what he'd left unspoken was a statement of want and desire, raw and primitive and male.

It was three in the morning. She was alone in her room with a man twice her size, a man who wore his anger like a second skin...

A man more beautiful, and overwhelmingly masculine, than any she'd ever imagined or known in her entire life.

To her horror, she'd felt her body begin to quicken. A slow heat coiled low in her belly; her breasts lifted and her nipples began to harden so that she almost gasped at the feel of them thrusting against the thin cotton of her T-shirt.

He saw it, too.

His eyes went to her breasts, lingered, then lifted to her face. Amanda felt her heart leap into her throat as he took a step forward.

"Sire."

He moved toward her, his eyes never leaving hers. The heat in her belly swept into her blood.

"Sire!"

Amanda blinked. A little man in a shiny black suit had come into the room. He scuttled toward the sheikh, laid his hand on the sheikh's muscled forearm.

"My lord, I have located your sister."

The sheikh turned to the man. "Where is she?"

The little man looked at his hand, lying against the sheikh's tanned skin, and snatched it back. "Forgive me, sire. I did not mean to touch—"

"I asked you a question."

Abdul dropped to his knees and lowered his head until his brow almost touched the floor. "She awaits your will, Lord Rashid, in the office of the Dean of Students."

That had done it. The sight of the old man, kneeling in

obeisance to a surly tyrant, the thought of Dawn, awaiting the bully's will…

Amanda's vision cleared.

"Get out," she'd said fiercely, "before I have you thrown out. You're nothing but a—a savage. And I pity Dawn, or any woman, who has anything to do with you."

The sheikh's mouth had twisted, the hard, handsome face taking on the look of a predator about to claim its prey.

"Sire," the little man had whispered, and without another word, Nicholas al Rashid had spun on his heel and walked out of the room.

Amanda had never seen him again.

He'd taken Dawn out of school, enrolled her in a small women's college. But the two of them had remained friends through Amanda's change of careers, through her marriage and divorce.

Over the years, her encounter with the sheikh had faded from her memory.

Almost.

There were still times she awoke in the night with the feel of his eyes on her, the scent of him in her nostrils—

"Mandy," Dawn said, "your face is like an open book."

Amanda jerked her head up. Dawn grinned.

"You're still mortified, thinking about how Nicky stormed into our room all those years ago, when he was trying to find me."

Amanda cleared her throat. "Yes. Yes, I am. And you know, the more I think about this, the more convinced I am it's not going to work."

"What's not going to work? I told you, he won't remember you. And even if he does—"

"Dawn," Amanda said, reaching for the purse she'd dropped on one of the glass-topped tables on the enormous terrace, "I appreciate what you've tried to do for me. Honestly, I do. But—"

"But you don't need this job."

"Of course I need it. But—"

"You don't," Dawn said, striking a pose, "because you're going to make your name in New York by waving a magic wand. 'Hocus-pocus, I now pronounce me the decorator of the decade.'"

"Come on, Dawn," Amanda said with a little smile.

"Not that it matters, because you've found a way to pay your rent without working."

Amanda laughed.

"Well, what, then? Have you changed your mind about taking money from your mother?"

"Taking it from my stepfather, you mean." Amanda grimaced. "I don't want Jonas Baron's money. It comes with too many strings attached."

"Taking alimony from that ex of yours, then."

"Even more strings," Amanda said, and sighed. This was not a good idea. She could feel it in her bones—but only an idiot would walk away from an opportunity like this. "Okay," she said before she could talk herself out of it again, "I'll try."

"Good girl." Dawn looped her arm through Amanda's. The women walked slowly from the terrace into the living room. "Mandy, you know this makes sense. Doing the interior design for Sheikh Nicholas al Rashid's Fifth Avenue penthouse will splash your name everywhere it counts."

"Still, even if your brother agrees—"

"He has to. You're my birthday gift to him, remember?"

"Won't he care that he'll be my first client?"

"Your first New York client."

"Well, yeah. But I didn't really work when I lived in Dallas. You know how Paul felt about my having a career."

"Once I tell Nick you designed for Jonas Baron, and for Tyler and Caitlin Kincaid, he'll be sold."

Amanda came to a dead stop. "Are you nuts? Me, decorate my stepfather's house? Jonas would probably shoot anybody who tried to move a chair!"

"You did your mother's sitting room, didn't you?"

"Sure. But that was different. It was one room—"

"The room's in the Baron house, right?"

"Dawn, come on. That's hardly—"

"Well, what about the Kincaids?"

"All I did was rip out some of the froufrou, replace it with pieces Tyler had in his house in Atlanta and suggest a couple of new things. That's hardly the same as redoing a fourteen-room penthouse."

Dawn slapped her hands on her hips. "For heaven's sake, Mandy, will you let me handle this? What do you want me to say? 'Nick, this is Amanda. Remember her? The last time you met, you chewed her out for being a bad influence on me. Now she's going to spend a big chunk of your money doing something you really don't want done, and by the way, you're her very first real client.'"

Amanda couldn't help it. She laughed. "I guess it doesn't sound like much of a recommendation."

"No, it doesn't. And I thought we both just agreed you need this job."

"You're right," Amanda said glumly, "I do."

"Darned right, you do. At least redo the suite Nicky lets me use whenever I'm in town. Did you ever see such awful kitsch?" Dawn gave Amanda a quick hug when she smiled. "That's better. Just let me do the talking, okay?"

"Okay."

Dawn quickened her pace as they started up the wide staircase that led to the second floor. "We'll have to hurry. You put on that slinky red dress, fix your hair, spritz on some perfume and get ready to convince my brother he'd be crazy to turn up his regal nose at the chance to have this place done by the one, the only, the incredible Amanda Benning."

"You ever think about going into PR?"

"You can put me on the payroll after the first time your name shows up in the—oh, damn! We never finished our tour. You haven't seen Nick's suite."

"That's all right." Amanda patted the pocket of her silk trousers. "I'll transfer my camera into my evening bag."

"No, don't do that." Dawn shuddered dramatically as she

opened the door to her rooms. "If Nick sees you taking pictures, he'll figure you for a media spy and..." She grinned and sliced her hand across her throat. "How's this? You shower first, get dressed, then grab a quick look. His rooms are at the other end of the hall."

"I don't think that's a good idea," Amanda said quickly. "What if the sheikh comes in while I'm poking around?"

"He won't. Nicky promised he'd be on time, but he's always late. He hates stuff like this. You know, public appearances, being the center of attention. The longer he can delay his entrance, the better he likes it."

Amanda thought about the walking ego who'd shoved his way into her room, unasked and unannounced.

"I'll bet," she said, and softened the words with a smile. "But I'd still feel more comfortable if you were with me."

"I promise I'll join you just as soon as I turn myself into the gorgeous, desirable creature we both know I am. Okay?"

Amanda hesitated, told herself she was being an idiot, then nodded. "Okay."

"Good." Dawn kicked off her shoes. "In that case, the shower's all yours."

Twenty minutes later, Amanda paused outside the door to the sheikh's rooms.

If anybody took her pulse right now, they'd probably enter the result in the record books. She could feel it galloping like a runaway horse, but why wouldn't it?

It wasn't every day she sneaked into a man's bedroom to take pictures and make notes. Into the bedroom of a man who demanded people address him as "Lord". A man to whom other men bowed.

Instinct told her to turn tail and run. Necessity told her to stop being a coward. She was wasting time, and there really wasn't much to waste. Ten minutes, if Dawn was wrong and the sheikh showed up promptly.

She ran a nervous hand through the short, pale gold hair

that framed her face, took the tiny digital camera from her evening purse and tapped at the door.

"Sheikh Rashid?"

There was no answer. The only sounds that carried through the vastness of the penthouse were snatches of baroque music from the quartet setting up in the library far below.

Amanda straightened her shoulders, opened the door and stepped inside the room.

It was clearly a man's domain. Dawn had said her brother hadn't changed any of the furnishings in the penthouse and Amanda could believe that—everywhere but here. This one room bore a stamp that she instantly knew was the sheikh's.

She didn't know why she would think it. Asked to describe a room Nicholas al Rashid would design for himself, she'd have come up with mahogany furniture. Dark crimson walls. Velvet drapes.

These walls were pale blue silk. The furniture was satin-finished rosewood, and the tall windows had been left unadorned to frame the view of Central Park. The carpet was Persian, she was sure, and old enough to date back to a century when that had been the name of the country in which it had been made.

A sleek portable computer sat open on a low table.

The room spoke of simplicity and elegance. It spoke, too, of a time older than memory that flowed into a time yet to come.

Amanda began taking photos. The room. The bed. The open windows and the view beyond. She worked quickly while images of the sheikh flashed through her mind. She could see him in this room, tall and leanly muscled, stiff with regal arrogance. He belonged here.

Then she saw the oil painting on the wall. She hesitated, then walked toward it, eyes lifted to the canvas.

The room was a sham. All the sophistication, the urbanity...a lie, all of it. This was the real man, the one she'd met that night, and never mind the jeans and T-shirt he'd worn then, and the nonsense about his half-American ancestry.

The painting was of Nicholas al Rashid dressed in desert robes of white trimmed with gold, seated on the back of a white horse that looked as wild as he did. One hand held the reins; the other lay on the pommel of the elaborate saddle.

And his eyes, those silver eyes, seemed to be staring straight at her.

Amanda took a step back.

She was wrong to have come here, wrong to have let Dawn convince her she could take this job, even if the sheikh permitted it.

Wrong, wrong, wrong—

"What in hell do you think you're doing in my bedroom?"

The tiny camera fell from Amanda's hand. She swung around, heart racing, and saw the Lion of the Desert, the Heir to the Imperial Throne of Quidar, standing in the doorway, just as he'd been doing that night in her dormitory room.

No jeans and T-shirt this time.

He wore a dark gray suit, a white-on-white shirt and a dark red tie. He was dressed the same as half the men in Manhattan—but it was easy to imagine him in his flowing robes and headdress, with the endless expanse of the desert behind him instead of the marble hall.

Maybe it had something to do with the way he stood, legs apart, hands planted on his hips, as if he owned the world. Maybe it was the look on his hard, handsome face that said he was emperor of the universe and she was nothing but an insignificant subject....

Get a grip, Amanda.

The man had caught her off guard that night, but it wouldn't happen again. She wasn't eighteen anymore, and she'd learned how to deal with hard men who thought they owned the world, men like her father, her stepfather, her ex-husband.

Whatever else they owned, they didn't own her.

"Well? Are you deaf, woman? I asked you a question."

Amanda bent down, retrieved her camera and tucked it into her beaded evening purse.

"I heard you," she said politely. "It's just that you startled

me, Sheikh Rashid.'' She took a breath, then held out her
hand. ''I'm Amanda Benning.''

''And?'' he said, pointedly ignoring her outstretched hand.

''Didn't your sister tell you about me?''

''No.''

No? Oh. Dawn? Dawn, where are you?

Amanda smiled politely. ''Well, she, um, she invited me
here tonight.''

''And that gives you the right to sneak into my bedroom?''

''I did not sneak,'' she said, trying to hold the smile. ''I
was merely…'' Merely what? Dawn was supposed to handle
all this. It was her surprise.

''Yes?''

''I was, um, I was…'' She hesitated. ''I think it's better if
Dawn explains it.''

A chilly smile angled across his mouth. ''I'd much rather
hear your explanation, Ms. Benning.''

''Look, this is silly. I told you, your sister and I are friends.
Why not simply ask her to—''

''My sister is young and impressionable. It would never
occur to her that you'd use your so-called friendship for your
own purposes.''

''I beg your pardon?''

The sheikh took a step forward. ''Who sent you here?''

''Who *sent* me?'' Amanda's eyes narrowed. Nearly eight
years had gone by, and he was as arrogant and overbearing as
ever. Well, she wasn't the naive child she'd been the last time
they'd dealt with each other, and she wasn't frightened of bul-
lies. ''No one sent me,'' she said as she started past him. ''And
there's not enough money in the world to convince me to—''

His hand closed on her wrist with just enough pressure to
make her gasp.

''Give me the camera.''

She looked up at him. His eyes glittered like molten silver.
She felt a lump of fear lodge just behind her breastbone, but
she'd sooner have choked on the fear than let him know he'd
been able to put it there.

"Let go of me," she said quietly.

His grasp on her wrist tightened; he tugged her forward. Amanda stumbled on her high heels and threw out a hand to stop herself. Her palm flattened against his chest.

It was like touching a wall of steel. The cover photo from *Gossip* sprang into her head. Savage, the caption had called him, just as she had, that night.

"Or what?" His words were soft; his smile glittered. "You are in my home, Ms. Benning. To all intents and purposes, that means you stand on Quidaran soil. My word is law here."

"That's not true."

"It is true if I say it is."

Amanda stared at him in disbelief. "Mr. Rashid—"

"You will address me as Lord Rashid," he said, and she saw the sudden memory spark to life in his eyes. "We've met before."

"No," Amanda said, too quickly. "No, we haven't."

"We have. Something about you is familiar."

"I have that kind of face. You know. Familiar."

Nick frowned. She didn't. The pale hair. The eyes that weren't brown or green but something more like gold. The elegant cheekbones, the full, almost pouty lower lip...

"Let go of my wrist, Sheikh Rashid."

"When you give me your camera."

"Forget it! It's my cam — Hey. Hey, you can't..."

He could, though Nick had to admit, it wasn't easy. The woman was twisting like a wildcat, trying to break free and keep him from opening her purse at the same time, but he hung on to her with one hand while he dug out her camera with the other.

She was still complaining, her voice rising as he thumbed from image to image. What he saw made him crazy. Photos of his home. The terrace. The living room. The library. The bathrooms, for God's sake.

And his bedroom.

She had done more than invade his privacy. She had stolen

it and would sell it to the highest bidder. He had no doubt of that.

He looked up from the digital camera, his eyes cold as they assessed her.

She was a thief, but she was beautiful even in a city filled with beautiful women. She seemed so familiar…but if they'd met before, surely he'd remember. What man would forget such a face? Such fire in those eyes. Such promised sweetness in that lush mouth.

And yet, for all of that, she was a liar.

Nick looked down at the little camera in his hand.

Beautiful, and duplicitous.

She played dangerous games, this woman. Games that took her into a man's bedroom and left her vulnerable to whatever punishment he might devise.

He lifted his head slowly, and his eyes met hers.

"Who paid you to take these pictures?"

"I can't tell you."

"Well, that's progress. At least you admit you're doing this for money."

"I am. But it isn't what you—"

"You came here in search of information. A story. Photos. Whatever you could find that was salable." A muscle flexed in his jaw. "Do you know what the punishment in my country is for those who steal?"

"Steal?" Amanda gave an incredulous laugh. "I did not—"

"Theft is bad enough," he said coldly. "Don't compound it by lying."

His eyes were flat with rage. Amanda's heart thumped. Dealing with her father, her stepfather, even her ex, was nothing compared to dealing with a man who ruled a kingdom. She wasn't one of his subjects, but she had the feeling this wasn't exactly the time to point that out.

If Nick finds out, Dawn had said, *he'll be angry at me.*

But Dawn was among the missing, the sheikh was blocking

the doorway, and clearly, discretion was not the better part of valor.

"All right." Amanda stood straighter, even though her heart was still trying to fight its way out of her chest. "I'll tell you the truth."

"An excellent decision, Ms. Benning."

She licked her lips. "I'm—I'm your surprise."

Nick frowned. "I beg your pardon?"

"My services. They're your gift. What Dawn talked about, on the phone."

His gift? Nick's brows lifted. His little sister had a strange sense of humor, but how far would she go for a joke? It could be that Amanda Benning was willing to tell one gigantic whopper as a cover story.

"Indeed," he purred.

Amanda didn't like the tone in his voice.

"I'll have you know that I'm much sought after." *Oh, Amanda, what a lie.* "And expensive." Well, why not? She would be, one day.

"Yes," Nick said softly. "That, at least, must be the truth."

And then, before she could take a breath, Nick reached for the blonde with the golden eyes and the endless legs, pulled her into his arms, and crushed her mouth under his.

CHAPTER THREE

IF THERE was one thing Nick understood, it was the art of diplomacy.

He was the heir to the throne of an ancient kingdom. He represented his people, his flag, his heritage. And he never forgot that.

It was his responsibility to behave in a way that gave the least offense to anyone, even when he was saying or doing something others might not like. He understood that obligation and accepted it.

But when the spotlight was off and Nick could be himself, the truth was that he often had trouble being diplomatic. There were instances when diplomacy was about as useful as offering condolences to a corpse. Sometimes, being polite could distract from the truth and confuse things.

He wanted no confusion in Amanda Benning's mind when it came to him. She was sophisticated and beautiful, a woman who lived by her wits as well as her more obvious charms, but he was on to her game.

And he wanted to be sure she knew it.

That was the reason he'd taken her in his arms. He was very clear about the purpose, even as he gathered her close against him, bent her back over his arm and kissed her.

He'd caught her by surprise. He'd intended that. She gasped, which gave him the chance to slip his tongue between her lips. Then she began to fight him.

Good.

She'd planned everything so carefully. The tiny camera that he should never have noticed. The sexy dress. The soft scent of her perfume. The strappy black silk shoes with the high, take-me heels…

32

Seduction first, conveniently made simple by his foolish sister, whose penchant for silly jokes had finally gotten out of hand. And then, having bedded the Lion of the Desert, the Benning woman would sell her photographs and a breathless first-person account of what it was like to sleep with him.

Nick caught Amanda's wrist as she struggled to shove a hand between them. What a fool Dawn had been to hire a woman like this and bring her into their midst. But he'd have been a greater fool not to at least taste her.

He wouldn't take her to bed. He was too fastidious to take the leavings of other men, but he'd give her just enough of an encounter to remember. Kiss her with harsh demand. Cup her high, lush breasts with the easy certainty that spoke of royal possession.

When she responded, not out of desire but because that was her job, he'd shove her from him, let her watch him grind her camera under his heel. After that, he'd call for Abdul and direct him to hustle the lady straight out the door.

Then he'd go in search of his sister. Dawn needed to be reminded how dangerous it was to consort with scum. A few months in Quidar, under the watchful eye of their father, would work wonders.

That was Nick's plan anyway.

The kiss, the reality of it, changed everything.

Amanda had stopped struggling. That was good. She'd been paid to accept his kisses, welcome his hands as they caressed her pliant body...except, he suddenly realized, she wasn't pliant.

She was rigid with what seemed to be fear.

Fear?

She'd cried out as his mouth covered hers. A nice touch, he'd thought coldly, that little intake of breath, that high, feminine cry. Righteous indignation didn't go with the dress or the heels, certainly not with the face or the body, but he could see where she might try it, just to heighten the tension and his arousal before her ultimate surrender.

There were games men and women played, and a woman

like this would know them all. Either Amanda Benning was
an excellent actress or he'd started the game before she was
ready.

Was she the kind who wanted to direct the performance and
the pace? Or was her imagination running wild? Innocent
maiden. Savage sheikh. The story wasn't new. Nick had come
across women who hungered for it and would accept nothing
else, but he never obliged. It was a stereotype, a fantasy that
offended him deeply, and he refused to play it out.

Sex between a man and a woman involved as much giving
as taking or it brought neither of them pleasure.

But this was different.

He had neither wooed the Benning woman nor won her.
She hadn't seduced him with a smile, a glance, a touch. She
was here because his sister had decided it would be amusing
to give her to him as a gift.

In other words, none of the usual rules applied.

The woman was his. He could do as he wanted with her.
And if what she thought he wanted was some rough sex, he
could oblige. He could play along until it was time to toss her
out.

A little rough treatment, maybe even a scare, was exactly
what Amanda Benning deserved. She was a creature of no
morals, willing to offer her body for information she could
sell to the highest bidder.

Oh, yes. A little scare would do Amanda Benning just fine.

She was struggling in earnest now, not just trying to drag
her mouth from his but fighting him, shoving her fists against
his chest, doing her best to free herself from his arms.

Nick laughed against her mouth, spun her around, pressed
her back against the silk-covered wall. He caught her wrists,
entwined his fingers with hers and flattened her hands against
the wall on either side of her.

She tried to scream. He caught her bottom lip in his teeth,
moved closer, brushed his body against her.

God, she was so warm. Heat seemed to radiate from her
skin. And she was soft. Her breasts. Her belly. Her mouth.

Her hot, luscious mouth. He could taste it now, not only the fear but what lay beyond it, the sweet taste of the woman herself.

His body hardened, became steel. There was a roaring in his ears. Nick wanted to carry her to the bed, strip her of her clothes, bury himself deep inside her. Need for her sang in his blood, raced through every muscle.

The part of his brain that still functioned told him he was insane. He was kissing a woman his sister had bought as a joke, a woman with a bag filled with professional tricks. She was pretending she didn't want him, and he was, what?

He was getting turned on.

It was just that she fitted his arms so well. That her hair felt so silken against his cheek. That she smelled sweet, the way he'd assumed she would taste. The way he wanted her to taste, he thought. The hell with it. She wanted to give a performance? All right. He would comply, but he was changing the rules.

He wasn't going to take her. He was going to seduce her.

"Amanda," he said softly.

Her lashes flew up. Her eyes met his.

"Don't fight me," he whispered, and kissed her. Gently. Tenderly. His mouth moved against hers, over and over; his teeth nipped lightly at her bottom lip. And, gradually, her mouth began to soften. She made a little sound, a whimper, and her body melted against his.

Nick groaned at the stunning sweetness of her surrender. He wanted to let go of her wrists and slide his hands down her spine, stroke the satin that was her skin, cup her bottom and lift her up into the urgency of his erection. When her hands tugged at his, seeking freedom, pleasure rocketed through him. He understood what she wanted, that she sought the freedom to touch him, explore him. It was what he wanted, too. He'd forgotten everything except that he was on fire for the woman in his arms.

He touched the tip of his tongue to the seam of her lips as he let go of her wrists and took her face in his hands. His

palms cupped her cheeks; he tilted her head back so that her
golden hair feathered like silk over the tips of his fingers, so
that he could slant his mouth hungrily over hers—

*—so that her knee could catch him right where he lived and
drive every last breath of air from his lungs.*

A strangled gasp of agony burst from his lips. Nick doubled
over and clutched his groin.

"Amanda?" he croaked, and got his chin up just in time to
see her coming at him again.

"You no-good bastard!"

He was hurting. The pain was gut-deep, but he fought it,
jumped out of her path, caught her as she flew by and flung
her on the bed. She landed hard, rolled to her side, sat up and
almost got her feet on the floor, but by then he'd recovered
enough to come down on top of her.

She called him a name he'd only heard a couple of times
in his life and pummeled him with her fists.

"Get off me!"

It was like wrestling with a wildcat. She was small and
slender but she moved fast, and it didn't help that it still felt
as if his scrotum was seeking shelter halfway up his belly.

Nick took a blow on his chin, another in the corner of his
eye. He grabbed for her hands, captured them and pinned them
high over her head.

"You little bitch," he said, straddling her hips.

Amanda bucked like an unbroken mare, her hips arcing up,
then down.

"Stop it." He leaned toward her, his eyes hot with anger.
"Damn you, woman, did you hear what I said? Stop!"

She didn't. She bucked again, her body moving against his,
her breasts heaving, her golden hair disheveled against the
blue silk pillows. Her eyes were wild, the pupils huge and
black and encircled by rims of gold. She was panting through
parted lips; he could see the flash of her small white teeth, the
pink of her tongue. Her excuse of a dress was ruined; one thin
red silk strap hung off her shoulder, exposing the upper curve
of a creamy breast. The skirt had ridden up her hips. He could

see the strip of black lace that hid the feminine delta between her thighs.

And all at once, he felt fine. No more pain, just the realization that he was hard, swollen and aroused, separated from the woman beneath him by nothing but his trousers and that scrap of sexy lace.

The air in the room crackled with electricity.

He became still. She did, too. Her eyes met his, and for the first time, what he saw in them took his breath away.

"No," she whispered, but his mouth was already coming down on hers.

She held back; he could feel her tremble.

"Yes," he said softly, and kissed her again. "Amanda..."

She moaned. Her lashes fell to her cheeks and she opened her mouth to his. Her surrender was real. Her need was, too. He could feel it in the pliancy of her body, taste it in the silken heat of her kiss.

Nick let go of her hands and gathered her against him. She moaned again and dug her hands into his hair, clutching the dark curling strands with greedy fists.

Greedy. Yes, that was the way she felt. Greedy for his mouth, for his touch. For the feel of Nicholas al Rashid deep inside her.

It was crazy. She didn't know this man, and what little she did know, she didn't like. Moments ago, she'd been fighting him off....

Her breath caught as he rolled onto his side and took her with him. He stroked his hand down her spine, then up again. All the way up, so that his thumbs brushed lightly over her breasts.

"Tell me you want me," he said.

His voice was as soft as velvet, as rough as gravel. His breath whispered against her throat as he licked the flesh where her neck joined her shoulder, and she moaned.

"Tell me," he urged, and she did by seeking his mouth with hers.

Nick sat up, tore off his suit jacket and his tie. She heard the buttons on his shirt pop as he stripped it off. Then he came back down to her, cupped her breasts in his hands and took her mouth.

His skin was hot against hers. She made a little sound of need, nipped his bottom lip. "Yes," she said, "yes, oh, yes…"

His knee was between her thighs. She lifted herself to it, against it; his thumbs rolled across her silk-covered nipples and she was caught up on a wave of heat, up and up and up. She cried out his name, shut her eyes, tossed her head from side to side.

"Look at you," Nick whispered. "Just look at you."

And as quickly as that, it was all over.

Amanda froze. Disgust, horror, anguish…a dozen different emotions raced through her, brought back by those simple, unforgotten words. They took her back seven years to that dormitory room, to the terrifying intruder named Nicholas al Rashid who'd branded her as immoral even as he'd looked at her and wanted her.

Bile rose in her throat. "Get off me," she said.

The sheikh didn't hear her. Couldn't hear her. She looked up at him, hating what she saw, hating herself for being the cause. His silver eyes were blind with desire; the bones of his face were taut with it.

Nausea roiled in her belly. "Get—off!"

She struck out blindly, fists beating against his chest and shoulders. He blinked; his eyes opened slowly as if he were awakening from a dream.

"You—get—the—hell—off," she said, panting, and struck him again.

He caught her flailing hands, pinioned them. "It's too late to play that game."

His voice was low and rough; the hands that held her were hard and cruel. She told herself not to panic. This was Dawn's brother. He was arrogant, imperious and all-powerful…but he wasn't crazy.

"Taking a woman against her will isn't a game," she said, and tried to keep the fear from her voice.

"Against her will?"

His eyes moved over her and she flushed at the slow, deliberate scrutiny. She knew how she must look. Her dress torn. The hem of her skirt at her thighs. Her lips bare of everything but the imprint of his.

A thin smile started at the corner of his mouth. "When a woman all but begs a man to take her, it's hardly 'against her will'."

"I'd never beg a man for anything," she said coldly. "And if you don't let go and get off me, I'll scream. There must be a hundred people downstairs by now. Every one of them will hear me."

"You disappoint me." The bastard didn't just smile this time; he laughed. "You sneaked into my home—"

"I didn't sneak into anything. Your sister invited me."

"Did she tell you that once the party begins, no one will be permitted on this floor?"

Her heart thumped with fear. "They will, if they hear me screaming."

"My men would not permit it."

"The police don't need your permission."

"The police can't do anything to help you. This is Quidaran soil."

"It's a penthouse on Fifth Avenue," Amanda said, trying to free her hands, "not an embassy."

"We have no embassy in your country. By the time our governments finish debating the point, it will be too late."

"You're not frightening me."

It was a lie and they both knew it. She was terrified; Nick could see it in her eyes. Good. She'd deserved the lesson. She was immoral. She was a liar. A thief. She was for sale to any man who could afford her.

What did that make him, then, for still wanting her?

Nick let go of her hands, rolled off her and got to his feet. "Get out," he said softly.

She sat up, moved to the edge of the bed, her eyes wary. She shot a glance at the door and he knew she was measuring her chances of reaching it. It made him feel rotten but, dammit, she wasn't worth his pity. She wasn't worth anything except, perhaps, the price his foolish sister had paid for her.

"Go on," he said gruffly, and jerked his head toward the door. "Get out, before I change my mind."

She rose from the bed. Smoothed down her skirt with hands that shook. Bent and picked up her purse, grabbed the camera and put it inside.

She stumbled backward as Nick came around the bed toward her.

"No," she said sharply, but he ignored her, snatched the purse from her hands and opened the flap. "What are you doing?"

He looked up. He had to give her points for courage, he thought grudgingly. She'd lost one of her ridiculously high heels in their struggle. Her dress was a mess and her hair hung in her eyes.

Those unusual golden eyes.

He frowned, reached for a memory struggling to the surface of his mind….

"Give me my purse."

She lunged for the small beaded bag. He whipped it out of her reach. She went after it, lifting up on her toes and batting at it with her hands.

"Dammit, give me that!"

Nick took out the camera and tossed the purse at her feet. "It's all yours."

"I want my camera."

"I'm sure you do."

Grinding the camera to dust under his heel would have been satisfying, but the carpet was soft and he knew he might end up looking like an ass if the damned thing didn't break. Instead, he strolled into the bathroom.

"What are you…?"

Nick pressed a button on the camera, took out the tiny recording disk and dumped it into the toilet. He shut the lid, flushed, then dropped the camera on the marble floor. Now, he thought, now it would smash when he stepped on it.

It did.

Amanda Benning was scarlet with fury. "You—you bastard!"

"My parents would be upset to hear you call me that, Ms. Benning," he said politely. He walked past her, pleased that the toilet hadn't spit the disk back—it had been a definite possibility and it surely would have spoiled the drama of the moment.

A little more drama, and he'd send Amanda Benning packing.

He swung toward her and folded his arms over his chest. "Actually, addressing me in such a fashion could get you beheaded in my homeland."

Amanda planted her hands on her hips. "It could get you sued in mine."

He laughed. "You can't sue me. I'm—"

"Believe me, I know who you are, Mr. Rashid."

"Lord Rashid," Nick said quickly, and scowled.

What was he saying? He didn't care about his title. Everyone used it. It was the custom but occasionally someone forgot, and he never bothered correcting them. The only time he had was years ago. Dawn's roommate...

The girl with the golden eyes. Strange that he should have remembered her after so long a time. Stranger still that he should have done so tonight.

"...and ninety-eight cents."

He blinked, focused his eyes on Amanda Benning. She hadn't moved an inch. She was still standing in front of him, chin lifted, eyes flashing. He felt a momentary pity that she was what she was. A woman as beautiful, as fiery as this, would be a true gift, especially in a man's bed.

"Did you hear me, *Lord* Rashid?" Amanda folded her arms, tapped her foot. "You owe me $620.98. That includes the film."

One dark, arched brow lifted. It made him look even more insolent. She was boring him, she thought, and fought back a tremor of rage.

"I beg your pardon?"

"The camera." She marched past him, plucked her purse from the floor, dug inside it and pulled out a rumpled piece of paper. "The receipt. From Picture Perfect, on Madison Avenue."

She held it out. Nick looked at it but didn't touch it.

"An excellent place to buy electronic devices, or so I've been told."

"I want my money."

"What for?"

"I just told you. For the camera you destroyed."

"Ah. That."

"Yes. Yes, 'Ah, that.' You owe me six hundred and—"

Nick reached for the phone. "Abdul?" he said, never taking his eyes from her, "come to my rooms, please. Yes, now." He put the telephone down, leaned back against the wall and tucked his hands into his trouser pockets. "Your escort is on the way, Miss Benning. Abdul will escort you down to the curb where the trash is usually left."

Enough was enough. Amanda's composure dissolved in a burst of temper. She gave a shriek and flew at him, but Nick caught her shoulders, held her at arm's length.

"You rat," she said, her breath hitching. "You—you skunk! You horrible, hideous savage—"

"What did you call me?"

"You heard me. You're a skunk. A rat. A—"

"A savage." He swung her around, pinned her to the wall. The memory, so long repressed, burst free. "Damn you," he growled. "You're Dawn's roommate."

"Her immoral, American roommate," Amanda said, and showed her teeth. "How brilliant of you to have finally figured it out. But then, I never expected a baboon to have much of a brain."

The door swung open. Dawn al Rashid stepped into the

room. She stared at her shirtless brother, her red-faced best friend, and swallowed hard.

"Isn't that nice?" she said carefully. "I see that you two have already met."

CHAPTER FOUR

AMANDA stared at Dawn. Dawn stared back.

"Dawn," Amanda said, "thank God you're here! Your brother—"

"Did you invite this woman into my home?" Nick's icy words overrode Amanda's. He took a step toward his sister and Dawn took a quick step back. "I want an answer."

"You'll get one if you give me a min—"

"Did you invite her?"

"Don't browbeat your sister," Amanda said furiously. "I already told you that she asked me to come here tonight."

"I will do whatever I please with my sister." Nick swung toward Amanda. His face was white with anger. "You take me for a fool at your own risk."

"Only a fool would imagine I'd lie my way into your home. I know it may come as a shock to you, Sheikh Rashid, but I don't give a flying fig about seeing how a despot lives."

"Amanda," Dawn muttered, "take it easy."

"Don't tell me to take it easy!" Amanda glared at the sheikh's sister. "And where have you been? Just go take a look at my brother's rooms and I'll meet you there, you said."

"I know. And I'm sorry. I tore my panty hose, and—"

"It's true, then. You not only invited this person into my home, you told her she was free to invade my private rooms."

"Nick," Dawn said, "you don't understand."

"No," the sheikh snapped, "I don't. That my own sister would think I would welcome into my presence the very woman who corrupted her—"

"How dare you say such things?" Amanda stepped in front of Nick. "I never corrupted anyone. I came here as a favor to your sister, to do a job I really didn't want to do because I already knew what you were like, that you were a horrible man with a swollen ego.''

Her eyes flashed. This was pointless and she knew it. Her rage was almost palpable. She yearned to slap that insufferably smug look from Nicholas al Rashid's face, but he'd never let her get away with it. Instead, she moved around him.

''I'm out of here. Dawn, if your brother, the high-muck-a-muck of the universe, lets you use the phone, give me a call tomorrow. Otherwise—''

Nick's hand closed on her arm. ''You will go nowhere,'' he growled, ''until I have answers to my questions.''

''Dammit,'' Amanda said, gritting her teeth and struggling against his grasp, ''let go of me!''

''When I'm good and ready.''

''You have no right—''

''Oh, for heaven's sake!'' Nick and Amanda looked at Dawn. She was staring at the two of them as if she'd never seen them before. ''What in hell is going on here?''

''Don't curse,'' Nick said sharply.

''Then don't treat me like an imbecile.'' Dawn slapped her hands on her hips and glared. ''Yes, I invited Amanda here tonight.''

''As my 'gift','' Nick said, his mouth twisting.

''That's right. I wanted to give you something special for your birthday.''

''Did you really think I'd find it appealing to have you provide a woman for my entertainment?''

''Holy hell,'' Amanda snarled, ''I was not provided for your entertainment! And don't bother telling me not to curse, Your Dictatorship, because I don't have to take orders from you.''

''I can't imagine what my sister was thinking when she made these arrangements.''

''I'll tell you what your sister was thinking. She thought—''

Dawn slammed her fist against the top of the dresser. ''Why not let *me* tell you what I was thinking?'' she snapped.

''Stay out of this,'' Nick said.

''This is unbelievable. All this fuss because I decided your apartment looked like an ad for the No-Taste Furniture Company!'' Her mouth thinned as she glared at Nick. ''What a mistake I made, fixing you up with the services of an interior designer.''

Nick blinked. ''A what?''

''A designer. Someone trained to figure out how to turn this—this warehouse for overpriced, overdone, overvelveted garbage into a home.''

''Oh, go on,'' Nick said with a tight smile, ''don't hold back. Just tell me what you really think.''

''You know it's the truth.'' Dawn waved her arms in the air. ''This apartment looks more like a—a mortician's show-room than a home. So I called Amanda, who just happens to be one of the city's best-known designers. Isn't that right, Amanda?''

Amanda glanced at the sheikh. He was looking at her, and the expression on his face wasn't encouraging.

''And one of its most modest,'' Dawn added hurriedly. ''She was booked up to her eyeballs. The mayor's mansion. The penthouse in that new building on the river. You know, the one that was written up in *Citylights* a couple of weeks ago.''

''Dawn,'' Amanda said, and cleared her throat, ''I don't think—''

''No. No, you certainly didn't. I didn't think it, either. Who'd imagine my brother would want to turn down such a gift from his favorite sister?''

''My only sister,'' Nick said dryly.

''The gift of a brilliant interior designer,'' Dawn said, ig-noring the interruption, ''who made room in her incredibly busy schedule solely as a favor to an old friend…'' She paused dramatically. ''And what have you done to her, Nicky?''

Color slashed Nick's high cheekbones. ''What kind of ques-tion is that?''

''A logical one. Just look at her. Her dress is torn. Her hair's a mess. She's missing a shoe—''

"Excuse me," Amanda said. "There's no need to take inventory."

"And you, Nicky." Dawn huffed out a breath. "I had no idea my brother, the Lion of the Desert, was in the habit of conducting business with his shirt off."

Amanda shut her eyes, opened them and looked at the sheikh. The flush along his cheeks had gone from red to crimson.

"I have no need to explain myself to anyone," he said brusquely.

"And a good thing, too, because how you could possibly explain this—"

"But since you're my sister, I'll satisfy your curiosity. We fought over Ms. Benning's spy camera."

"My what?" Amanda laughed. "Honestly, Dawn. This brother of yours—"

Nick's eyes narrowed. "Be careful," he said softly, "before you push me too far."

"Well, you've already pushed *me* too far." Dawn marched to Amanda's side and took her hand. "We'll be in my room, Nicky, when you're ready to apologize."

The sheikh stiffened. The room went still. Even the distant sounds of the party—the strains of music, the buzz of conversation that had begun drifting up the stairs a little while before—seemed to stop.

Amanda sensed that a line had been crossed.

She looked at Dawn, who seemed perfectly calm—but the grip of her hand was almost crushing. The women's eyes met. Hang on, Dawn's seemed to say and we can get away with this.

Together, they started for the door. It was like walking away from a stick of dynamite with a lit fuse. One step. Two. Just another few to go—

"An admirable performance, little sister."

Dawn let out her breath. Amanda did, too. She hadn't even realized she'd been holding it. Both of them turned around.

"Nicky," Dawn said softly, "Nicky, if you'd just calm down—"

"Do as you suggested. Take Ms. Benning to your room." His eyes swept over Amanda. She fought back the urge to smooth down her skirt, grasp her torn strap, fix her hair. Instead, she lifted her chin and met his look without blinking. "Give her something to wear. Let her make herself respectable and then bring her downstairs."

"I am not a package to be brought downstairs or anywhere else, for that matter. Who do you think you are, giving orders to your sister about me? If you have something to say to me—"

"The matter is settled for the moment."

"The matter is settled permanently." She tore her hand from Dawn's tight grasp. "I wouldn't so much as pick out the wallpaper for your kitchen, let alone—"

"Get her out of here." Nick waved an imperious hand. He knew he sounded like an ass, but what else was there to do? Dawn's story had holes in it the size of the Grand Canyon. He was angry at her, angry at the Benning woman, but he was furious at himself for losing control in the bed that seemed to loom, stage center, a thousand times larger than life.

What in *hell* had he been thinking, to have almost made love to her?

He hadn't been thinking, he decided grimly. That was the problem. His brain had gone on holiday, thanks to Amanda Benning's clever machinations. A far more dangerous part of his anatomy had taken over.

But his thought processes were clear now. He wasn't about to let this situation deteriorate any further, nor was he about to permit Amanda to walk away before he was certain of what she'd been up to.

"Go on," he said to his sister. "Get her out of here and I'll deal with you both when the night ends."

"Deal with us?" Amanda's voice rose. "You'll deal with us?"

"Oh, he doesn't really mean—"

"Silence!"

The command roared through the room. Amanda caught her breath. She'd never heard a man speak to a woman that way. Her own father had been strict, her stepfather could be crude, and her ex had specialized in sarcasm, but this was different. Nicholas al Rashid's voice carried the ring of absolute authority. Shirtless and disheveled, there was still no mistaking the raw power that emanated from him.

She looked at Dawn and waited for her to respond, to stand up to her brother and tell him that she didn't have to take orders.

To her horror Dawn bowed her head. "Yes, my lord," she whispered.

Amanda stepped in front of her friend. "Now wait just a minute—"

"As for you," Nick barked, "you will speak only when spoken to."

"Listen here, you—you pathetic stand-in for a real human being—"

Nick grabbed her by the elbows and hoisted her to her toes. "Watch how you speak to me."

"Watch how you speak to *me*, Your Horribleness. You might have your sister bowing and scraping like a slave, but not me!"

"Mandy," Dawn pleaded, "stay out of this. Let me explain—"

"Yes," Nick said. He let go of Amanda and folded his arms. "Do that. Now that I think about it, why should I wait until later for an explanation? Explain to me why I found your so-called friend, your interior designer, taking photographs of my things with a spy camera."

"I told you, it wasn't a spy camera."

"It was designed to be concealed."

"It was designed to fit inside a pocket or a purse!"

Nick gave a cold smile. "Exactly."

"It was *not* a spy camera, and if you hadn't stomped it into pieces, I could prove it!"

"You will learn to speak when spoken to," he growled. "And if you cannot manage that, I'll lock you away until I've finished with my sister. Do you understand?"

Amanda's heart bounced into her throat. He would do it, too. She could see it in his eyes.

"You're despicable," she said in a choked whisper. "How I could ever have let you—"

Nick said something in a language she didn't understand. She shrieked as he picked her up, slung her over his shoulder and strode toward a large walk-in closet.

"Put me down. Damn you, put me—"

He yanked the door open, dumped her inside the closet. She dived for the door, but she was too late. It shut in her face, and then she heard a scraping sound against the wood. Amanda rattled the knob, pounded her fist against the door until she was panting, but it was useless.

The sheikh must have jammed a chair under the doorknob. She was trapped.

All she could do was listen to the murmur of voices. The sheikh's angry, Dawn's apologetic. After a while, she couldn't hear anything, not even a whisper. She could imagine Dawn, cowed into submission, while her abominable brother stood over her, glowering. Glowering was what he seemed to do best.

"Bastard," Amanda said softly.

Tears welled in her eyes. Tears of anger.

"Oh, hell," she whispered. Who was she kidding? They were tears of shame. Her rage at the sheikh's accusations, at what he'd done to her camera, at how he'd treated her, was nothing compared to the rage she felt at herself.

How could she have kissed him? Because she had kissed him; she'd have done more than that if she hadn't mercifully come to her senses just before Dawn came into the room. She'd lost control of herself in Nicholas al Rashid's arms. Done things. Said things. Felt things...

Let go, her husband used to say. *What's the matter with you? Why are you such a prude when it comes to sex?*

Well, she hadn't been a prude tonight. She'd behaved as if she were exactly what the sheikh had accused her of being.

"Oh, hell," Amanda said again, and she leaned back, slid to the floor, wrapped her arms around her knees and settled in to wait until His Royal Highness, the Despot of Quidar, deigned to set her free.

It wasn't a very long wait. But when the door opened, it wasn't the despot who stood outside. It was Dawn.

Amanda scrambled to her feet. "What happened?"

"Nick is furious."

"Not half as furious as I am." She peered past Dawn. "Where is he? I haven't finished telling him what—"

"He took his stuff and went to one of the guest rooms to change." Dawn glanced at the diamond watch on her wrist. "By now, he's probably downstairs."

"Yeah, well then, that's where I'm—"

"Mandy." Dawn caught Amanda's hand. "What happened before I got here?"

Color swept into Amanda's face. "Nothing happened," she said, and wrenched her hand free. She smoothed down her dress, tugged uselessly at the torn strap and wished she knew what had happened to her other shoe. "Your brother caught me in here and jumped to all the wrong conclusions."

"Uh-huh." Dawn managed a smile. "So he thought I'd arranged a gift for his, uh, for his pleasure?"

"He most certainly did. As if I'd ever—"

"I know. Sometimes it's not easy dealing with Nicky."

"That's because his head is as hard as a rock."

"Do us both a favor, okay? Don't say things like that to him. You can't call him names, not when he's angry. It isn't done."

"Maybe not in your country, but this is America." Amanda hobbled past Dawn, eyes on the carpet as she searched for her shoe. "Freedom of speech, remember? The Bill of Rights? The Constitution? Ah. There it is." She bent down, picked up her shoe and grimaced. "The heel is broken. Okay, okay,

that's it. Tell your brother he owes me for the camera and now
for a pair of shoes.''

"One dress, too, from the looks of it." Dawn hesitated.
"You guys must have really tussled over that camera."

Amanda was glad she had her back to Dawn. "Yes. Yes,
we did."

"The thing is, I never figured you'd get caught alone in his
bedroom. I was sure I'd get here before he came home."

"Well, you didn't." Amanda heard the sharpness in her
own voice. She stopped, drew a breath and turned around.
"Look, what happened isn't your fault. Anyway, now that
your brother knows the truth—"

"Well, he's not sure he does."

"You mean he still thinks you arranged for me to—"

"No. No, not that." Dawn sat down on the edge of the bed,
sighed and crossed her legs. "Mandy, try to see things from
his perspective. I mean, you saw that awful photograph on the
cover of *Gossip*. People try to get close to him all the time
just so they can find out personal stuff about his life."

"I'd sooner get close to a python."

"I know how you feel. But Nick is sensitive about invasions
of his privacy."

"Your brother is about as sensitive as a mule. And you
know damn well that I wasn't invading anything."

"Of course. And he'll know it, too." Dawn blew out her
breath. "Just as soon as the party is over."

"Yeah, well, you can explain it to him by yourself."
Amanda slung her evening purse over her shoulder and limped
to the door. "Because I am out of here."

"You can't."

"Oh, but I can." She looked back as she curled her hand
around the knob. "I feel sorry for you, Dawn. You're trapped
with His Arrogance, but I'm… Dammit! This—door—is—
stuck!" Dawn said something so quietly that Amanda couldn't
hear it. "What?" she said, and rattled the knob again.

"I said, the door isn't stuck. It's locked."

Amanda stood perfectly still. When she let go of the knob

and looked around, her face was a study in disbelief. "From the outside?"

"Uh-huh." Dawn swung her foot back and forth. She seemed to be contemplating her black silk pump. "I guess some nutcase owned this penthouse before Nicky did. Lots of the doors have locks on the—"

"I don't care who owned it, dammit!"

"I'm just explaining..." Dawn licked her lips. "Nicky locked the door."

"Nicky locked..." Amanda clamped her lips together. Be calm, she told herself, be very calm. "Let me understand this. Your brother locked this door the same way he locked me into the closet?"

Dawn peered intently at her shoes. "Right."

"And you let him do it?"

"I didn't *let* him do anything." Dawn looked up. "He just did it. He has the right." Amanda laughed. Dawn's face pinkened. "Mandy," she said, "I know this seems strange to you—"

"Strange? Strange, that a man I hardly know doesn't think twice about locking me up?" Amanda grabbed for her dangling shoulder strap. "That he feels free to try to rip my clothes off? To tumble me into his bed?"

A grin, a real one, curled across Dawn's mouth. "Oh, wow," she said softly. "So that wasn't true, huh? Nicky's little speech about losing his shirt when you were fighting over the camera."

"The truth," Amanda said stiffly, "is that your dear, devoted brother is a lunatic. And so are you, for letting him lock that door."

Dawn shot to her feet. "I didn't 'let' him. I told you that. Nobody 'lets' him, don't you see? My brother is the future ruler of our kingdom. His word is law."

"For you, maybe. And for anybody else who's willing to live in the Dark Ages."

"Now, you just wait a minute before you say—"

The door suddenly swung open. Amanda spun around and glared at the man she despised.

How calm and collected he looked. While she'd been cooling her heels behind locked doors, the Sheikh of the Universe had been readying himself for his party. His dark hair was still damp from the shower; his jaw was smooth. She could see a tiny cut in the shallow cleft in his chin.

Good, she thought grimly. Maybe he wasn't as calm as he looked. The son of a bitch had cut himself while he shaved. She only hoped she was the reason for his unsteady hand on the razor. From the way he'd looked at her before and from how he was looking at her now, it was pretty obvious that Nicholas al Rashid wasn't accustomed to having anyone, especially a woman, talk back to him.

Women probably told him lots of other things, though. That he was exciting. That he was gorgeous, especially in that tux and pleated white shirt. That he could make a woman forget everything, even the code she lived by, with one kiss....

Amanda drew herself up. Snakes could be handsome, too. That didn't make them any less repulsive.

"You have one hell of a nerve," she said, "locking us in this room."

Nick looked at his sister. "Dawn?"

"This is the United States of America in case you haven't—"

"Dawn, our guests are here."

Amanda strode toward him. "Are you deaf?" Her words were rimed with ice. "I'm talking to you."

Nick ignored her. "Thanks to this unpleasant incident, I am not at the door to greet them."

Dawn cast her eyes down. "It's my fault, Nicholas. I apologize."

"I've decided to forgive you."

A glowing smile lit Dawn's face. "Thank you, Nicky."

Amanda made a little sound of disgust. Nick decided to go on pretending she was invisible.

"But this is the last time. One more transgression and you return home."

"Oh, give me a break."

Dawn shot Amanda a horrified look. Nick merely tilted his head toward her. "Did you have something you wished to say, Ms. Benning?"

"How generous of you to notice."

"Is that a yes?"

Amanda limped toward him. "It is indeed."

Nick looked at his watch, then at her. "Say it, then. I'm in a hurry, thanks to you."

"And I'm out a camera, a dress and a pair of shoes, thanks to you." It wasn't easy to maintain your dignity with one shoe three inches higher than the other, but Amanda was determined to manage it. "I'm going to send you a bill for—" she paused, furiously adding the numbers in her head "—for nine hundred and eighty dollars."

"Really."

Damn him for that annoying little smirk! "Yes," she said with a smirk of her own, "really. That camera was expensive."

"Oh, I'm sure it was." He folded his arms and raked her with a glance, his gaze settling, at last, on her face. "I'm just surprised that your dress and shoes would be so costly, considering what little there was of both."

Actually, Nick thought, that was overstating it. A wisp of red. Two slender straps. A pair of high-heeled sandals that made her legs long and endless...

One sandal. The other was broken, now that he took a closer look. That was the reason she'd lurched toward him. Still, those legs were as long and endless as he'd remembered. As long and glorious as they'd felt, wrapped around him when he'd tumbled her down onto the bed.

The feel of her beneath him. The soft thrust of her breasts. The scent of her hair. The taste of her mouth...

Nick frowned.

Terrific. He'd found a conniving little schemer in his bedroom, and just remembering what she'd felt like in his arms was enough to send his hormones into a frenzy.

Disgusted, he walked past her and paused before the mirrored wall that faced his bed, supposedly to straighten his tie when what actually needed straightening was his libido.

What was the matter with him? All right. Amanda Benning was beautiful. She was as sexy as sin. So what?

All his women were beautiful and sexy, but he hadn't stumbled across any one of them hiding in his bedroom, snapping photos with a camera that would have made James Bond envious, then coming to life in his arms when she'd decided the situation was desperate enough to require a distraction.

This was a setup. Nick was positive of it. What else could it be? His little sister, complaining about the furnishings of his apartment? It didn't ring true. Dawn never noticed her surroundings unless it was the once-a-year encampment their father demanded of her, and she only noticed then because she hated the heat, the dust, the inconvenience of sleeping in a tent.

As for Amanda—if she was an interior designer, then the moon was made of green cheese. And, dammit, she brought out the worst in him.

First he'd mauled her. No point in pretending, not to himself. He'd come on to her with the subtlety of a freight train, or never mind all his rationalizations about playing her game, or teaching her a lesson, or whatever nonsense he'd used to justify wanting to kiss her.

Then he'd come to his senses, started to let her go, but ended up trying to seduce her instead. That didn't make sense, either. Why would he try to seduce a woman whose motives for being in his bedroom were, at the very least, questionable?

And then there was the icing on the cake. The way he'd talked to Dawn, as if he really were the tottering ghost of old Rudy Valentino. Just thinking about it was humiliating. Nicholas al Rashid, stepping straight out of an outdated Hollywood flick, complete with flaring nostrils, attitude, and macho enough to make a camel gag.

The only thing he'd left out was the shoe-polish hair.

Yeah, he thought, yeah, he'd made a fool of himself.

And for what? Because he'd found Amanda Benning in his bedroom? He'd destroyed her disk, broken her camera. Abdul would give him a report on her in a little while and then he'd put the fear of God in her.

Nick's mouth twitched. The fear of his lawyers, to be specific. One well-worded threat and she'd be out of his life for good.

The world was full of women, lots of them as beautiful as this one. There was nothing special about her. His mouth thinned. There hadn't been anything special about her seven years ago, either, when his panic over Dawn was all that had stood between him and insanity—

"...an itemized bill."

Nick scowled at his reflection, turned and looked at Amanda, who'd come up to stand behind him. "What?"

"I said, I'll send you an itemized bill if you don't believe that I paid almost three hundred dollars for the dress."

"There's no need for that. Abdul—my secretary—will write you a check before you leave tonight."

"Good old Abdul," Amanda said pleasantly. "Still crawling around on his hands and knees, is he?" Her chin lifted. "Tell him to get busy, then, because I'm going straight out the front door the instant I get down—"

"No."

"No? But you just said—"

"You're not leaving so quickly, Ms. Benning."

"On the contrary, Sheikh Rashid. As far as I'm concerned, I'm not leaving quickly enough."

"You will leave here after I'm done with you, Dawn." Nick smiled. "People are asking for you."

"Oh. But you said—"

"I know what I said. I've changed my mind. I'd prefer not to have to try to explain your absence."

"What's the matter?" Amanda said nastily. "Are you

afraid people might be put off if they knew you were in the habit of locking women in your bedroom?''

The sheikh smiled at his sister. "Just behave yourself."

"Just behave yourself," Amanda said in wicked imitation. "What does that mean? Is she supposed to walk two paces to the rear?"

"Go on." Nick kissed Dawn's cheek. "Go downstairs and tell our guests I've been momentarily detained."

Dawn hesitated. "What about Amanda?"

Nick's smile thinned. "I'll take care of her."

"Dawn?" Amanda said, but Dawn shook her head and hurried out of the room. Abdul seemed to materialize in the doorway.

"There you are, Abdul," Nick said.

"My lord."

"Has it arrived?"

"Yes, my lord."

Nick nodded. Abdul bent down, then straightened up with two elaborately wrapped boxes in his arms.

"On the bed, please."

The little man walked to the bed and put the boxes down. Then he bowed his body in half and backed out of the room.

"Those are for you."

Amanda looked at the things lying on the bed as if they might start ticking.

"A dress," Nick said lazily, "and a pair of shoes."

"Are you crazy?"

"I would be, if I let you slip away without confirming your reasons for being here." He jerked his head at the boxes. "I guessed at your sizes."

"I'm sure you're an expert," she said coldly.

"And," he said, ignoring the taunt, "I did my best to describe the style of your things to the concierge."

"How nice for the concierge." She folded her arms and lifted her chin. "But you should have told her to order them in her size."

"In his size," Nick said with a little smile, "but I doubt if they're quite to his taste."

"Maybe you didn't hear me before, Sheikh Rashid. I said I wanted a check to pay for my things, not replacements."

"And you shall have a check. But I've no intention of letting you go just yet, Ms. Benning. Dawn's things won't fit you. And I certainly won't permit you to insult my guests by moving among them while you look like something no self-respecting cat would drag home."

Amanda's brows rose. "If you honestly think I want to go to your party—"

"I'm not interested in what you think, honestly or otherwise. But I must attend my party, as must my sister. And, since I need to keep you here for another few hours, I have no choice but to subject my guests to your presence."

Heat swept into her face. "You are the most insulting man I've ever had the misfortune to meet."

"Ah, Ms. Benning. That breaks my heart." Nick pointed a commanding finger at the boxes. "Now, take those things into the dressing room. Change your dress and shoes. Fix your hair and do whatever is required to make yourself presentable. Then you will emerge, take my arm, stay at my side all evening, comport yourself with decorum and speak to no one unless I grant permission for you to do so."

"In your dreams!"

"If you do all that, and if your so-called interior design credentials check out, you will be free to leave. If not…"

"If not, what?" Amanda's jaw shot out. "Will you lock me in the dungeon?"

His smile was slow and heart-stopping in its male arrogance. "What a fine idea."

"You—you…"

Nick looked at his watch. "You have five minutes."

"You're a horrible man, Sheikh Rashid!"

"I'm waiting, Ms. Benning." He looked up, his cold silver eyes locked on hers. "Perhaps you require my assistance."

Amanda snatched the boxes from the bed and fled into the

dressing room. Angry tears blinded her as she stripped off her dress and kicked her shoes into a corner. Then she opened the packages and took out what Nick had bought her.

The dress looked almost like the one he'd ruined, except it had surely cost ten times as much and seemed to have been fashioned of cobwebs instead of silk. The shoes were elegant wisps of satin and slid on her feet as if they'd been made for her.

Nick rapped sharply on the door. "One minute."

She looked at herself in the mirror. Her eyes were bright. Her cheeks were pink. With anger, she told herself. Of course with anger. And it was anger, too, that had sent her heart leaping into her throat.

She ran her fingers through her hair, bit her lips to color them. Then she threw back her head, unlocked the door and stepped into the bedroom.

Nick was leaning back against the wall, arms folded, feet crossed at the ankles. He gave her a long, appraising look, from the top of her head to her feet, then up again. "I take it the dress and shoes fit."

His tone was polite, but when his eyes met hers, they were shot with silver fire. She could feel the heat swirling in her blood.

"I despise you," she said in a voice that sounded far too breathless.

He uncoiled his body like a lazy cat and came toward her. "Liking me isn't a prerequisite for the night we're about to spend together."

"We aren't," she said quickly, even though she knew he was baiting her, that he was really just referring to the time she'd be with him at his party. "There's no way in hell I'd spend the night with—"

He bent and brushed his mouth over hers. That was all he did; the kiss was little more than a whisper of flesh to flesh, but the intake of her breath more than proved she was lying.

She knew it. He knew it. And she hated him for it.

"The Sheikh," she said, her eyes cool.

"I beg your pardon?"

"*The Sheikh,* starring Rudolph Valentino. It's an old movie. You'd love it. Be sure and rent the video sometime."

Nick laughed. "I can see we're going to have a delightful evening." He held out his arm. She tossed her head. "Take it," he said softly, "unless you'd rather I lift you into my arms and carry you."

Amanda took his arm. She could feel the hardness of his muscles, the taut power of his body through his clothing—but mostly, she could feel the race of her own heart as he led her out of his bedroom and to the wide staircase that led downstairs.

CHAPTER FIVE

AMANDA knew all about making an entrance.

Her father, a California businessman who owned a department store and had hopes of building it into a chain, had put his three beautiful little daughters in front of the cameras whenever he could. They'd promoted everything from baby clothes to barbecue grills.

"Lick your lips, girls," he'd say just before he'd walk them out. "And give 'em a big smile."

The small-town lawyer she'd married had turned into a publicity-hungry politico looking for national office before she'd had time to blink.

"Smile," he'd say, and he'd put his arm around her waist as if he really cared, just before walking her into a room filled with strangers.

Her stepfather, Jonas Baron, was the exception. Jonas owned almost half of Texas but he didn't much care about entrances or exits. He never sought public attention but he couldn't escape it, either.

Still, nothing could have prepared her for what it was like to make an entrance on the arm of the Lord of the Desert.

"Oh, hell," Nick said softly when they reached the top of the stairs.

Oh, hell, indeed, Amanda thought as she looked down.

A million faces looked back. And oh, the expressions on those faces! All those eyes, shifting with curiosity from the sheikh to her...

She jerked to a stop. "Everyone is watching us," she hissed.

"Yeah." Nick cleared his throat. "I should have realized this might happen. It's because I'm late."

"Well, that's not my fault!"

"Of course it's your fault," he growled.

"I'm not going down there. Not with you."

Nick must have anticipated that she'd move away because his free hand shot out and covered hers as it lay on his arm. To the people watching, it would have looked like a courtly gesture, but the truth was that his hand felt like a shackle on hers.

"Don't be ridiculous. They've all seen us. As it is, tongues will wag. If you run off now, there'll be no stopping the stories."

"That's your problem, Lord Rashid, not mine."

He looked at her, his eyes narrowed and hard. "You're my sister's oldest friend." Slowly, he began descending the steps with Amanda locked to his side. "And you've come to pay her a visit."

"I'm the immoral creature who led her astray. Isn't that what you mean?"

"You haven't seen each other in ages, not since—when?"

She looked at him. His mouth was set in a polite smile.

"How charming," she said coolly. "You can speak without moving your lips."

"When did you and Dawn last see each other?"

"Two weeks ago, at lunch. Not exactly 'ages', is it?"

Nick's hand tightened over hers. "Just keep your story straight. You're Dawn's friend. You've kept in touch over the years. She heard you were in town and invited you to her birthday party."

They were halfway down the steps. Amanda looked at all those upturned faces. The only thing lacking was a trumpet fanfare, she thought, and bit back a hysterical bark of laughter.

"Did you hear me, Ms. Benning?"

"I heard you, Lord Rashid. But I'm not visiting New York. I live here. I know you'd prefer to think I live in Casablanca and that I'm a spy."

"What I think, Ms. Benning, is that you watch too many old movies."

"What am I supposed to say if people ask why you and I came downstairs together?"

It was, Nick decided, an excellent question. "Tell them…tell them I hadn't seen you in a long time."

"Not long enough," Amanda said, smiling through her teeth.

"You and I were catching up on old times."

"Ah. Is that some quaint Quidaran idiom that means you were trying to jump my bones?"

Nick stopped so abruptly that she stumbled. He caught her, his arm looping tightly around her waist.

"Listen to me," he growled. "You are to behave yourself. You will smile pleasantly, say the proper thing at the proper moment. And if you don't—"

"Don't threaten me, Lord Rashid. I'll behave, but not because I'm afraid of you. It's because I've no desire for ugly publicity."

"Afraid it might ruin your image?" he said sarcastically.

"Being seen with you will be enough to do— What are they doing?"

The question was pointless. She could see, and hear, what all those people down there were doing. They were applauding.

"They're applauding," Amanda said, and looked at him.

Nick gave her a smile so phony she wondered if it made his mouth hurt.

"I know."

"Well, why are they—"

"The applause is for me."

She looked down again, into that sea of smiling faces, at the clapping hands. Then she looked at Nick. Definitely, that smile had to be painful.

"They're clapping for you?" she said incredulously.

"Must I repeat myself?" A muscle tightened in his cheek. "It is the custom."

"The custom?"

"Do you think you're capable of making a statement, Ms.

Benning, instead of following each question with another?
Yes. It is the custom to applaud the prince on his birthday.''

"Well, it's dumb.''

Nick laughed. Really laughed. "It is indeed.''

"Then why do you permit it?''

He thought of a hundred different answers, starting with
three thousand years of history and ending with the knowledge
that had come to him only after more than a decade of trying
to push his country into the twenty-first century—the simple
realization that not even he could accomplish such a thing
quickly.

He could tell Amanda Benning all of that, but why should
he? She wouldn't understand. And the odds were excellent that
if he did, she'd rush to sell that morsel of news to the highest
bidder.

As it was, he was doing everything possible not to think
about her trying to sell the sordid little tale of what had gone
on in his bedroom. Surely his lawyers' threats would stop her.
And if that didn't do the trick, he'd deny whatever she said.
But would he be able to deny the memory of those moments
to himself? The feel of her in his arms? The taste of her on
his tongue?

Of course he would, he thought calmly.

"I permit the applause,'' he said, "because it is the custom.''

"That's ridiculous.''

"We have other customs you would probably call ridiculous, as well, including one that demands a woman's silence
in my presence until I grant her permission to speak.''

"Is that a threat?''

"It's a promise.''

Amanda shook her head in disbelief. "I have no idea how
Dawn tolerates you.''

"And I have no idea how someone like you managed to
insinuate yourself into my sister's life. Now, smile and behave
yourself.''

"You're a horrible man, Lord Rashid.''

"Thank you for the compliment, Ms. Benning."

They reached the bottom of the steps. Nick smiled. So did Amanda. The crowd surged forward and swallowed them up.

An hour later, Nick was still leading Amanda from guest to guest.

If her ex could only see her now, she thought wryly.

Not wanting to be stage center was one of the first things they'd quarreled over, but that was where she'd been all evening. If there'd been a spotlight in the room, it would have been beamed at her head.

Nicholas al Rashid might be the Lord of the Realm, the Lion of the Desert, the Heir to the Imperial Throne and the Wizard of Oz, but not even he could control people's tongues. And those tongues were all wagging. Wagging, Amanda thought grimly, at top speed.

"My sister's friend," he said each time he introduced her. "Ms. Amanda Benning."

The answers hardly varied. "Oh," people said, "how…interesting."

She knew that what they really wanted to say was that if she was Dawn's friend, why had she made such a spectacular entrance on his arm, with no Dawn in sight? For that matter, where was Dawn now?

On the other side of the room, that was where. Dawn had smiled and waggled her fingers, but clearly, she was going to adhere to the rules and keep her distance.

As Nick was walking her toward another little knot of people, Amanda snagged a glass of wine from a waiter and took a sip.

Rules. The sheikh was full of rules. And, fool that he was, he seemed to think people abided by them.

"You see?" he'd said smugly, after he'd marched her around for a while. "No one's asking any questions. It wouldn't be polite."

Idiot, Amanda thought, and took another mouthful of wine.

Etiquette could keep people from *saying* what they were

thinking, but nothing could stop the thoughts themselves or the buzz of speculation that followed them around the room.

Finally, she'd had her fill.

"I don't like this," she murmured. "Everyone is talking about me."

"You should have thought of that possibility before you sneaked into my bedroom. Keep moving, please, Ms. Benning."

"They think I'm your—your—"

"Probably." Nick's jaw knotted; his hand clasped her elbow more tightly as he steered her toward the terrace door. "That's why it's important to show no reaction to the whispers."

"There isn't anything to whisper about," Amanda said crossly. "Can't you tell them that?"

Nick laughed.

"I'm glad you find this so amusing." She yanked her arm free of his hand as they stepped into the cool night air. "Can't you tell them—"

"Sire?"

Amanda looked over her shoulder. Abdul, looking more like a pretzel than a man, came hurrying toward them.

"Your slave approacheth," she said, "O Emperor of the World."

Nick ignored her as Abdul dropped to one knee. "What is it, Abdul?"

The old man lifted his head just enough to give her a meaningful look. Nick sighed, eased his secretary to his feet and led him a short distance away. He bent his head, listened, then nodded.

"Thank you, Abdul."

"My lord," Abdul said, and shuffled backward into the living room.

"He's too old to be doing that whenever he comes near you."

"I agree. But—"

"Don't tell me. It's the custom, right? And we wouldn't

want to ignore the custom even if it means that poor little man has to keep banging his knees against the floor.''

Nick's jaw shot forward. "Abdul was my father's secretary. He was my grandfather's apprentice clerk. This is the way he's always done things, the way he expects to do..." He stopped talking. Amanda was looking at him as if he were some alien species of life. "Never mind," he said coldly. "I'm not going to spend the evening in debate."

"Of course not, because you know you'd lose."

"What I know," Nick said even more coldly, "is that Abdul's just reminded me of some things that need my attention. You're on your own."

Amanda raised her hands and flexed her wrists. "Off with the handcuffs," she said brightly.

"You're to keep away from Dawn."

"Certainly, sire."

"You're not to bother anyone with personal questions."

"Darn," she cooed, batting her lashes. "And here I was, hoping to ask the governor what he wore to bed."

"Other than that, you're free to move among my guests unattended."

"Does that mean I passed the background check?"

"It means I'm too busy to go on playing baby-sitter, and that if you try to leave before I'm done with you, you'll be stopped by my security people."

"How gracious of you, Lord Rashid."

Nick flashed a grim smile. "What man would not wish to be gracious to you, Ms. Benning?" he answered, and strolled back into the brightly lit living room.

"Good riddance," Amanda muttered, watching him.

"Nicky!"

He was halfway across the room when Deanna Burgess launched herself into the sheikh's arms. Amanda's eyebrows lifted. It was a warm greeting, to say the least, but the look she shot over his shoulder was far from warm.

Obviously, Deanna Burgess knew Nick had made his entrance with her on his arm. Of course she knew, Amanda thought grimly. She drank some more wine. Two hundred and fifty absolute strangers had witnessed that entrance and the odds were excellent that most of them were still talking about it.

Oh, if only she could get that sort of publicity for Benning Designs.

Amanda lifted her glass to her mouth. It was empty. She tilted it up and let the last golden drops trickle onto her tongue. Time for another drink, she thought, and strolled into the living room.

There had to be a way to turn this disaster into something useful. Dawn's original plan certainly wasn't going to work now. No way would the sheikh agree to let Benning Designs decorate the penthouse.

Amanda smiled at the bartender, put down her empty glass and exchanged it for a full one.

Think, she told herself, think. What would Paul do? Her ex, with his toothpaste smile, had been unsurpassed at turning political liabilities into political bonuses.

She took a drink. Mmm. The wine was delicious. And cooling.

Jonas, then. Her stepfather was the sort of man who'd never let a difficult situation stop him. What would Jonas do?

"...old friend, or so he..."

The whispered buzz sounded as clearly as a bell in the seconds it took the chamber quartet to segue from Vivaldi to Mozart. The little knot of people that had produced it looked at her. Amanda looked back, lifted her glass. One man colored and lifted his, too.

The bastards were, indeed, talking about her.

She buried her frown in her glass.

If only they'd talk about Benning Designs instead of Amanda Benning, but there was no way that would happen. Not even Jonas Baron could turn this silk purse into a sow's ear. Or maybe it was the other way around. Even old Jonas would be helpless in this situation. The best he'd do would be to come up with some creaky saying.

Like, you had to roll with the punches. Like, those were the breaks. Like, when life hands you lemons...

"Make lemonade," Amanda said, and blinked.

"Sorry?"

She swung around, gave the bartender a big smile. "I said, could I have another glass of wine, please?"

Glass in hand, smiling brilliantly, she headed straight for the little group of whisperers.

"Hello," she said, and stuck out her hand. "I'm Amanda Benning. Of Benning Designs. I apologize for making His Highness late for his own party, but I had him all excited." She smiled modestly and wondered if the woman to her left knew her mouth was hanging open. "He's so private, you know."

"Oh," the woman with the hanging jaw said, "we know!"

"He probably thought it would upset me if he told anyone what we'd really been doing upstairs."

Four mouths opened. Four heads leaned toward her. Amanda tried not to laugh.

"I'd just shown him some fabric swatches, and he—Nicky—well, he just loved them." She did laugh this time, but in a way that made it clear she was sharing a charming anecdote with her new acquaintances. "And then he wanted to see some paint chips, and before we knew it, the time had just flown by."

Silence. She knew what was happening. She hoped she did anyway. The little group of guests was processing what she'd said. Come on, she thought impatiently, come on! Surely one of you wants to be first—

"You mean," the man who'd had the decency to blush said, "you're the sheikh's interior decorator?"

"His interior designer." Amanda smiled so hard her lips ached. "And I can hardly wait to get started. I had to shift my calendar around to make room for the sheikh—"

"Really."

"Yes. Really." Amanda curled her free hand around the slender shoulder strap of her evening purse and hoped nobody could see her crossed fingers. "The vice president will be a bit put out, I know, but, well, when the Lion of the Desert makes a request—"

"The vice president? And the sheikh?" The woman with the drooping jaw was almost drooling as she leaned closer. "Isn't it funny? That you should mention interior decorating, I mean?"

"Design," Amanda said, and smiled politely.

"Oh. Of course. But what I meant is, we've been thinking of redoing our cottage in the Hamptons."

Amanda arched a brow. A cottage in the Hamptons. She knew what that meant. A dozen rooms, minimum. Or maybe fifty.

"Really," she said with what she hoped was the right mix of politeness and boredom. "How nice."

A waiter floated by with a tray of champagne. She grabbed his elbow, swapped her now empty glass for a flute of bubbly and took a drink. Her head felt light. Well, why wouldn't it? She hadn't eaten in hours.

"I wonder, Ms Benning…would you have time to fit us in?"

Thank you, God. Amanda frowned. "I don't know. My schedule "

"We'd be grateful if you could just come out and take a look."

"Well, since you're friends of the sheikh—"

"Old friends," the woman said quickly.

"In that case…" Amanda opened her evening purse and whipped out a business card. "Why don't you phone me on Monday?"

"Oh, that would be wonderful."

Wonderful didn't quite do it. Incredible was more like it. She fought back the desire to pump her fist into the air, made a bit more small talk and moved on to the next group of guests.

Before long, her cards were almost all gone. Everybody seemed to want one now that they knew she was Amanda

Benning, the sheikh's designer. It wasn't a lie. Not exactly. She'd have been his designer if Dawn's plan hadn't backfired.

"Ms. Benning," someone called.

Amanda smiled, relieved a waiter of another flute of champagne and started toward the voice. Whoa. The floor was tilting. She giggled softly. You'd think a zillion-billion-million-dollar penthouse wouldn't have warped—

"Amanda."

A pair of strong hands closed on her shoulders. She looked up as Nick stepped in front of her. Wow. His head was tilting, too.

"Are you enjoying yourself?"

How come he wasn't smiling? Amanda gave him a loopy grin. "How 'bout you, Nicky? Are you envoy—enboy—enjoying you'self?" she said, and hiccuped.

Nick marched her through the room, out the door and onto the terrace. It wasn't deserted as it had been before. He clutched her elbow, kept her tightly at his side as he walked her past little clusters of guests.

"Hello," he kept saying. "Having a good time?"

"Hello," Amanda sang happily. "Havin' a goo' time?"

Someone laughed. Nick laughed, too, but his laughter died once they turned the corner of the terrace. "Just what do you think you're doing?" he demanded in a furious whisper.

Amanda blinked owlishly. It was darker out here. She couldn't see Nick's face clearly, but she didn't have to. He was angry, angry that she'd finally been having fun.

"Half my guests are marching around, clutching your address and phone number."

She giggled. "Only half?" Champagne sloshed over the edge of her glass as she raised it to her lips. "Jus' let me finish this and I'll— Hey," she said indignantly as he snatched the flute from her hand. "Give me that."

"Who told you that you could hand out business cards?"

"Who *told* me? Nobody told me. I didn't ask. I wouldn't ask! People don't need permission to hand out business cards."

"They do when they're in my home."

"Tha's ridiculous."

"I won't have you bothering my guests."

"Oh, for goodness' sake, I wasn't bothering anybody." She laughed slyly. "Matter of fact, your guests are eager to meet me."

"I'll bet they are."

"Ever'body wants the sheikh's designer to do their house."

"You're not my designer," he said coldly. "And as soon as they realize that, your little scheme will collapse."

"A minor teshnic—technic—a minor inconvenience."

Nick's eyes narrowed. "And you're drunk."

"I'm not."

"You are."

"No, I'm not," she said, and hiccuped again.

"Have you eaten anything tonight?"

"No."

"Why not?"

Amanda lifted her chin. "I was too busy drinking wine."

Nick said something under his breath. She looked at him.

"Was that Quidaran again? Must have been. I couldn't understand it."

"Be glad you didn't," he said, his voice grim. "Let's go, Ms. Benning."

"Go where?"

"You need a pot of strong coffee and a plate of food."

The mention of food made her stomach lurch. "No. I'm not hungry."

"Coffee, then. And something for your head before it starts to ache."

"Why should it...?" She caught her breath. "Ow," she whispered, and put the back of her hand to her forehead. "My head hurts."

"Indeed." Nick pulled her into the circle of his arm and led her to the end of the terrace.

"Is that a door?"

"That's what it is. Let me punch in the code."

The door swung open. Amanda took a step and faltered. Nick lifted her into his arms, carried her inside, kicked the door shut and switched on the light. She threw her arm over her eyes. "Agh. That's so bright."

"I'll turn it down. Okay. Sit here. And don't move."

She sat. It didn't help. Her head spun. Or the room spun. Either way, she felt awful.

"Nick?"

"Here I am. Open your mouth."

She opened an eye instead. He was holding out a glass and four tablets.

"What's that?"

"I know you'd like to think it's poison, but it's only water and something that'll make your head feel better."

"How about my stomach?" she said in a whisper.

Nick grinned. "That, too. Go on. Take them."

She took the tablets and gave them a wary look. "Are they from Quidar?"

Nick didn't just grin, he laughed. "They're from a pharmacy in Bond Street. Come on. Swallow them down."

She did. He took the glass from her.

"Now, put your feet up." His voice sounded far away, but he was right there, beside her. She could feel his hands, lifting her. Shifting her so her head was propped on something. A bed? A pillow?

His lap.

"Where are we?" she mumbled, and opened one eye.

"My study," Nick said.

The room was small, with an interior door that she assumed led into the rest of the penthouse. It was cozy, she thought. Everything looked lived in: the threadbare old rug, the battered leather sofa and the equally battered desk.

"Dawn didn't show me this."

"No." His voice hummed with amusement. "She doesn't have the combination, so it wouldn't have been on the dollar tour. Shut your eyes and let the tablets do their job."

She did. For five minutes. For an hour. Time passed; she

had no idea how long she lay there. A hand stroked her forehead and she sighed and turned her face into it.

A knock sounded at the door.

Nick lifted her head gently from his lap. She lay back, eyes closed, heard a door open, heard him say, "Thank you," heard the door swing shut.

"Coffee," Nick said. "Freshly ground and brewed."

"It's wonderful to be king," Amanda murmured.

"Wonderful," he said dryly. "Can you sit up?"

She did. He held out an enormous mug, filled to the brim with liquid so black it looked like ink.

She took it, held it in both hands. "It's hot."

"Clever of you to figure that out."

"It's black."

"Clever again."

"I like cream and sugar in my coffee."

"Drink it," he said, "or I'll grab your nose and pour it into your mouth."

He looked as if he might do just that. Amanda drank, shuddered, and drank again. When the cup was empty, she gave it to him. He refilled it, looked at her, sighed and put it down on the desk. Then he took a chair, turned it backward, straddled it and sat.

"Better?"

"Yes." Amazingly, it was true. "What was in those tablets?"

Nick smiled. "You'll have to let me take you to London to find out."

The words were as teasing as his smile, but they made her breath catch.

"You're not being a tyrant," she said.

"It's late, and I'm tired. It takes too much energy to be a tyrant twenty-four hours a day." He folded his arms along the back of the chair, propped his chin on his wrists. "Abdul finished checking you out."

"Ah. Am I Mata Hari?"

"He says you live alone."

Amanda sighed, shut her eyes and laid her head back. "He's a genius."

"He says you're divorced."

She put her index finger to her mouth, licked it, then checked an imaginary scorecard in the air.

"Why?"

Amanda's eyes popped open. "Why what?"

"Why are you divorced?"

"That's none of your business."

"You made everything about you my business when you crept into my room and started taking photographs."

"God, are we back to that? I told you—"

"You were getting data so you could redo my apartment." He reached down, picked up her foot. Amanda tried to jerk it back.

"What are you doing?"

"Taking off your shoes." His hands were gentle though the tips of his fingers felt callused. Why would a sheikh who never did anything except order people around have callused fingers? she wondered dreamily, and closed her eyes as he began massaging her arch.

"Mmm."

"Mmm, indeed." Nick cleared his throat. What in hell was he doing? Well, he wasn't a complete idiot. He *knew* what he was doing; he was sitting in the one room in the overblown, overfurnished, overeverythinged penthouse that really belonged to him with a woman's foot in his lap. And he was thinking something insane. Something totally, completely crazy.

He let go of Amanda's foot, shoved back his chair and stood up.

"You didn't do the mayor's mansion."

Amanda opened her eyes. "No," she said wearily. "I didn't do that penthouse, either."

"Then why did you lie?"

"Dawn lied, not me. I'm a designer, but not the way she said."

"Meaning?"

"Meaning, I've never had a real client."

Abdul had said as much. "Not one?"

"Not unless you count my mother. And my stepbrother. But I'm a good designer. Damned good."

"Don't curse," Nick said mildly. "It isn't feminine."

"Is it feminine for a woman to curl around a man like a vine?"

"What?"

"Deanna Whosis. The woman in that magazine photo. I couldn't tell if she was trying to strangle you or say hello."

Nick grinned, hitched a hip onto the edge of the desk and folded his arms. "You're still tipsy, Ms. Benning."

"I'm cold sober." But if she was, why would she have asked him such a question? "She did it again tonight, too. She seems to think two objects can be in the same space at the same time."

"Jealous?" Nick said with a little smile.

"Why on earth would I be?"

"Maybe because it's a feminine trait."

"You haven't answered my question."

"You haven't really asked one."

"I did."

"You didn't. You asked me about vines and the laws of physics, but what you really want to know is if I'm involved with Deanna."

"I didn't ask you that."

"You didn't have to. And the answer is no, I'm not. Not anymore."

The answer surprised her. "But I saw—"

"I know what you saw. And I'm telling you, Deanna Burgess is history."

Amanda licked her lips. "As of when?" she said softly, and held her breath, waiting for the answer.

"As of the minute I kissed you tonight," Nick said, and as he did, he knew it was the truth.

Amanda stared at him. Then she got to her feet. "It's late," she said, because it was all she could think of to say. Had he really gotten rid of Deanna Burgess because of her? No. The idea was preposterous. It was crazy.

Mostly, it was incredibly exciting.

Nick rose, too. "Deanna is gone, Amanda. From my home and from my life."

"I don't—I don't know why you're telling me this."

"Yes, you do." He put his hand under her chin and tilted her face up. "And I know why you asked."

"I don't know what you're…" Her breath hitched. He was moving his thumb gently over her mouth, tracing its contours. "Nick?"

"I like the way you say my name."

He bent his head, his eyes locked to hers and followed the path his thumb had taken with his lips.

"Kiss me," he said in a rough whisper. "Kiss me the way you did before."

"No," she said, and thrust her hands into his hair, pulled his head down to hers and kissed him.

Moments later, centuries later, she shuddered and pulled back.

"I didn't come here for this."

"No." Nick bent his head, pressed his open mouth to the pulse racing in the hollow of her throat. "Neither did I."

"Nick." She put her hands on his chest to push him away. Instead, her fingers curled into the lapels of his tux. "I'm not a woman who sleeps around."

"That's fine. Because I'm not a man who believes in sharing."

"And I'm not looking for a relationship. My divorce wasn't pleasant. Neither was my marriage. It will be a long, long time before I get involved with another—"

Nick kissed her again, his mouth open and hot. She moaned, swayed, and his arms went around her.

"My life is planned," she whispered. "I was my father's devoted daughter, my mother's rock, my husband's puppet."

"I don't want any of that from you."

"What do you want, then?"

He took her face in his hands. "I want you to be my mistress."

CHAPTER SIX

IT WAS, she realized, a joke.

A bad joke, but a joke all the same. What else could it be?

A man she hardly knew, a man she'd done nothing but argue with, had just told her that he wanted her to be his mistress. He'd said it—no, he'd announced it—with certainty, as if it were an arrangement they'd discussed and agreed to.

A joke, absolutely. Or a sign of insanity...but was what the sheikh had said any more insane than what she'd been doing? Kissing him. Hanging on to him. Aching for him, this rude, self-important stranger...

This gorgeous, sexy, incredible man who'd held her gently when she felt ill.

Amanda's head whirled. She stepped back, tugged down her skirt, smoothed a shaking hand over her hair. Homey little gestures, all of them. Well, who knew?

Maybe they'd restore her equilibrium.

Or maybe she'd misunderstood him. That was possible. After all, just a little while ago, she'd felt as if a crazed tap dancer was loose inside her skull. Could a headache make you hear voices? Could it leave you suffering from delusions?

Was she crazy, or was he?

"Amanda?"

She looked up. Nick's face gave nothing away. He looked like a man waiting for a train. Calm. Cool. Collected. Surely he wouldn't look like that if he was waiting for her to say yes.

Heat spiraled through her, from the pit of her belly into her breasts and her face. What in hell was she thinking? She wouldn't. In fact, she should have slapped his face at his words. The sheikh wanted a new sexual toy and he figured she'd be thrilled to discover she was it.

He wasn't only crazy; he was insulting. She told him so, succinctly, coldly, carefully. And the SOB just smiled.

"I should have kept count of the number of times you've called me crazy tonight."

"Yes, you should. It might tell you something about your behavior, Lord Rashid."

"It's a little late for formality."

"It's never too late for formality and it's certainly not too late for sanity. Did you really think I'd agree to your offer?"

"Actually," he said, his mouth twitching just a little, "I thought you might slug me."

"An excellent idea." She stepped back, her hands on her hips, a look of contempt on her face. "I suppose it's been your experience that women become delirious with joy when you offer them such a wonderful opportunity."

Nick tucked his hands into his pockets. "I don't know. I've never, ah, made the offer before."

"Uh-huh. I'll just bet. Nicholas al Rashid, Lion of the Desert, Heir to the Imperial Throne, Lord of the Realm...and Celibate of the Century." She lifted a hand, examined her fingernails with care before looking at him again and flashing a toothy smile. "You never asked a woman to be your mistress?"

"No." He leaned back against the edge of the desk, crossed his feet at the ankles. "Usually the relationship simply...develops."

"Ah. You usually show a bit more finesse." She smiled brightly. "How nice."

Clearly, her sarcasm didn't impress him. He shrugged, his expression unchanging.

"Our situation is different. It called for a bolder move." His eyes, silver as rain, met hers. "You want a commission." The quiet tone in his voice changed just a little, took on a husky edge. "I want you."

Say something, Amanda told herself. Tell him he's being offensive, that he can't go around saying things like this to women. But he wasn't saying it to "women," he was saying it to her. She was the one he wanted. And she, heaven help her, and she...

Stop it!

She stood up straighter, cocked her chin and flashed a cool smile. "I see. You get a night in the sack. I get a job."

"No."

"Don't 'no' me, Lord Rashid." Amanda's tone hardened. "That's what you said. I'll sleep with you, and you'll give me a job. Do you have any idea how incredibly insulting and sleazy that offer is?"

Nick sighed and shook his head. "You're never going to make a success of—what was it? Benning Designs?"

"You're wrong. I'll make a huge success of it and I'll do it without accepting your charming proposition," she said caustically, "because I'm good. Damn good."

"You won't succeed," he said calmly, "unless you learn to pay attention." He folded his arms, lowered his chin, looked at her as if she'd just flunked the final exam in her business administration course. "I didn't say I wanted to sleep with you. I said I wanted you to be my mistress."

"It's the same thing."

"Not at all." Nick smiled coolly. "Sleeping with you would mean an hour of pleasure. Taking you as my mistress means pleasure for as long as our desire for each other lasts."

Heat seeped into her blood again, warmed her flesh and turned her bones to jelly. How could he talk so calmly about such a thing? Odder still, how could she hear those calm words and feel as if he were touching her skin?

"Either way, I'm not going to do it. I'd never trade my body for your checkbook."

"And a lovely body it is," Nick said, and uncoiled from the edge of the desk.

Amanda took a quick step back. The warning was there, burning in his eyes. "Nick," she said, "wait a minute—"

Her shoulders hit the wall as he moved forward. And when he reached for her, her heart leaped like a rabbit.

"I'll fight you," she said in a breathless whisper. "Nick, I swear..."

His hands encircled her wrists. That was all. He didn't kiss her, didn't gather her to him. Just that, the feel of his fingers on the pulse points in her wrists, but it was enough to turn her body liquid with desire.

"A spectacular body," he said softly. "And a face more beautiful than any I've ever seen." Nick lowered his head. She lifted hers. Lightly, lightly, he brushed his mouth across her slightly parted lips. "But I'm not asking for either in trade."

"No?" Amanda cleared her throat. Her voice sounded small and choked. "Then—then what's this all about?"

His eyes fell to her lips, then returned to lock with hers. "It's about desire," he murmured, and he bent his head and nuzzled the hair back from her face, pressed his hot mouth against her throat.

Don't, she thought, oh, don't. Don't fight. Don't move. Don't respond to him at all. But she trembled and made a little sound she couldn't prevent, and she knew that her pulse leaped under the stroke of his fingers.

"We're both intelligent adults, Amanda."

"Exactly. That's why I expect you to understand that what you want is impossible."

He smiled. "Anything is possible when you really want it."

She gave a little laugh that sounded forced even to her own ears, but it was the best she could manage at the moment. "Do you think I'm stupid? Or is that the plan, Nick? You're going to convince me of how foolish I am unless I agree to sleep..." She took a breath. Why was she arguing with him? He wanted something. She didn't. That was that. "Let go of me," she said.

He did. It was what she'd wanted, but she felt chilled without his hands on her, and that was silly. The night was warm. So was the room. And yet, without Nick to hold her...

Amanda swallowed, turned her back and walked to the window. It was very late. The moon had gone down and a breeze sighed around the windows. It made the shrubs that lined the terrace tremble under its touch, just as she had trembled under Nick's.

"You're right," she said, her voice low. "We're both adults. I'm not going to be coy and pretend I don't know what happens when you touch me. But I don't intend to give in to it." She took a breath, slowly let it out. "What went on in your bedroom? That wasn't me. You probably won't believe it, but I've never…I mean, no one has ever—"

"Except for me."

He spoke from just behind her, so close that all she had to do was take a step back to be in his arms again.

"Yes." She felt his hand move lightly over her hair and she fought back the urge to shut her eyes and give herself up to the caress. "But it won't happen again."

"I regret what happened, too." His voice thickened and he cleared his throat. "I've never come on to a woman with so little tact. I know I should apologize, but—"

"Don't." She spun around, looked at him, her cheeks on fire, her eyes glittering. "You wanted honesty. Well, the truth is that we were both at fault."

"We wanted each other. There's no fault in that."

"I don't much care how you choose to explain it, Nick. It was wrong. And I'm not going to change my mind about sleeping with—"

She gasped as he pulled her to him. "I could take you to bed right now."

"You could." Her chin rose and her eyes locked with his. "You're much stronger than I am."

His eyes went flat and cold. "Do you think I'm the kind of man who takes a woman by force?"

She didn't. She couldn't imagine him forcing himself on a woman any more than she could imagine a woman walking away from his bed.

"No," she whispered. "You're right. You wouldn't do that."

He shifted his weight, slid his hands up her body, leaving a trail of heat in the wake of his palms.

"All I'd have to do is kiss you. Touch you. How long would it take before you'd be naked in my arms, begging me to finish what we began in my bedroom hours ago?"

"No," she said again, but her voice trembled, and she couldn't meet his eyes.

"Yes," he said. "But that's not what I want. I want more. Much more."

He dropped his hands to his sides, turned away and walked across the small room. He stood with his back to Amanda, his hands clenched in his pockets.

Earlier tonight, in his bedroom, he'd wanted nothing more than a quick, hard ride. The blonde with the golden eyes beneath him, her skin slick with heat, her head thrown back...

That would have been enough.

Later, watching her drift from group to group at the party, seeing her make the best of what he knew had to be a difficult situation, he'd smiled a little, decided it might be pleasant to spend not an hour but a night with Amanda Benning in his bed.

Deanna had caught him looking. She'd said something cutting that was meant to remind him that his loyalty was supposed to be to her, but all she'd done was make him face what he'd known, and not admitted, for weeks.

He'd had enough of Deanna.

She was beautiful, but she was proof of the old adage. Beauty was, after all, only skin-deep. And so he'd taken her aside, gently told her that they were finished, and after a scene that had been uglier than he'd expected, he'd come back into the living room, taken one look at Amanda and realized she was drunk.

"Shall I deal with the lady, Lord Rashid?" Abdul had whispered, and Nick had sighed and said no, he'd take care of it...but somewhere between the living room and his study, he'd realized that he was wrong.

One night with Amanda wouldn't be enough.

He was hungry for her, and she was hungry for him, and only a fool would have imagined they'd have enough of each other between sunset and sunrise.

No, Nick thought, watching her face, one night wouldn't be sufficient. He wanted time to learn all the textures and tastes of this woman's mouth. Of the secret places of her body. She was a feast that would keep a man busy for a month of nights.

He turned and looked at her. "Have you ever gambled, Amanda?"

The sudden shift in conversation made her blink. "Gambled?"

"Yes. Did you ever bet on something?"

"No. Well, yes. I went to Las Vegas once. With my sisters. Sam played the slots. Carin played poker. I watched a roulette wheel for a while." Her brow furrowed. "What's this have to do with anything?"

"Indulge me," Nick said with a smile. He sat on the edge of the desk. "Did you bet? On the wheel, I mean?"

"Eventually."

"And?"

"And," she said, her chin lifting, daring him to say anything judgmental, "after I'd lost a hundred bucks, I quit."

Nick lifted his brows. "Interesting."

"I couldn't see the sense in losing more money."

"Ah. And you figured why bother betting unless you had a better chance of winning."

"Something like that."

"Suppose somebody offered you the chance to make a bet where you controlled the odds."

Something had changed in his smile. It made her uncomfortable. This whole conversation made her uncomfortable. She knew it was ridiculous, but talking about his wanting to sleep with her made her less uneasy than talking about bets and stakes and odds.

"Well," she said, "that, um, that would be, um, interesting."

Not as interesting as the way he was looking at her. His gaze was intense, as if she were the only thing in the universe worthy of his attention. It was flattering. It was disturbing. It reminded her of something she'd almost forgotten.

Once, just after her mother had married Jonas and gone to live at Espada, she'd visited the ranch and gone horseback riding in the hills that surrounded it. She'd dismounted beside a clear-running stream, tied the reins to a tree branch, strolled maybe a hundred yards—and come almost face-to-face with a cougar.

The cat had looked at her. She'd looked at the cat. And when it finally hissed and melted into the trees, she'd known that she'd gotten away because it had chosen to let her go, not because she'd been brave enough to stare it down.

That was how she felt now. Her heart gave a little shiver. As if she'd gone for an innocent stroll and ended up face-to-face with a cougar.

Nick reached back, slid open a drawer in the desk, took something from it. A coin, she saw. A bright silver coin. He smiled, tossed it, caught it in his hand. "Heads or tails," he said. "What do you think?"

"I think it's time I went home. Good night, Nick. It's certainly been—"

"Scared?"

She sighed, rolled her eyes, folded her arms over her chest. "Heads."

"Heads it is." The coin spun through the air. Nick caught it, showed it to her. "Good guess. How about another try?"

"Oh, for heaven's... Heads."

He tossed the coin again, caught it, held out his hand. The silver piece lay, heads up, in his palm.

"Great," she said with an artificial smile.

"One last time." Nick tossed the coin. It spun like quicksilver before he caught it and closed his fingers around it. "What's it going to be this time? Heads or tails?"

"This is… Okay, I'll humor you. Tails. It has to be. I remember enough of my college stats course to know that the odds of it coming up heads again are…"

He opened his hand. She blinked.

"…One in six," she said, and frowned. "How'd you do that?"

He smiled, tossed the coin to her. She caught it, examined it, then looked at him.

"Heads on both sides," she said. "It's a phony."

"The gentleman who gave it to me preferred to refer to it as a device for assuring a positive outcome."

Nick grinned. She almost smiled back at him. He had, she thought, a wonderful smile…but then she thought of the cougar, of how she could never have matched either its strength or its cunning, and she felt more like running than smiling.

"If there's a point here," she said carefully, "I don't get it."

He rose to his feet, came slowly toward her, his smile gone. The room seemed to have reduced in size until there was barely space in it for the both of them. Foolishly, she held out the coin. Nick shook his head, took her hand, folded her fingers around it.

"Keep it," he said softly.

"I—I don't want it. I don't—"

"Amanda." He clasped her shoulders, slid his hands down her arms, twined his fingers with hers. "We're going to make a bet, you and I." A slow, sexy smile curled across his mouth. "A bet that will assure you of a positive outcome."

"Nick, I told you. I don't gamble. Just that one time…"

"You're going to give me a week of your life."

Her eyes widened. "A week of my—"

"One week." He kissed her, his mouth tender, soft against hers. "Just seven days."

"Nick, listen to me. You can't just—"

"When the week ends, I'll sign a contract with Benning Designs."

"Damn you!" Amanda jerked her hands free. "Haven't you heard a word I said? I won't sleep with you for a contract."

"No," he said softly, "I'm sure you won't."

"Great. We understand each other. Now, I'm going to open this door. And you're not going to stop me."

"I'll sign the contract whether you've slept with me or not."

"What?" She moved past him, dragged a hand through her hair. "What is this? Another quaint custom straight from the homeland? I wasn't born yesterday. Do you really think I believe life is like that coin of yours? Heads on both sides?" She frowned, opened her hand and looked at the quarter. "Where'd you get this anyway?"

Nick sighed. "It's a long, dull story."

"Amazing." She smiled brightly. "I just happen to be in the mood for a long, dull story."

"I was sixteen, and I stopped to watch a guy working a three-card-monte game in Greenwich Village. Each time he thought a mark—"

"A what?"

"A player." Nick grinned. "Or, more accurately, a loser. Whenever he thought a loser was going to leave, he'd take a coin from his pocket, show it and say, 'Call it. Double or nothing.' It never came up anything but heads."

"And the reason the Heir to the Imperial Throne was standing on a corner, betting against a street hustler, was…?"

"Well, it was fun."

"Fun," she said dryly.

"Yeah. I was at a private prep school."

"Of course," Amanda said politely.

"My tuition was paid, but my father was strict about my allowance. I wanted more money for something—I don't recall what. And my mother was in Europe, making a movie.

Anyway, I was pretty good with cards. It was a weekend and I had nothing better to do—"

"So you went down to the village and got hustled." She narrowed her eyes at him. He had to have invented the story. The Lion of the Desert, a cardsharp? "And, what? The guy gave you the coin?"

He laughed softly. "I paid him twenty bucks for it. I figured it made a great souvenir."

"Uh-huh. He hustled you. And now you're trying to hustle me. Did you really think I'd fall for that?" Amanda tossed the coin on the desk. "The 'you give me a week and I'll give you a contract' routine?"

"Well, no." Nick put one hand on the wall beside her and slid the other around the back of her head. "Actually, I didn't."

"Ha," she said, and tried to pretend she didn't feel the drift of his fingers along the nape of her neck. "I knew there was a catch."

He gave her the kind of smile that made her heart try to wedge its way into her throat. "I meant what I said. You'll give me a week. If we become lovers, you get the contract. If we don't…" He took her hand and brought it to his mouth. "If we don't, you still get the contract." His eyes met hers, and what she saw in them made her feel dizzy. "But if you do give yourself to me," he said softly, "then you'll agree to be my mistress. To be available only to me, accessible only to me, for as long as it suits us both." A quick smile angled across his mouth. "Despite what you may think, I believe in equality of the sexes."

His words, the way he was looking at her, conjured up images more erotic than anything she'd ever experienced in a man's arm. Talk, that was all it was. Not even Nicholas al Rashid could really expect her to accept such a proposition.

"I mean every word," he said softly.

She tilted her head up, stared into his eyes and knew, with breathtaking certainty, that he did.

He turned her hand over, brought it to his mouth again, kissed the soft flesh at the base of her thumb. "Are you afraid to trust yourself?"

Amanda laughed. "Such modesty. Do you really think—"

He kissed her even though he knew it was a mistake. The last thing a wise man would do right now was give Amanda Benning graphic proof of how sure he was he'd win the bet.

But he'd underestimated her. She made a little sound as their mouths met, but that soft, sweet whisper of breath was the only sign she gave of the emotional storm he knew raged within her. It made what lay ahead all the more exciting.

"You're very sure of yourself, Lord Rashid."

"As are you, Ms. Benning." He smiled. "You'll be a worthy adversary."

"*If* I were to accept your proposition. But it's out of the question. It's so outlandish."

"Is it?"

She started to answer, caught herself just in time and wondered if this was really happening.

Yes. Yes, it was.

Twenty-five stories below, a siren wailed through the night. Music from the party drifted under the door. Life was going on all around them; people were doing the things people did on a warm evening in Manhattan...and she stood here, discussing whether or not she'd agree to become the mistress of a man she hardly knew.

It wouldn't happen. There wasn't even a remote possibility she'd let Nick seduce her. He was handsome. All right. He was gorgeous. He was rich and powerful and he ruled a desert kingdom.

But a man would need more than that to get her into his bed. She was a twenty-first-century American woman. She was educated and independent and she couldn't be lured into a man's arms like some trembling virgin.

What she *could* do was win the bet.

A week. That was all he'd asked. Seven days of what would

basically be simple dating. And, at the end of those days, she'd walk away from Nicholas al Rashid with her virtue intact, a contract in her pocket. She'd give the man who thought he could buy everything a lesson in how to choke down a large helping of humble pie.

She had to admit the possibility was intriguing.

"Well?" Nick said.

Amanda looked at him. She could read nothing in his face, not even desire. Oh, yes. He'd be very good, playing cards.

"Tell me," she said softly, "have you ever wanted something you couldn't have?"

"You're doing it again. Answering a question with a question."

"You've asked me to allow you to try to seduce me." She smiled tightly. "I think that entitles me to ask as many questions as I like."

"Are you afraid I'll succeed?"

"Seduction requires a seducer and a seducee, Lord Rashid. You can't succeed unless I cooperate." This time, her smile was dazzling. "And I promise you, I'd never do that."

"Is that a yes?"

Her eyes met his. She could see something there now, glinting in the silver depths. *What do you think you're doing, Amanda?* a voice inside her whispered.

"There'd have to be rules," she said.

"Name them."

"No force."

"I'm not a man who believes in forcing himself on a woman."

"No tricks."

"Certainly not."

"And I don't want anybody to know that we've entered into this—this wager." She hesitated. "It would be difficult to explain."

"Done."

He held out his hand as if they were concluding a business

deal. She looked at it, then at him. *Amanda,* the voice said desperately, *Amanda...*

She took a quick step back. "I'll—I'll think about it," she said, the words coming out in a rush.

Nick reached for her. "You already did."

And then his mouth was on hers, she was curling her arms tightly around his neck, and the wager was on.

CHAPTER SEVEN

AT FOUR forty-three in the morning, Nicholas al Rashid, Lion of the Desert, Lord of the Realm and Sublime Heir to the Imperial Throne of Quidar, gave up all attempts at sleep. He threw back the blankets, swung his legs to the floor, ran his fingers through his tousled hair and tried to decide exactly when he'd lost his mind.

A man had to be crazy to do the things he'd done tonight. He'd found a woman going through his things, accused her of spying, made passionate love to her, locked her in his closet and, in a final show of lunacy, fast-talked her into a wager so weird he still couldn't believe he'd come up with it.

"Hell," Nick muttered.

He rose, paced back and forth enough times to wear a path in the silk carpet, pulled on a pair of jeans and went quietly down the stairs.

Not quietly enough, though. He'd hardly entered the kitchen when a light came on in the hallway that led to Abdul's rooms. A moment later, the old man stood in the doorway, wearing a robe and blinking against the light.

"Excellency?"

It was, Nick thought with mild surprise, the first time he'd ever seen Abdul wearing anything but a black, somewhat shiny, suit.

"Yes, Abdul. It's me."

"Is something wrong, sire?"

"No, nothing. I just... Go on back to bed, Abdul."

"Did you want a sandwich?"

"Thank you, no."

"Some tea? Coffee? I shall wake the cook."

94

"No!" Nick took a breath and forced a smile to his lips. "I don't need the cook, Abdul. I just—I'm thirsty, that's all."

"Of course, sire." Abdul bustled into the kitchen. "What would you like? Mineral water? Spirits? Sherry? You're right, there's no need to wake the cook. I'll—"

"Abdul," Nick said pleasantly but firmly, "go back to bed."

"But, my lord—"

"Good night, Abdul."

The little man hesitated. Nick could see that he wanted to say something more, but custom prevented it. And a good thing, too, he thought grimly, because he had the feeling his secretary had developed as many doubts about his sanity as he had.

"Very well, Lord Rashid. If you change your mind—"

"I'll call you."

Abdul nodded, bowed and backed out of the room. Nick waited until the hall light went out. Then he opened the refrigerator, peered inside, found a bottle of the New England ale he'd developed a taste for back in his university days, and popped the cap. Bottle in hand, he walked through the darkened apartment and out onto the terrace.

The city lay silent below him.

At this hour on a Sunday morning, traffic was sparse, the sound of it muted. Central Park stretched ahead of him, its green darkness broken by the diamond glow of lamps that marked its paths

Nick leaned against the low wall, tilted the bottle of ale to his lips, took a long drink and wished he were home. There'd been times before when he'd felt like this, when thoughts had whirled through his head and sleep had refused to come. The night before he'd left for Yale and a course of study that he knew would set him irrevocably on the path toward eventual leadership of his people. The night word had come of his mother's death in a plane crash. The night before he'd left for New York and the responsibilities that came with representing his country's financial affairs...

Nick took another drink.

Each time, he'd found peace by riding his Arabian stallion into the desert, alone under the night sky, the moon and the majestic light of the stars.

He sighed, turned his back to the city and swallowed another mouthful of ale. There was no desert to give him solace now. He was trapped in the whirlwind of his thoughts and the knowledge that nothing he'd done tonight made sense.

He wasn't a man who'd ever forced himself on a woman, yet he'd come close to doing that with Amanda Benning. Not that he'd have needed force. The way she'd melted against him. The way she'd returned his kisses, fitted her body to his...

Nick held the bottle of ale against his forehead, rolled it back and forth to cool his skin.

And that proposal he'd made her. Give me a week, he'd said. If I can seduce you, you'll agree to be my mistress.

Talk about acting like a second-rate Valentino, he thought, and groaned again. It was ludicrous. Besides, who knew if he'd even want her more than once? The lady might turn out to be a dud in bed instead of a smoldering ember just waiting to be fanned into an inferno.

"Dammit!"

Nick swung around and glared out over the quiet park. What was wrong with him? He was standing alone in the middle of the night, thinking about a woman he hardly knew, and doing one fine job of turning himself on.

Okay, so she'd probably be good in bed. Terrific, even. There really wasn't much doubt about that. Still, a man needed more than sex from a mistress. Well, he did anyway. She had to be interesting and have a sense of humor. She had to like some of the things he liked. Riding, for instance. Walking in the rain. Could she watch the film, *When Harry Met Sally,* for the third or fourth time and still laugh over that scene in the delicatessen?

Nick frowned. What was he thinking? So what if it turned out Amanda didn't like those things? Deanna certainly didn't.

Rain made her hair frizzy, she said. Movies were boring the second time around. And riding was best done in a limousine, not on a horse.

The women who'd come before her had tastes different from his, too.

All he'd ever asked of a woman was that she be attractive, fun and, of course, good in bed. If Amanda had those qualifications, fine. He wanted to sleep with her, not live with her. And she'd agreed.

He was making a mountain out of a molehill. It was a bet, that was all it was. And he'd win it. He had no doubt about that. They'd go to bed together and he'd take it from there.

The sky was lightening, changing from the black of night to the pink of dawn. Somewhere in the leafy bowers of the park, a bird chirped a sleepy homage to that first hint of day.

Nick yawned and stretched, then decided he felt much better. Amazing what a little clear thinking could do. Okay, then. In a while, he'd tell Abdul to call Amanda and inform her that his car would pick her up at, say, seven this evening. That would get her here by seven-thirty for drinks and dinner.

If they ever made it to dinner, he thought with a little smile. As wagers went, this was the best he'd ever made. How come he'd wasted half the night figuring that out?

He strolled back through the darkened penthouse, put the empty bottle neatly on the kitchen counter, went up to his bedroom, pulled off his jeans and threw himself across the bed on his belly. He closed his eyes, yawned, punched his pillow into shape...

Twenty minutes later, he was still awake, lying on his back with his hands clasped under his head as he stared up at the ceiling. The distant whisper of the fax machine came as a relief.

Nick put on his jeans and went down to his study. The fax was long and still coming in. He plucked the first page from the basket, smiled as he read his father's warm greeting, but his smile changed to a frown as he read further.

His father, whose Arabian horses were world renowned, had

reached agreement with an old American friend. He'd arranged to fly a stallion to the States in exchange for the friend's gift of a Thoroughbred mare. He hated to impose upon Nicholas on such short notice, etc. etc., but would he meet with the friend and work out the details in person?

Nick huffed out a breath. He would do it, of course. It would mean a day, perhaps two, spent out of the city, time during which he wouldn't be able to do what he had to do to win his wager with Amanda.

"Oh, for God's sake," Nick said, and tossed the fax on the table.

Enough was enough. The truth was, the bet was a bad one. A man didn't win a woman as if she were the stakes in a hand of poker. He didn't tempt her into his arms with a contract.

A smart man wouldn't want Amanda Benning at all. She was as prickly as a porcupine, as unpredictable as the weather. She was city heat; she was desert night. She was either the roommate who'd pointed his sister toward trouble seven years ago or the one who'd been wise enough to avoid it.

The one, the only, thing she absolutely was, was female.

So what?

He'd wearied of Deanna. That had to be the reason he'd been attracted to Amanda. Right?

"Right," Nick muttered.

Well, he could be attracted to another woman just as easily. He could have any woman he wanted. He could have his choice—blondes, brunettes and redheads in such profusion they'd cause a traffic jam, just lining up outside the door.

Nick went back upstairs, pulled on a white T-shirt and tucked it into his jeans. He put on sneakers, grabbed his wallet, his keys and his cell phone, went down the steps and into his private elevator. There was only one way to deal with this. He'd go to see Amanda, tell her the bet was off and put this whole foolish episode behind him.

He was in the elevator, halfway to the underground garage, when he realized he didn't have the slightest idea where she lived.

"Hell," he said wearily, punched the button for the penthouse and headed back the way he'd come. Was she in the phone book? he wondered as the door slid open...but he didn't have to bother checking. There, lying forlornly on a table, was one of those little business cards she'd been handing out like souvenirs.

Nick picked it up, lifted it to his nostrils. The card still bore a trace of her perfume. He shut his eyes, saw her as she'd gone from guest to guest, chin up, back straight, facing down the whispers and making the best of a difficult situation.

He frowned, looked at the address, then tucked the card into his pocket and rode the elevator down again. If the situation had been tough, it was her fault, not his. The only thing he cared about now was making sure she understood that he wasn't the least bit interested in following through on their bet.

Not in the slightest, he thought as his Ferrari shot like a missile into the quiet of the Sunday morning streets.

Amanda sat cross-legged in the center of her bed and watched the hands of the clock creep from 6:05 to 6:06.

Was the clock broken? She reached for it, held it to her ear. *Ticktock,* it said, *ticktock,* which was what it had been saying since she'd checked it the first time, somewhere around four.

She frowned, set the clock down on the night table and wrapped her arms around her knees. The only thing that wasn't working was her common sense.

What on earth had she done?

"You said you'd sleep with Nicholas al Rashid," she muttered. "*That's* what you've done."

No. Her frown deepened as she unfolded her legs and got out of bed. No, she thought coldly, she most definitely had not done anything as simple as that.

What she'd done was agree to become Nick's newest sexual toy, assuming he managed to seduce her in the next seven days.

God, it was hot in here!

She padded to the window where an ancient air conditioner wheezed like the Boston terrier her mother had once owned. She put her hand to the vents and waggled her fingers. An anemic flow of cool air sighed over her skin.

"Great," she said. No wonder she couldn't sleep.

Amanda jerked her nightgown over her head, marched into the bathroom and stepped into the shower, gasping at the shock of the cold water. It was the only way to stay cool in this tiny oven of an apartment. The place was so hot that when she'd awakened at four, she'd been drenched in very unlady-like sweat.

She lowered her head and let the water beat against the nape of her neck,

She'd been dreaming just before she awoke. A silly dream, something straight out of a silent movie. Nick had been dressed in a flowing white robe and riding a white horse. She'd been seated behind him, her arms tight around his waist, her cheek pressed to his back. And then the scene had shifted, and he'd been carrying her into a tent hung with royal-blue silk.

"Amanda," he'd said softly as he lowered her to her feet, and she'd sighed and lifted her mouth for his kiss....

Shower or no shower, she was hot again. But not from the dream. Certainly not from the dream. It was the apartment, she thought briskly. The stuffy, awful apartment.

Amanda turned off the water and blotted herself dry. She ran her fingers through her hair, tugged an oversized cotton T-shirt and cotton bikini panties over her still-damp skin and headed for the kitchen.

"Forget about sleep," she muttered.

Obviously, it wasn't a very good idea to drink lots of champagne before bedtime, especially if you spent the time between the wine and the attempt at sleep in the arms of a man who thought he could talk you into something he was certain you couldn't possibly refuse.

She filled the kettle with water, set it on the stove and turned on the burner.

Thought, Amanda?

"Let's be honest here," she said.

Nick *had* talked her into it. And—to stay with the honesty thing—he hadn't had to work all that hard to do it.

What a smooth character he was. Proposing a wager like that, making it sound so simple…

But, of course, it was.

Amanda sighed, walked to the window and gazed at the view. It wasn't exactly Central Park, but she could see a tree. All she had to do was stand on her toes, crook her neck, tilt her head and aim at a spot beyond the fire escape.

Nick wouldn't know what that was like. To have to contort yourself for a view. For anything. What Lord Rashid wanted, Lord Rashid got.

And Lord Rashid wanted her.

Well, he wasn't going to have her. And wouldn't that come as a huge surprise? All he'd get out of their wager was a handsomely furnished home. As for a woman to warm his bed—he'd always have plenty of those. A man like that would.

The kettle whistled. She turned off the stove, took a mug from the cupboard, dumped a tea bag into it and then filled it with water. She looked at the sugar bowl, turned away, then looked at it again.

"The hell with it," she said, and reached for the bowl.

Calories didn't count tonight. Comfort did, and if that meant two, well, three heaping spoonfuls of that bad-for-you, terrible-for-your-teeth and worse-for-your-waistline overprocessed white stuff, so be it.

"Ah," she said after her first sip.

The tea tasted wonderful. Funny how a hot liquid could make you feel cooler. She hadn't believed it until she'd spent a couple of weeks visiting her mother in Texas last year.

"Hot tea cools you off," Marta had insisted, and when Amanda finally tried it and agreed it was true, she'd hugged her and smiled. "You just come to me for advice, sweetie, and I'll always steer you right."

Amanda took another sip of tea as she walked through her

postage-stamp living room, sank into a rocker she'd rescued from a sidewalk where it had awaited death in the jaws of a garbage truck, and watched the sun claw its way up the brick sides of the city.

What advice would her mother offer about Nick? That was easy. She knew exactly what Marta would say.

"Mandy, you have to telephone that man this minute and tell him you can't possibly agree to the wager. A lady does not bet her virtue."

Excellent advice it would be, too.

Not that she was afraid she'd lose the bet. Amanda took a drink of tea and leaned back in the rocker. A woman who didn't want to be seduced couldn't be seduced. It was just that the implications of the wager were—well, they were...

Sleazy? Immoral?

"Humiliating," she mumbled.

Yes, she would call Nick and tell him the wager was off. She'd reached that conclusion hours ago. How best to do it, though? That was the problem.

She'd thought about calling Dawn for suggestions, but then she'd have to tell her all the details, and what, exactly, was there to say?

Hi, sorry we didn't get the chance to spend any time together last night. Are you okay? And oh, by the way, I've agreed to become your brother's mistress if he can first lure me into his bed.

No way. Discussing this with Dawn wasn't even an option. Neither was discussing it with Marta. How could a daughter tell her mother she'd even considered a proposal like that?

Amanda drank some more tea.

She could call one of her sisters for help, but there wasn't much sense in that, either. Carin would just tell her, in that irritatingly proper tone of voice, that if a deal sounded too good to be true, it probably was. As for Samantha...she couldn't begin to imagine what Sam would say unless it was something outrageously facetious, maybe that the deal sounded like lots of fun if it weren't for all the bother involved.

"Fun," Amanda muttered, and drained the last sugary drops from the mug.

Okay, then. She'd just have to do the deed without consulting anybody but herself. Phone Nick, tell him she was sorry but she'd changed her mind. Not that she was afraid she'd lose their bet, but...

Amanda scowled. Why did she keep telling herself that? Certainly she wouldn't lose it.

Someday she'd tell her sisters the story. They'd laugh and laugh; the whole thing would be one big joke.

"He was a sheikh," she'd say, "and he said, 'Come wiz me to zee Casbah.'"

Except he hadn't. If only he had. If he'd played the scene as if he'd stolen it from a bad movie, with a smoldering look and a twirl of his mustache...

She groaned and closed her eyes.

The truth was, Nick was gorgeous and sexy. He could have any woman he wanted, but he wanted her.

She had to admit it was thrilling. Maybe that was the reason she'd lost all perspective. Maybe it was why she'd let him fast-talk her into agreeing to a bet on her own morality.

Was that the doorbell? Amanda sat up straight. Who'd be at her door at this hour? This building had awful security, but still, did burglars really ring the bell and announce themselves?

The bell rang again. She rose to her feet and hurried to the door. "Who is it?"

"It's Nick."

Nick? Her heart thumped. She opened the peephole, peered out. It *was* Nick, and he didn't look happy.

"Nick." Her mouth felt as dry as cotton. "Nick, you should have called first. I—"

"I didn't want to wake you."

"You didn't want to wake me? What did you think leaning on my doorbell at—at what, six in the morning, would do?"

"It's seven-thirty, and if you want to have a discussion about the propriety of phoning first, I'd prefer having it in your apartment. Open the door, please, Amanda."

Open the door. Admit Nick into this tiny space. Into *her* space, where he'd seem twice as tall, twice as big, twice as commanding.

"Amanda." There was no "please" this time. She jumped as his fist thudded against the door. "Open up!"

She heard a lock click, a door creak open. Oh, God. Her neighbors were preparing themselves for a bit of street theater. New Yorkers might live on the same floor in an apartment building, collect their mail at lobby boxes ranged side by side and never so much as make eye contact, but she suspected none of them would pass up a little drama going on right in the hall.

Amanda rose on the balls of her bare feet, put her eye to the peephole and looked at Nick. "People are listening," she whispered.

"And watching," he said coldly. "Perhaps you'd like to sell tickets."

She stepped back, slipped the lock, the chain and the night bolt. The door swung open and he stepped inside.

"An excellent decision," he said, and shut the door behind him.

"What are you doing here, Nick?"

What was he doing there? Just for a second, he couldn't quite remember. Amanda was standing before him, barefooted. She was wearing a loose T-shirt and nothing else. Nothing he could see anyway. Her hair was tousled, her face was scrubbed and shiny, and he couldn't imagine anything more urgent than finding out if she tasted as sweet and fresh as she looked.

But that wasn't why he'd come here, Nick reminded himself, and folded his arms. "I want to talk," he said.

"Good." She lifted her chin. "That's—that's really good. Because I—I..." She stopped, the words catching in her throat, and stared at him.

"What's the matter?"

"You're not wearing a tux."

"No." His smile was all teeth. "No, actually, I've been known to get through an entire day without feeling the need to put on a pair of pants with satin stripes down the legs."

"I didn't mean—it's just that you look—you remind me—"

"Of the night we first met." She was right, he thought, and gave her a long, measuring look, except she was older now, and the soft curves outlined beneath the cotton shirt were more lush. "Instant replay," he said, and flashed a smile that upped the temperature in the room another ten degrees.

Amanda stepped back. "I'm not dressed," she said, and blushed when she realized how stupid she sounded. "For company. If you'll just wait—"

"I've been awake half the night. I'll be damned if I'll wait any longer."

"Look, Nick, I want to talk, too. About that bet. Just let me put on some clothes."

"You're already wearing clothes." His voice turned husky as he took a step toward her. "What else would you call what you have on?"

Provocative, he thought, silently answering his own question, although how a T-shirt could be provocative was beyond him to comprehend. He liked his women in silk. In lace. In things that flowed and shimmered.

"Nick?"

"Yes." Somehow, he was standing a breath away from her. Somehow, his hands were on her hips. Somehow, he was bunching the cotton fabric in his hands, lifting it, sliding it up her skin and revealing the smallest pair of white cotton panties he'd ever seen.

"Nick." Her voice was barely a whisper. Her head was tilted back; her eyes were huge, luminous and locked with his. "Nick, the bet is—"

He bent his head, brushed his mouth over hers. She gave a delicate moan, and he cupped her breasts, felt the delicate weight and silken texture of them in his palms. He feathered his thumbs over the crests and Amanda moaned again, trembled against him and lifted herself to his hungry embrace.

He kissed her over and over, offered her the intimacy of his tongue, groaned when she touched it with her own, then sucked it into the heat of her mouth. He backed her against the wall; she gave a cry of protest as he took his lips from hers to peel off her shirt, then his.

Oh, the feel of her satin skin against his, when he took her back into his arms. The softness of her breasts against the hardness of his chest. He trembled, felt the air driven from his lungs.

"Amanda," he whispered, and she sighed and kissed him, breathed a soft "yes" against his lips as he lifted her off her feet and into his arms—

A buzz sounded from his pocket.

"Nick?"

His pocket buzzed again.

"Nick." Amanda tore her mouth from his. "Something's buzzing."

He lifted his head, his breathing harsh. She was right. His cell phone was making sounds like an angry wasp. He mouthed an oath, let her down to her feet, kept an arm firmly around her as he dug the phone from his jeans.

"What?" he snarled.

"Sire."

Nick's eyes narrowed. "Abdul. This had better be important."

"It is, my lord. There is a fax from your father. I thought you would wish to know of it."

The color was high in Amanda's cheeks. He could read her eyes, see her growing embarrassment. She looked up at him, shook her head and tried to step away. Nick bent quickly and kissed her, his mouth soft against hers until, at last, she kissed him back.

"Lord Rashid? There is a fax—"

"I already saw it, Abdul. Goodbye."

"Excellency, it is a second fax and arrived only moments

ago. Your father asks if you would fly to this place called Texas—"

"He asked me that in the first fax. Dammit, Abdul—"

"He asks if you would fly there today. The stallion he sent arrived much sooner than expected, and the animal has been hurt in transit."

Nick uttered a violent oath. The only place he wanted to be right now was in Amanda's bedroom, but he knew the importance of duty and obligation. Would the woman in his arms be as understanding?

"Call the pilot," he said gruffly. "Have him ready the plane. You are to pack me some clothes, Abdul. Meet me at the hangar in an hour with the things I'll need."

Abdul was still speaking when Nick hit the disconnect button, tossed the phone aside and tried to gather Amanda close to him again, but she was unyielding, moving only her arms, crossing them over her naked breasts in a classic feminine gesture that somehow went straight to his heart.

"It's good that you're leaving." Her voice was steady, but her face was pale. "You're not to come here again, Lord Rashid. I know I agreed to the terms of our wager, but—"

"The wager is off, Amanda. I came here to tell you that." Her golden eyes widened; he knew it wasn't what she'd expected him to say. He wanted to draw her close and kiss her until the color returned to her cheeks. Instead, he picked up her discarded shirt and wrapped it gently around her. "Here," he said softly. "You must be cold."

Cold? She was swimming in heat from his touch, from imagining what would have happened if Abdul hadn't called— but she knew better than to let him know that.

"Thank you," she said stiffly.

"I don't want you as my mistress because of a bet," Nick said, his eyes locked to hers. "I want you to be mine because you desire no other man but me. Because you find joy only in my arms."

Her heartbeat stumbled, but the look she gave him was sharp and clear.

"You amaze me," she said with a polite smile. "You're always so sure you'll get what you want."

"We'd be making love right now if that call hadn't interrupted us."

"I'm not going to argue with you."

"No." He smiled. "You won't, because there's nothing to argue about. You know that I'm right."

She took a step back. "I want you to leave. Right now."

"I don't think that's what you want at all."

He moved quickly, drew her into his arms and kissed her. She told herself his kisses meant nothing, that she wouldn't respond...but it was Nick who ended the kiss, not she.

"All right," she said stiffly, "you've proved your point. Yes, I—I've thought about what it would be like to—to..." She gave a shuddering breath. "But it would be wrong. I know that. And, unlike you, I don't always give in to my desires."

"Why would it be wrong?"

"Why?" Her laugh was forced and abrupt. "Well, because...because...dammit, I don't have to justify my decision to you!"

"You can't even justify it to yourself." Nick put his hand under her chin and tipped her head up until their eyes met. "I can't get out of this trip, Amanda. Do you understand?"

"I'm not a child," she said coldly. "Certainly I understand. You're going away on business and you'd like me to be waiting for you when you get back. Well, I'm sorry to disappoint you, Lord Rashid, but I won't be."

"You won't have to be, not if you go with me."

"What?"

"We'll only be gone a day or two." He bent his head, brushed his mouth over hers. "Come with me, Amanda."

"No!" She laughed again and tried to wrench free of his hands. "You must think I'm an idiot!"

"I think you're a woman with more courage than she gives herself credit for. And I think you want to say yes."

"Well, you think wrong. We've agreed our wager is—"

"Off. And it is." *And what, exactly, was he doing?* He

never mixed business with pleasure. Then again, this wasn't really a business trip. It was just a couple of days on a ranch in Texas. "Come with me," he urged, rushing the words together, knowing that his thinking was somehow flawed, that it would be dangerous to think too long or hard about what he was asking her to do. "We'll simply be a man and a woman, getting to know each other."

"I know you already. You're a man who can't take no for an answer. Besides, I can't just—just up and leave. I have a business to run."

"And I'm your client. Don't look so surprised, sweetheart. I said our wager was off. I didn't say I wanted to go on living in an apartment that looks like an expensive hotel suite." Nick linked his hands in the small of Amanda's back. "If you come with me, you can ask me all the questions you like. About my tastes. My preferences. You need to know them in order to decorate my home, don't you?"

"Yes." She chewed on her lip. "But..."

But what? He was making it sound as if going away with him was the most logical thing in the world, but it wasn't. She'd just trembled in his arms. His hands had been on her breasts, and oh, she'd wanted more. Much more. She'd wanted to touch him as he'd touched her. To lie naked in his arms, to feel the weight of him as he filled her—

"Amanda?"

His voice was low and rough. She didn't dare look at him because she knew what she'd see in his eyes.

"We'll talk. Only talk, if that's what you want." Nick raised her face to his. "Say you'll come with me."

She knew what her answer should be. But she gave him the answer they both wanted—with her kiss.

CHAPTER EIGHT

NICK wouldn't tell her where they were going.

"It's a surprise," he said, when she asked.

He knew it was crazy not to tell her, but what if he said they were flying to a ranch in Texas and she said she hated ranches and everything about them? What if she said she didn't like riding fast and hard across the open range? It might turn out she'd never seen a horse except maybe in Central Park and that would be all right just so long as she smiled and said yes, that would be wonderful, when he offered to teach her to ride.

"Hell," Nick muttered as he paced the length of Amanda's living room.

Maybe he really was crazy. He'd met this woman last night. Well, he'd met her years ago, but he'd never gotten to know her until last night, never held her in his arms until then. What did it matter if she liked horses or hated them? If she didn't want to sit behind him in the saddle, her arms wrapped around his waist, her breasts pressed to his back as they rode not across the green hills of north-central Texas but over the hot desert sands?

Crazy was the word, he thought grimly, and swung toward the closed bedroom door. All right. He'd knock on the door, tell her politely that he'd changed his mind. She was right. There was no reason for her to go with him. He'd phone when he got back and they'd have drinks, perhaps dinner....

The door opened just as he reached it. Amanda stood in the opening, holding a small carry-on bag. "I packed only what you said I'd need. Jeans. Shirts." She gave a little laugh. "I don't know why you're being so mysterious about this trip. I mean, it's hard to know what to take when you don't know the destination. What is it, Nick?''

Her face was flushed, her eyes bright. She was wearing jeans and a cotton shirt, she hadn't bothered putting any makeup on her face, and he wanted to tell her he'd never seen a more beautiful woman in his life.

''Whatever you've packed is fine,'' he said gruffly, and he took the carry-on from her, linked his fingers through hers and tried to figure out exactly what was happening to him.

His plane was a small, sleek jet.

Amanda had flown in private aircraft before. Two of her stepbrothers owned their own planes. Her stepfather did, too; in fact, Jonas had a small jet, similar to Nick's in size—but Jonas's plane didn't have a fierce lion painted on the fuselage.

Nobody bowed to Jonas, either, but half a dozen people bowed as Nick approached the jet, half-prostrating themselves even though he waved them all quickly to their feet.

The Lion of the Desert, Amanda thought. Goose bumps rose on her skin. Yesterday, the words had been nothing but a title. A silly one, at that. Now, for the first time, she looked at the stern profile of the man walking beside her and realized that he was, in fact, a prince.

She tore her hand from his and stumbled to a halt.

''Amanda?''

''Nick.'' She spoke quickly, breathlessly. Her heart was racing as if she'd run here from her apartment instead of riding in Nick's Ferrari. ''I can't go with you. I can't —''

Nick clasped her shoulders and turned her to face him. ''My people won't blink an eye if I lift you into my arms and carry you on board,'' he said softly. ''You could scream and kick, but they'd ignore you. Kidnapping a woman and keeping her in his harem is still the prerogative of the prince of the realm.''

He was smiling. He was teasing her; she knew that. Still, she could imagine it happening. Nick, scooping her up in his arms. Carrying her onto the plane. Taking her high into the clouds, stripping away her defenses as he stripped away her clothes because yes, she wanted him. Wanted him...

"I made you a promise, sweetheart. And I'll keep it. You'll be safe. I won't touch you unless you want me to."

He held out his hand. She hesitated.

Have you ever gambled, Amanda?

The question, and her answer, were laughable. What was losing a hundred dollars at the roulette wheel compared to what she stood to lose now? And, thinking it, she put her hand in his.

He led her into a luxurious compartment done in deep shades of blue and gold. A pair of comfortable upholstered chairs flanked a small sofa. Everywhere she looked she saw the embroidered image of the same fierce lion that was painted on the outside of the plane.

"The Lion of the Desert," she said softly.

To her surprise, Nick blushed. "I suppose it seems melodramatic to someone who's lived only in the United States, but it's the seal of Quidar. It's been the emblem of my people for three thousand years."

"It's not melodramatic at all." Amanda looked at him. "It must be wonderful, being part of something so ancient and honorable."

"Yes," he said after a few seconds, "it is. Not everyone understands that. In this age of computers and satellites—"

"Of small, swift jets," she said with a little smile.

"Yes. In these times, it would be easy to forget the old ways. But they're important. They're to be honored even when it's difficult..." He paused in midsentence and smiled back at her. "Forgive me. I don't normally make speeches so early in the day." He bent down, pressed a light kiss to her forehead. "I'll be back in a minute, sweetheart. I just want to talk with Tom."

Who was Tom? she wondered. More importantly, who was this man who spoke with such conviction of the past? This man who'd taken to calling her "sweetheart"? It was far too soon for him to address her that way. She could tell him that,

but it would have seemed silly, even prissy, and what was
there in a word, anyway? He'd probably called a hundred other
women "sweetheart." Set a hundred other women's hearts to
beating high and fast in their throats.

Taken them away with him, as he was taking her.

But she wasn't those other women. She wasn't going to let
anything happen between them. This was just a trip. A chance
for her to discuss business with Nick. Business, she reminded
herself when he came back into the cabin, sat on the sofa and
drew her down beside him.

"We'll be in the air in a few minutes."

"Good," she said, and cleared her throat. "Who's Tom?"

"The pilot." Nick laced his fingers through hers. "I'm usually up there in the cockpit. But today I decided I'd rather be
back here, with you."

"Ah," she said with a little smile. "So the prince sits beside
his pilot and makes him nervous, hmm?"

He grinned. "The prince sits beside his *co*-pilot and flies
the plane himself."

"You know how to fly?"

Nick settled back, put his feet up on the low table before
the sofa and nodded. "I learned when I was just a kid.
Distances are so vast in Quidar...flying is the easiest way to
get from place to place."

"My stepbrothers say the same thing."

"It's the logical thing to do, especially when you're expected to put in appearances."

"Expected?"

"Uh-huh. It was one of my earliest responsibilities back
home. Standing in for my father."

Amanda tried to imagine a boy with silver eyes taking on
the burden of representing an absolute monarch.

"Back home. You mean, in Quidar."

"Yes." He lifted her hand, brought it to his mouth and
brushed his lips over her knuckles. "I've spent a lot of my
life in the States. My mother kept a home in California even

after she married my father. But Quidar has always been 'home'. What about you?''

"Don't…'' Her breath hitched. "Nick, don't do that.''

His brows rose. "Don't ask about your childhood?''

She made a sound she hoped would pass for a laugh. "Don't do—what you're doing. Kissing my hand. You said you wouldn't. You said—''

"You're right.'' He closed his fingers over hers, then put her hand in her lap and folded his arms. "Tell me about yourself. Where is home for you?''

Her hand tingled. She could almost feel the warmth of his mouth still on her skin.

"I don't really think of anyplace as 'home','' she said briskly. "I was born in Chicago, but my parents were divorced when I was ten.'' *Why had she stopped him from holding her hand? There was nothing sexual in it.*

"And?''

"And,'' she said, even more briskly, "my mother got a job in St. Louis, so we moved there. After a year or so, she sent us—my two sisters and me—to boarding school. We'd go to visit her some holidays and my father on others.'' *Take my hand, Nick. It was silly telling you not to. I like the feel of your fingers entwined with mine.* "So, when I think of 'home','' she said, stumbling a little on the words, "sometimes it's Chicago. Sometimes it's St. Louis. Sometimes it's Connecticut, where I went to school. And there are times it's Dallas, where I lived when I was married.''

"What was he like? Your husband?''

"Like my father,'' she said, and laughed. "I didn't realize it, of course, when I married him, but he was. Self-centered, removed…I don't think he ever thought of anyone but himself.'' Her breath hitched. Nick had taken her hand again. He was playing with her fingers, examining them as if they were new and remarkable objects.

"Did you love him?''

She blinked. He'd lifted his head. He was looking at her now, not at her hand, and he was still smiling, but the smile

was false. She could see the tautness in his face, the glint of
ice in his silver eyes.

"I thought I did. I mean, I wouldn't have married him if
I—"

"Do you still?"

"No. Actually, I don't think I ever really...Nick? You're
hurting my hand."

Nick looked at their joined hands. "Sorry," he said quickly,
"I just— I..." He frowned, wondered why it should matter if
Amanda Benning still carried the torch for her ex, then answered the question by telling himself he wouldn't want to
bed any woman if she was still thinking about another man.
"Sorry," he said again, and let go of her hand. "So." His
tone was brisk, his smile polite. "You left Dallas and moved
east. That must have been quite a change."

Amanda smiled. "Not as big a change as it must have been
for you, going from Quidar to New York."

"Well, I spent lots of time in the States, growing up. And
I went to school here." His smile softened. "But you're right.
New York is nothing like Quidar."

"What's it like? Your country?"

He hesitated. Did she really want to hear about the desert,
about the jagged mountains to the north and the sapphire sea
to the south? She looked as if she did and, slowly, he began
telling her about his homeland, and the wild beauty of it.

"I'm boring you," he said after he'd been talking for a long
time.

"Oh, no." She reached for his hand, curled her fingers
around his. "You're not. It sounds magnificent. Where do you
live when you're there? In the desert, or in the mountains?"

So he told her more, about Zamidar and the Ivory Palace
set against the backdrop of the mountains, about the scented
gardens that surrounded it, about long summer nights in the
endless expanse of the desert.

He told her more than he'd ever told anyone about his
homeland and, he suddenly realized, about himself. And when
he fell silent and she looked at him, her golden eyes shining,

her lips bowed in a smile, and said Quidar must be incredibly beautiful, he came close to saying yes, it was. Very beautiful, and he longed to show it to her.

At that moment, the phone beside him buzzed. He picked it up, listened to his pilot give him an update on their speed and the projected time of arrival. He let out his breath and knew he'd never been so grateful to hear such dry statistics. The interruption had come at just the right time. Who knew what he might have said, otherwise?

The path back to reality lay in the sheaf of papers he knew he'd find inside the leather briefcase on the table beside him.

Carefully, he let go of Amanda's hand, reached for the case and opened it. "Forgive me," he said politely. "But I have a lot of reading to do before we reach our destination."

She nodded. "You don't have to explain," she said, just as politely. "I understand."

She didn't. He could see that in the way she shifted away from him. He'd hurt her. Embarrassed her. Taking his hand was the first gesture she'd made toward him and he'd rejected it.

Nick frowned and stared at the papers in his lap as if he really gave a damn about what they said. He was the one who'd direct their relationship. He would make no move unless she made it clear that was what she wanted, but inevitably, the start—and the finish—of an affair was up to him. It had always been that way, would always be that way.

Nick stopped thinking. He reached out, put his arm around Amanda's shoulders and drew her close.

"Come here," he said a little gruffly. "Put your head on my shoulder and keep me company while I wade through this stuff."

"Really, Nick, it's all right. I don't want to distract you."

"It's too late to worry about that," he said with a little laugh. "Sorry. I just—I have some things on my mind, that's all."

"Second thoughts about this trip?" she said, her tone stiff.

"Yes," he said bluntly, "but not about you."

"I don't understand."

"No, I don't, either." She looked up at him, her eyes filled with questions, and he sighed. "My brain is in a fog. Thinking about you kept me awake most of the night."

"That makes it unanimous."

"Well, why don't you take a nap, sweetheart? It'll take a few hours for us to get to Texas."

Amanda lifted her eyebrows. "Is that whe-ah we're a'goin'?" she said in a lazy drawl. "To Tex-as?"

Nick groaned. "That's terrible," he said, and grinned at her.

Amanda grinned back. "It's the best I can do. I'm not a native Texan."

"Better watch that phony accent." He touched the tip of her nose with his finger. "Our host is known for having a temper."

She yawned and burrowed closer, inhaled the scent of him. "Must be a Texas tradition. He can't have more of a temper than my stepfather. Are we going to a ranch? Is that why you told me to pack jeans?"

"Clever woman." She was cuddled up to him like a kitten, all warm, soft and sweet-smelling. Nick turned his head, buried his nose in her silken hair. "Yes. We're going to a ranch."

"Oh, that's nice," she said, and gave another delicate yawn. "It is?"

"Uh-huh. Maybe we'll get the chance to go riding. I like horses. And I love to ride."

"Do you?" Nick said, knowing he was grinning like an idiot. "Like to ride, I mean?"

"Mmm."

"I do, too. My father breeds Arabian horses. They're an ancient breed. Graceful, fast "

"Mmm. I know something about Arabians."

He smiled. "Really?"

"Arabian horses," she said, and laughed. Her warm breath tickled his throat. "My stepfather has a weakness for them."

"Well, so does the owner of the ranch we're going to. My

father shipped a stallion to him, but something must have gone wrong during the flight.''

''Where is this ranch? What part of Texas?''

''It's near Austin. Do you know the area?''

''A little. I've spent some time there. My mother and step-father live nearby.''

Nick put the briefcase aside, leaned back and gathered Amanda closer. He didn't much care about reading through the papers Abdul had provided. Not right now. All he wanted to do was enjoy the feel of Amanda, nestled in his arms.

''Perhaps they're familiar with the ranch we're going to.''

''What's it called?'' She smiled. ''The Bar Something, right?''

Nick grinned and kissed her temple. ''Wrong. It's called Espada.''

Her body, so soft and sweetly pliant seconds ago, became rigid in his embrace.

''Espada?'' She sat straight up and stared at him. ''We're going to Espada?''

''Yes. Do you know it?''

''Do I…?'' Amanda barked a laugh, pulled free of his arms and shot to her feet. ''Yes, I know it. For heaven's sake, Nick! Jonas Baron owns Espada.''

''Right. He's the man we're going to see.''

''Jonas is married to my mother.''

It took a minute for the message to sink in. ''You mean— you mean, he's your stepfather?''

Amanda chuffed out a breath. ''That's exactly what I mean.''

Nick couldn't believe it. How could something like this have happened? The irony was incredible. He'd never taken a woman with him on a business trip until today—and now, his business trip was taking Amanda straight into the bosom of her family.

No, he thought, and bit back a laugh. No, it was impossible.

He never got involved with the families of the women he dated. Oh, he met mothers and fathers from time to time. You couldn't live the life he did and not have that happen. New York seemed like a big city to outsiders but the truth was that the inner circle, made up of financiers and industrialists, politicians and public figures, was surprisingly small.

After a while, the Joneses knew the Smiths and the Smiths knew the Browns and the Browns, of course, knew the Joneses. The names and faces all took on an almost stultifying familiarity.

But that wasn't the same as spending a weekend—a weekend, for God's sake—with a woman's parents.

He'd always been scrupulously careful about that. He'd turned down simple invitations to spend days in the country or on Long Island if it meant Daddy or Mommy would be there, and it hadn't a thing to do with anything as simple as the propriety—or the impropriety—of sharing the bed of the daughter of the house.

It had to do with far more delicate matters.

Family weekends were complications. They were far too personal. They created expectations he never, ever intended to fulfill.

"Dammit, Nick, say something! Didn't you hear what I said?"

He looked at Amanda. She was standing in front of him, her hands on her hips.

"Yes," he said slowly, as he rose to his feet. "I heard you."

"Well, I can't go there. To Espada. You'll have to tell Tim—"

"Tom," he said as if it mattered.

"I don't care what the pilot's name is!" She could hear her voice rising and she took a deep breath, told herself to calm down. "Nick, I'm sorry, but you'll have to take me back to New York. Or—or have your pilot—have Tom—land at an airport, any airport. I can take a commercial flight back to—"

"Amanda." He took her hands. "Take it easy."

"Take it easy?" She snorted, looked at him as if he were out of his mind. "Do you know what they'll think if I show

up with you? Do you have any idea what my mother will—
what Jonas will... Oh, God!''

She swung away. Nick caught her, drew her to him and
wrapped his arms tightly around her. She was stiff and unyielding, but he didn't care. If anything, that was all the more
reason to hold her close.

''They'll think we didn't want to be apart,'' he said roughly.

''Nick—''

''They'll think we just met and yes it's crazy, but the
thought of being away from each other, even for a couple of
days, was impossible.''

''Nick,'' she said again, but this time her voice was soft
and her eyes were shining when she lifted her face to his.

''They'll think I'm the luckiest man in the world,'' he whispered, and then her arms were around his neck, her mouth was
pressed to his, and nothing mattered to either of them but the
joy and the wonder of the moment.

CHAPTER NINE

THE afternoon sun was high in the western sky as Marta Baron settled into her chair on the upper level of her waterfall deck, smiled politely at her guests and wondered what on earth she was supposed to say to the stranger who was her daughter's lover.

At least, she assumed Sheikh Nicholas al Rashid was Amanda's lover.

It hadn't been a very difficult assumption to make.

The expression on the sheikh's handsome face when he looked at Amanda, the way he kept his arm possessively around her waist, even the softness in his voice when he used her name, were all dead giveaways.

He might as well have been wearing a sign that read, This Woman Belongs To Me.

Amanda was harder to read.

There was a delicate pink flush to her cheeks, and she had a way of glancing at the sheikh as if they were alone on the planet, but Marta thought she'd noticed an angry snap in her daughter's eyes when the sheikh's arm had closed around her—a look he had studiously ignored as he drew her down beside him on the cushioned teak glider.

"...so I said, well, why would I want to buy a horse from a man who couldn't tell the front end of a jackass from the rear?" Jonas said, and Marta laughed politely, along with everybody else.

She'd always considered herself a sophisticated woman, even before she'd assumed her duties as the wife of Jonas Baron. She'd lived through the sexual revolution, looked the other way when her girls were in college and one or the other of them had brought a boy home for the weekend. Not that

121

she'd put them in one room, but she'd known that closed doors hadn't kept them from sleeping—or not sleeping, she thought wryly—in the same bed.

Not Amanda, though.

Marta smiled at something the sheikh said, but her attention was focused on her middle daughter.

Amanda had never brought a boy home. She'd never brought a man home, either; surely that ex-husband of hers didn't qualify. He'd been a self-serving, emotionless phony. Marta had only figured out why Amanda married him after the marriage ended, when she realized her daughter had been looking for the father she'd never really had.

Marta lifted her glass of iced tea and took a delicate sip.

One thing was certain. No one could ever mistake Sheikh Nicholas al Rashid for a father figure. He was, to use the indelicate parlance of the day, a hunk.

And she had to stop thinking of him as Sheikh.

"Please," he'd said, lifting her hand to his lips, "call me Nick."

She looked at him, seated beside Amanda. He was watching Jonas, listening to him, but his concentration was on the woman at his side. There was no mistaking the deliberate brush of that hard-looking shoulder against hers, the flex of his hand along her hip.

If Nick and Amanda weren't yet lovers, they would be, and soon. This was a man who always got what he wanted, and he wanted Amanda. But would he know what to do with her once he had her?

No, Marta thought, he wouldn't.

Nick was like a much younger version of her own husband. He was strong, powerful and determined. He was also, she was certain, often unyielding and immovable. A successful monarch needed those traits to run his empire—Jonas to rule Espada, Nick to rule Quidar.

Men like that were difficult to deal with. They could break a woman's heart with terrifying ease. It didn't help that they also attracted women as readily as nectar attracted hummingbirds. And because men were men, they'd always want the freshest little flower with the brightest petals.

Marta sighed.

She waged a constant battle against time's cruel ravages, but, paradoxically enough, time was her ally in matters of the heart. She'd come along late enough in Jonas's life so that she could be fairly certain she was the last woman he'd want to taste. It wasn't an especially sentimental view but it was a realistic, even reassuring one, because she loved her husband and would never willingly have given him up.

Amanda was enough like her so that she'd love the same way, once she found the man she really wanted. Marta could only hope Nick wasn't that man. He had the look about him of a man who would love one woman with heart-stopping intensity, but only on his terms.

For a woman like her daughter, that would not work.

Amanda, Marta thought, Amanda, sweetie, what are you doing?

"...have known it instantly, Mrs. Baron, even if we'd met accidentally."

Marta blinked. Nick was smiling at her, but she had no idea what he'd said.

"Sorry, Your Highness—"

"Nick, please."

"Nick." Marta smiled, too. "I'm afraid I missed that."

"I said, I'd have known you were Amanda's mother even if no one told me. You look enough alike to pass as sisters."

"And you must have a bit of Irish in your blood," Marta said, her smile broadening, "to be able to spout such blarney without laughing."

Nick grinned. "It's the truth, Mrs. Baron, though, actually, my mother always claimed she had an Irish grandfather."

"Please. Call me Marta. Yes, now that you mention it, I think I've read that your mother was American."

"She was, and proud of it, as I am proud of my American half. I've always felt very fortunate to be the product of two such extraordinary cultures."

"One foot in the past," Marta said, still smiling, "and one in the future. Which suits you best, I wonder?"

"Mother," Amanda said, but Nick only chuckled.

"Both have their advantages. So far, I've never found it necessary to choose one over the other."

"No. Why would you, when you can have the best of both worlds? Here you are, blue jeans and all—"

"It's difficult to handle horses in a suit," Nick said, and smiled.

Marta smiled, too. "You know what I mean, Nick. Any time you wish, you're free to turn into the ruler of your own kingdom, do as you will, come and go as you please, answering to no one."

"Mother, for heaven's sake—"

"No." Nick took his arm from around Amanda, lifted her hand to his mouth and kissed it. "No, your mother's quite right. Perhaps it's a simplification, but it's pretty much an accurate description of my life." He rose to his feet. "Marta? I noticed a garden behind the house. Would you be kind enough to walk me through it?"

"Of course." Marta rose, too. "Do you like flowers, Nick?"

"Yes," he said simply. "Especially those that are beautiful and have the strength to flourish in difficult climes."

Marta smiled and took his arm as they strolled down the steps, along the path and into the garden.

"There aren't many flowers that can manage that," she said after a few minutes.

"No, there aren't." Nick paused and turned toward her. "Let's not speak in metaphors, Marta. You don't like me, do you?"

"It isn't that I don't like you. It's..." Marta hesitated. "Look, I'm not old-fashioned. I'm not going to ask you what your intentions are with regard to my daughter."

"I'm glad to hear it." He spoke politely, but his words were edged with steel. "Because it's none of your business. Our relationship, Amanda's and mine, doesn't concern anyone but us.''

"I know. Like it or not, my little girl is all grown up. But her welfare does concern me. I don't want to see her hurt.''

Nick jammed his hands into the back pockets of his jeans. ''And you think I do?''

"No, of course not. It's just… A man like you can hurt a woman unintentionally.''

"A man like me,'' he said coldly. ''Just what is that supposed to mean?''

"Oh, I'm not trying to insult you…'' Marta gave a little laugh. ''But I'm doing a fine job of it, aren't I?'' She put her hand lightly on his arm. ''Nick, you remind me of my husband in so many ways. All the things that make you successful can be difficult for a woman to deal with.''

"Are you saying being successful is a drawback in a relationship?''

"On the contrary. It's a wonderful asset. But sometimes success can lead to a kind of selfishness.'' Marta clicked her tongue. ''Just listen to me! I sound like one of those horrible newspaper advice columnists.'' She looped her arm through Nick's and drew him forward. ''Jonas would tell me I'm meddling.''

"Well, he'd be right.'' Nick softened the words with a grin. ''But I understand. You love your daughter. And I—I…'' God, what was he saying? ''I can promise you, Marta, I care about her, too.''

"Good. And now, let me show you the vegetables I grow, way in the back garden. Tomatoes, actually. Hundred-dollar tomatoes, Jonas calls them.'' Marta smiled. ''And, Nick? I'm very happy to have you here at Espada. Whatever happens, a woman should have at least one man in her life who looks at her the way you look at Amanda.''

"Every man who sees her must look at her that way,'' Nick said, and cleared his throat.

"Well, let me put that another way, then. I've never seen a man look at her the way you do.''

Nick stopped in his tracks. "Not even her husband?"

Marta shook her head. "Especially not her husband."

"He must have been an idiot."

Marta laughed. "What a perceptive man you are, Nicholas al Rashid!"

Nick spent most of the remaining afternoon at the stables with Jonas, the ranch foreman and the vet. By evening, he was satisfied that the Arabian stallion was suffering from nothing more serious than a minor sprain and a major case of nerves.

"Who could possibly blame him?" Nick had said when he'd come back up to the house. "He's gone from Quidar to Texas. That's a one-hundred-eighty-degree change in any life."

A one-hundred-eighty-degree change indeed, Amanda thought as she slipped into the emerald-green dress Marta had loaned her to wear for dinner.

Before last night, the only thing she'd known about Nick was that she didn't like him. She liked him now, though. More than was reasonable or logical...or safe.

Her mother had tried to tell her that when she'd brought her the dress and a matching pair of shoes.

"Good thing we're about the same size," Marta had said with a smile. "Not that you don't look charming in denim, but Jonas likes to dress for dinner. He'd never admit it, of course. He lays the blame on me."

Amanda sighed. "I just wish I hadn't listened to Nick when he told me to pack nothing but jeans."

"A good thing his valet didn't." Marta grinned. "That was a delightful story the sheikh told, about unpacking his bag and finding a dark suit tucked in with his riding boots."

"Mmm. That was probably the work of his secretary. That's what Nick calls him anyway, this funny little man who bows himself in and out of rooms."

Marta plucked a loose thread from the dress's hem. "Well, after all, sweetie, Nick is heir to the throne of Quidar."

Amanda held the dress up against herself and looked in the mirror. "It's perfect. Thanks, Mom."

"I gather you didn't even know you were coming to Espada."

"No. Nick didn't mention it. He just said we were flying somewhere."

"And you said you'd go with him."

Was that a gentle note of censure in her mother's voice? Color rose in Amanda's cheeks as the women's eyes met in the mirror.

"Yes. Yes, I did."

"And no wonder. He's a fascinating young man. Charming, intelligent, Incredibly good-looking. And, I would think, very accustomed to getting his own way." Marta smiled. "Actually, he reminds me of Jonas."

Amanda turned around. "Nothing's going on between us," she said flatly.

"Oh, I think you're wrong, sweetie. I think a lot is going on. You just aren't ready to admit it."

"Mom—"

"You don't owe me any explanations, darling. You're a grown woman. And I have every confidence in your ability to make your own decisions." Marta reached for her daughter's hands and clasped them tightly. "I just don't want to see you get hurt."

"Nick would never—"

"There are different ways of being hurt, Mandy. Loving a man who may not be able to love you back in quite the same way is perhaps the worst pain of all."

"I don't love Nick! I admit, I'm—I'm infatuated with him, but—"

Marta had smiled and put her finger over Amanda's lips. "Go on," she'd said gently, "make yourself beautiful for your young man."

Beautiful? Amanda thought as she finished dressing. She wondered if Nick would think so. There'd certainly been more

stunning women at the party last night, and she'd never be an
eye-catching knockout like Deanna Burgess.

But she wanted Nick to like what he saw tonight. Any
woman would. That didn't mean she was in love with him...

And then she opened her door to Nick's polite knock and
knew, without any hesitancy, that she was. Everything her
mother had said was true.

"Hi."

"Hi yourself." Her heartbeat stuttered. Amanda took a
breath, dredged up a smile. "You're right on time."

"Always."

He grinned, and she wondered frantically how it could have
happened. She hadn't been looking to fall in love. And if she
had, it wouldn't have been with the Lion of the Desert.

"My father drummed it into me."

"What?"

"The importance of being on time. Sort of the eleventh
commandment. You know, 'Thou shalt never be late.'"

"Yes." She swallowed dryly, fought to hang on to whatever remained of her composure. *How? How could she have
fallen in love so quickly?* "Well, it worked. You're certainly
prompt."

His smile tilted. "And you," he said softly, "are incredibly
beautiful."

His words, the velvet softness of them, even the way he was
looking at her, ignited a slow-burning heat in her bones.

"Thank you. It's my mother's dress. I didn't—"

"I know. I should have anticipated that the Barons would
expect us to dine with them." A muscle danced in his jaw.
He moved toward her, his eyes a burnished silver. "But I
didn't think of anything except you. Since last night I haven't
been able to think of anything but you."

"Nick..."

Gently, he took her face in his hands, lifted it to his. He
could feel her trembling with the same excitement that burned
inside him.

"One kiss," he said softly, "just one, before we go downstairs."

"All right. Just—"

His mouth closed over hers. Amanda moaned, closed her eyes, lifted her hands and laid them against his chest. His heart was racing, but no faster than hers. She moved closer to him, closer still, and he swept his arms around her, gathered her against him so that she could feel his hunger.

"Nick," she said in a choked whisper, "oh, Nick..."

He took her hand from his chest, brought it down his body, cupped it over his arousal. He groaned, or maybe it was she who made that soft, yearning sound. It didn't matter. Her needs, and his, were the same.

"To hell with dinner," he whispered. "Amanda, I want to touch you. To undress you. To bury myself inside you while you lift your arms to me and cry out my name."

"Oh, yes! It's what I want, too." She took a shaky breath, lifted her hand from the heat and hardness of him and leaned back in his arms. "But Jonas and Marta expect us to join them."

Nick bent his head, nipped gently at her throat. "I don't give a damn what they want."

Amanda gave a breathless laugh. "Nick, that's my mother downstairs."

He laughed, too, or made the attempt. "I'm sorry, sweetheart. Of course it is. Okay. Just give me a minute. Then we'll make our entrance, pretend we're interested in drinks and dinner and polite conversation for a couple of hours—"

"Only for a couple of hours."

He tugged her towards him and she went willingly, thrust her hands into his hair, dragged his mouth down to hers and kissed him.

Nick felt the kiss pierce his heart like an arrow.

A couple of hours, he'd said. Since when could a couple of hours seem like an eternity?

Drinks first, out on the deck, where they were joined by

Tyler and Caitlin Kincaid. They lived nearby, Jonas said. He clapped Tyler on the back, gave him a proud smile and said Tyler was his son and Caitlin his stepdaughter.

Any other time, Nick would have found that intriguing. A son who didn't bear the old man's name. A stepdaughter, but obviously not of Marta's blood. Interesting, he thought—but then his curiosity faded.

His only interest was Amanda.

Still, he went through the motions. Made pleasant small talk. Murmured something about the excellence of the wine. Agreed that dinner was a masterpiece. He supposed it was. Everybody said so. The thing was, he couldn't taste any of it.

Nothing had any flavor. How could it, when the only taste that mattered was Amanda's? That last kiss lingered on his mouth. The memory of it. The way she'd pulled his head down to hers, the way she'd initiated that all-consuming, hungry kiss...

Ah, hell. Nick shifted uneasily in his chair.

He was too old for this. Boys worried about their hormones making them look foolish, and he was far from being a boy. But just thinking about her...the heat of her in his arms; the sweet sounds she made when he kissed her; the way she fitted herself against him...

Hell, he thought again, and cleared his throat.

"...oil strike?"

He blinked, looked around the table blindly. Everyone was looking at him.

"Sorry," he said, and cleared his throat again. "Tyler? Did you say something?"

"I was just wondering about that oil strike in Quidar last year. Was it really the gusher our people said it was?"

"Oh. Oh, yeah. Absolutely. The field was huge, bigger than..."

Nick talked about oil. He talked about oil prices. And all the time part of his brain was doing such sensible things, another part was wondering what Amanda was thinking. She was seated beside him, and every now and then when he trusted

himself to do it without pulling her into his arms, he looked
at her. Her golden eyes were wide; her cheeks were flushed.
And when he took her hand under the table, he could feel her
tremble.

Was she aching, as he was, for these endless hours to pass
so that she could come into his arms and ask him to take her?
Because she had to ask. He'd told her that she had to ask, and
he was a man of his word, would remain a man of his word,
even if it killed him. It would, if he didn't have her. If he
didn't make her his.

"Nick?"

And if any son of a bitch tried to take her from him, he'd—

"Nick?"

Nick frowned. They were on the deck again, just he and
Tyler Kincaid, though he had only the haziest recollection of
finishing dessert and agreeing it would be great to go outside
for a breath of air.

"Yes." Nick inhaled deeply, then let out his breath. "Kincaid. Tyler. I…hell, I'm sorry. You must think I'm—"

"What I think," Tyler said with wry amusement, "is that
if you and Amanda don't get behind a closed door pretty damn
soon, the rest of us are going to be in for an extremely interesting night."

Nick swung toward him, eyes narrowed. "What's that supposed to mean, Kincaid?"

"It means that the temperature goes up a hundred degrees
each time you look at each other," Tyler said carefully. "And
that if you think you'd rather work it off by taking me on,
you're welcome to try it."

The two men stared at each other and then Nick gave a
choked laugh. "Sorry. Damn, I'm sorry. I just—"

"Yeah, I know the feeling." Tyler leaned back against the
deck rail. "Amazing, isn't it? What falling in love with a
woman can do to a perfectly normal, completely sensible
male?"

"In…?" Nick shook his head. "You've got it wrong. I'm
not—"

"Tyler?" Caitlin Kincaid smiled as she came toward them. "Tyler, darling, it's late. We really should be leaving. It was lovely meeting you, Nick."

"Yes." Nick took her hand and brought it to his lips. "I gave your husband my card. Give me a call the next time you're in New York."

Caitlin rose on her toes and kissed his cheek. "I think it's wonderful," she whispered.

Nick felt bewildered as she stepped back into the arc of her husband's arm. "What's wonderful?"

Tyler looked at Nick, started to say something, then thought better of it. "Well," he said, and held out his hand, "it's been a pleasure meeting you."

"Yeah," Nick said. "Uh, Tyler? You're definitely wrong. About what you said. I mean, I'm not—I'm certainly not—"

"Of course you're not," Tyler said solemnly.

Nick thought he heard Kincaid chuckle as he and his wife walked into the house. Not that it mattered. The laugh was on Tyler if he thought any rational man would ever confuse lust with love.

After a while, the lights in the house went off. He straightened up, looked at the lighted dial of his watch. How long had he been out here? Had Amanda gone to her room? Had he misread what he'd seen in her eyes all evening?

"Nick?"

He turned and saw her standing in the doorway, a beautiful shadow in the soft light of the moon. The sight of her almost stopped his heart, but then, desire—lust—could be a powerful thing. Any thinking man knew that.

"Nick," she said again, and Nicholas al Rashid, the Lion of the Desert, stopped thinking, went to the woman he wanted, the woman he'd always wanted since the beginning of time, took her in his arms and kissed her again and again until he could no longer tell where she left off and he began.

CHAPTER TEN

THE world was spinning out of control, the stars racing across the black Texas sky like a kaleidoscope gone mad.

"Tell me, sweetheart." Nick's voice was hoarse and urgent. "Tell me what you want."

Amanda looked up at this man who'd turned her life upside down, this dangerous, gorgeous, complex stranger, and framed his face with her hands. "You," she said softly. "I want—"

Nick's mouth closed hungrily over hers. His hands slipped down her spine, cupped her bottom, lifted her into his heat and hardness.

Desire sparkled in her blood. She moaned, caught his lip between her teeth, bit gently into the soft flesh and traced the tiny wound with the tip of her tongue. His arms tightened around her and he whispered something in a language she couldn't understand, but words didn't matter.

Not now.

Nick drew back, just enough so he could see Amanda's face in the pearlescent glow of the moon.

"You're so beautiful," he whispered, and kissed her again, heating her mouth with his, parting it with his, feasting on the taste of her, on the little sounds she made as she returned his kisses. She was trembling in his arms, straining against him, fitting her body to his until nothing but the whisper of their clothing separated them.

Nick knew he couldn't take much more of this sweet torment.

The moon slipped behind the surrounding hills. The silver-shot night swooped down, embraced them in a cloak of velvet darkness.

He drew Amanda closer, settled her in the inverted vee of

his legs. His erection pressed against her belly and she sighed his name.

"Please," she whispered, "Nick, please…"

"Amanda." His voice was raw. "Sweetheart, come upstairs with me."

"Please," she said again, and kissed him, took his tongue into her mouth, and he was lost.

He bunched the silk of her skirt in his fists and pushed it up her thighs. She was wearing stockings and a small triangle of silk. His brain registered that much and, in some still-functioning part of it, he thought about how exciting it would be to see her now, see those long, elegant legs, that scrap of silk, but then she moved her hips and he forgot everything but the uncontrollable need to possess her.

"Amanda," he groaned, and he slipped his hand between her thighs and cupped her, felt the heat of her, and the dampness. He moved against her, moved again, and she moaned.

She slid her hands up his chest, shoved his jacket half off his shoulders, fumbled at his tie, at the buttons of his shirt, and put her hands on his skin. She felt her knees go weak. Oh, the feel of him! The hot male skin. The whorls of silky hair, the ridges of hard muscle.

Nick caught her hands, held them against the thudding beat of his heart.

"Amanda." He dragged air into his lungs, told himself to breathe, to think, to slow down. He'd waited all these years for this moment. He knew it now, knew that he'd lived with the memory of the woman in his arms since he'd first seen her. Now, at last, she would be his—but not like this.

She was as soft as the petals of a rosebud, as lovely as a dream. He wanted to pleasure her slowly, take her slowly, see her eyes turn blind with passion as he took her to the brink of ecstasy over and over again before they tumbled over the edge and fell through time, joined together for eternity.

Nick shuddered.

Unless she moved against him. Yes, like that. Unless she lifted herself to him like that. Just like that. Unless her delicate tongue searched for his. Unless she rubbed her hot, feminine core against his palm…

A cry broke from his throat. He drew her closer into his embrace, deeper into the inky silence of the moonless night, and pressed her back against the railing.

"Look at me," he whispered, and when her eyes met his, he ripped away the bit of silk between her thighs, found the tiny bud that bloomed there. Touched her. Stroked her. And kissed her, kissed her and drank in her cries as she came against his hand.

She sobbed his name, pulled down his zipper, found him, held him, stroked him, and then, oh then, she was a hot silken fist taking him deep inside her.

Nick strove for sanity. Wait for her, he told himself, dammit, wait.

Amanda trembled and arched like a bow in his arms, tore her mouth from his and sank her teeth into his shoulder. The sound, the feel, the heat of her surrender finished him. He stopped thinking, slid his hand around the nape of her neck, took her mouth with his and exploded deep within her satin walls.

For long moments, neither of them moved. Then Nick let out a breath, pulled down her skirt and gently kissed her lips. "Sweetheart," he whispered.

She shook her head, made a weak little sound and tried to turn her face from his, but he caught her chin, kissed her again and tasted the salt of her tears.

Nick cursed, damned himself for being such a selfish fool. He enfolded her even more closely in his arms, cupped her head and brought it to his shoulder.

"Forgive me, sweetheart," he murmured, rocking her gently in his embrace. "I know it was too quick. I meant to go slowly, to make it perfect."

Amanda lifted her head, silenced him with a kiss. "It *was* perfect."

"But you're crying."

She gave a soft little laugh. "I know. It's just…" *It's just that my heart is full,* she thought. Full with love, for the first time in her life. She smiled, put her hand to his cheek. "Those weren't sad tears," she whispered. "This was—what we just did—I've never…"

He felt his heart swell with joy. "Never?"

She shook her head. "Never."

He kissed her again until she was breathless with desire. Then he put his arm around her, led her into the sleeping house and took her, at last, to bed.

Amanda awoke to Nick's kisses just before dawn.

"Hello, sweetheart," he whispered.

Safe and warm in the curve of his arm, she smiled up at him. "Good morning."

He bent to her, kissed her mouth with lingering tenderness. "You slept in my arms all night."

"Mmm."

"I liked having you there."

"Mmm," she said again, and laced her fingers into his dark hair.

He smiled, nipped gently at her bottom lip. "You're not a morning conversationalist, huh?"

Amanda laughed softly. "I'm not a morning anything. I don't… " Her breath hitched. "Nick?"

"You see, sweetheart?" His voice roughened as he caressed her breast, licked the nipple and watched it bead. "It isn't true that you're not a morning anything. You just need to find something that appeals to you."

She caught her breath, lifted herself to his mouth.

"Like this for instance. Or…" He shifted, moved farther down her warm flesh and gently parted her thighs. "Or this."

He loved the soft sound she made as he put his mouth against her, loved the sweet taste of her, like honey on his tongue. And the scent of her, of aroused woman, filled him with hot pleasure. How could he want her again? He'd had her endless times during the long, miraculous night.

But he would never have her enough, he thought suddenly,

and he rose above her, looked down into her passion-flushed face and spoke her name.

Her lashes flew up. Her wide golden eyes looked into his as he entered her and he saw the blur of pleasure suffuse her face. He withdrew, slid into her again, drove deeper, saw her eyes darken and her lips form his name.

"Yes," he whispered, "yes," and he caught her hands, laced his fingers through hers and stretched her arms to the sides, still moving, still seeking not just that incredible moment when they would fly into the sun together but something more, something he'd never known.

"Nick," she moaned, just that, only that, but he could hear—he thought he could hear—everything a man could hope for, long for, in the way she said his name.

"Come with me," he said, "Amanda, love..."

She wrapped her legs around his hips, sobbed his name, and Nick stopped thinking, stopped wondering, and lost himself in the woman in his arms.

Afterward, they lay in a warm, contented tangle, her head on his chest, his arms holding her close.

He gave a dramatic groan. "I'm never going to be able to move again."

She laughed softly, propped her chin on her wrist and looked at him. "Be sure and explain that to the housekeeper when she finds your naked body in my bed."

"I'll just smile and tell her that I died and went to heaven."

"Uh-huh. My mother will probably love that explanation."

"Hell," Nick grumbled. She squealed as he rolled her onto her back, gently drew her hands above her head and manacled them with his. "Let me be sure I understand this, Ms. Benning. You expect me to get up, get dressed and beat it back to my room before the sun rises." He bent his head, kissed her mouth. "Is there no pity in your heart for a man who's given his all?"

Amanda gave a little hum of satisfaction. "But you haven't given your all," she said huskily, and shifted beneath him. "Or am I imagining things?"

"What?" Nick said with mock indignation. "You can't be referring to this."

"But I am."

And then, neither of them was laughing.

"Amanda," he whispered, "sweetheart."

He drew her into his arms and they made love again, slowly, exploring each other, tasting each other, coming at last to a climax no less transcendent for all the sweet, gentle steps that had led them to it.

Nick held Amanda close for long moments, savoring the slowing beat of her heart against his. How could he have thought he knew what sex was, when he'd lived without ever knowing this sense of completion in a woman's arms?

He'd been with many women, all of them beautiful, almost all of them skilled in bed. Amanda was beautiful, yes. And she was eager, even wild in his arms, but skill...?

He drew her more tightly into his embrace.

She wasn't skilled. There'd been moments during the night when she'd caught her breath at some of the things he'd done. "Oh," she'd whispered once, "Nick, I never..."

Shall I stop? he'd said, even though stopping would have half killed him, but there was nothing he wouldn't do to please her. And she'd sighed and touched him and said no, please, no, don't ever stop.

Which, he thought, staring up at the ceiling, just about terrified him. Because he didn't want to stop. Not ever. Not just making love to her, although he suspected he could do that for the rest of his life without ever tiring of it.

The thing of it was, he didn't want to stop being with Amanda. Laughing with her. Talking with her. Even arguing with her. He didn't want any of that to stop.

And it scared the hell out of him.

What was happening here? He'd met this woman less than two days ago under what could only charitably be called suspicious circumstances. He didn't know very much about her. And now, he was thinking—he felt as if he might be—he had this idea that—

Nick slid his arm from beneath Amanda's shoulders and sat up.

"It's getting late," he said, and flashed a quick smile as he got out of bed, stepped into his trousers and pulled on his shirt. "The sun's coming up."

"Nick?" Amanda shifted against the pillow, rose on her elbows and looked at him. "What's the matter?"

"Nothing. Nothing's the matter. I just, uh, I dropped a cuff link."

He bent down, collected the rest of the clothing he'd practically torn off last night, then searched the carpet vigilantly for a cuff link that had gone astray. It was much easier to think he might have lost a cuff link than a far more vital part of himself, one he'd never given any woman—one he wasn't sure he could retrieve.

"Found it," he said, straightening up, holding out the link and smiling again as he quickly made his way to the door. "I'll see you at breakfast. Okay?"

She nodded, then drew the blanket to her chin. She looked lost and puzzled, and he came within a breath of dropping his stuff, going back to her and taking her in his arms.

"Go on," she said, "before you turn into a pumpkin. Or whatever it is sheikhs turn into when the moon goes down and the sun comes up. Dammit, Nick, I can smell coffee. Someone's awake, and I don't want them to find you here."

Her voice had taken on strength. She looked neither lost or puzzled, just annoyed. Annoyed, because he wasn't getting out of her room fast enough? Because someone might find him with her?

Nick's mouth thinned. What if he told her he damned well wasn't going anywhere? That he belonged in her bed just as she belonged in his arms?

"Will you please leave?"

"Of course," he said politely, and shut the door after him.

Amanda stared at the closed door. She wanted to roll over on her belly, clutch her pillow and weep. Instead, she grabbed the pillows, first his, then hers, and hurled them at the door.

What a fool she'd been, thinking this had been anything more than sex to Nick. And what a fool she'd been, thinking she was in love with him. She was far too intelligent to fall for a man like Nicholas al Rashid. What woman would want a man who could never love anyone as much as he loved himself?

This, she thought grimly, this was what he'd been after, all along. To sleep with her and add another conquest to his list.

She hadn't been a fool, she'd been an idiot.

No wonder he'd called off their wager. He'd known she'd sleep with him. After all, he was irresistible. He thought so, anyway. But why saddle himself with keeping her, or having her, or whatever the hell you called the responsibility a man like that assumed when he took a mistress?

Look at how easily he'd rid himself of Deanna. No second thoughts. No hesitation.

Amanda sucked in her breath. "Stop it," she said.

She rose quickly, stepped over the little pile of silky clothing that lay on the carpet. She wouldn't think about how Nick had undressed her, how they'd barely closed the door before he'd been pulling off his clothes and hers, arousing her so fast, so completely, that they'd only just made it to the bed before he was inside her again.

Don't look, she told herself hotly, not at the clothes, not at the mirror...

Too late.

She'd already turned, sought out her reflection in the glass and found a stranger. A woman with tousled hair and a kiss-swollen mouth. With the marks of a man's possession on her body.

There, on her mouth. At the juncture of shoulder and throat. On her thighs.

Amanda trembled.

Nick hadn't hurt her, but he'd marked her. Marked her as his own. No man had ever done that. Well, there'd only been one other man. Her husband. And his idea of sex had been something done quickly, almost clinically. Like—like brushing your teeth. That was how she'd assumed it was supposed to be. A couple of kisses, a fast, slightly uncomfortable penetration.

How could she have known that making love could be wild one moment and tender the next? That nothing in the world could compare to what happened when you spun out of control in the arms of your lover, and he came apart in yours?

Tears blurred her vision. She swung away from the mirror and hurried into the bathroom.

What was done, was done. She didn't regret it. Why should she? she thought, as she stepped into the shower. Actually, she owed Nick a debt of gratitude for the night they'd spent together. He'd taught her things about herself, about her capacity for passion and pleasure, she might never have known.

She turned off the water, reached for a towel and dried herself briskly.

This wasn't some Victorian melodrama. She wasn't a virgin whose innocence had been sullied. Neither was she a woman who could possibly fall in love with a man in, what, forty-eight hours? She'd only told herself that because facing the truth—that she'd wanted to sleep with a stranger—had been too difficult.

"Silly," she murmured, and looked into the mirror again and smiled at her self-confident, coolly-contained reflection.

She dressed quickly in a silk T-shirt and jeans and went down the stairs. Her mother was having coffee in the breakfast room.

"Good morning, darling," Marta said. "Did you sleep well?"

"Very well," Amanda replied. She could feel herself blushing and she went straight to the buffet and poured herself coffee. "Where's Jonas?"

Marta smiled. "Oh, he was up hours ago. He's outside somewhere, probably driving his men crazy." She took a sip of coffee. "Have you seen Nick?"

"No," Amanda said quickly. Too quickly. She saw her

mother's eyebrows lift. "I mean, how could I have seen him? He's probably still sleeping."

"He isn't," Marta said slowly. "Sweetie, he had a phone call a few minutes ago. I don't know what it was about, but he said he had to leave for home right away."

"Ah." Amanda smiled brightly, as if the news that he hadn't even wanted to say goodbye to her was meaningless. "I see. Well, that's no problem. I'll call the airport and book myself a seat—"

Strong hands closed on her shoulders. She gasped as Nick swung her toward him. His eyes were dark, his expression grim.

"Is that what you think of me?" he said coldly. "That I'd leave you without a word?"

"Yes," she said. Her voice trembled, but her chin was raised in defiance. "That's exactly what I thought."

Nick's mouth twisted. He wrapped his fingers around her wrist and started for the door. "Excuse us, please, Marta." He spoke politely, but there was no mistaking that the words weren't a request, they were a command.

"Amanda?" her mother said.

"It's all right, Mother."

It wasn't. Did Nick think he had to add to her humiliation by dragging her after him like a parcel? Amanda wrenched free of his grasp as soon as they were in the hall.

"Just who in hell do you think you are?" she said in an angry whisper. "Strolling out of my bedroom without so much as a look. Making some pathetic excuse so you can fly back to New York. Grabbing me as if you owned me, right in front of my mother—"

"I'm not flying back to New York."

"Frankly, Lord Rashid, I don't give a damn where you're—"

"I'm flying to Quidar. My father's having political problems. Serious ones."

Amanda folded her arms. As excuses went, this was a good one but then, a man who was the son of an absolute monarch wouldn't be reduced to pleading absence because of a sick grandmother.

"It's the truth."

It probably was. Nick might not have much loyalty to the women who warmed his bed, but she had no doubt that he was loyal to his king and to his kingdom.

"I'm sorry to hear it," she said stiffly.

"I'll be gone a week. Or a month. I can't be certain."

"You don't have to explain yourself to me, Your Highness."

"Dammit," Nick growled, clasping her elbows and lifting her to her toes, "what's the matter with you?"

"Nothing's the matter with me."

"Don't lie to me, Amanda."

"Why not? I asked you that same question a little while ago. Remember? 'What's the matter?' I said, and you gave me the answer I just gave you."

"Yeah, well, I lied." His hands tightened on her. "You want an answer? All right. I'll give you one." He took a deep breath. "I was afraid."

"Of what?"

"Of..." He let go of her, ran his hands through his hair. Color striped his cheekbones. "I don't know." He hesitated. "Dammit, I was afraid of you."

"The Lion of the Desert? Afraid of me?" She laughed and took a step back. "Nice try, Your Loftiness, but—"

Nick pulled her into his arms. "This isn't a game! I'm trying to tell you what happened to me this morning. When I kissed you, when I knew it was time to leave you..." His throat constricted. "Amanda." He drew her close, cupped her face and looked into her eyes. "Come with me."

"Come with you?"

"Yes. I don't want to leave you. I *can't* leave you." He kissed her, then looked into her eyes again. "Come with me, sweetheart."

"No!" Marta Baron's voice rang out like the hour bell from a campanile. Amanda spun around and saw her mother, standing in the entrance to the breakfast room. "Amanda, darling, don't go. Please. I have this feeling…"

"Amanda," Nick said softly, "I want you with me."

What was the good of pretending? Amanda turned to the man she loved. "And I want to be with you."

An hour later, they were in the air, en route to an ancient kingdom where the word of the Lion of the Desert was law.

CHAPTER ELEVEN

NICK wasted no time once Amanda said she'd go with him.

They were in the air in record time. Shortly after takeoff, he took out his cell phone and made a flurry of calls. Then he sat back and took Amanda's hand.

"Abdul will meet us in Quidar."

"You've asked Abdul to fly to Quidar?"

"Yes, of course. He's familiar with the situation back home. He's worked with me for years, and before me—"

"I know. Your father, and your grandfather, too."

"Exactly." Nick brought her hand to his mouth and kissed it. "You don't like Abdul, do you?"

"I don't know him well enough not to like him. It's just...I get the feeling he doesn't like me." Amanda looked at their joined hands, then at Nick. "I doubt if he'll be very happy when he sees you've brought me with you."

"He's my secretary. He's not required to think about anything other than his duties. My private life isn't his concern."

"You don't really believe that," she said with a little laugh. "Everything about you is Abdul's concern."

"No, sweetheart, you're wrong. The duties of the secretary to the heir to the throne are very clear. It is—"

"—the custom," Amanda said, more sharply than she'd intended.

"Yes. Such things are very important in my country."

"Customs. Duties. And rules."

"Sweetheart, don't look like that."

"Like what?" she said, and even she could hear the petulance in her voice.

Nick put his arm around her. "You'll like Quidar." He smiled. "At least, I hope you will."

145

Amanda sighed and let herself lean into him. "How long is the flight?"

"Too long for us to try to make it in this plane. We'd have to stop for refueling at least twice, and I don't want to waste the time. We'll board a commercial jet in Dallas. And…" He glanced at his watch. "And twelve hours from now, we'll step down on the soil of my homeland."

The soil of his homeland. A place called Quidar. A country so remote, so ancient, that it had only opened its borders to outsiders under the rule of Nick's father…

Amanda sat up straight. "Nick. I just realized I don't have my passport."

He smiled and reached for her hand. "That's not a problem."

"But it is. They won't let me out of the country without—'

"You only need a passport to get back into the States. And, of course, to enter Quidar." He tugged gently on her hand and drew her close to his side. "You forget, sweetheart. You're traveling with me. I'll see to it you'll have no difficulty reentering your country." His smile tilted. "And I can guarantee you'll be allowed to enter mine."

"But…"

She hesitated, trying to find the right words. His explanation was simple. What wasn't simple was the sudden panic she felt at the thought of leaving everything familiar and going into the unknown with a man she hardly knew.

Without a passport, she'd be totally dependent on Nick. And she knew what that kind of dependency could do to a woman after seeing the mistakes of her mother's two marriages and experiencing the problems of her own.

"I'd just feel better if I had my passport." She tried to soften the words with a smile. "It would seem strange to travel abroad without—"

The phone beside Nick buzzed. He picked it up.

"Yes?" he said brusquely, and then he frowned. "Please tell my father I'm on my way. No, no, I'm glad you called.

Yes. I understand.'' He put the phone down slowly, his face troubled.

''Nick? What is it?''

A muscle knotted in his cheek, a sign she'd come to know meant he was worried.

''That was my father's physician. My father hasn't been well. And now this added stress…'' He fell silent, then cleared his throat. ''Well,'' he said briskly, ''what were we talking about?''

Amanda twined her fingers through his. ''You were explaining why I didn't need my passport.''

''And you were explaining why you did.''

''Well, I was wrong.'' She brought his hand to her face and pressed it to her cheek. ''Ah, the joys of traveling with the Lion of the Desert,'' she said lightly.

Nick looked deep into her eyes. ''I'm not the Lion of the Desert when I'm with you,'' he said, and he drew her into his arms and kissed her.

They changed planes in Dallas and settled into the first-class cabin of the commercial flight that would take them to Quidar.

The flight attendant who brought them champagne recognized Nick and dropped a quick curtsy. ''Your Highness. How nice to have you with us again.''

She turned brightly curious eyes on Amanda. Nick took her hand.

''Thank you,'' he said politely, and asked something inconsequential about the projected flight.

''Forgive me for not introducing you,'' he said softly when they were alone again.

''That's all right.'' It wasn't. Amanda knew how stiff her words must sound. ''You're under no obligation to—''

''Sweetheart.'' Nick leaned close and brushed his lips over hers. ''I'm only protecting you from reading about yourself in tomorrow's papers.''

''Are you serious?''

''Deadly serious. I've no reason to distrust the attendant,

but why take chances? There's a heavy market in celebrity gossip."

"Yes, but..." But you're not a celebrity, she'd almost said because she didn't think of him that way. He was a man to her, a man with whom she'd fallen in love, but to the rest of the world, he was the stuff of tabloid headlines. She sighed and rubbed her forehead against his sleeve. "It must be awful," she murmured. "Never having any privacy, never being able to let down your guard."

"That's the way it's been most of my life...until now." Nick put his hand under Amanda's chin and smiled into her eyes. "I've let down my guard with you, sweetheart."

"Have you?" she said softly.

He nodded. "I've told you more about myself than I've ever told anyone. And I've never taken anyone with me to Quidar."

Her heart leaped at what he'd said.

"No one?"

"No one," he said solemnly. "You're the first." He leaned closer. "The first woman I've ever—"

"Dom Pérignon or Taittinger, Your Highness?" the flight attendant asked cheerfully.

"It doesn't matter," Nick said, his eyes locked on Amanda's face. "What we drink doesn't matter at all."

They ate dinner, though Amanda was too wound up to do more than pick at hers. What would her first glimpse of Nick's homeland be like? What would his father think about her being with him? What would Nick tell him?

She stole a glance at Nick. He'd opened his omnipresent briefcase and read through some papers. Then he'd reached for the telephone and made several calls, sounding more purposeful, even imperial, with each conversation. He even looked different, his mouth and jaw seemingly set in sterner lines, as if he were changing from the man who'd made such passionate love to her into the man who was the heir to the throne of his country.

Her throat tightened.

"Nick?" she said as he hit the disconnect button.

He frowned, blinked, stared at her as if, just for a moment, he'd all but forgotten her presence.

"Yes," he said a little impatiently, and then he seemed to give himself a little shake. "Sorry, sweetheart." He put his arm around her, drew her close. "I wanted to take care of some things before we land."

"Have you told your father that you're bringing me with you?"

Nick hesitated. "Yes, I told him."

"And?"

"And what?"

"And what did he say?"

"He said he hoped you were even more beautiful than Schehcrazade," Nick said lightly. "I assured him that you were."

"I don't understand."

"There's an ancient legend that says Scheherazade visited Zamidar and the Ivory Palace centuries ago."

Amanda gave him a puzzled smile. "The same Scheherazade who saved her neck by telling that sultan all those stories?"

"The very one." Nick smiled. "Unfortunately, she didn't tell any tall talcs whcn shc visitcd thc monarch of Quidar."

She grinncd. "Your grandpa, no doubt, a zillion times removed. Well, why didn't she? Tell him stories, I mean."

"There was no reason."

"Ah." Amanda tucked her head against Nick's shoulder. "Nice to know."

"Hmm?"

"That the monarch of Quidar didn't have the power to..." She sliced her hand across her neck and Nick laughed.

"Of coursc hc did."

"He did?"

"Yes." He tipped her chin up and lightly folded his hand around her throat. "He still can," he said softly. "The rulers of my country have always held life-and-death power over those who cross into the kingdom."

"Oh." Her heart skipped a beat. "Does that include the heir to the throne?"

Nick smiled into her eyes, then brushed his mouth over hers. "I can do anything I want with you, once we reach Quidar."

His tone was light, his smile gentle. Still, even though she knew it was foolish, she couldn't help feeling a little uneasy.

"That sounds ominous," she said, and managed a smile in return.

Nick kissed her again. "Come on. Put your head on my shoulder. That's it. Now, love, shut your eyes and get some sleep."

She let him draw her head down, let him gently kiss her eyes closed.

He could do anything he wanted with her, he'd said. And what he wanted was to bring her to the Ivory Palace and call her his love.

They changed planes in Paris, going from the commercial jet to a smaller plane, similar to the one they'd flown to Espada. It, too, bore the emblem of Quidar on the fuselage.

Butterflies were beginning to swarm in Amanda's stomach.

"How much longer until we reach your country?" she asked.

"Just a few hours." Nick took her hand. "Nervous?"

"A little," she admitted.

Why wouldn't she be? She was flying to an unknown place to meet a king. The king was Nick's father, and yes, Nick was a prince—but the Nick she knew was only a man, and her lover.

So long as she kept sight of that, she'd be fine.

The final leg of their journey went quickly. Nick held her hand but spoke to her hardly at all. He seemed—what was the right word? Preoccupied. Even distant. But he would be, considering that all his energies would have to be centered on the problems that had brought him home.

The plane touched down, coasted to a seamless stop. Nick rose to his feet, held out his hand and she took it.

"Ready?" he said softly, and she nodded, even though her heart was pounding, and let him lead her to the exit door.

Blinking, she stepped out into bright sunlight.

All during the past few hours, she'd tried to envision what she'd find at the end of their long journey. She'd conjured up an endless strip of concrete spearing across a barren desert.

What she saw was a small, modern airport, graceful palm trees and, just ahead, the skyline of a small city etched in icy-white relief against a cerulean sky. A line of limousines stood waiting nearby, but she'd lived in New York long enough to have seen strings of big cars before.

The only really startling sight was at their feet, where a dozen men, all wearing desert robes, knelt in obeisance, their foreheads pressed to the concrete runway.

Amanda shot a glance at Nick. His face seemed frozen, as if an ancient, evil wizard had changed him into a stranger.

One of the men stirred. "My Lord Rashid," he said, "we bid you welcome."

"English?" Amanda whispered.

Nick drew her beside him. "English," he said softly, a touch of amusement edging his voice. "The Royal Council usually uses it when addressing me. It's their very polite way of reminding me that I am not truly of Quidar."

"I don't understand."

"You couldn't understand," he said wryly, "without roots that go back three thousand years."

He stepped forward, thanked the council members for the greeting and told them to rise. He didn't mention her or introduce her, but she felt the cold glances of the men, saw their stern expressions.

A shudder raced along her skin.

"You didn't introduce me," she said to Nick as their limousine and the others raced toward the city.

"I will, when the time is right."

"Won't those men wonder who I am?"

"They know you're with me, Amanda. That's sufficient."

The shudder came again but stronger this time.

"Nick?" She took a deep breath, let it out slowly. "Nick, I've been thinking. Maybe...maybe I shouldn't have come with you."

"Don't be ridiculous."

"I mean it. I want to go back."

"No."

"What do you mean, no? I'm telling you—"

"And I said, no."

Amanda swung toward Nick. He was staring straight ahead, arms folded, jaw set.

"Don't speak to me that way," she said carefully. "I don't like it."

Seconds passed. Then he turned toward her, muttered something under his breath and took her in his arms. "Sweetheart, forgive me. I have a lot on my mind. Of course you can leave if that's what you really want. I'm hoping it isn't. I want you here, with me."

"I want to be with you, too. It's just that...I think—"

Nick stopped her with a kiss. "Remember what I once told you? Stop thinking."

She knew he was teasing, but the throwaway remark still angered her. "Dammit," she said, pushing free of his arms, "that is such a miserably chauvinistic—"

"Okay. So I'm a chauvinist." Nick put his hand under her chin and gently turned her face away from him. "Chew me out later, but for now, wouldn't you like to take a look at the Ivory Palace?"

"No," she said tersely. "I'm not the least bit..."

Oh, but she was.

The Ivory Palace rose from the dusty white city of Zamidar like a fairy-tale castle. Ornate, brightly polished gates swung slowly open, admitting them to a cobblestone courtyard. Flowers bloomed everywhere, their colorful heads nodding gently in a light breeze. Beyond the palace, jagged mountain peaks soared toward the sky.

Their limousine stopped at the foot of a flight of marble steps. Amanda reached for Nick's hand as a servant opened the door, then all but fell to the ground as they stepped from the car. Nick didn't give any sign that he'd noticed. He didn't seem to notice the servants who lined the steps as they mounted them, either, even though each one bowed to him.

It was, Amanda thought dazedly, like being passed from link to link along a human chain that led, at last, into the vast entry hall of the palace itself, where Abdul, shiny black suit and all, waited to greet them.

Until that moment, she hadn't realized how good it would be to see a familiar face.

"Abdul," she said, holding out her hand, "how nice to—"

"My lord," the old man said, and bowed. "Welcome home."

"Thank you, Abdul. Is my father here?"

"Your father has been called away from the palace. He says to tell you he is happy you have returned and that he will dine with you this evening. I trust you had a pleasant journey."

"Pleasant but tiring." Nick gathered Amanda close to his side. "Ms Benning and I will want to rest."

"Everything is in readiness, sire."

"You will call me when you know my father is en route."

"Of course, Lord Rashid. May I get you something to eat?"

"Not now, thank you. Just have a tray sent to my quarters in an hour or so."

"Certainly, my lord."

Abdul bowed. Nick stepped past him and led Amanda through the hall, past walls of pink-veined marble and closed doors trimmed with gold leaf, to a massive staircase. Halfway to the second floor, she peered over her shoulder.

"Nick?"

"Hmm?"

"He's still bent in half."

"Who?"

"Abdul. Aren't you going to tell him to stand up?"

"No."

"For heaven's sake—"

Nick's arm tightened around her. "Keep walking."

"Yes, but—"

"There is no 'yes, but.' This is Quidar. Things are different here. The customs—"

"Damn your customs! That old man—"

She gasped as Nick swung her into his arms, strode down the hall, elbowed open the door to one of the rooms, stepped inside and kicked it shut.

"Watch what you say to me, woman," he growled, and dumped her on her feet.

"No, *you* watch what you say to me!" Amanda slapped her hands on her hips. "Who do you think you are, talking to me like that?"

"I'm the Lion of the Desert. And you would do well to remember it."

"My God," she said with a little laugh, "you're serious!"

"Completely serious."

"So much for what you said on the plane. About not being the Lion of the Desert when you're with me."

"My private life isn't the same as my public life," Nick said sharply. "Those customs you think so little of matter a great deal to my people."

"They're antiquated and foolish."

"Perhaps they are, but they're also revered. If I were to tell Abdul not to bow to me, especially on Quidaran soil, he would be humiliated."

"I suppose that's why you left that lineup of slaves standing on their heads outside the palace."

"They're not slaves," Nick said, his voice cold. "They're servants."

"And you like having servants."

"Dammit!" He marched away, turned and marched back. "It's an honor to serve in the royal household."

Amanda gave a derisive snort.

"You might not understand that, but it's true. And yes, that's exactly why I didn't stop them from bowing to me. Only my father, the members of his council and, someday, the woman I take as my wife, will not have to bow to me."

"I'm sure that will thrill her."

Nick grabbed Amanda's arms, yanked her against him and kissed her.

"You can't solve every problem that way," she gasped, twisting her face from his, but he caught hold of her chin, brought her mouth to his and kissed her again and again until her lips softened and clung to his.

"I don't want to talk about Quidar," he said softly, "or its rules and customs. Not right now."

"But we have to—"

"We don't," he murmured, and slipped his tongue between her lips.

She moaned, lifted her hands and curled them into his shirt. "Nick—"

"Amanda." He smiled and kissed her throat.

"Nick, stop that. I'm serious."

"So am I. I'm seriously interested in knowing which you'd rather do—debate the historical and social validity of Quidaran culture or take a bath with Quidar's heir to the throne."

She drew back in his encircling arms and tried to scowl, but Nick's eyes glinted with laughter and, after a few seconds, she couldn't help laughing, too.

"You're impossible, O Lion of the Desert."

"On the contrary, Ms. Benning. I'm just a man who believes in cleanliness."

She laughed again, but her laughter faded as he began unbuttoning her blouse.

"What are you doing?" she said with a catch in her voice.

"I'm doing what I've ached to do for hours," he whispered. Slowly, his eyes never leaving hers, he undressed her. Then he stepped back and looked at her, his gaze as hot as a caress. "My beautiful Amanda." He reached for her, gathered her against him until she could feel the race of his heart against hers. "Tell me what you want," he said as he had done once before, and she moaned and showed him with her mouth, her hands, her heart.

Nick lifted her into his arms and carried her into an enormous bathroom, to a sunken marble tub the size of a small swimming pool. Water spilled into the tub from a winged gold swan; perfume-scented steam drifted into the air like wisps of fog.

Amanda sighed as he stepped down into the tub with her still in his arms. "Mmm. Someone's already run our bath. How nice."

"Uh-huh." Nick lowered her gently to her feet, linked his hands at the base of her spine. "Another little benefit you get when you're known as a lion."

She laughed softly and stroked her hands down his chest. "Lions are pussycats in disguise."

Nick caught his breath as she curled her fingers around him. "I've always liked cats," he said thickly. He drew her against him with one arm, slipped his hand between her thighs. "I like to hear them purr when I stroke their silken fur."

Amanda caught her breath. "Nick. Oh, Nick…"

He stepped back, sat on the edge of the tub, then drew her between his legs. "Your breasts are so beautiful," he whispered, and bent his head to taste them. "I could feast on them forever."

I could love you forever, she thought. *I could be yours, Nicholas al Rashid. I could—*

He clasped her hips, drew her to him. "Come to me, sweetheart," he said softly.

She put her hands on his shoulders. Then, slowly, she lowered herself on him, impaled herself on him, took him deep into her silken softness until his velvet heat filled her. Nick groaned, lifted her legs, wrapped them around his waist.

"Amanda." He cupped her face in his hand, kissed her deeply. "My beloved."

My beloved. The words had the sweetness, the softness, of a promise. Her heart filled with joy.

"You'll be mine forever," he said quietly. "I'll never let you leave me."

"I'll never want to leave you," she said in a broken whisper, and then he moved, moved again until she was clinging to his shoulders and sobbing his name.

She collapsed in his arms as he drove into her one last time. They stayed that way, she with her face buried against him, he with his arms tightly around her. At last he stirred. He kissed her mouth, her breasts, swung her into his arms, carried her to his bed and held her until she drifted into exhausted sleep.

When she awoke, night held the room in moonlit darkness. She was alone in the bed; Nick was gone and she smiled, imagining him talking with his father, telling him what he had told her, that he loved her, that she would be with him forever.

Tonight, she thought, tonight she would say the words.

"I love you, Nicholas al Rashid," she whispered into the silence. "I love you with all my heart."

A knock sounded at the door.

"Nick?" she said happily. But Nick wouldn't be so formal. Ah. Of course. He'd told Abdul to have a tray sent to his rooms. "Just a minute."

She reached for the lamp on the table beside the bed and switched it on. What was protocol in such a situation? She had no robe. Would it be all right to stay where she was, wrapped in the silk sheet like a mummy? Was that the custom for the woman who was the beloved of the Lion of the Desert? The woman who would spend her life with—

The door swung open. Amanda grabbed the sheet and dragged it up to her chin. "Excuse me. I didn't…Abdul?"

The little man stood in the doorway, but he didn't look quite so little now. He stood straight, arms folded, a look of disdain on his face. Two robed figures flanked him—two tall, muscular figures whose stance mimicked his.

A whisper of fear sighed along Amanda's skin, but she spoke with cool authority. "Is it the custom to enter a bedroom before you're given permission?"

"You are to come with me, Ms. Benning."

"Come where? Has Lord Rashid sent for me?"

"I act on his command."

That wasn't the answer to her question. Amanda licked her lips. "Where is he? Where is the prince?"

The old man jerked his head and the robed figures advanced toward the bed.

"Dammit, Abdul! Did you hear what I said? When I tell Lord Rashid about this—"

"Lord Rashid has given orders that you are to be moved to different quarters. It is your choice if you come willingly or if you do not."

Amanda's heart banged into her throat. "Moved?"

"That is correct."

"But where—where am I to be moved?"

The old man smiled. She had never seen him smile before.

"To the harem, Ms. Benning, where you will be kept in readiness for the pleasure of the Lion of the Desert for so long as he may wish it."

CHAPTER TWELVE

AMANDA shrieked like a wild woman.

She cursed and kicked, and was rewarded by a grunt when her foot connected with a groin, but she was no match for the two burly men.

They subdued her easily, wrapped her in the sheet and carried her through the palace as if she were an oversize package, one man supporting her knees, the other holding her shoulders. Abdul headed the little procession up stairs and down, through endless corridors.

She kept screaming and kicking, but it did no good.

Her captors ignored her, and though they passed other people in the halls, nobody took notice. Nobody cared. As frightened as she'd been when Abdul's henchmen grabbed her, that was the most terrifying realization of all.

Finally, the men came to a stop before a massive door. Abdul snapped out an order, the door groaned open, and Amanda's captors stepped across the threshold and dumped her, unceremoniously, on the floor.

Abdul clapped his hands and the men backed from the room. The door swung shut. Amanda, shaking as much with rage as fear, kicked free of the sheet and sat up. She looked at Abdul, standing over her. He'd traded his shiny black suit for a long, heavily embroidered robe; his face was expressionless.

"You horrible old man!" Panting, weeping, she struggled to her feet, clutching the sheet around her. "You'll rot in hell for this, Abdul, do you hear me? When I tell the sheikh what you've done to me..."

"I have done nothing to you, Ms. Benning. My orders to

my men were very clear. They were not to hurt you, and they have not.''

''They trussed me up like a—a Christmas gift!''

An evil smile creased Abdul's leathery face. ''More like a birthday gift, I think.''

''What's that supposed to mean?''

''All will be explained in due time.''

''Listen, you miserable son of a—''

''Women do not use obscenities in Quidar,'' the old man said sharply. ''It is against our rules and customs.''

''Oh, no. No, that's not the custom. Brutalizing women. Kidnapping them. *That's* the custom.'' She hung on to the sheet with one hand and pointed a trembling finger at Abdul. ''You're finished. I just hope you know that. When Lord Rashid hears what you've done—''

''There is food and drink in the next room, and clothing, as well.''

''I don't care what's in the next room!''

''That is your prerogative,'' Abdul said calmly. ''At any rate, Lord Rashid will be with you shortly.''

''You mean Lord Rashid will be with *you,* you bastard! And when he does, he'll have your head.''

Abdul laughed. First a smile, now a laugh? Amanda knew that wasn't good. She was more frightened than ever, but she'd have died rather than let the old bastard know it, so she drew herself up and glared at him.

''What's so funny?''

''You are, Ms. Benning. You see, it was Lord Rashid who instructed me to have you brought here.''

''Don't be ridiculous. Nick would never...''

Abdul turned his back to her, walked to the door and opened it. Amanda made a leap for it, but the door swung shut with a thud. She heard the lock click as the bolt slid home, but she grabbed the knob anyway, pulled, tugged...

The door didn't move.

For a moment, for a lifetime, she stood absolutely still, not moving, not blinking, not even breathing.

"No," she finally whispered, "no…"

Her voice rose to a terrified wail. She fell against the door, pounded it with her fists. The sheet she'd wrapped around herself fell, forgotten, to the floor.

"Abdul," she shouted, "old man, you can't do this!"

But he could. The silence on the other side of the door was confirmation of that. Her screams faded to sobs of despair. She gave the door one last jarring blow, then slid to the carpet.

God, what was happening? What was Abdul up to? What had he meant when he said Nick had told him to bring her here? It wasn't true. It couldn't be. And that nonsense about taking her to the harem. Harems didn't exist anymore, except in bad movies.

Okay. She had to calm down instead of panicking. Abdul had done this to frighten her, but she wouldn't let that happen. She'd take deep breaths. Slow and easy. Breathe in, breathe out. Good. She could feel her pulse rate slowing. It was only a matter of time before Nick realized she was missing. He'd come looking for her. He'd find her—

"Ms. Benning?"

Amanda jerked her head up. A dark-haired woman stood over her, holding a pale green caftan over her arm.

"Would you like to put this on, Ms. Benning? Or would you prefer to choose something for yourself?"

"Thank God!" Amanda clutched at the sheet and shot to her feet. "Look, there's been some horrible mistake. You have to get word to Nick—to Lord Rashid—"

"My name is Sara."

Her name was Sara? Who cared about her name?

"Sara. Sara, you must find the sheikh and tell him—"

"Let me help you with this," Sara said pleasantly. "Just let go of that…what is that anyway?" She gave Amanda a little smile. "It looks like a sheet."

"It *is* a sheet! Two men came into my room—into Lord Rashid's quarters—and—"

"Raise your arms, Ms. Benning. Now let me pull this over your head. That's it. Oh, yes. The pale green is perfect for you.'' Sara smoothed her hand over Amanda's hair. "Such a lovely color," she said, "but so short. Well, it will grow out, and when it does, I'll plait it with flowers. Or perhaps Lord Rashid would prefer emeralds—''

Amanda slapped the woman's hand away. "I'm not a doll! And I'm not going to be here long enough for you to plait my hair with anything.''

"I'm sure you will, Ms. Benning," Sara said soothingly. "A favorite may be kept for months. Years, perhaps.''

"Dammit, I've no intention of becoming a 'favorite'. If you know what's good for you, you'll find Lord Rashid and tell him—''

"Tell him what, Amanda?''

Amanda spun around. Nick stood in the doorway.

"Nick! Oh, thank God you've…''

Her words trailed to silence. It *was* Nick, wasn't it? He looked so different. No jeans, no T-shirt. No carefully tailored suit and tie. Instead, he wore a flowing white robe trimmed in gold. He looked exactly as he'd looked in the *Gossip* photo. Tall. Proud. Magnificently masculine…

And heart-stoppingly dangerous.

He looked past her to Sara, who had dropped to the floor at the sound of his voice. "Leave us," he said brusquely.

Sara scrambled to her feet and backed quickly from the room.

Nick shut the door and folded his arms. "Well? What did you wish Sara to tell me?''

"Why—why, about this. About what Abdul did to me…''

Amanda fell silent. He was looking at her so strangely. She wanted his arms around her, his heart beating against hers. She wanted him to hold her close and tell her that this was all a terrible mistake or a bad joke gone wrong. She wanted anything but for him to stand as he was, unmoving, a stranger with a stern face and cold eyes.

"Nick?" Her voice was a dry whisper. "Nick, what's going on?''

Nick almost laughed. This woman who had slept with him,

who had stolen his heart and sold its contents to the world, wanted to know what was going on. She said it with such innocence, too—but then, why wouldn't she?

She had no way of knowing that Abdul, with his usual efficiency, had managed to get a copy of the lead article in next week's *Gossip* and that he'd brought it to Nick, trembling as he did, wringing his hands and whispering, "Lord Rashid, the American woman has betrayed you."

"I had you moved to new quarters," Nick said with a tight smile. "Don't you like them? This is the oldest part of the Ivory Palace. I thought it would appeal to you, considering your supposed interest in interior design." He eased away from the door, strolled around the room, pausing at an intricately carved chair, then at a table inlaid with tiny blocks of colored woods. "These things are very old and valuable. There's great interest in them at Christie's, but I've no wish to sell—"

"Dammit!" Amanda strode after him, hands clenched, her terror rapidly giving way to anger. "I'm not interested in tables and chairs."

"No. You most certainly are not."

He'd tossed the words out like a barb, but she decided to ignore them. What she wanted were answers, and she wanted them fast.

"I want to know why you had me brought here. Why you let Abdul and his—his goons wrap me up like laundry, dump me in a heap and lock the door!"

Nick turned toward her. "They brought you here because it is the custom."

"The custom. Well, damn the custom! If I hear that word one more time…" She took a breath and reminded herself to stay calm. "What custom?"

"The Quidaran custom, of course."

God, he was infuriating. That insulting little smile. That I'm-so-clever glint in his eyes. Staying calm wasn't going to be easy.

"Everything is a Quidaran custom," she said coldly. "But if abusing women falls into that category, I'm out of here."

Nick's brows lifted. "No one has abused you, Amanda."

"No? Well, what do you call it, then? Your thugs burst into my room, dragged me out of my bed—"

"It is *my* room," he said softly. "And my bed."

"I know that. I only meant—"

"And I no longer wanted you in either one."

His words skewered her heart and put a stop to the anger raging through her.

"But you said…." Her voice trembled. She stopped and took a deep breath. "You said you wanted me to be yours forever."

Yes. Oh, yes, he thought, he had. The memory was almost more painful than he could bear. He knew it would be years—a lifetime—before he managed to put it aside.

What a fool he'd been to want her. To call her his beloved. To have told his father he'd found the missing half of his heart, the part of himself each man searches for, without knowing it, from the moment he first draws breath….

"Nick." Her voice was filled with pleading. "Nick, please, tell me this is all some awful joke."

"Did I say I wanted you with me forever?" He smiled coolly, lifted his shoulders in an expressive shrug. "It was a figure of speech."

Amanda stared at him. "A figure of speech?"

"Of course." Nick forced a smile to his lips. "'Forever' is a poetic concept." He walked slowly toward her, still smiling, and stopped when they were only inches apart. "Don't look so worried," he said softly. "It won't be forever, but it will be a long time before I tire of you."

"Please," she said shakily, "stop this. You're scaring me. I don't—I don't know what you're talking about."

Slowly, he wrapped his hand around the nape of her neck and tugged her to him. She stumbled, put out her hands and laid them against his chest.

"Don't you?"

"No. I don't understand why you had me brought here. I don't even know where I am. The oldest part of the palace, you said."

"Indeed." Nick's eyes dropped to her mouth. Her sweet, beautiful, lying mouth. "I had you brought here because it's where you belong." His gaze lifted, caught hers. "You were my birthday present, darling. Remember?"

She stared at him. "A birthday...? But that was just a joke. You misunderstood what Dawn meant—"

"Nonsense."

"It's not nonsense. I explained everything. That I was a designer. That Dawn only wanted me to do your apartment."

Nick laughed softly. "You're a designer all right. Your 'design' was to worm your way into my life." He reached out a finger, traced the outline of her mouth with its tip. "What you are is a man's dream come true. And now you're right where you belong." His smile was slow and sexy. "Welcome to the harem, Amanda."

She jerked back as if the touch of his hand had scorched her. "What?"

Nick smiled, bent his head, brushed his mouth over hers. She didn't move, didn't respond, didn't so much as breathe.

"Didn't Abdul tell you?"

"He said something about a harem, yes. But I thought..."

His hand cupped her throat, his thumb seeming to measure the fluttering race of her pulse.

"You don't... Harems don't exist," she said quickly. "Not anymore. That's all changed."

"This is the kingdom of Quidar. Nothing changes here unless the king—or his heir—wishes it."

"Do you really expect me to believe you—you have a harem? A bunch of women you keep as—as sexual slaves?" She gave a weak laugh. "Honestly, Nick—"

"Do you recall what I told you about your use of that word, 'slaves'?" Nick cupped her shoulders, drew her stiff body to his. "I assure you, it's an honor to warm my bed."

"This isn't funny, dammit. Surely you can't think I'd—"

She gasped as his mouth covered hers in a long, drugging kiss.

"I must admit, I found you enjoyable," he said calmly, when he finally lifted his head and looked into her eyes. "You have a beautiful body. A lovely face. And you've proven an apt pupil in the ways to pleasure a man."

Her face whitened. She tried to pull free of him, but his hands dug into her flesh.

"So, I've decided to keep you. For a while, at any rate." She cried out as he thrust his hand into her hair and tugged her head back so that her face was raised to his. "Don't look so shocked, darling. You'll enjoy it, I promise. And think of the excellent material you'll have to sell when I finally tire of you and send you home."

"Sell? What 'material'? What are you—"

"Damn you!" Nick's smile vanished. "Don't pull that wide-eyed look on me! You were too impetuous. If only you'd waited…but I suppose you thought you'd be back in New York, safe and sound, before the next issue of that rag hit the streets."

"What rag? I have no idea what—"

"'My Days and Nights with Nicholas al Rashid'," Nick said coldly. He thrust her from him hard enough so she stumbled. "Such a trite title, Amanda. Or does *Gossip* write its own headlines?"

Amanda stared at him in disbelief. "What has *Gossip* to do with this?"

Nick's mouth thinned. He reached inside his robe, took out a sheet of paper and shoved it at her. She gave it a bewildered glance.

"What is this?"

"Take it," he said grimly. "Go on."

She looked down at the paper he'd pushed into her hand. It was a copy of what appeared to be an article bylined, "Special to *Gossip,* from Amanda Benning."

"'My Days and Nights with…'" she read in a shaky whisper. Her face paled, and she looked up. "Nick, for God's sake, this is a hoax. Surely you don't think I'd write something like this."

"Read it."

His voice flicked over her like a whip. Amanda looked at the paper and moistened her lips. "'My Days and Nights with...'" Color rushed into her face. "'With the sexy sheikh...'" She looked at him again. "Whoever wrote this is talking about—about—"

"About what it's like to make love to..." Nick's jaw tightened. "What was the phrase? Ah, yes. I remember now. "To 'an elegant, exciting savage'." His mouth twisted. "I've been called a lot of things, Ms. Benning, but never that."

"Nick. Listen to me. I'd never do this. Never! How could you even think...? Someone else did it. Wrote this—this thing and used my—"

"Read the final paragraph," he commanded. "Aloud."

She drew a shaky breath. "'As it turns out, the Lion of the Desert is...'" She stopped and lifted imploring eyes to his. "No," she whispered. "Nick, I can't—"

"'As it turns out,'" he said coldly, calling up the ugly words that had been forever burned into his brain, "'the Lion of the Desert is more than a stud. He also has a talent for three-card monte. The sexy sheikh has a souvenir from that time, a two-headed coin that's a reminder of the days when he hustled his school chums...'" Nick looked directly into Amanda's eyes. "I never told that story to anyone," he said softly. "Not to anyone but you."

"And you think..." The paper fell from her hand. She reached out to Nick, her fingers curling into his sleeve. "I swear to you, I didn't write this!"

"Perhaps you didn't hear me. No one knows about that coin except you."

"Someone knows. Someone wrote this, put my name on it. Don't you see? This is a lie. I'd never—"

She cried out as he grabbed the neckline of the silk caftan and tore it from the hollow of her throat to the hem. She tried to tug the edges together, but Nick captured her hands. "Don't play the terrified virgin with me. Not when you've shared the intimate details of my life with millions of strangers.''

"Nick. I beg you—"

"Go on. Beg me. I want you to beg me!" He dragged her into his arms, clamped her against him, caught her face in his hands and forced it to his. "So, I'm a savage, am I?" His teeth showed in a quick, feral grin. "That's fine. I think I'm going to enjoy living down to that description."

"Don't. Nick, don't do this. I love you. I love—"

He kissed her, hard, his mouth covering hers with barely suppressed rage, his teeth and tongue savaging her while his fingers dug into her jaw.

"Don't speak to me of love, you bitch!"

He kissed her again and again, deaf to her pleas, unmoved by her desperate struggles, lifted her into his arms, tumbled her onto a pile of silk cushions and straddled her.

"Speak to me of what you know. Of betrayal. Of mindless sex. Of how it feels to be a whore."

The sound of her hand cracking against his cheek echoed through the room like a gunshot. Nick's head jerked back; he raised his hand in retaliation.

"Go on," Amanda said. Her voice trembled, but her gaze was steady. "Hit me. Dishonor me. Do whatever you came here to do because you couldn't possibly hurt me any more than you already have."

Nick stared down at her while the seconds slipped away. God, he thought, oh, God, how close she'd come to turning him into the savage she'd called him. He cursed, shot to his feet, grabbed Amanda's wrist and dragged her after him.

"Abdul!" he shouted as he flung the door open.

The little man stepped forward. "Yes, my lord?"

"Bring the woman her clothes."

"But, sire…"

Nick shoved Amanda into the corridor. "She will dress and you will take her to the airport. See to it she's flown to Paris and put on the next plane for New York."

Abdul bowed low. "As you wish, Lord Rashid."

"Get her out of my sight!" Nick's voice shook with rage and the pain of betrayal. "Get her out of my sight," he whispered again, once he was back in his own rooms with the door closed and locked.

Then he sank onto the bed, the bed where he'd finally admitted that he'd fallen in love with Amanda Benning, buried his face in his hands and did something no Lion of the Desert had ever done in all the centuries before him.

Nicholas al Rashid, Lord of the Realm and Sublime Heir to the Imperial Throne of Quidar, wept.

An hour later, Abdul knocked on the door. "Lord Rashid?"

Nick stirred. He'd changed back into jeans—the truth was, he always felt like a fool in that silly white-and-gold robe. He was even feeling a little better.

After all, he'd get over this. Amanda was only a woman, and the world was filled with women....

"Lord Rashid? May I come in?"

It had been his mistake, that he'd opened his heart. He should have known better. Everyone always wanted something from him. The instant celebrity of being seen in his company. The right to mention his name in seemingly casual conversation. The supposed status that came of saying he was a friend or, at least, an acquaintance.

That was just the way things were. He knew it; he'd known it all his adult life. Why should he have expected things to be different with Amanda?

Why should he have let himself think, even for a moment, that she loved him for himself, not for who he was or what he might do for her?

The knock sounded again, more forcefully. "Sire. It is I. Abdul."

Nick sighed, switched on a lamp and went slowly to the door. "Yes?" he said as he pulled it open. "What is it?"

Abdul knelt down and touched his forehead to the floor. "I thought you would wish to know that it is done, my lord. The woman is gone."

"Thank you."

"You need trouble yourself with thoughts of her no longer."

"Did she…?" Nick cleared his throat. "Did she say anything more?"

"Sire?"

"Did she send any message for me?"

"Only more lies, my lord."

"More lies…"

"Yes. That she had not done this thing."

Nick nodded. "Yes. Of course. She'll deny it to the end." He looked down at the old man, still doubled over with his forehead pressed to the tile. "Abdul. Please, stand up."

"I cannot, sire. It is not the custom."

"The custom," Nick said irritably. "The custom be damned!" He grabbed the old man's arm and hoisted him to his feet. "You're too old for this nonsense, Abdul. Besides, it's time for some changes in this place."

"I think not, my lord. Your father would wish—"

"My father agrees."

"About change?" Abdul laughed politely. "That cannot be, sire. Your father understands the importance of things continuing as they always have. He may not have understood it once, but—"

"What's that supposed to mean?"

Abdul bit his lip. "Nothing, sire. Just—just the meandering thoughts of an old man."

"Well, prepare yourself for some upsets, Abdul." Nick crossed the room and switched on another light. "My father is going to abdicate the throne."

"Already? I assumed he would wait until he was much older, but that is good, sire. Putting the kingdom in your hands while you are still young is—"

"He's not abdicating for me."

The old man paled. "They why would he abdicate?"

"It's time Quidar entered the twenty-first century. There

will be elections. The people will choose a council. There'll be no more bowing and scraping, no more—"

"That woman. May her wretched soul burn in hell!"

Nick turned around, his head cocked. "What?"

"Nothing, sire. I, ah, I'll go and arrange for your meal to be served. You must be hungry—"

"Are you referring to Ms. Benning?"

The old man hesitated, then nodded. "I am, my lord. There is no reason not to admit it now. She was not good for you."

"What is good or not good for me is my affair," Nick said sharply.

"Of course. I only meant—"

"Yes. I know." Nick sighed and raked his fingers through his hair. "It doesn't matter. She's gone. And you're right. She wasn't good for me."

"Indeed, she was not. A woman who would pretend illness just to gain access to your study—"

"Access to my...?"

"The night of your birthday party, my lord." Abdul snorted. "Such a lie, that she had a headache."

Nick looked at the old man. "How did you know she had a headache?" he asked softly.

Abdul hesitated. "Well, I—I... You rang for aspirin, sire."

"I rang for coffee."

"Ah, yes. Of course. I meant that. You rang for coffee, and then you told her the story of the two-headed coin." Abdul clamped his lips together.

Nick's eyes narrowed. "You were listening," he said. "At the door."

"No. Certainly not."

"You were listening," Nick repeated grimly. "Otherwise, how would you know I'd told her about the coin?"

"I, ah, I must have..." A fine sheen of sweat moistened Abdul's forehead.

"Must have what?" Nick walked slowly toward his secretary. "How could you know I told her about the coin that night?"

The old man dropped to his knees and grasped the cuff of Nick's jeans in his fingers. "I did it for you," he whispered. "For you, and for Quidar."

"Did what?" Nick reached down, grabbed Abdul by the shoulder and hauled him to his feet. "Damn you, what did you do for me and for Quidar?"

"She was wrong for you, sire. As wrong as your mother had been for your father. Foreign women know nothing of our ways."

"Tell me what you did," Nick said through gritted teeth, "or so help me, Abdul..."

"I did my duty."

"Your duty," Nick said softly.

Abdul nodded.

"How did you 'do your duty', old man?"

"Miss Burgess called while you were in Texas with Ms. Benning. She was angry."

"Go on."

"She said—she said to give you a message, sire. She was writing a piece for *Gossip* that would teach you that you couldn't make a fool of her."

Nick let go of Abdul. He clenched his fists and jammed his hands into the back pockets of his jeans. He knew that was the only way he could keep from wrapping them around the old man's scrawny throat.

"And?" he said carefully.

"I offered money for her silence. She laughed and said there wasn't enough money in the world to keep her quiet. Oh, I paced the floor for hours, sire, searching for a solution, but I could think of none."

"And you didn't think to call me?"

"I didn't wish to upset you, my lord." Abdul clasped his hands together in supplication. "I wished to help you, sire, and to help Quidar. If I couldn't stop the Burgess woman from writing the *Gossip* article, I would use it, just as I'd used that picture of you and her on the beach."

Nick stared at Abdul. "Are you telling me that you sold that photo to *Gossip*?"

"I did not 'sell' it, Lord Rashid. I would never..." Abdul took a quick step back. "Sire, don't you understand? I could see what you could not. These foreign devils, tormenting you—"

"What the hell are you talking about?"

"The Benning woman was the worst. She was a temptress. A succubus. And you were falling under her spell."

"For the love of God!" Nick barked out a laugh and raked his hand through his hair. "This isn't the Dark Ages, man. I wasn't succumbing to a spell. I was falling in love!"

Abdul stood as straight as Nick had ever seen him. "The Lion of the Desert must marry a woman who understands our ways."

"The Lion of the Desert must try damned hard not to slam you against the wall," Nick growled. "Go on. What did you do next?"

"I telephoned Miss Burgess. I suggested we could help each other."

"Meaning?"

"I..." For the first time, the old man hesitated. "I gave her some information. I said she might consider using it, along with a different identity," He made a strangled sound as Nick grabbed him by the neck and hoisted him to his toes. "Lord Rashid." Abdul clawed at the powerful hand around his throat. "Sire, I cannot breathe."

Nick let go. The old man collapsed on the floor like a bundle of dirty clothes.

"You son of a bitch," Nick whispered. "You told Deanna about that coin."

"For the good of Quidar, sire," Abdul gasped. "It hurt no one. Surely you can see that. A simple tale about a coin—"

"A simple tale that I thought proved I'd been betrayed by the woman I love."

Nick swung away from the huddled form at his feet and

strode toward the door. Abdul pulled himself up and hurried after him.

"Lord Rashid? Where are you going?"

"To Paris," Nick said. "To New York. To the ends of the earth, until I find Amanda." He looked at Abdul; the old man cowered under that icy gaze and fell to his knees. "And you'd better not be within the borders of this kingdom when I return," he said softly, "or I'll revive one old custom and have your neck on a chopping block."

"Sire. Oh, sire, I beg you. Don't banish me. Please…"

Nick slammed the door. Half an hour later, he was on a jet, hurtling through the night sky toward Paris.

CHAPTER THIRTEEN

WEARY travelers sprawled across the seats in the departure lounge at Paris's Charles de Gaulle Airport.

Their New York–bound plane was still on the ground, its takeoff already delayed by more than three hours. The mechanics had yet to solve a perplexing electrical problem. Until they did, the passengers wouldn't be going anywhere. There was no substitute plan available, so they'd just have to wait it out.

Waiting was the last thing Amanda felt like doing. She knew it was childish but all she wanted was to get home, not just to the States and New York but to her own apartment, where things were familiar and real. Maybe then she could erase the past few days from her head and heart, and start putting things into their proper perspective.

"I just don't understand it!" a querulous voice said.

Amanda turned toward the gray-haired matron who'd dropped into the seat next to hers. "Sorry?"

"The airline," the woman said. "The lie it keeps feeding us. Just look at that airplane out there. Anyone can see there's nothing wrong with it. Why would they expect us to believe an electrical problem is the reason for this awful delay?"

"I'm sure that's what it is," Amanda said politely.

"Nonsense. Electricity is electricity. That's what I told the man at the desk. 'Whom do you think you're fooling?' I said. 'Just put in a new fuse.' And he said..."

The woman's voice droned on. After a while, Amanda closed the magazine she'd been pretending to read and rose to her feet. "Excuse me," she said, and walked to a seat at the far end of the waiting area.

There was no point in trying to change the woman's mind.

If there was one thing the past few days had taught her, it was that people would always believe what they wanted to believe, no matter what anyone told them.

Nick had wanted to believe the very worst about her, that she'd tell the entire world about him, about their most intimate secrets—

"Hi."

She blinked, looked up. A man was standing over her. He was good-looking. Handsome, actually. He had a nice smile and a great face—but that was all he had, all he'd ever have, because he wasn't Nick.

"Miserable, huh? This long delay, I mean—"

"Excuse me," Amanda said for the second time.

She stood up, tucked her hands into the pockets of her jacket and walked out of the waiting area toward the end of the terminal where there were lots of empty seats. The lights were turned low. That was fine. She was in the mood for shadows and darkness.

The man she'd cut dead probably thought she was rude or crazy or maybe both. Well, what was she supposed to have said?

Look, this is a waste of time. I'm not interested in men just now. Or maybe she should have explained that she was too busy thinking about another man to manage even small talk with a stranger.

Oh, hell.

There was no point in thinking about Nick. She'd done nothing except think about him and the humiliation he'd heaped on her. That was all he'd done ever since Abdul had marched her out of the Ivory Palace.

Somewhere along the way, self-doubt had taken the place of anger. What would have happened if only she'd said this thing or that; if she'd somehow forced Nick to listen to her. And then, finally, she'd faced the truth.

Torturing herself wouldn't change a thing. Nick would believe what he wanted to believe no matter what she said. It wasn't as if she'd let some chance to make him see the truth slip through her fingers.

The only mistake she'd made was to have gotten involved with him in the first place.

End of story.

Their affair, their relationship, whatever you wanted to call it, was over. Feelings changed, things ended, you moved on. Her mother had done that. She had, too.

I'm so riddled with guilt, she'd told Marta after her divorce. *Marriage is supposed to be forever. How will I ever put this behind me?*

And Marta had hugged her and said, *Sweetie, you just do it, that's all. You move on.*

She knew Marta had given her good advice. Excellent advice, really. There was no more logic in agonizing over her failed marriage than there was in wasting time wishing this thing with Nick had never happened or in trying to convince the woman with gray hair that you couldn't fix an airplane's electrical problems by changing a fuse.

You couldn't judge a man's heart by his performance in bed, either.

It was a cold realization but it was honest, and if she'd been fool enough to think Nick's whispered words, his kisses, his caresses, were anything but part of sex, that was her problem.

Amanda sighed, strolled into one of the empty lounges and sank wearily into a chair facing the windows. The jet that would take her home squatted on the tarmac. Mechanics scuttled purposefully around it. Problems were being solved, life was going on, and why wouldn't it?

What had happened with Nick—what she'd been stupid enough to let happen—was nothing but a blip in the overall scheme of things. The planet would go on spinning, the stars would go on shining, everything would be exactly the same.

Certainly they would. She'd be home soon, and Nick would be a distant memory. Thank goodness she'd already figured out that she'd never actually fallen in love with him.

"Mesdames et messieurs…"

The impersonal voice droned from the loudspeaker, first in French, then in English. The flight was still delayed. The airline regretted the inconvenience. Another hour or two, blah, blah, blah.

Amanda stood up and walked closer to the window. The sky was darkening. Was a storm blowing toward them or was night coming on? She couldn't tell anymore. Night and day seemed to have gotten all mixed up, just like her emotions.

Mixed up? That was a laugh. Her emotions had gone crazy. Otherwise, how could she possibly have imagined she loved Nick?

The lengths a woman would go to just to avoid admitting the truth—that she'd succumbed to lust. And lust was what she'd felt for Nicholas al Rashid. Good old garden variety, down-and-dirty lust. Wasn't it pathetic she'd had to tell herself it was love?

This was the twenty-first century. The world had long ago admitted that the female of the species could have the same emotions as her male counterpart. Why should she be any different? One look at the Lion of the Desert and pow, her hormones had gone crazy.

Why wouldn't they? He was gorgeous. It had been as flattering as hell to know he wanted to sleep with her because she'd certainly wanted to sleep with him.

And she had.

Most definitely the end of the story…or it should have been.

The trouble was, no matter how many times she told herself that, the *real* end of the story intruded.

Amanda leaned back against the wall and closed her eyes. The scene played in her mind over and over like a videotape caught in a loop.

Nick, hatred blazing in his silver eyes.

Nick, calling her a whore.

Nick, believing that she'd written that article, that she would ever hurt him or betray him. How could he think it? Didn't he know how much she loved him? That her heart would always long for him, want him, ache for him?

She drew a shaky breath, then slowly let it out.

Okay. So—so maybe she'd loved him just a little. What did it matter? They'd only spent a handful of days together. Surely that didn't really add up to "love."

Love didn't come on with the speed of a hurricane. It didn't overwhelm you. It grew slowly into something deep and everlasting.

And the foolishness of thinking Nick loved her... Oh, it was laughable! He didn't. He never had. He'd called her beloved, said he wanted her with him forever, but so what? She wasn't naive. Men said lots of things they didn't mean in the throes of passion.

Love—real love—wasn't only about sex. It was about little things. Things like taking walks in the rain. Like laughing, maybe even crying, over a movie you've seen before. It was about trust.

Especially trust.

If Nick had loved her, he'd have taken one look at the *Gossip* piece and known it was a fake. "It's a lie," he'd have said if he loved her. And then he'd have set out to discover who'd actually written those horrible things, who'd lied and used her name to drive them apart.

But he hadn't done any of that. He'd turned on her in fury, humiliated her, terrified her, believed she'd violated his confidence, talked about the things they'd done together in bed—

"It was a lie," a husky masculine voice whispered.

Amanda's heart skittered into her throat.

"I know it now, beloved. I only hope you can forgive me for not knowing it then."

The world stood still. Please, she thought, oh, please...

She turned slowly, wanting it to be him, afraid it would be him.

Nick stood in the shadows as still as if he'd been carved from stone.

Her knees buckled. He moved quickly and caught her. "Sweetheart. Oh, sweetheart, what have I done to you?"

His face was inches from hers. She longed to touch his

stubbled jaw, to trace the outline of his mouth with the tip of her finger, but he had broken her heart once and she wasn't about to let him do it again.

"Let go of me, Nick."

He swung her into his arms.

"No," she said breathlessly. "Put me down."

"Hey. Hey!"

Nick turned, still holding Amanda. The man with the nice smile and the great face came toward them.

"What's going on here?"

Nick looked at him. Whatever the man saw in his eyes made him retreat a couple of steps before he spoke up again.

"Say the word, lady, and I'll send this dude packing."

"You'll try," Nick said softly, "But you won't succeed." His arms tightened around Amanda. "This woman belongs to me."

"I don't belong to you! I don't belong to anybody."

His eyes met hers. "Yes, you do." He bent his head and kissed her gently. "You'll always belong to me, and I to you, sweetheart, because we love each other."

The words he'd spoken stunned her. She wanted to tell him she didn't love him, she'd never loved him. She wanted to tell him he'd never loved her—but he smiled into her eyes and she saw something in those cool silver depths that stole her breath away.

"Lady?"

Nick lifted his head. He was smiling, the way he'd smiled after they made love the very first time. "The lady is fine," he said quietly, his eyes never leaving hers.

The man looked from Amanda to Nick and back again. "Yeah," he said with a little laugh, "yeah, I can see that."

Nick set off through the terminal, Amanda still in his arms. She saw the startled faces all around them, the wide eyes of the women, the smiles on the lips of the men. Her cheeks flushed crimson and she buried her face in his shoulder. Doors opened and shut; she felt the rush of cool air against her hot face, the silence of enclosed space.

When she lifted her head and looked up again, they were in Nick's private plane. He let her down slowly. And when her feet touched the floor, her sanity returned.

"What do you think you're doing, Nick?"

He smiled and linked his hands at the base of her spine. "I love you, Amanda."

"Love?" She laughed. "You don't know the meaning of the—"

Nick lifted her face to his and kissed her. She felt her heart turn over, felt the longing to put her arms around him sweep through her blood, but she would not make a fool of herself ever again.

"If you really think you can—you can just pretend what you did never happened..."

Nick put his arm around her, led her into the cockpit.

"What are you doing?"

"Sit down," he said calmly. "And put on your seat belt."

"Don't be ridiculous. I will not—"

He sighed, pushed her gently into the co-pilot's seat and buckled the belt around her.

"Dammit," she sputtered, "you can get away with kidnapping in Quidar, but this is France. You can't just—"

Nick silenced her with a kiss. She moaned; she didn't mean to, but the feel of his mouth on hers, the soft pressure of it, was almost more than she could bear.

"Neither can you," he said with a little smile. He leaned his forehead against hers. "You can pretend you don't want me, sweetheart, but your kisses speak the truth."

"The truth," she said coolly, "is that I'm as human as the next woman. You're a charming man, Lord Rashid."

Nick grinned as he took the pilot's seat. "A compliment! Who'd have believed it?"

"Charming, and good-looking, but—"

"Very good-looking. That's what women always tell me."

"And clever," Amanda said crisply. "But I'm not going to be taken in again."

"Do you think I flew all the way to Paris to charm you, sweetheart?"

She looked away from him, folded her arms and stared straight out the windshield. "I don't know why you came, and I don't care. I am not going anywhere with you."

"You *do* care, and you are going with me."

"You're wrong, Lord Rashid."

"I came because I love you, and you love me. And we're never going to be separated again."

"You found me enjoyable." Her voice wobbled a little and she silently cursed herself for even that tiny show of weakness. "Enjoyable, Your Highness. That was your very own word."

Nick sighed. "A bad choice, I admit." He smiled. "True, though. You were wonderful in bed."

Color scalded her cheeks. "Which is why you regret getting rid of me before finding a replacement."

"Amanda. I know I hurt you, sweetheart, but if you'd listen—"

"To what? More lies? More whispers about—about wanting me forever?" Tears rose in her eyes. Angrily, she dashed them away with the back of her hand. "Look, it's over. I slept with you and I don't really have any regrets. It was—it was fun. But now it's time to go back to New York and pick up my life."

"Deanna wrote that article."

"Am I supposed to go saucer-eyed with shock?"

"Hell." Nick sat back and rubbed at the furrow that had appeared between his eyebrows. "Amanda, please. Just give me a chance to explain."

"The same chance you gave me?"

"All right." He swung toward her, eyes glittering, and grabbed her hands. "I was a fool, but now I'm trying to make it right. I'm telling you, Deanna wrote that thing—with Abdul's help."

"Frankly, Lord Rashid, I don't really give a…" Her mouth dropped open. "Abdul? He helped her do such a terrible thing to you?"

"He saw what was happening between us."

"Sex," Amanda said with a toss of her head. "That's what was happening between us."

"He saw," Nick said gently, taking her face in his hands, "that we were falling in love."

"What an ego you have, Your Excellency! I most certainly did not—"

Nick kissed her again. It was a tender kiss, just the whisper of his lips against hers, but it shook her to the depths of her soul. All her defenses crumpled.

"Nick." Her voice trembled. "Nick, I beg you. Don't do this unless you mean it. I couldn't bear it if you—"

"I love you," he said fiercely. "Do you hear me, Amanda? I love you." He lifted her hands to his lips and pressed kisses into each palm. "Abdul listened at the door the night I told you about the double-faced coin."

"He eavesdropped? But why?"

"He must have sensed something even then." Nick stroked a strand of pale blond silk back behind her ear. "The old man knew the truth before I was willing to admit it. I was falling in love with you."

"And he didn't trust me?"

"He wouldn't trust any female unless she was born in Quidar." Nick smiled. "And it would probably help if she had a hairy mole on her chin and weighed only slightly less than a camel."

Amanda laughed, but her laughter faded quickly. "But you believed I'd written that—that piece of filth. How could you have thought that, Nick? If you loved me, if you really loved me—"

"I was wrong, sweetheart. Terribly wrong. And I'll spend the rest of my life making up for it." A muscle flickered in Nick's jaw. "I know it's not an excuse, but—but once I was a man, the only person who loved me for myself was my father. People see me as a—a thing. A commodity. They want what they can get from associating with me. But not you. You wanted what was in here," he said softly, and placed her hand over his heart. You looked beyond all the titles and saw a man, one who loved you. It's just that I was too stupid to trust my own heart.''

''Not stupid,'' Amanda said, and slipped her arms around his neck. ''You were afraid, Nick. And I was, too. That's why it took me so long to admit I loved you.'' She laughed. ''Well, maybe not so long. We've known each other, what, four days?''

''We've known each other since the beginning of time,'' Nick whispered, and kissed her again.

''I love you,'' she sighed. ''I'll always love you.''

''You're damned right you will,'' he said gruffly. ''A man expects his wife to love him forever.''

Amanda's eyes glittered. ''Yes, my lord,'' she said, and smiled.

''I have so much to tell you, sweetheart. Things are changing in Quidar. I may not be the Lion of the Desert for much longer.''

Her smile softened. She framed his face in her hands and drew his mouth to hers. ''You'll always be the Lion of the Desert to me.''

Sheikh Nicholas al Rashid, Lion of the Desert, Lord of the Realm and Sublime Heir to the Imperial Throne of Quidar put his arms around the woman who'd stolen his heart and knew that he had finally found what he'd been searching for all of his life.

Liz Fielding started writing at the age of twelve, when she won a writing competition at school. After that early success there was quite a gap – during which she was busy working in Africa and the Middle East, getting married and having children – before her first book was published in 1992. Now readers worldwide fall in love with her irresistible heroes, adore her independent minded heroines. Visit Liz's website for news and extracts of upcoming books at www.lizfielding.com

CHAPTER ONE

'THERE was a journalist on the plane, Partridge.' Prince Hassan al Rashid joined his aide in the rear of the limousine. 'Rose Fenton. She's a foreign correspondent for one of the television news networks. Find out what she's doing here.'

'There's no mystery about it, Excellency. She's convalescing from pneumonia. That's all.' Hassan favoured the man with a look that doubted his sanity. But then Partridge was young, British and unbelievably innocent when it came to politics, whereas he had learned the game at his grandfather's knee and suspected it would be very far from 'all'. 'She's Tim Fenton's sister,' Partridge added helpfully. As if that explained everything. 'He's the new Chief Veterinary Officer,' he continued, when he realised it didn't. 'He thought a little sun would help with his sister's recuperation.'

'Did he?' How convenient. 'And since when did being related to the CVO entitle anyone, let alone a journalist, to a seat on Abdullah's private jet?'

'I believe that His Highness thought Miss Fenton would appreciate the extra comfort, after being so ill. He's apparently a great admirer...' Hassan's response was a dismissive wave of the hand, but Partridge stuck to his guns. 'And since you were coming home anyway—'

'I only learned about the flight when I asked the embassy to organise my own travel arrangements. We both know that Abdullah wouldn't fly a kite for my convenience. As for offering his personal flying palace...'

'I think His Highness is fully aware of your opinion of his extravagance.'

'Yes, well, even the Queen of England flies on a commercial airliner these days.'

'His Highness doesn't want the Queen of England to write a flattering piece about him for one of the major news magazines.'

Not that innocent, then. 'Thank you, Partridge.' Hassan briefly acknowledged his aide's unusually wry touch of humour. 'I was sure you would get to the point eventually.'

Unfortunately it was not something to laugh about. Rose Fenton would doubtless be fêted and flattered as part of the Regent's charm offensive while Faisal, the youthful Emir, was conveniently out of the country studying American business methods and showing no great eagerness to return home. His own return, Hassan thought grimly, had been precipitated by a friendly whisper that Abdullah was on the point of turning his Regency into something more permanent.

'Is she aware what's expected of her?' he asked.

'I shouldn't think so.'

Hassan wasn't convinced. 'What about her brother? Have you met him?'

'At the sports club,' he said. 'On the social circuit. Tim Fenton's good company. He asked for leave to go home when his sister was taken ill and before he knew what was happening His Highness had issued a personal invitation for her to visit Ras al Hajar to convalesce.'

'And when my cousin makes up his mind to something, it's a foolish man who argues.' And why would Rose Fenton argue? Abdullah kept foreign journalists out of Ras al Hajar as a matter of policy. And there weren't any local ones. This must have seemed like a gift.

'I don't think you need worry, sir. Miss Fenton's reputation as a journalist is formidable. If your cousin is looking for some flattering publicity I'd say he's chosen the wrong woman.'

'Maybe. Tell me, does Tim Fenton like his job here?'

Partridge's silence was all the reply he required. Rose Fenton wouldn't need to have it spelt out for her in words of one syllable either; she was far too clever for that. And Abdullah would make it easy for her. He'd tell the woman what a great job he was doing, and to prove it he'd whisk her in air-conditioned luxury from the new medical centre to the new shopping mall, via the new sports facilities. Progress in stainless steel and reinforced concrete.

He'd keep her sufficiently busy so that she wouldn't have time to go looking for anything that might give her other ideas. Even if she had a mind to. After all, a one-to-one interview with the media-shy Regent would be a serious scoop for any journalist, no matter how formidable her reputation.

Hassan wasn't as enamoured of journalists as his aide, even when they came packaged like the lovely Rose Fenton.

He changed tack. 'Tell me, Partridge, since you're so well informed, what entertainments has my cousin arranged to keep the lady amused while she's here? I imagine he *does* have plans to keep her amused?' The idea was distasteful, but he knew that if Abdullah admired the lady it was for her lovely face and fiery red hair rather than her journalistic skills. Partridge's quick flush demonstrated exactly the effect Miss Fenton produced on susceptible males. 'Well?'

'There have been some activities arranged,' he confirmed. 'A dhow trip along the coast, a feast somewhere in the desert, a tour of the city...'

'She appears to be getting the full red carpet treatment.' Although he suspected her feet wouldn't touch the ground long enough for her to feel it. 'Anything else?'

'Well, there's a cocktail party at the British Embassy, of course...' Then he hesitated.

'Why do I have the feeling that you're saving the best until last?'

'His Highness is hosting a reception at the palace in her honour.'

'Practically a State visit, then,' he said, all his worst fears confirmed. 'But rather an exhausting schedule for a woman convalescing from pneumonia, wouldn't you say?'

'She *has* been ill, Excellency. She collapsed reporting to camera from somewhere in Eastern Europe. I saw it happen. She just pitched forward...for a moment I thought she'd been shot by a sniper. How did she look?' He asked anxiously, 'You did see her on the plane?'

'Only briefly. She looked...'

Hassan paused briefly to consider exactly how Rose Fenton had looked. A little flushed, perhaps. The ruffled collar of her white blouse had provided a frame for a face that was a little thinner than the last time he'd seen her on a satellite news broadcast. Maybe that was why her dark eyes had seemed so large.

Dressed for warmth against the raw chill of the weather, she'd been wearing a scarlet sweater that should have clashed horribly with her red hair, but hadn't. On the contrary; the effect had been riveting.

She'd looked up from a book she was holding and met his glance with frank curiosity; it had been a confident look that avoided being in any way flirtatious but had still managed to convey the suggestion that she'd welcome his company to while away the tedious hours in the air.

Honesty forced him to concede that he'd been tempted, his own curiosity thoroughly roused by her presence on his cousin's private jet. And he was not impervious to the pleasure of a beautiful woman's company to help pass the time.

At one point he'd got as far as summoning the steward to invite her forward. In the few seconds it had taken the man to respond, common sense had reasserted itself.

Mixing with journalists was not a good idea. A man just never knew what they'd print next. Or rather he did know. Too late, he'd learned that it was far easier to gain a reputation than lose it, especially if the reputation suited a certain highly placed individual.

And Abdullah would certainly hear about any conversation they'd shared the minute the wheels touched down. Being seen with him would do her no good at all in palace circles.

She'd be safer sticking to her book, no matter how

unexpected her choice. Fantasy was always less dangerous than the real thing.

He realised that Partridge was still waiting for his answer. 'She looked well enough,' he said irritably.

Rose Fenton stopped to catch her breath as she stepped out of the chill of the air-conditioned arrival hall of the airport and into the midday heat of Ras al Hajar.

Despite the brave show of daffodils in the parks, London hadn't quite made spring, and Rose had been bundled up in thermal underwear and a heavy sweater by her unusually anxious mother.

'Are you all right, Rose? You must be tired from the journey.'

'Don't fuss, Tim.' Her brother's anxious query made him sound exactly like their mother and she wasn't used to being fussed over. It made her realise just how sick she'd been. She peeled off the sweater. 'I'm not an invalid, just hot,' she snapped, her irritability a sure indication that she wasn't feeling quite as lively as she would have everyone believe. She'd been very bad-tempered the week before she collapsed with pneumonia, but Tim's obvious concern made her instantly contrite. 'Oh, heck, I'm sorry. It's just that for the last month Mum's been treating me like some nineteenth-century heroine about to expire from consumption.' Her smile took on a slightly mischievous slant as she hooked her arm through his. 'I thought I'd escaped the leash.'

'Yes, well, I have to admit you don't look quite as bad as I'd expected from the way she's been fretting,' he retaliated, easily slipping into the old habit of brotherly teasing, not in the least in awe of her distinguished reputation as a foreign correspondent. 'I was beginning to wonder if I should rent a bath-chair for your visit.'

'That really won't be necessary.'

'Just a walking stick, then?'

'Only if you want me to beat you with it.'

'You're definitely on the mend,' he said, laughing.

'I had two choices: recover quickly, or die of boredom. Mum wouldn't let me read anything more taxing than a three-year-old magazine,' she told him as he ushered her in the direction of a dusty dark green Range Rover. 'And when she discovered I was watching the news, she threatened to confiscate my TV.'

'You're exaggerating, Rose.'

'As if I would!' Then she relented. 'Well, maybe. Just a bit.' And she grinned. 'But I'm not tired, really. Travelling in the Emir's private jet had about as much in common with flying economy as a bicycle has with a Rolls Royce.' She grinned. 'It's flying, Tim, but not as we know it.' She breathed in the warm desert air. 'This is what I need. Let me get out of these thermals,' she said, 'and you won't be able to stop me.'

'I warn you, I'm under strict orders to keep you from doing anything too physical.'

'Spoilsport. I was banking on being whisked away on a fiery black stallion by some hawk-nosed desert prince,' she teased, but, since her brother looked less than impressed with that idea, she squeezed his arm reassuringly. 'Just kidding. Gordon gave me a copy of *The Sheik* to read on the plane.' Her news editor's idea of a joke, no doubt. He had an odd sense of humour. Or maybe it had been an excuse to hand over the bookshop carrier that contained all the information he'd been able to dig up on the situation in Ras al Hajar right under her mother's watchful eyes. She patted the bag slung over her shoulder. 'I'm not sure whether it was meant as inspiration or warning.'

'You mean you actually read it?'

'It's a classic of women's fiction,' she protested.

'Well, I hope you took it as a warning. I've had my instructions from Ma and, believe me, horse riding of any description is definitely off the agenda. You're allowed to lie in the shade by the pool with a little light reading in the morning, but only if you promise not to go in the water—'

'I've had weeks of this, Tim. I am not promising anything.'

'Only if you promise not to go in the water,' he repeated, with a broad grin, 'and have a little nap in the afternoon.' Then, more gently, 'You gave us all a terrible fright, you know, collapsing in the middle of the evening news.'

'Very bad form,' she agreed briskly. 'I'm supposed to report the news, not make it...' Her voice trailed off as she watched a long black limousine, windows darkened, speed away from the airport.

The car's occupant was undoubtedly the reason for the flight of the Emir's private jet on which her brother had managed to hitch her a ride. Wearing an immaculately tailored dark suit, a discreetly striped shirt and a silk tie, he could have been the chairman of any large public company boarding his private plane moments before take-off. But he wasn't.

Their gazes had met and mutual recognition had been

instant before the door to her cabin had been hurriedly
shut by an apologetic stewardess more used to travelling princesses than nosy journalists.

Which had been a pity. Prince Hassan al Rashid came
very high on her must-meet list. Amongst the pile of
news clippings, the photograph of the hawkish face
with piercing grey eyes had been the only one that had
caught her attention and held it. If Rose had been seriously seeking her own personal fantasy adventure
with a sheikh, on a horse of any colour, he would have
fulfilled the role admirably.

Prince Hassan had paused as he'd entered the aircraft, and in the moment before the door was shut those
grey eyes had fixed her with a look that had brought a
flush of colour to her cheeks and made her want to tug
her calf-length skirt closer to her ankles. It was a look
that had left her feeling entirely female, entirely vul
nerable in a way that for a twenty-eight-year-old journalist was almost embarrassing.

A twenty-eight-year-old journalist, with one marriage, one war and half a dozen in-depth interviews with
prime ministers and presidents behind her.

But she was quite capable of recognising a seriously
dangerous man when she saw one, and his photograph,
a posed, expressionless, formal portrait, hadn't even
come close to the real thing.

What, if any, impression she had made upon him was
impossible to tell. In the few moments before the door
had been closed discreetly between them, his expression
had given nothing away.

It was her first taste of purdah and, despite the fact
that she'd been treated throughout the flight like a prin-

cess, she didn't much like it. She knew that, by his own standards, Prince Hassan was showing her far more respect by ignoring her presence than if he had joined her, but as a journalist she could scarcely help being disappointed. It was her disappointment as a woman that disturbed her more.

Besides, such respect seemed strangely at odds with his reputation as a playboy prince whose wealth, according to gossip, was pumped straight from his country's oil wells to the wrists and necks of beautiful women, and the world's most exclusive gaming tables.

But at home in Ras al Hajar he apparently chose to at least nod to convention. When he had disembarked before her, to be greeted by the officials lined up on the tarmac, he had dispensed with the expensive Italian tailoring and was wearing the trappings of a desert prince. A black prince.

The breeze had tugged impatiently at the gossamer-thin camel hair cloak thrown over his black robes, at the black *keffiyeh* held in place by a simple, unadorned camel halter. And she had sensed his own impatience with the ceremonial honour paid him as each man stepped forward to take his hands and bow deeply over them.

Tim saw her glance drawn to the limousine as the morning sun flashed from the darkened windows. 'Prince Hassan,' he murmured.

'Prince who?' she asked, feigning ignorance. She had long since learned that people told her far more that way.

But Tim did not leap in with the local gossip as she

had hoped. 'No one for you to get worked up about, Rose. He's only the local playboy.'

'Really? From all the bowing and scraping when he got off the plane, I thought he must be next in line to King around here.'

'He's not next in line to anything.' Tim shrugged. 'Hassan warrants all that "bowing and scraping", as you so eloquently put it, because his father took a bullet meant for the old Emir. Several bullets, in fact.'

'Oh?' Act dumb, Rosie, just act dumb. 'He was shot?'

Tim's disbelieving glance warned her that she might have gone a bit over the top, but he indulged her curiosity. 'Yes, he was shot, and his reward for a bullet in the shoulder and a smashed leg was the hand of the old Emir's favourite daughter and a life of ease. Not that he lived long enough to enjoy it.'

'He didn't survive the attack, then?'

'He made a pretty fair recovery, by all accounts, but he was killed in a car accident a few months after the wedding.'

'How terrible.' Then, 'Was it an accident?'

Her brother's mouth straightened in a knowing grin. 'Quick for a girl, aren't you?' Then he shrugged. 'Your guess is as good as mine and that's all anyone can do— guess.'

'Well, he lived long enough to father a son,' she said, regret stirring at deeply buried memories. 'That's as close to immortality as any of us ever gets.'

'Rose,' Tim prompted gently.

She responded with a distracted, 'Mmm,' as she continued to watch the limousine speed away from the airport. It might be her job to be interested in anyone who was so close to the throne yet could never aspire to it, but something else was prompting her curiosity about the man behind those grey eyes.

She'd met men who could command the most undisciplined rabble with no more than a look from eyes like that. It wasn't the colour that mattered, it was the strength, the conviction behind them. His weren't the eyes of a playboy. And if he was pretending? The thought strayed into her head and stirred the down on the nape of her neck.

Then, realising that Tim was still patiently holding the door for her, she smiled. 'So, I like a good human interest story. Tell me about him. His father must have been dead before he was born.'

'He was. Perhaps that's why Hassan was so indulged by the old man. He was raised as a favourite.' Tim glanced back at the limousine, disappearing at speed in the direction of the open desert. 'Too much money, too little to do; it was bound to lead to trouble.'

'What kind of trouble?'

He shrugged. 'Women, gambling… But what can you expect? A man has to do something, and despite the title he's effectively barred from palace politics.'

'Oh? Why's that?' She was too quick with the question and Tim suddenly realised that he was being pumped for information.

'Leave it, Rose,' he said firmly. 'You're here for rest and recuperation, not to ferret out a non-existent story.'

'But if you don't tell me why he can't get involved in politics I'll just worry about it,' she said, quite reasonably, as Tim helped her up into the air-conditioned comfort of the four-wheel drive. 'I just won't be able to help myself.'

'Try. Very hard,' he suggested. 'This isn't a democracy and nosy journalists are not welcome.'

'I'm not nosy,' she said, with a grin. 'Just interested.' Prince Hassan interested her a lot. Men with eyes like that didn't waste time playing...not without good reason.

'And I'm Charley's Aunt. You're here as Prince Abdullah's guest, Rosie. Break the rules and you'll be on the first flight out of here. And so will I, so drop it. Please.'

It was years since Tim had called her Rosie, and she suspected that this was his way of reminding her that, despite the fact that she was a well-known and respected journalist, she was still his little sister. And this was his territory. So she shrugged and let the subject drop. For now. Besides, she knew, or suspected she knew, the answer to her question. Hassan's father might have been a hero, but he'd been a foreigner, a Scot who'd been drawn to the desert. She had the press cuttings to prove it.

But it wouldn't do to let Tim know that. 'Sorry, it's just force of habit. And boredom.'

'Then we'll have to make sure that you don't get bored. I've arranged a small party to introduce you to some people, and Prince Abdullah has pulled out all the stops to make sure you have a good time.'

Rose allowed Tim to run on about the receptions and parties lined up and waiting for her pleasure, not pushing the subject she was most interested in. After all, receptions and parties were the places to hear all the latest gossip and, with luck, meet the local playboy.

'What was that about a reception at the palace?' she asked, tuned in for the important words even while her brain was thinking about something else.

'Only if you feel up to it,' he added. He glanced across at her and pulled a little face. 'I should warn you that the ride in Abdullah's private plane might have strings attached. He's not above trying to charm you into recording a flattering interview with him.'

'Well, he's out of luck,' she said, mentally scratching the interview with Abdullah, number two on her Ras al Hajar must-do list. A pity, but it would give her more time to concentrate on Prince Hassan. After all, she was on holiday and entitled to a treat. 'I'm here to relax.'

'Since when did relaxation get in the way of work? I can't see you turning down an exclusive interview with the ruler of a strategically important and oil-rich country, no matter how sick you've been.'

'Regent,' she reminded him, abandoning all pretence. 'Isn't the young Emir due back from America soon? Or could it be that now he's had a taste of life at the top, Prince Abdullah is reluctant to step down? I mean, once you've been King anything else has to be something of an anticlimax. Doesn't it?' Tim frowned, his glance suddenly anxious. She grinned and put a reassuring hand on his arm. 'I'll just stick to lying quietly by the pool with a little light reading, shall I? Relaxing.'

He swallowed. 'Perhaps that would be best. I'll tell His Highness that you're too weak for partying just yet.'

'Don't you dare! Tell him... Tell him, I'm just to weak to work.'

Hassan remained deep in thought for a long time after the car had come to a halt. 'You'll have to go to the States, Partridge. It's time Faisal was home.'

'But Excellency—'

'I know, I know.' He waved impatiently. 'He's enjoying the freedom and he won't want to come, but he can't put it off any longer.'

'He'd take it better from you, sir.'

'Maybe, but the fact that I feel unable to leave the country will ram home the message more effectively than anything either of us can say.'

'What do you want me to say?'

'Tell him...tell him if he wants to keep his country, it's time to come home before Abdullah takes it from him. I can't put it plainer than that.'

He climbed from the limousine and strode towards the huge carved doors of the coastal watch-tower he had made his home, his feet ringing on the stone slabs of the courtyard.

'And Miss Fenton?' Partridge asked, his pace slower as he leaned heavily on his walking stick.

Hassan paused at the entrance to his private apartments. 'You can safely leave Miss Fenton to me,' he said sharply.

Partridge paled, swinging round in front of him and forcing him to a halt. 'Sir, you won't forget she's been ill—'

'I won't forget that she's a journalist.' Hassan's face darkened as he saw the anxiety in the man's face. Well,

well. Lucky Rose Fenton. Needed by a fabulously rich
and totally powerful older man for her ability to make
him look good, desired by a young and foolish one with
nothing in his head but romantic nonsense. All in one
day. How many women could start a holiday with that
kind of advantage?

It occurred to him that Rose Fenton, blessed with
both brains and beauty, probably started every holiday
with that kind of advantage.

'What are you planning to do, sir?'

'Do?' He wasn't used to having his intentions questioned.

Partridge might be nervous, but he wasn't cowed.
'With Miss Fenton.'

Hassan gave a short laugh. 'What do you *think* I'm
going to do with her, man?' The image of the book she
had been holding swept into his mind. 'Abduct her and
carry her off into the desert like some old-time bandit?'

Partridge immediately flushed. 'N-no.'

'You don't sound very certain,' he pressed. 'It's what
my grandfather would have done.'

'Your grandfather lived in a different age, sir,'
Partridge said. 'I'll go and pack.'

Hassan watched him go. The young man had guts,
and he admired him for the way he coped with disabil-
ity and pain, but he wouldn't put up with dissent from
anyone. He'd do whatever he had to.

Thirty minutes later he handed Partridge the letter he
had written to his young half-brother and walked with
him to the Jeep that would take him down to the jetty.
The courtyard was full of horsemen with hawks at their
wrists, long-legged silky-coated Salukis at their heels.

Partridge's eyes narrowed. 'You're going hunting? Now?'

'I need to heat the London damp out of my bones and get some good, clean desert air in my lungs.' And it occurred to him that if Abdullah was planning a quiet coup, it might be wise to take himself to his desert camp where his presence would be less noticeable. 'I'll speak to you tomorrow.'

'This is it.'

'It's beautiful, Tim.' The villa was out of the town, set on the hillside overlooking the wild and rugged coast near the royal stables. Tim's title might give him control of the country's veterinary services, but his main concern was the Regent's stud. Below them was a palm grove and around the house there were oleanders in flower, bright birds... 'I expected desert...sand dunes...'

'Hollywood has a lot to answer for.' The door opened at their approach and Tim's servant bowed as Rose crossed the threshold. 'Rose, this is Khalil. He cooks, cleans and looks after the place so I can concentrate on work.' The young man returned her smile shyly.

'Good grief, Tim,' Rose said, once she'd admired everything, from the exquisite rugs laid over polished hardwood floors to the small swimming pool in the discreetly walled garden beyond the French windows. 'It's a bit different from that scruffy little house you had in Newmarket.'

'If you think this is luxury, just wait until you see the stables. The horses have a much larger swimming pool than me and I have a fully equipped hospital, anything I ask for—'

'Okay, okay!' She grinned at his enthusiasm. 'You can give me the grand tour later, but right now I could do with a shower.' She lifted her hair from her neck. 'And I need to change into some lighter clothes.'

'What? Oh, sorry. Look, why don't you make yourself at home, have a rest, something to eat? Your room is through here.' He shepherded her through to a large suite. 'There's plenty of time to see everything.'

She stopped in the doorway, but it wasn't the splendour of her room that surprised her. It was the fact that every available surface was obscured by baskets full of roses. 'Where on earth did all these come from?'

'Wherever roses are grown at this time of year.' Tim shrugged, obviously embarrassed by the excess. 'I should have thought you were used to it by now. I don't suppose anyone ever sends you lilies, or daisies or chrysanthemums. Do they?'

'Rarely,' she admitted, looking for a card, but finding none. 'But they usually come in dozens. These appear to have been ordered by the gross.'

'Yes, well, Prince Abdullah sent them over this morning so that you'd feel at home.'

'He thinks I live in a florist's shop?'

Tim pulled a face. 'They do everything on a grander scale here.' He glanced anxiously at his watch. 'Rose, can you look after yourself for an hour or so? I've a mare about to foal...'

She laughed. 'Go. I'll be fine.'

'If you're sure? If you need me—'

'I'll whinny.'

His face relaxed into a smile. 'Actually, I think you'll find the telephone system is perfectly adequate.'

Alone, she turned back to the roses. Creamy white, perfect florist's blooms. She resisted the urge to count them; instead she thoughtfully riffled the satiny petals of a half-open bud with the edge of her thumb. The flowers were beautiful, but scentless, a sterile cliché without any real meaning.

And her thoughts wandered back to Prince Hassan al Rashid. The playboy prince was something of a cliché too. But those grey eyes suggested something very different behind the façade.

Prince Abdullah might woo her co-operation with his private jet and his roses, but it was Hassan who had her undivided attention.

CHAPTER TWO

'WHAT do you mean, you can't find him?' Hassan could barely contain his anger. 'He has bodyguards who watch him night and day—'

'He's given them the slip.' Partridge's voice echoed faintly on the satellite link. 'Apparently there's a girl involved—'

Of course there would be a girl. Damn the boy. And damn those blockheads who were supposed to look after him…

Except that he'd been twenty-four himself, once, centuries ago, and remembered only too well how it felt to live every waking moment under watchful eyes. Remembered just how easy it was to lose them when there was a girl…

'Find him, Partridge. Find him and bring him home. Tell him…' What? That he was sorry? That he understood? What good would that do? 'Tell him there isn't much time.'

'I'll do whatever is necessary, Excellency.'

Hassan stood at the entrance to his tent, Partridge's words ringing in his head. *Whatever is necessary…* His dying grandfather had used those words to him on the day he'd named his younger grandson, Faisal, his heir, and his nephew, Abdullah, as Regent. *Whatever is necessary for my country.* It had been an apology of sorts, but, hurting and angry at being dispossessed, he had

24

refused to understand and had behaved like the young
fool that he'd been.

Older, wiser, he understood that for a man to rule he
must first accept that the wishes of the heart must always be sacrificed to necessity.

In a few short weeks Faisal would be twenty-five,
and if his young half-brother was to take on the burden
of kingship he too would have to learn that lesson. And
quickly.

In the meantime something would have to be done
to disrupt Abdullah's attempt at coup by media. His
cousin might not encourage the press to come calling
at his door, but he understood its power, and he would
not let the chance slip to have someone like Rose
Fenton in his pocket.

She'd already been given the official grand tour of
the more fragrant parts of city, and it would be so easy
to be fooled into believing everything was wonderful if
you weren't looking too hard. And Abdullah had it in
his power to distract her in all manner of ways.

She might not succumb to the gifts, the gold and
pearls that would be showered upon her. It was unlikely—he had little faith in the myth of the crusading,
incorruptible journalist—but Abdullah had never been
a one-plan dictator. If money wouldn't do it, he had her
brother as a hostage to her co-operation.

Well, two could play at that game, and, although he
was sure she wouldn't take the same view of the situation, Hassan reasoned that he would actually be doing
Miss Fenton a favour if he took her out of circulation
for a while.

And dealing with her frantic family, the British

Foreign Office, the unkind comments of the British media, would give his cousin something more pressing to worry him than usurping Faisal's throne. It might even prompt him to bail out. While Abdullah enjoyed the tribute that went with his role as stand-in Head of State, he wasn't nearly so keen on the responsibilities that accompanied the role.

Partridge would doubtless be outraged, but, since his aide was clearly aware of the urgent necessity of doing whatever it took, he could be relied upon to keep his own counsel. In public, if not in private.

'Horse racing?' Rose helped herself to a slice of toast. It was six years since she'd been to a racetrack. It might not have been a deliberate decision, but she had always found some pressing reason to decline the many invitations to Ascot and Cheltenham that came her way. 'At night?'

'Under floodlights. It's cooler then. Especially in summer,' Tim added, then grinned. 'There'll be camel racing, too. Would you want to miss that?'

'Would I?' She pretended to think. 'Yes.'

For a moment she thought he was going to say something. Give her the 'it's been nearly six years' speech. He clearly thought better of it, because he shrugged and said, 'Well, it's up to you.' If he was disappointed by her decision he didn't let it show, and she could hardly believe that he was surprised. 'I have to be there for obvious reasons, but I can come back and pick you up afterwards.'

She glanced up from the careful application of butter to her toast. 'Pick me up?'

Tim indicated the square white envelope propped up against the marmalade. 'We've been invited out to dinner after the races.'

'Again?' Didn't anyone ever stay in for a pizza and a video in Ras al Hajar? 'Who by?'

'Simon Partridge.'

'Have I met him?' she asked, picking up the envelope and extracting a single sheet of paper. The handwriting was bold and strong. The note oddly formal. 'Simon Partridge requests the pleasure…'

'No, he's Prince Hassan's aide.'

About to plead tiredness, a headache, anything to get out of another formal evening, the night in with a video suddenly lost its appeal. She hadn't seen the playboy prince since he got off the plane. She'd looked for him, listened out for his name, but he appeared to have vanished from the face of the earth.

'You'll like him,' Tim said. She was sure her brother meant Simon Partridge rather than Hassan, but she didn't ask; she had the feeling that it would be wiser not to draw attention to her interest. 'He was desperately keen to meet you, but he's been out of town.'

'Really?' And then she laughed. 'Tell me, Tim, where do you go when you go "out of town" in Ras al Hajar?'

'Nowhere. That's the point. You leave civilisation behind.'

'I've done that.' She'd been in some very uncivilised places in the last few years. Too many. 'It's overrated.'

'The desert is different. Which is why, if you're someone like Hassan, the first thing you do when you get home is take your hounds and your hawks out into the desert and go hunting. And if you're his aide, you go with him.'

'I see.' What she saw was that if Simon Partridge was back in town, then so was Prince Hassan. 'Tell me about him. Simon Partridge. It's unusual for someone like Hassan to have a British aide, surely?'

'His grandfather had one and lived to tell the tale.'

'Did he?'

Tim frowned. 'Hassan's father. He was a Scot. Didn't I say?'

'No, you didn't.' Well, he hadn't. 'It explains a lot.'

Tim shrugged. 'Maybe he feels he can rely on Partridge one hundred per cent to be his man, with no divided tribal loyalties, no family feuds to get in the way.'

'A back to get in the way should someone feel like stabbing him in it?' she pondered. 'What does Simon Partridge get out of it?'

'Just a job. He's not Hassan's bodyguard. Partridge *was* in the army, but his Jeep got into a bit of an argument with a landmine and he was invalided out. His Colonel and Hassan were at school together…'

'Eton,' she murmured, without thinking.

'Where else?' Tim had assumed it was a question. 'Partridge, too.' He looked pleased at her apparent interest in his absent friend and Rose sighed, suspecting a little furtive matchmaking. 'So?' Tim retrieved the invitation. 'What shall I tell him?'

That was easy. The racing might be a non-starter, but Rose wasn't going to miss out on a chance to meet Hassan's aide. She handed him back the note. 'Tell him… Miss Fenton accepts…'

'Great.' The phone rang and Tim answered it, listened, then said, 'I'll be right there.' He was halfway to the door before he remembered Rose. 'Simon's number is on the note. Will you call him?'

'No problem.' She picked up the receiver, dialled the number. As it rang, she looked again at the bold cursive and decided Tim was right for once. She was sure she would like the owner of such a decisive hand.

'Yes?'

'Mr Partridge? Simon Partridge?'

There was the briefest pause. 'I believe I have the pleasure of speaking to Miss Rose Fenton.'

'Er, yes.' She laughed. 'How did you know?'

'If I told you I was psychic?' the voice offered.

'I wouldn't believe you.'

'And you would be right not to. Your voice is unmistakable, Miss Fenton.'

While Simon Partridge sounded rather older than she had expected from Tim's description of him, his voice was low, deeply authoritative, velvet on steel. Not that she was about to drool into the phone.

'That's because I talk too much,' she replied crisply. 'Tim's had to rush off to the stables, but he asked me to ring you and say that we're delighted to accept your invitation to dinner this evening.'

'I have no doubt that the delight will be all mine.'

His formality was so very…foreign. She wondered how long he had been in Ras al Hajar. She'd assumed it was a fairly recent thing, but maybe not. 'You know he has to go to the races first, of course—'

'Everyone goes to the races, Miss Fenton. There is nothing else to do in Ras al Hajar. You will be there?'

'Well…'

'You must come.'

Must she? 'Yes,' she said, rapidly changing her mind. She rather thought she must. After all, she reasoned, if everyone went to the races, Hassan would be there. 'Yes, I'm looking forward to it.' And suddenly she was. Very much.

'Until this evening, Miss Fenton.'

'Until then, Mr Partridge,' she replied. And she put down the receiver feeling just a touch breathless.

Hassan switched off the cellphone that had been purchased in the souk that morning and registered in an entirely fictitious name and tossed it on the divan. Beyond the opening of the huge black tent he could see the lush palm grove watered by the small streams that ran from the craggy mountainous border country. In spring it was paradise on earth. He had the feeling that Rose Fenton might not view it in quite the same way.

'Come home quickly, Faisal,' he murmured. At the sound of his voice the hound at his feet rose and pushed a long silky head against his hand.

Rose was thoroughly dissatisfied with her small wardrobe. She'd felt like an absolute dowd at the embassy cocktail party. She'd assumed that it would be smart but casual. Tim had been absolutely no help and in the end she'd decided on her crush-proof go-anywhere little black dress. In the event, of course, all the other women had taken the opportunity to wear their latest designer creations, leaving the black dress looking as if it had already been around the world and back again. Well, it had.

She hadn't anticipated so much socialising, and besides, she had nothing that could possibly cover an evening outdoors at the races followed by a private dinner.

She would normally have asked her hostess what would be suitable. But there was no hostess, and something about Simon Partridge had precluded that kind of informal chattiness. It was the same something that urged her to make a real effort, pull out all the stops, and she decided to wear the *shalwar kameez* that she'd been given on a trip to Pakistan and packed in the hope of an interview with the Regent. Something she'd been doing her best to avoid ever since she'd arrived, although even she had begun to run out of convincing excuses.

The trousers were cut from heavy slub silk in a dull mossy shade, the tunic a shade or two lighter and the hand-embroidered silk chiffon scarf paler still. She should have worn it to the embassy.

'Wow!' Tim's reaction was unexpected. He didn't usually notice what anyone wore. 'You look stunning.'

'That's worrying. I suddenly get the feeling that everyone else will be wearing jeans.'

'Does it matter? You're going to absolutely knock Simon's eyes out.'

'I'm not sure that's the effect I'm striving for, Tim.' Remembering the effect of his voice on her ability to breathe, she thought she might just be kidding herself. 'At least not until I know him better.'

'In that outfit he'll definitely want to get to know you

better.' He glanced at his watch. 'We'd better go. Got everything?'

'Hanky, safety pin, ten pence for the telephone,' she said solemnly. Her cellphone, tape recorder, notebook and pen went without saying. And she didn't say anything because she had the feeling they would make her brother uneasy.

Tim laughed. 'I'd forgotten the way Mum used to say that.' He put his arm beneath her elbow and helped her up into the Range Rover.

'How far is it?'

'Oh, just a couple of miles beyond the stables. Once you get through these low hills there's a good flat piece of ground that's perfect for racing.' He pulled a face as they bumped over the rough track. 'Sorry about this. The Emir's had a dual-carriageway road laid from town, but this way's much quicker for us.'

'Hey, this is "Front-line" Fenton you're talking to. A few bumps aren't going to... Oh, look out!'

A pale riderless horse leapt from a low bluff and landed in front of them, turning to rear up in front of the car, mane flying, hooves pawing at the air. Tim swung to avoid it, throwing the car into a sideways skid that seemed to go on for ever on the loose gravel.

'It's one of Abdullah's horses,' he said, as he brought the Range Rover under control. 'Someone's going to be in trouble—' The moment they stopped, he flung open the door and leapt down. 'Sorry, but I'll have to try and catch it.'

'Can I do anything?' She turned as he opened the tailgate and took out a rope halter.

'No. Yes. Use the car phone to call the stables. Ask them to send a horsebox.'

'Where?'

'Just say between the villa and the stables; they'll find us.'

The interior light had not come on and she reached up, clicked the switch, but nothing happened. She shrugged, lifted the phone, but there was no dial tone. Great. She picked up her bag and dug out the new mobile phone that Gordon had included in the carrier with the book and the cuttings. It was small, very powerful and did just about everything except play the national anthem, but she wasn't confident enough with it to press buttons in the dark, so slid down from her seat to check it out in the headlights. Her feet had just touched the ground when the headlights went out.

She could hear her brother, some distance off, gentling the nervous horse, hear the scrabbling of hooves against the rough ground as the lovely creature danced away from him. Then that sound, too, abruptly stopped as the horse found sand.

It was so quiet, so dark in the shadow of the bluff. There was no moon, but the stars were brilliant, undimmed by light pollution, and the sand reflected the faintest silvery shimmer against which everything else was jet-black.

A shadow detached itself from the darkness.

'Tim?'

But it wasn't her brother. Even before she turned she knew it wasn't him. Tim had smelt faintly of aftershave, was wearing a light-coloured jacket. This man had no scent that she could discern and he was dressed from head to foot in a robe of a blackness so dense that it absorbed light rather than reflecting it. Even his face was concealed in a black *keffiyeh* worn so that nothing but his eyes were visible.

His eyes were all she needed to see.

It was Hassan. Despite the charge of fear that fixed her to the spot, despite the adrenalin-driven panicky race of her heart, she knew him. But this was not the urbane Prince boarding a private jet in expensive Italian tailoring; this was not Hassan in playboy prince mode.

This was the man promised by granite-grey eyes, deep, dangerous and totally in command, and something warned her that he wasn't about to ask if she needed help.

Before she could do more than half turn to run, before she could even think about shouting a warning to her brother, he'd clamped his hand over her mouth. Then, with his free arm flung around her, he lifted her clear of the ground as he pulled her hard against his body. Hard enough for the curved weight of the dagger at his waist to dig into her ribs.

Definitely not from the local branch of auto rescue.

She might have done a self-defence course but so apparently had he, because he knew all the moves. Her elbows were immobilised, and with her feet off the ground she had no platform from which to launch a counter-move. Not that it would do her any good. She might make the high ground, but what then? There was nowhere to run to and, although she couldn't see anyone else, she doubted that he was alone.

She struggled anyway.

He simply tightened his grip and waited, and after a

moment she stopped. There was no point in wearing herself out unnecessarily.

When she was quite still except for the unnaturally swift rise and fall of her breast as she tried to regain her breath, he finally spoke. 'I would be grateful if you did not shout, Miss Fenton,' he said, very quietly. 'I have no wish to hurt your brother.' And his voice was like his hand, like his eyes, hard, uncompromising, not playing games.

He knew who she was, then. This wasn't some random snatch. No. Of course it wasn't. It might have been some days since they'd exchanged that momentary glance on the plane that had brought her to Ras al Hajar, but she'd heard the voice much more recently. Heard it insisting that she must go to the races. And she had blithely assured him that she would be there. That had been the reason for the invitation; he'd wanted to be sure she would be there so he could plan exactly where and when to abduct her.

Not Simon Partridge, then. But Hassan. She realised that she wasn't as surprised as she might have been. The voice was a much better fit.

But what did he want? Just because she'd read a few pages of *The Sheik* in an idle moment, that didn't mean she subscribed to the fantasy. She didn't think for a minute that he was about to carry her off into the desert for the purposes of ravishment. She was a journalist, and not given much to flights of fancy. And why would he bother when, with the click of his fingers, he could bring just about any woman he desired to his side?

'Well?' He was offering her a choice? Not much of one. She nodded, once, promising her silence.

'Thank you.' The formal courtesy was unmistakable. As if she had had any choice but surrender! But, as if to prove that he was a gentleman, Hassan immediately removed his hand from her mouth, set her feet to the ground, eased his grip on her. Maybe he was so used to obedience that it didn't occur to him that she wouldn't keep quiet, keep still. Or maybe it didn't matter all that much. There was only Tim, after all, and with a sudden sense of dread she recalled the sudden silence.

'Where is Tim? What have you done with him?' she demanded as she spun back to face him, her own voice hushed in the absolute still of the desert night. Hushed! She should be screaming her head off...

'Nothing. He's still chasing after Abdullah's favourite stallion.' The eyes gleamed. 'I imagine he'll be gone some time. This way, Miss Fenton.' Her eyes, quickly adjusting to the darkness, saw the uncompromising shape of a Land Rover waiting in the shadows. Not one of the plush, upmarket jobs that her brother drove, but the basic kind that took to hard terrain like a duck to water. The kind used by military men the world over.

Far more practical than a horse, she didn't doubt, any more than she doubted that she would go wherever he was taking her. Her only alternative was to run for it, try and dodge him in the rocky outcrops of the rising ground behind her. As if he anticipated she might try it, Hassan tightened his hold and urged her towards the waiting vehicle.

Despite the prickle of fear that was goosing her flesh, all her journalist instincts were on red alert. But, although her curiosity was intense, she didn't want him to think she was going willingly. 'You've got to be kidding,' she said, and dug in her heels.

'Kidding?' He repeated the word as if he didn't understand it. Then he raised his head, looked beyond her. The moon was rising, and as she turned she saw the dark silhouette of her brother in the distance. He had managed to get the head rope on the stallion and was leading him quietly back towards the Range Rover, completely oblivious to her plight, to the danger he was walking into.

Hassan had seriously underestimated his skill, his empathy with even the most difficult of horses, and, realising it, he swore beneath his breath. 'I don't have time to argue.'

She wasn't about to let Tim walk into trouble, but even as she drew a ragged breath to shout a warning she was enveloped in blackness. Real blackness, the kind that made starlight look like day, and she was wrapped, parcelled, bundled, lifted off her feet and slung over his shoulder.

Far too late she stopped being the cool correspondent, absorbing every last detail for her report, and began to struggle in dreadful earnest. Too late she realised she should have yelled when she'd had the chance. Not for help, since that would surely be pointless, but to make sure that Tim called her news editor to tell him what had happened.

She kicked furiously in an effort to free her head, not wasting her breath in shouting, because her voice wouldn't make it beyond the confines of the heavy cloth. But although her feet were free to inflict whatever damage she could manage they appeared to make no impression upon her captor. If only she could free her hands! But they were pinned uselessly to her sides... Well, not quite uselessly. One them was still gripping the little mobile phone. She almost smiled. The mobile. Well, that was all right, then. She'd call the news desk herself...

Then she was dumped unceremoniously on the floor of the truck, and even through the thick muffling cloth she could hear the sound of an engine, smell hot diesel oil. Diesel oil? Where were the horses? Where was the glamour?

Right now, according to the book she'd read on the plane, she should be racing across the desert crushed against her captor's hard body and struggling desperately for her honour...

She almost laughed. Times had certainly changed. Her honour was the last thing on her mind. She'd been kidnapped and all she could think about was calling in the story.

Well, not quite all. There had been a moment as she'd been crushed against Hassan's chest, with his hand clamped across her mouth and his gaze locked with hers, when swooning would have been very easy. And it didn't need a particularly vivid imagination to picture his body hard against hers, holding her tightly as she continued to fight him even as the Land Rover sped away.

Only three days ago she'd been joking about being swept off by a desert prince. Bad mistake. It wasn't a bit funny. She was being jolted hard against the Land Rover floor and, as if he realised it, her captor rolled so that he was beneath her, taking the worst of it.

Although whether lying on top of a man hell-bent on abduction could be described as an improvement... But with his arm still clamped about her, she didn't have any choice.

Maybe it would be wiser to stop struggling, though, put the fantasy firmly from her mind, ignore the intimacy of their tangled legs and try and work out what on earth Hassan thought he was doing. Ask herself why he had taken such a crazy risk.

It would be easier to think without the suffocating weight of the cloak depriving her of her senses, without his arms wrapped tightly about her.

She supposed she should be afraid. Poor Tim would be frantic. Then there was her mother. So much for the constant nagging to be prepared. For the first time in her life she had a real use for the safety pin, could have jabbed it into His Highness's thigh hard enough to make him seriously regret grabbing her, maybe even hard enough to make him let go so that she could throw off the covering.

Unfortunately her handbag, containing the pin, was sitting on the floor of Tim's Range Rover. Along with the clean hanky and the ten pence piece for the emergency telephone call.

This situation certainly fell into the emergency telephone call category, although how many public telephones was she likely to find in the desert? Her mother hadn't thought of that one.

Still, when she found out that her daughter was missing, Pam Fenton would spend far more than ten pence on the telephone giving the Foreign Office hell.

If she found out her daughter was missing. Rose had

the feeling that her disappearance would be kept out of the news if Abdullah could manage it. And he probably could. Tim wouldn't be too hard to convince that her safety depended upon it. And the embassy would do whatever they thought was most likely to achieve her safe return. Just as well she had the mobile, then; Gordon would never forgive her for failing to turn in this scoop.

Oh, Lord! Whatever had happened to her fright-or-flight mechanism? She wasn't afraid; she wasn't planning escape. The primary emotion flowing through her system was indignation at the unromantic manner of her abduction.

She should just be grateful that Hassan hadn't hurt her, that he hadn't tied her up, or gagged her. Well, he hadn't needed to. She hadn't yelled when she could have, should have. Even now she was lying still and doing nothing at all to make life difficult for the man. That was because curiosity was running indignation a close second.

What did Hassan *want*?

Not just a cosy chat. If he'd wanted that he could have knocked on the villa door any time and she'd have been happy to offer him a cup of tea and a chocolate digestive. It was the way they did it in Chelsea. Maybe they did things differently in Ras al Hajar.

Or maybe he had an entirely different agenda.

Think, Rose! Think! What possible reason could Hassan al Rashid have for kidnapping her? What reason did anyone have?

Ransom? Ridiculous.

Sex? There was a momentary wobble somewhere

low in her abdomen at the thought, then she dismissed the idea as errant nonsense.

Could this be the playboy prince's idea of a joke? After all, his cousin the Regent would be seriously ticked off by the kind of publicity this little escapade would generate, and rumour suggested there was no love lost between the two men. She could just imagine the headlines, the news bulletins…

Suddenly everything clicked into place. That had to be it. Headlines. This was no joke. Hassan wanted Ras al Hajar in the news. More than that, he wanted to embarrass Abdullah…

Quite suddenly, she lost her temper. Drat the story! Here she was, wrapped up like a parcel of washing, her bones rattling like stones in a cup, and all because Hassan thought it would be amusing to irritate his cousin with bad headlines and she happened to be a handy source of aggravation.

She felt aggrieved. Seriously aggrieved. She was a woman. Not film star material, maybe, but she had all the right bits in all the right places. Her hair… All right, she might have personal reservations about her hair, but there was no doubt that it was an unmissable shade of red. Her eyes might be plain old brown, but they did the job and came complete with the regulation set of lashes. Her nose… Oh, what the heck. She stopped the inventory and, digging her knees into whatever part of his anatomy happened to be in the way, she heaved herself up and back.

Surprise, or maybe pain, together with the serendipitous lurching of the Land Rover as it raced over the rough terrain, combined to loosen Hassan's grip. She just had time to fling off the cloak before he recovered, caught her and pinned her against the floor. And, as she dragged great gulps of fresh air into her lungs, she was once again staring up into those dangerous grey eyes.

Her situation was not lost upon her. She was vulnerable and utterly at the mercy of a man she did not know, whose motives were less than clear. One of them had better say something. And quickly.

'When you ask a girl to dinner, Your Highness, you really, really mean it, don't you?'

CHAPTER THREE

'DINNER?' Hassan repeated.

Rose blew away an errant curl that was threatening to make her sneeze. 'That *was* you, this morning? "Simon Partridge requests the pleasure..." Tell me, does Mr Partridge know that you've taken his name in vain?'

'Ah.'

Ah? That was it? 'Well?' she demanded. 'Is dinner off? I warn you, I don't do well on bread and water. I'm going to need feeding—'

'Dinner has been arranged, Miss Fenton, but I'm afraid you'll have to accept Mr Partridge's regrets. He's at present out of the country and, in answer to your first question, no, he has no idea that I have used his name. He is, in fact, entirely blameless in this affair.'

The significance of that was not lost on her. Investigations would quickly establish that this was a carefully planned snatch, that someone had used a known friendship to ensure her presence at the races. But when the authorities checked out the telephone number on that invitation, she just knew that it would lead absolutely nowhere.

'Well,' she said, after a moment, 'I hope he gives you a piece of his mind when he does find out.'

'I think you can rely on that.'

Actually, Rose had been planning to give him a piece

of her own mind, but Hassan's voice did not encourage liberties and she thought that it might be wiser to leave it to Simon Partridge. Wherever he was. She hoped he wouldn't be away long. The sneeze threatened again and, inspired, she changed tack. 'You didn't have to bundle me up like that, you know.' She gave a little cough. 'I've not been well.'

'So I've been told.' He didn't sound totally convinced by her act, and she realised that playing for sympathy would get her nowhere. 'You seem to be managing to have a good time, though. Personally, I wouldn't have thought that a busy round of cocktail parties, receptions, public relations tours of the city were at all good for you—'

'Oh, I *see*! You're doing me a *kindness*. You've abducted me so that I shouldn't over-exert myself.'

'That is a point of view.' Hassan's eyes creased in a smile. It was not a reassuring smile, however. 'I'm afraid my cousin has no thought but his own pleasure—'

'And mine. He told me so himself.' She had not been entirely convinced by that, either. Prince Abdullah seemed terribly keen that she should get a very positive image of the country. The curtained windows of the limousine that had taken her around the city at high speed had, she felt sure, hidden a multitude of sins.

She'd been planning to put on one of the all-enveloping black *abbayahs* worn by the local women and, heavily veiled to disguise her red hair, have a closer look around on her own. Not that she had proposed to involve Tim in her little outing. She strongly suspected he would disapprove.

'And as for standing about in the night air at the race course,' Hassan continued. 'Most unwise. It's almost certain to lead to a relapse.'

Except that until she'd spoken to him she hadn't planned on going anywhere near the race course. She didn't bother to mention it, though. She didn't want him to know he'd had anything to do with her changing her mind. 'Your concern is most touching.'

'Your appreciation is noted. You are in Ras al Hajar for rest and relaxation and it will be my pleasure to see that you get it.'

His pleasure? She didn't care for the sound of that. 'Prince Hassan al Rashid, the perfect host,' she responded sarcastically, easing her shoulder from the hard floor of the Land Rover in as pointed a manner as she could manage, considering that she was practically being sat on.

The gesture was wasted. All she got for her trouble was the slightest bow of his head as he acknowledged his name. 'I do my best.' He ignored her snort of disbelief. 'You came to my country for pleasure, a holiday. A little romance, perhaps, if the book you were reading on the plane is anything to judge by?'

Oh, good grief! If he was into fulfilling holiday fantasies, she was in big trouble. She swallowed. 'At least *The Sheik* had style.'

'Style?'

'A Land Rover is no substitute for a stallion.' She realised she was letting her mouth run away with her. Nerves, no doubt. She might refuse to admit to fear but she was entitled to be a little nervous. 'Black as night, with the temper of the devil,' she prompted. 'That's the more usual mode of transport for desert abductees. I have to tell you that I feel short-changed.'

'Do you?' He sounded surprised by that. Who could blame him? 'Regrettably our destination is too far for us to ride there doubled up on a horse.' His eyes smiled, and this time there was no doubt about it; there was not a thing to be reassured about. 'Especially when you've been unwell.' *Oh, very funny.* 'I will make a note for the future, however.'

'Oh, please. Don't trouble yourself.' She attempted to sit up, but he did not move.

'The ground is rough, I wouldn't want you thrown about. You'll be safer lying down.'

With the length of his body covering hers? Did she have any choice? But he was probably right. It would be safer...

What? She couldn't believe she was even thinking that! This man might fulfil all the criteria of the fantasy but that was all it was, a fantasy. He'd kidnapped her and she was far from safe.

She swallowed. Tried to gather her wits. The network briefed staff on this kind of situation before sending them to dangerous parts of the world. She knew that she was supposed to keep the man talking. Make him see her as a person.

The way he was looking at her, the fact that his legs straddled her, that his hips were pressed firmly against her abdomen suggested that he could do little other than see her as a person. A *female* person.

All the more reason to talk. 'You've gone to a lot of trouble for my company. If you wanted to talk to me, why didn't you come and join me on the plane? Or call at my brother's house—'

Maybe he was getting the same thoughts, because without warning he moved, shifting to her side so that he was lying alongside her, eyeing her warily. 'You knew who I was, didn't you? Back there?'

Instantly. She had no intention of flattering him, though. 'I shouldn't think too many of the local bandits went to an English public school. And very few of them have grey eyes.' Even in the darkness, his eyes had been unmistakable. 'And of course there was your voice. I heard that just a few hours ago. If you'd wanted to remain anonymous, you should have sent one of your henchmen to capture me.'

'That would have been unthinkable.'

'You mean your men mustn't handle the goods? That's very possessive of you.' And distinctly unnerving. Or it would be if she wasn't already thoroughly unnerved.

'You are very cool, Miss Fenton.' He reached up to unwrap the *keffiyeh*. The moonlight was shining through the windscreen and into the rear of the truck so that his face was all black and white angles. Harsher than she remembered. 'But you shouldn't be deceived by my education. My mother is an Arab, my father was Highland Scots. I am not one of your English gentlemen.'

No. She felt, finally, a tiny quiver of something closer to fear than she cared to admit to, even in her head. Closer to fear. But not quite fear. She moistened her dry lips and refused to back down. 'Well, I suppose that's something,' she said, with reckless bravado.

There was a flash of white teeth in the darkness before he said, 'Are you really so brave?'

Sure she was. Everyone knew that. Rose 'Front-line' Fenton didn't know the meaning of the word fear. Not much. But this had nothing to do with courage. She'd recognised the danger at twenty feet as he'd stepped on the plane. At twenty inches his magnetism was likely to prove fatal, but it was entirely possible that she would die happy.

It was just as well that the moonlight did not reach her face. She would not like him to read her thoughts.

'Have you no interest in where I'm taking you?' he demanded.

The noisy rattling had stopped a little while ago and they were making speed on a good road. But which one? And in which direction? 'If I asked you, would you tell me?'

'No,' he snapped. Her bravado, it seemed, was beginning to irritate him. 'But be assured I have not carried you off for the pleasure of your conversation, although I have no doubt it will be an unexpected bonus.'

A bonus? To what?

'I wouldn't count on it.' Oh, heck. The golden rule in situations like this was listen and learn, but she couldn't help it. She just couldn't be all girly and pathetic, apparently not even to save her life. Or anything else. Well, that was how myths were made. With a big mouth.

But, for all her bluff, her heart stepped up a gear. Could she be wrong? Could it be that he regularly carried off visiting females? 'Tell me, do you do this sort of thing often?' she asked. Well, that was what she did.

Asked questions. 'Do you have a harem of women like me stashed away in some desert encampment?'

'How many women like you could one man stand?' he demanded, finally exasperated with her and clearly far from amused that she could conceive of such an idea. That pleased her. Whatever he had in mind for her, she would like to be an original.

But he was waiting for her answer. His eyes gleamed darkly as he waited for her to ask why he had carried her off, what he intended to do with her. Unbridled curiosity was undoubtedly her greatest strength, but it was also a weakness. She just never knew when to stop. And her curiosity about this man had been aroused long before she'd set eyes upon him.

His face was above her in the harsh white moonlight, hard planes and dark shadows. His expression was closed, his eyes steeply hooded. She didn't want him to hide from her, wanted no shadows, and without thinking she raised her hand to his face.

Startled by her touch, he pulled back an inch or two. But where could he go? In the rear of the Land Rover he was as much her prisoner as she was his, and, emboldened, she flattened her palm against his cheek, felt the rough stubble of an hours-old beard. This time he held fast, submitted to her exploring touch as she rubbed the side of her thumb along the hard edge of his jaw. She shouldn't be doing this, but there was an excitement about the danger, and as she trailed the tips of her fingers over the chiselled lines of his lips she felt him swallow.

In that brief moment she was the predator, not

Hassan, and in the darkness she smiled and gave him her answer.

'If a man was fortunate enough to have one woman like me, Your Highness, I would make it my life's work to ensure that he wanted no other.' For a moment she let her fingers linger against his mouth, and then she took them away.

Hassan bit back a caustic retort. What could he say? He believed her. And he recognised it not as an invitation but as a warning. What a woman! She hadn't turned a single strand of that beautiful red hair when he seized her. She had not cried out when she might have, but had defied him, was still defying him with her words and with her body, even though she had no idea what her fate might be.

It was fortunate indeed for Rose Fenton that he was nothing like the bitter, twisted man in the old novel she had been reading, or he would have been seriously tempted to put her courage to the test.

If he were honest with himself, he'd admit that he was tempted anyway. She was quite different from any woman he had ever met. She wasn't coy, she wasn't flirtatious, she wasn't afraid…or maybe it was just that she'd had more practice in hiding fear than most women of his acquaintance.

He found himself wanting to reassure her, but suspected she would despise him for such dishonesty. She would be right too. And he realised that it would be wise to put some distance between them.

He had never intended to keep her so personally his captive. For one brief, exhilarating moment he'd even thought that she would come freely, that she could ride up front with him. Maybe if she hadn't seen help so close at hand she would have come quietly.

But the moment had been lost and she was hard to read. The last thing he wanted was to have her throwing herself out of the vehicle. Not at the speed they were travelling. He moved to his knees, gathered the discarded cloak, wadded it into a pillow, then hesitated, unwilling to touch her, risk a repeat of the sizzling impact of her skin against his. But the Land Rover lurched and rattled as they took to the desert again, shaking them both, and, gritting his teeth, he cupped her neck in his hand.

His fingers were cool, firm, insistent against the sensitive skin of her neck, and for a moment Rose thought he was taking her at her word. 'Lift your head,' he said as she resisted, his voice as firm as his touch. 'Try and make yourself comfortable.' And he pushed the cloak beneath her head. 'We've some way to go.'

'How far?' she asked, as he moved away to sit cross-legged against the side of the Land Rover, between her and the rear door. Barring any attempt at escape. Did he think she was that foolhardy? When she had first been snatched she might have thought of it, but not now. She would be lost, hurt, and it would be a long cold night in the desert before she could hope for rescue. 'How far?' she repeated. Hassan's look suggested she was pushing her luck. 'Won't there be people looking for us by now?' she pressed. Helicopters, Jeeps…they could follow the tyre marks until they reached the road, but not until it was light. Nine or ten hours from now at the earliest.

'Maybe.' He glanced at his wristwatch, black, like

everything else he wore, against the pallor of his wrist. 'Your brother has no phone, no way of calling for help and he's hampered by Abdullah's favourite stallion. Will he put you or the horse first?'

'You broke into Tim's car and disconnected the car phone?' she asked, avoiding a direct answer. 'Removed the bulb from the interior light?'

'Not personally.'

No. There was only one person who could have done that. Khalil, who smiled and bowed and served her brother with such eagerness.

'And you let loose Abdullah's horse.' Personally or not, the intent had been his. Hassan's preparations had been thorough, Rose realised. And using the horse had been particularly clever. Tim would never leave one of Abdullah's valuable horses running wild where it might get hurt. She hadn't been in Ras al Hajar for long, but she had quickly realised that no one would be foolish enough to steal it.

'And let loose Abdullah's horse,' he agreed. 'What will your brother do?' Hassan persisted.

'What would you do?' she countered.

'I would have no choice. I would come after you.' With murder on his mind, she had no doubt. She sensed rather than saw him shrug. 'The horse will return to his stable as soon as he's hungry.'

'I expect that's what Tim will do, then,' she said.

'But he's an Englishman.'

'An English gentleman to his boot straps,' she agreed. 'But does that preclude the passionate response?'

'I would anticipate reason rather than passion, but you know him. Is your brother a passionate man?'

How tempting to say that her brother would come after her and kill the man who'd dishonoured her. Perhaps it was fortunate that Tim was exactly the reasoned, sensible man Hassan imagined. Not that she was going to reassure him.

'I've absolutely no idea what Tim's reaction will be,' she said truthfully, banging the makeshift pillow into a more comfortable shape and deliberately turning away from him. 'I've never been kidnapped before.'

By the time the truck finally shuddered to a halt, Rose was stiff in every limb. They had left the smooth, fast highway long since, and the rattling of the chassis, the thrumming of the powerful engine had combined with tension to give her a seriously bad headache. She didn't move even when the rear door was flung open.

'Miss Fenton?' Hassan had jumped down and was now inviting her to descend under her own steam, which suggested there was nowhere she could run for help. Well, she had expected nothing else. The fact that his voice was gentler than before did nothing to help. 'We have arrived.'

'Thanks,' she said, not looking up, not moving, 'but I'm not stopping.'

There was a brief exclamation of irritation. 'Stay there, then, stubborn woman. Stay and freeze.' There was a brief pause, presumably while he waited for her to see sense. In answer she pulled the cloak from beneath her head and covered herself with it. He swore...at least she assumed he was swearing; why else would he do it under his breath? She didn't intend to be prissy about it, after all, she hadn't planned to make his day. But his anger had nothing to do with her declaration of independence. 'You're shivering.'

Mmm. The truck had stopped shaking, but she hadn't. It wasn't anything to do with the cold, though. It was the kind of uncontrollable shivering that started after an accident, the result of shock. She'd had sufficient time to regret her show of bravado while her mind had been taking her on a tour of the realities of her situation. Shock seemed about right.

Maybe if she'd screamed, cried, gibbered with fear when he'd grabbed her, Hassan would have thought twice about carrying her off, whatever his reason. In her experience men would do almost anything to avoid that kind of thing. Unfortunately she didn't have much practice in weeping hysterics.

So, no tears, no hysterics. She had even resisted, with difficulty, the temptation to press the call button on her telephone. The Land Rover was dark and noisy, but Hassan had been close enough to hear if she'd tried to call for help. She had to save the phone for a moment when she could be sure that she wouldn't be overheard.

Maybe she shouldn't even do that, but save the battery for an emergency, although she preferred not to think how much worse things could get. So she had tucked the telephone down in the seam pocket of her trousers where, with any luck, it would not be found.

She felt the rocking movement of the truck as Hassan stepped up beside her. 'Come on,' he said. 'You've done more than enough to justify your reputation.' He didn't wait for further argument but gathered her up, cloak and all, and, holding her close, carried her across the sand.

She considered protesting that she could walk perfectly well by herself, but in the end decided to save her breath. At five foot ten she was no lightweight. Maybe he'd put his back out carrying her. It would be no more than he deserved.

She saw the flicker of firelight, the shadowy shapes of men and palm trees against the night sky, and then she was inside one of those huge black tents that she had seen in some television documentary.

There was a brief glimpse of a lamplit room furnished with rugs and a divan before he elbowed aside a heavy drape and put her down on a large bed. A bed! She swung her legs to the floor and, clutching the cloak about her, stood up with a speed that sent the blood rushing from her head. She swayed and he caught her, held her for a moment, then lowered her back onto the bed, lifted her feet, removed her shoes.

That was it. Shoes were far enough.

'Go away,' she said, through gritted teeth. 'Just go away and leave me alone.'

Hassan ignored her, dropping her shoes beside the bed. He remained at her side, eyes narrowed as he watched her. And Rose felt the colour flush rapidly back to her cheeks. Apparently satisfied, he nodded, took a step back.

'You'll find hot water, everything you need through there,' he said, indicating yet another room beyond more thick dark hangings. 'Come through as soon as you've freshened up and we'll eat.' And with that he swung round and disappeared into the living apartment.

Eat! He expected her to tamely wash and brush up and sit down to eat a civilised meal with him?

She was outraged.

But she was also hungry.

With a shrug of resignation, she sat up and looked about her. This might be a tent, this might be camping, but, rather like the private jet, it was not as she recognised it. The room was hung with richly worked cloth, furnished with antique brass-bound campaign furniture, and a large trunk that she guessed doubled as a dressing table.

She put her feet to the floor, felt the smooth silk of the carpet beneath her feet. It was warmer inside and she threw off the cloak, padded across to the trunk and lifted the lid. As she'd suspected there was a shallow tray containing a mirror, brushes, combs. There were other things. Things that brought the tremor back to her fingers.

There were fresh supplies of the make-up she wore, a jar of her favourite moisturising cream, the sunblock she used. The man had done his homework. He wanted her to be comfortable. Which might have been heart-warming except that it suggested her stay might be prolonged. Which was anything but.

The bathroom was similarly equipped with shampoo and soap that were familiar friends. She poured hot water from a jug into the basin, washed her hands and face, all her suspicions about Khalil confirmed. Who else would be able to disconnect the telephone in the Range Rover, remove the light bulb without suspicion? Not that she blamed the young man. In a country where loyalty was first and always to the tribe, the outsider would always be at a disadvantage.

A fact Hassan had discovered for himself when he'd been passed over for the throne.

She returned to the dressing table, freshened her make-up, combed her hair, brushed the dust from her *shalwar kameez*. Then she picked up the long silk chiffon scarf. About to loop it about her throat, leaving the ends to trail below the hem of her tunic, the way she had worn it earlier, she changed her mind. Instead she draped it over her head, modestly covering her hair in the traditional style. Only then did she join her insistent host.

Hassan raked his fingers through his hair as he paced the rug. He'd expected tears, He'd expected hysterics. He'd been prepared for them. What he hadn't expected was the kind of in-your-face defiance that dared him to do his worst even when her teeth were chattering with delayed reaction shock.

What on earth was he going to do with her? She'd have to be watched night and day or she'd probably kill herself trying to get back to town.

It would have been easier at the fort, where there were doors with locks. But also much harder.

Too many people came and went there, and not all of them could be relied upon. It would have been much more difficult to keep her presence a secret. Out here, with a few picked men, men he would trust with his life, men he would trust with *her* life, that would not be a problem.

Out here he had relied on distance and the desert to

keep her his prisoner. His first encounter with Rose Fenton suggested that it wouldn't be so easy. So he'd have to offer something to make her want to stay. Something important.

As he reached the edge of the rug and turned the hangings were pushed aside, and his breath caught at the sight of her. In the darkness he hadn't seen what she was wearing when he'd seized her. He'd assumed she would be dressed in something a modern western woman would consider suitable for an evening at the races to be followed by dinner with a man she did not know but who might be worth the effort. Something dressy. Modern. Sharp. The kind of clothes worn by the kind of woman who'd travelled the world, risked all kinds of danger for her job.

The *shalwar kameez* was beautiful, but unexpectedly demure. The long chiffon scarf draped over her vivid red curls was exactly the kind of covering his half-sisters, his aunts, his mother would have worn at a mixed family gathering.

It was a shock to see her wearing something like that. It made him feel as if he had somehow violated her, and after that first still moment, when movement had seemed beyond him, he crossed swiftly to pull back a chair for her.

She didn't immediately take it, but glanced about her, taking in the brass-bound map chest, the fold-out travelling desk. 'When you go camping,' she said, 'you certainly do it in style.'

Demure, but still full of fire. 'You have a problem with that?'

'Who, me?' She crossed to take the chair he held for

her, sat down with all the poise of his Scottish grandmother at a vicarage tea party. 'Hell, no, Your
Highness,' she said, dispelling the image as quickly as
she'd provoked it. And she took a linen napkin from
the table, flicked it open and laid it on her lap. 'If I
have to be abducted, I'd just as soon it was done by a
man with the good sense to install an *en suite* bathroom
in his tent.'

'I am not a Highness,' he snapped. 'Yours or anyone
else's. Call me Hassan.'

'You want to be friends?' She laughed. Laughed! A
few minutes ago she'd been shivering in his arms, her
teeth chattering.

'No, Miss Fenton, I want to eat.'

He crossed to the entrance to the tent and barked a
swift command before turning to rejoin her. His head
was bare, revealing the thick thatch of hair that, against
the unrelieved blackness of their surroundings, was not
as dark as she remembered.

In the lamplight a hint of red betrayed his Scottish
father's Highland roots. But everything else, the black
robes bound with a heavy sash, the *khanjar* he wore at
his waist, was from another world. The ornate filigree
silver scabbard was old and very beautiful, but the knife
it held was not an ornament.

It would be easy to forget that, to think of Hassan as
civilised. She was certain he could be charming. But
she wasn't fooled. There was a streak of steel through
the man, tempered in fire every bit as hot as the one
that had tempered the blade of his dagger. Sense told
her it would be wiser not to stir up the embers. Her

nature suggested she would be unable to resist the temptation. But not yet. Not yet.

They ate in silence. Lamb broiled over an open fire, rice spiced with saffron and pine nuts. Rose had thought she wouldn't be hungry, but the food was good and there was nothing to be gained from a hunger strike. It would be far wiser to conserve all her strength.

Afterwards one of Hassan's men brought dates and almonds and thin desert coffee scented with cardamom.

She took an almond, nibbled on it while Hassan drank his coffee and stared out into the darkness. 'Are you going to tell me what this is all about?' she asked eventually. He didn't move. Said nothing. 'I only ask because my brother will have been going out of his mind with worry for the last few hours and by now my mother will have joined him.' She paused. 'I would hate to think they should be put through that simply because you wanted to irritate your cousin.'

He glanced up sharply then. Her probing had evidently hit some tender spot. 'They are the only people who will worry about you? What about your father?'

She shrugged. 'My father is of the absentee variety. His only purpose in my mother's life was to provide the means to motherhood. She's a card-carrying feminist of the old school, you see. And a pioneer of single-parenthood. She's written books about it.'

'I wouldn't have thought the subject was so difficult that anyone would need to buy a book to discover how it was done,' he replied drily.

Well, fancy that. The man had a sense of humour.

'They are not do-it-yourself manuals,' she informed him. 'More in the line of philosophical commentary.'

'You mean she felt the need to justify her actions?'

Straight to the point and no messing. She liked that, and found it rather difficult to stop herself from smiling at his bluntness. 'Quite possibly,' she said. 'Maybe when this is over you should ask her.'

Her smile dared him. 'Maybe I will,' he said. 'Do you mind? Not having a father?'

He was getting rather close to her own tenderest spot. 'Do you?' she asked, and knew the answer even before the words were out of her mouth.

His look was thoughtful, and she thought perhaps she had given away rather more than she should have. Act dumb, Rosie, she reminded herself. Act dumb. But he let it go. 'Why did you come here?'

'To Ras al Hajar?' she asked. 'I thought you had that all worked out.'

'You could have gone to the West Indies for winter sun and fun.'

'Yes, I could. But my brother invited me here. It's a while since I've seen him.'

'Abdullah invited you here. Abdullah laid on his personal 747 to bring you here—'

'No,' she said. 'That was for you.' His gaze was unblinking. 'Surely? I mean, he wouldn't...'

'He wouldn't cross the road to shake my hand. I merely took advantage of a flight that had already been arranged. There seemed little to be gained by compounding the extravagance for a point of principle.'

'Oh.' Hassan was right. She should have accepted a long-standing invitation to visit Barbados.

'My cousin is planning to use you to further his political ambitions, Miss Fenton. What I want to know is whether you're an unwitting pawn, or whether you've come here specifically to help him.'

'Help him?' Apparently there was a lot more to this than embarrassing his cousin. 'I think you're overestimating my influence, Your Highness.' The flicker of irritation that crossed his face at her disobedience in insisting on the title was oddly pleasing.

'No, Miss Fenton. If anything I underestimated you. And I have asked you not to call me Your Highness. The title is Abdullah's. For the moment.'

So close to the throne, but never aspiring to it. Maybe. She wondered how Hassan had felt when he was passed over for a younger half-brother. Disinherited after being brought up as a favourite grandson. How old would he have been? Twenty? Twenty-one? There was certainly a battle for power going on here, but she was beginning to think that whoever came out on top it wasn't likely to be young Faisal.

Rose propped her elbows on the table and nibbled at another almond. 'I'll do a deal with you. If you don't call me Miss Fenton in that particularly irritating tone of voice again, I won't call you Your Highness. What do you say?'

CHAPTER FOUR

HASSAN almost laughed aloud. Almost. Rose Fenton was doing a pretty good job of making 'Your Highness' sound more like an insult than anything he could manage, and he doubted it was by chance.

'Am I allowed to call you Miss Fenton in any other tone of voice?' he enquired, as politely as dignity allowed. He just knew she would take advantage of any sign of weakness.

'Better stick to Rose,' she advised. 'It'd be safer. Now, about my mother—'

Oh, no. He wasn't getting involved in a cosy chat about her mother. 'I deeply regret the anxiety your disappearance will cause her. I sincerely wish I could allow you to call her and put her mind at rest.'

'In what way "at rest"?' She didn't feel the need to restrain her feelings, he realised as she laughed mirthlessly. A broad gesture took in her surroundings. 'What exactly would I tell her?'

'That you are in no danger.'

'That's for me to decide, Your Highness, and I have to tell you that the jury's still out.' Her eyes were dark, her look direct, and they told him that she wasn't interested in his fake platitudes. That his 'regret' cut no ice with her. 'And for your information I don't think my mother would be very impressed either.'

Not if she was anything like her daughter. 'You're close?' he asked.

Rose looked startled by that. 'Yes,' she said. 'I suppose so.' Not that close, he suspected. Two strong and independent-minded women would grate uncomfortably against one another. As if she realised that she wasn't being convincing, she added, 'She's very protective.'

'Good. She'll be far more useful to my cause if she's thoroughly roused.'

She let out a sharp, explosive little breath that betrayed her outrage at being tricked like that. 'What *is* your cause?' she demanded. 'What's so special that you think you've the right to do this?' He'd been waiting for the question, but he was sure she wouldn't expect a straight answer. He wasn't about to give her a crooked one, so he took a date from the dish, bit into the sweet flesh without answering her. She gave him a we'll-get-back-to-that-one look and changed tack. 'What'll you do if my mother decides to keep a low profile and leave all the fuss to the Foreign Office? I'm sure Tim will advise her to do that.'

'The more I see of you…' He checked himself. 'The more I *hear* of you, Rose, the more confident I become that she will do exactly what she wants. Almost certainly the opposite of any advice she is given.'

Was that a compliment? Rose couldn't be sure.

'And if she disappoints you? Won't all this have been a waste a time? I assume embarrassing Abdullah is the prime motive for my abduction?'

'Do you?'

She didn't, not for a minute. There was far more to

this than simply irritating Abdullah. But with luck she could provoke him into revealing his purpose.

Hassan sat back and watched her. He had anticipated that she would have done her homework, would quickly catch on to the tension underlying the deceptively peaceful surface of Ras al Hajar. He was right.

'What other reason could there be?' she asked, in a voice far too innocent.

To stop her being used by Abdullah, to distract him, to give Partridge time to get Faisal home. But now he had Rose Fenton sitting beside him, her character as fiery as her hair, he could think of any number of reasons for keeping her. All of them personal.

'Embarrassing Abdullah is not my prime motive. Just a happy side effect. Which is why I won't be leaving the public relations aspect to him.' He checked his watch. 'We're three hours ahead of London. There's plenty of time for your disappearance to make the mid-evening news.'

Rose, scarcely able to believe the arrogance of the man, managed to resist looking at her own wristwatch. 'Are you telling me you've issued a press release?'

'Not yet.' And he smiled. Smiled! 'Not until the last minute. I don't want to give your Foreign Office time to check the facts and hear Abdullah's pressing reasons for keeping the story under wraps. You'll be one of those "word is just coming in" stories. I'm sure you can fill in the gaps without my assistance.'

'Yes.' She could fill them in, all right. Just as she could imagine the buzz of adrenalin in the newsroom as the story broke while they were on air. Run with it? Don't run with it? Time it right and they wouldn't have a choice. Not unless they were prepared to allow some other network to grab a scoop on one of their own reporters being kidnapped. After all, Gordon knew where she was, had implied there was something brewing. He'd phone her mother first to warn her, if he could, check if she'd heard anything, but it was too big a story to ignore. 'How will you send it?'

Hassan smiled again at her apparently casual question. 'Not from here.'

No. She shrugged. 'Oh, well, it was worth a try.' If he thought she hoped to get to whatever communication equipment he had tucked away and yell for help, he would be less inclined to wonder if she had any of her own. 'Why don't you tell me what this is all about?' she asked. 'You seem to think I have some influence. I might be able to help.'

'You're hoping for a scoop?' That appeared to amuse him. 'Isn't *being* the story sufficient for you?'

'It's getting to be a rather dangerous habit.'

'There's no danger here,' he promised. Laughter did something wonderful to the lean features of his face and his voice was velvet-soft. 'Just a little celebrity. It should do wonders for your status. You'll be able to name your price when you negotiate your next contract.'

'I'm not in the entertainment business.'

'Oh, come on, Rose. We both know that news is very big business. Twenty-four-hour-a-day television. And if you can put a pretty woman in the front line it adds a certain frisson of excitement, a touch of glamour. Believe me, the world will be glued to its television sets worrying about the brave and lovely Rose Fenton.

Newsmen will be storming the embassy door for visas and poor Abdullah will have to let them come or risk being pilloried in the world's press. You news persons take these things so personally.'

His amusement angered her like nothing else. How dared he be amused? How dared he sit there, enjoying his coffee, while out there her family would be going out of their minds with worry? How dared he treat her like one of his namby-pamby bimbos with nothing on her mind but where the next diamond was coming from?

She was a journalist, a serious journalist, and if she and her family were being put through the grinder for his amusement she wanted the whole story. She was entitled to that. 'I've a right to know why I'm here.'

'You know why you're here. You're in Ras al Hajar to relax, recuperate. You can do that up here near the mountains far more pleasantly than you can in town. It's cooler, the atmosphere is drier. You can ride, swim in the stream, sunbathe. The food is good, the hospitality legendary.' He offered her an intricately wrought silver dish. 'You should try one of these dates. They're really good.'

She stood up abruptly, dashing the dish from his hand so that the fruit flew everywhere. 'Stuff your dates,' she said, and stormed out of the tent and into the night.

It was a grand gesture, but an empty one. Outside there was nothing but darkness and the desert. But Rose wasn't about to turn around and go back inside, face his further amusement at her total loss of self-control. She should be probing, questioning, keeping her mind completely detached from what was happening. But she couldn't. It was just too personal.

Aware that Hassan's men, gathered about a campfire a little distance from the tent, had stopped talking and had turned to see what she would do, she spun on her heel and headed in the direction of the Land Rover. She tried the door. It was unlocked.

Her scarf slipped back from her hair as she pulled herself up into the driving seat and she shivered a little. Hassan was right; it was cooler at the camp. Up here, he'd said. They must be near the mountains at the border. She tried to picture the map, but they were miles off the road and she had no idea which way the road was. North. She was sure it would be north. If she headed for the North Star she would eventually reach the coast. Maybe.

Not that anyone had left the keys conveniently in the ignition. Life wasn't that simple. Oh, well. She yanked out the wires and touched them together. The engine roared into life, startling her almost as much as the men, who until that moment had been idly watching her, grinning stupidly in the firelight.

They leapt up, falling over themselves to get to her. They would have been about twenty seconds too late. Hassan was not so slow. As she slammed the Land Rover into reverse he opened the door and, without bothering to ask what she thought she was doing, he lifted her bodily from the seat and the vehicle stalled. Then he tucked her beneath his arm and headed back towards the tent.

This time she did yell. She yelled and she screamed and would have punched him too, but her arms were trapped so all she could do was flail her hands uselessly at his body. He didn't appear to notice.

It wasn't that she'd expected to get away. In fact she wasn't at all sure she wanted to be racing over unknown terrain in the darkness. But she *was* sure that this was the most humiliating thing ever to happen to her. The fact that she'd brought it on herself did nothing to help.

'Let me go!' she demanded, using both hands in her attempt to lever his arm from around her waist.

'And if I did? Where would you run to?' He stood her up on the rug in the middle of the spilled dates, catching her wrists so that she couldn't strike out at him. 'Stop it. Stop acting like a silly girl and tell me what you planned to do.' She had no plan. He knew that as well as she did. But he wasn't leaving it. 'Come on, don't be coy, Miss Fenton, it's not your style to keep your thoughts to yourself. You've proved unexpectedly useful when it comes to hot-wiring a Land Rover. I applaud your spirit. But what next? Where were you going?' She didn't answer, but was pleased to note that he was no longer laughing. 'What's this? You have nothing to say? You're not normally so slow with a pithy response.'

Her response to this was both pithy and to the point. Whether he was happy with it was debatable, since his brows rose like a high-speed elevator.

'My interest is purely practical, Miss Fenton.' So, they were back to the sarcastic 'Miss Fenton'. 'I'd like to know what you have in mind so that in the unlikely event that you get beyond the perimeter of the camp there's some chance we'll find you before the sun bleaches your bones—'

'All right! You've made your point. I'm an idiot, but
what about you, Hassan?' She'd stopped bothering to
struggle. She was strong, but he was more than a match
for her. 'How can you do this?' She stared at him.
'You're an educated man. You know that this is wrong,
that even here, where you're apparently a real old-
fashioned warlord you've no right to do this.'

'Do what?' He yanked her towards him so that his
face was close enough for her to see the muscle working in his face, for her to see the blaze of anger heating
up the steely grey of his eyes. 'What exactly do you
think I'm going to do to you?'

Oh, heck, she'd done it now. She'd really done it,
but she wasn't going down without a fight. 'What exactly do you *think* I think, Your-Seriously-High-and-
Mightiness?' Sarcasm, after all, was a game for two.
'You've already kidnapped me,' she said, flinging the
words at him. 'You're keeping me here against my
will—' Far worse, he'd made her lose control. Even
when Michael had died, even when she'd been doing
reports live to camera with rockets landing all around
her and the crew, she'd never broken down and completely lost it the way she had just then. There were
tears stinging the back of her lids. Tears of pure rage
and utter frustration. 'You've got an imagination. Put
yourself in my shoes and use it!'

Somehow his hands, instead of grasping her wrists,
were at her back, gentling her. And her face was
pressed against his heart. There was a comfort in the
steady beat beneath her cheek, comfort in the warmth
of his arms about her as she sobbed into the blackness
of his robes. It was so long since she'd cried. Five

years. Nearly six. Longer since she'd let a man hold her close while she exposed her emotions, provoked a caring response.

Not that Hassan cared. Not really. He was just better at dealing with hysterics that most men of her acquaintance. If he went in for this sort of thing on a regular basis he probably got a lot of practice. It was a thought to tense the steel in her backbone and she pushed away from him, lifted her head, forced a smile to her lips.

'I'm sorry about that. Losing control is so...' She sniffed a little, palmed away a tear. 'So messy. Not my kind of thing at all. You'd better put it down to the kind of day I'm having. If you'll excuse me, I'll just go and lie down in a darkened...er...room for a while.' She turned, and was halfway to the bedroom when he said her name.

'Rose.' She didn't like her name very much. She'd shortened it from Rosemary, which she loathed. But Hassan said it as if it was the most beautiful word in the entire world. She stopped, could do nothing else, and waited with her back to him. 'Promise me that you won't do anything like that again.' Or what? She turned. His expression was no longer angry. She couldn't tell what he was feeling. Well, that was fine. She was totally confused herself. 'Please.'

She suspected that asking, rather than telling, did not come easily to him. 'I can't do that, Hassan,' she said, almost with regret. 'If I can escape, I will.'

'You're making this a lot more difficult than it has to be.'

She shrugged. If he was uncomfortable with the role he'd chosen, he would have to live with it. 'You could always let me go.' Then, maybe, she would stay of her own accord. It wasn't the company she objected to, just the manner of it.

'I was hoping I might persuade you to think of yourself as my guest. This way you force me to make you my prisoner.'

'You invite a guest,' Rose said, ridiculously disappointed. 'You could have invited me.'

'You'd have come?'

Maybe. Probably. In a heartbeat. But she couldn't tell him that. Not now. And they both knew that as a guest her presence wouldn't serve his purpose. Instead she extended her wrists to him, holding them close together, palm upward, offering them as if for the handcuffs. 'Perhaps it's time we both recognise the truth of the situation.'

For a moment he stared at her, his face livid in the flaring lamplight. Then he stepped up to her, took her proffered wrists and, holding them easily in one hand, pulled free the scarf that now trailed untidily from her neck. Without a word, he bound her wrists, wrapping the scarf around them once, twice, three times, in a purely symbolic gesture but one that left her in absolutely no doubt of the situation. As if to drive home the point, he caught the loose ends, wrapped them swiftly about his fist and yanked her towards him.

Her protest evaporated in a quick gasp as he caught her shoulders and pulled her hard against his body, so that her head had nowhere to go but backwards, leaving her vulnerable, exposed.

'Is this what you want?' She didn't believe it. She didn't believe he was going to do this. He wouldn't.

Even as she opened her mouth to warn him that he was making a big mistake, he did.

His lips were hard, demanding, punishing her for daring to defy him, for making him do this. But even while her head was telling her to fight, to kick, bite, make him pay with all the limited means at her disposal, feminine instinct kicked in with a ferocity that took away what little breath she had.

This man is strong, it told her. This man would protect her against the worst the world could throw at her, he would give her strong children and lay down his life to defend them.

It was primitive, the female picking out the strongest male in the group for her mate. It was elemental and savage. But beneath the insistent, provoking heat of his mouth, his tongue, Rose knew that in some way she didn't quite understand she had won.

And with that knowledge she melted, dissolved, and for long, blissful seconds she surrendered herself and gave him back everything she had, meeting the marauding silk of his tongue with all the siren sweetness at her command. Oh, yes, she wanted this. She wanted him. In more than five years she had never been tempted, but from the moment he had turned to look at her as he boarded Abdullah's 747 she'd known; this was the moment she had been waiting for.

Then, when she was quite boneless in his arms, his to take with a word, Hassan released her without warning, so that she swayed and staggered.

For a moment he continued to stare at her, as if he could not quite believe what he had done. Then he stepped back. 'I, too, hate to lose control,' he said, his face a mask of restraint. 'Now I believe we are quite even.' And with that he spun on his heel and walked from the tent.

Rose could scarcely catch her breath, could scarcely stand, and she clutched at the chair-back, at the table, staring at the pale silk that Hassan had used to bind her wrists.

She was still trembling, not with rage, but with un-fulfilled longings. She pulled her hands free, flung the scarf to the floor and raced to the opening of the tent, but Hassan had disappeared into the night. There was just a long-legged hunting dog stretched out across the entrance, and a little way off stood an armed man who, at her fierce glance, bowed respectfully.

No more silly grins, she noticed. Well, that was something. She was tempted to test her guard's purpose, but there seemed little point. She had pressed the point and she had got her answer, more answer than she was quite comfortable with. Now she would have to live with it.

She heard the Land Rover starting up, moving off at speed. Hassan, having been delayed by the need to put her firmly in her place, was presumably racing off to alert the world's media to her disappearance.

She lifted her chin a little and told herself she was glad to see him go. Yet the camp felt ridiculously empty without him, and, as if sensing her loneliness, the dog stood up and pushed a nose up against her hand. She stroked his narrow silky head on automatic, then turned away and surveyed her prison.

She checked at the mess of dates on the priceless rug and stooped to pick them up. Then she realised what she was doing and, angry with herself, stopped, backed off and skirted them as she retreated to the refuge of the bedroom. The dog followed her and lay at the foot of the bed.

Waiting, no doubt, for the return of his master, Rose thought. Well, tough. There was only one bed. It was a big bed, but she was there first and she wasn't in the mood to share. A small voice warned her that after the way she had kissed Hassan she could scarcely expect a choice. An even smaller voice suggested that she would be fooling herself if she pretended she wanted one.

She put her hand to her mouth. What on earth had she done? She wasn't in the habit of jumping into bed with just any man who abducted her. Just any man, full stop. She was too busy these days for the falling in love stuff. Been there, done that. Crossed it off the list.

Hassan certainly knew how to re-ignite a girl's interest.

Rose suspected that Hassan could ignite just about anything he chose to fix with eyes that had heated her from frost to meltdown faster than she could say it. She'd recognised him for what he was the moment she had set eyes on him. A very dangerous man.

She kicked off her shoes and flung herself on the bed. The telephone dug into her thigh.

Hassan put his foot hard on the throttle and drove from the camp as if the hounds of hell were after him. Did she know? Did she understand what she'd done? He was gripping the wheel so hard that even in the darkness the bones showed white through his skin.

Why did she have to be like that? It was hard enough

that she was beautiful. But he could resist beautiful. He'd resisted the charms of any number of beautiful women who would have been happy to be held captive in his desert encampment. Maybe that was the difference. Rose Fenton was wilful, strong. She fought him.

She scorned him for what he'd done and then held out her hands to him and dared him to do his worst. In that moment she'd jarred loose the civilised veneer he wore so casually over his desert heritage and laid him bare to the bone, stripped him back to the man his grandfather had been in his youth, a desert warrior who had fought for and taken whatever he wanted, whether it was land, or horses, or a woman.

He'd never had to do that and yet he hadn't thought twice about it. He'd made his plans, summoned the men who would do whatever he asked of them and he'd taken Rose Fenton from under the very nose of her brother.

He'd thought it would be difficult. She had a reputation for toughness and he'd thought she would fight him. It hadn't been like that. Her toughness had made it easier. She hadn't been afraid. She'd been cool, curious. She wanted the story. Or she had until her nerves momentarily let her down and she bolted.

Even then she'd defied him, mocked him, urged him to do his worst and, by heaven, he had come close. He'd bound her wrists as if she was some prize he'd captured in a raiding party, to do with as he willed. He'd bound her wrists and kissed her and had been a heartbeat from taking it all.

But even then she'd won. Not by fighting him. There had been no struggle for honour, nothing to heat his blood and drive him over the edge. She'd been cleverer than that. Cooler than he'd given her credit for. She'd called his bluff and kissed him right back, hot and sweet. Lava on snow.

It was just as well she had no idea it wasn't a bluff or one of them would have been in deep trouble.

He had a feeling it would have been him. If Partridge didn't find Faisal soon, it still might be.

Rose retrieved the telephone from her pocket and for once in her life found it hard to know what to do best. She knew she should contact someone, but who?

Not Tim. She wasn't involving him. Caught like some piggy in the middle between two feuding princes, he could only get crushed.

Gordon, then. Yes, Gordon. She really should call her news editor. Except he would be getting a press release courtesy of Hassan at any moment. All she could add was the name of her abductor, and she wasn't quite ready for that. That would mean choosing sides, and although her head suggested that Abdullah, as Regent, as her brother's employer, deserved her loyalty, her heart just wasn't in it. Tim's warning had been unnecessary; she'd quickly seen for herself that Abdullah intended to use her.

Wasn't that what Hassan was doing?

Maybe. But at least he was frank about it. And she wasn't prepared to hold the fact that Hassan could kiss a woman senseless against him. It didn't *necessarily* mean he was bad. The odds were against it, but she was prepared to give him a chance. Several chances, even.

So what had happened to the totally impartial journalist?

She was on hold. Waiting for the facts, waiting for the truth to emerge. And, since she had no option but stick around, she'd hold the call to the office until she had a story to file. The real story. No sense in wasting the battery after all.

Her mother. She could at least privately assuage Hassan's conscience and reassure her mother. Not that he would know about it, of course. She punched in the number. It was engaged and remained engaged, although she tried again every few minutes until it became quite obvious that she was too late; her mother had heard the news, presumably from Tim, and was already in full vent. And her mother understood the power of the press. Forget the Foreign Office; her first call would be to Gordon. Lucky Hassan.

She switched off, closed the phone and looked about her. She'd been fortunate so far that he hadn't thought to search her. Until that kiss she'd assumed he was being a gentleman. It seemed more likely that the women he knew who wore such traditional garments didn't carry mobile phones.

She could not rely on her luck holding out for ever, however. She needed a secure hiding place for her one link with the outside world. A link she might yet have a desperate need for. And she might not have much time.

There was a new box of tissues on the dressing table. She ripped open the top, removed some of the tissues to make a space, then pushed the palm-sized phone to the bottom of the box, tidied it, pulled a tissue up so that it looked as if she'd been using them.

She was left with a pile of tissues which she wadded extravagantly and used with the cleanser provided by her thoughtful host to remove her make-up. Then tossed them untidily beside the box to prove what she'd done with them.

She yawned. Nerves, tension, exhaustion, combining suddenly in a need for sleep. Yet the thought of stripping to her underwear was slightly unnerving. Except surely any man who had gone to such lengths to provide her with her favourite cosmetics wouldn't have overlooked the fact that she'd need a change of clothes? She pulled back the bedcover. No, he hadn't forgotten.

She picked up the nightdress that had been neatly folded and left beneath the cover for her, and shook it out. It was...it was... She found herself biting back a grin. It was such a thoroughly *reassuring* garment. So completely *respectable*. It was the kind of nightgown that a Victorian spinster would feel safe in. No man with ravishment on his mind would choose anything like it, not unless he planned to fight his way through yards and yards of winceyette and cotton lace. Presumably that *was* the point he was trying to make. The dog had lifted his head at her stifled giggle and now thumped his tail hopefully.

'All right,' she said 'So he's not all bad.' She held up the nightgown. 'But I'd like to know where on earth he found something like this. In his grandmother's attic, do you suppose?' It would have to have been his Scottish grandmother's attic. It was just the thing for a cold Highland night. She shivered. Just the thing for a cold desert night, too.

She slipped out of the silk two-piece that she'd chosen with such care, with such hopes of impressing the interesting Mr Partridge and his master. What a waste of time that had been. Simon Partridge wasn't actually in the country and Hassan would have abducted her even if she'd been wearing a pair of combats.

Although, on second thoughts, she doubted that combats would have drawn the same startled glance when she'd joined him for dinner. Unfortunately, she couldn't decide whether that was a good thing or not. Did she want to be that noticeable? She pulled a face as she picked up a hairbrush. Cursed with hair the colour of a Technicolor sunset, how could she be anything else?

When she finally climbed into the vast bed, settling the folds of the voluminous nightgown about her, she decided that her mother would have approved of it. It was draughtproof, oozed comfort, and what it lacked in length it more than made up for in width.

Her last thought before falling asleep was to wonder whether Hassan had raided the same wardrobe for her day-wear.

Would she wake up to find a good tweed skirt laid out for her? A cashmere twinset in a nice, sensible heather mixture? A pair of solid knickers with a double-stitched gusset and the kind of stout elastic that discouraged wandering hands...

The idea should have been reassuring. Somehow it wasn't.

Hassan sat beside the bed for a long time just watching her. How could a woman who had created such havoc sleep so peacefully? It was tempting to wake her, disturb her, except that he suspected he would be the one made to suffer.

She was so lovely, her skin so pale against the bright copper of her hair. She hadn't given him an inch all evening and even in sleep she had the power to disturb him more than any woman he'd known.

It wasn't a comfortable feeling. He didn't like it. But he suspected that when she went away it would be even worse.

CHAPTER FIVE

ROSE stirred. She felt warm and wonderfully comfortable and snuggled further beneath the covers, untroubled by any inclination to leap out of bed and get on with life. This was nice. She shifted slightly. The warm weight against her back shifted too, moulding itself snugly against the curve of her spine. That was nice too. It had taken her so long to get used to waking alone.

Rose froze, slowly opened her eyes, all senses on full alert.

She was not alone. *Not alone.*

The sunlight was being filtered softly through the black goathair of Hassan's tent. Her gaze flickered over the antique campaign chest, standing open in the corner, with her make-up scattered on the inner lid. Over the soft sheen of a priceless carpet. Over the heavy silk of her *shalwar kameez*, neatly folded on a camel stool next to the bed. And the weight at her back was a solid reality, definitely not a figment of some dream she was still waking from.

The fuzzy feeling of comfort rapidly evaporated as the events of the previous evening flooded back with vivid and terrible clarity. What was a girl to do? Should she turn and let her captor take her in his arms and finish what they had started last night? Or should she opt for outrage?

She quickly opted for outrage before she could weaken, erupting from the covers in a flurry of indignation. Her companion erupted too, leaping to his paws and barking excitedly.

It was the dog. Just the dog.

She fell back against the pillow and allowed her heart-rate to subside a little. Not Hassan. Relief warred with disappointment. She had definitely been alone too long.

The dog yawned widely, then settled down again with his head laid flat on her stomach. 'So, you get to sleep on the bed, do you?' she said, once she'd regained her breath. 'My mother would have a fit if she could see you.' She stroked his head. 'She doesn't approve of dogs on the bed.' She didn't approve much of husbands either. Only lovers received her seal of approval. It was one of those mother/daughter disagreements that still festered between them, long after the husband was no more.

Something, some movement out of the corner of her eye made her look up. Hassan, attracted no doubt by the noise, had swept the drapes aside.

'You slept well?'

Amazingly well, while he looked as if he'd had a very bad night indeed. But before she could ask her brain to compute a sensible answer they were interrupted.

'I knew it!' A small woman, heavily cloaked and veiled in an *abbeyah*, appeared at his side and, without waiting for an invitation, pushed past. Then, having confirmed her worst suspicions, turned on him. 'For heaven's sake, Hassan!' Outrage, heavily laced with exasperation. 'What on earth are you thinking of?'

Was it his wife? Rose hadn't even thought about a wife. It was a long time since she'd blushed, but faced with almost terminal embarrassment she discovered that she still remembered how.

Hassan did not immediately reply, or attempt to defend himself. The woman apparently had no expectation that he would, since she didn't wait, but swept up to the bed. Tossing aside the cloak and veil, she revealed herself as a young and very beautiful woman dressed, beneath the traditional trappings of purdah, in a heavy silk shirt and a beautifully cut skirt that stopped just short of her knee.

'Nadeem al Rashid,' she said, extending a small hand to Rose. 'I apologise unreservedly for my brother's behaviour. His heart is in the right place but, like most men, he has the brains of a donkey. You're coming home with me right now; you'll be safe there until Faisal returns. And in the meantime we can think of some way to explain your disappearance.'

Faisal? Rose's mind clicked into gear. This girl couldn't be more than Hassan's half-sister. That would make her Faisal's full blood sister, and yet she was clearly intent on mopping up Hassan's mess. Direct action seemed to be a family trait.

Rose glanced at him, but he appeared to be avoiding meeting her gaze and she bit down on her lip. It wouldn't do to be grinning too obviously; she'd just sit back and watch the fun as Nadeem turned on him.

'What on earth were you thinking of, Hassan?' She repeated the question, but didn't give him a chance to answer. 'No, don't tell me, I can guess. Have you spoken to Faisal?' Hassan sent her a warning look, which she ignored. 'Well?'

He could see there was no stopping her, so he shrugged and conceded the point. 'I sent Partridge to the States to bring him home but he's slipped his guards and taken off somewhere.'

'How inconsiderate of him,' she said drily. 'I wonder who taught him that trick?'

'I'm handling it,' he said, through gritted teeth. 'Just leave it to me.'

'I don't think so.'

'No one asked what you thought, Nadeem. I want you to leave now. This is my problem and I don't want to get anyone else involved.' He didn't want his sister getting into trouble and Rose found herself unexpectedly in sympathy with him.

'I am involved, idiot. Faisal is my brother, too.'

'If it goes wrong…'

'With you in charge? How can it?' Rose had thought she could do sisterly sarcasm, but this young woman could take the simplest sentence and make it really hurt. 'Take no notice of him,' Nadeem said, returning her attention to Rose. 'I've brought a spare *abbeyah*; no one will see you arrive at my house.' She turned on her brother. 'You've behaved disgracefully, Hassan. Miss Fenton is a guest in our country…' She slipped into Arabic and clearly vilified his character in no uncertain terms.

Rose watched the scene played out before her with a growing desire to laugh. There was something about a powerful man being roundly taken to task by one of his female relations that left her wanting to cheer. Then, over Nadeem's gesticulating arms, her glossy black hair, her gaze finally connected with that of Hassan. It was as if she could read his mind.

'Um, excuse me.' She waved a hand and Nadeem stopped her tirade long to enough to turn and stare at her. 'I hate to interrupt when you're clearly doing a fine job of reading Hassan his character, but do I get a say in this?'

And from behind his sister Hassan's eyes thanked her.

Well, that was great, but she wasn't doing it for him. This was a purely professional decision. The last thing she wanted was to be rescued by Princess Nadeem, no matter how well intentioned her motives. She'd be taken to town and kept out of sight and out of contact. At least here she was in the centre of things. Close to Hassan…where everything was happening.

Nadeem, though, misunderstood, and came and sat down on the bed, took her hand in her own. It was tiny, exquisitely manicured, beautifully painted in hennaed arabesques. She made Rose feel like some ungainly giantess.

'Miss Fenton, I realise that you simply want to go back to your brother's house and resume your holiday, but we have something of a problem. Abdullah is close to seizing the throne and Faisal, stupid boy, has chosen this moment to…well…let's say his timing is a little off.' She spat some words at Hassan that undoubtedly involved the stupidity of men in general and of her brothers in particular. 'The uproar caused by your disappearance will keep Abdullah in check for a few days, and if you'll stay with me until everything is sorted out I am sure Hassan will make sure your sacrifice does not go unrewarded.'

'Unrewarded?' She repeated the word. What was Nadeem saying? She'd get the Ras al Hajar equivalent of the Order of Merit?

'Well, Rose,' he said, softly. He was standing behind his sister and she looked up at him. 'It would seem that you can name your own price. A *lakh* of gold…a rope of pearls—'

'"And Thou Beside me singing in the Wilderness"?' Not honour, then. Just plain old gold, she thought, as she completed his alternative version of the line from *The Rubaiyat of Omar Khayyam*.

'Whatever you wish,' he replied.

That momentary glimpse of the man behind the eyes, a man capable of love, would do to be going on with. '*Can* you sing?'

'Like a nightingale.' *Oh, sure.* 'Or was it a crow?'

'The story, Hassan,' she snapped. 'That's all I want. The story, the whole story and nothing but the story. And I stay here.'

Nadeem looked momentarily startled. 'But you can't—'

'She can and she must.' Hassan, with her co-operation assured, regained mastery of the situation. 'I assure you that Miss Fenton's sacrifice will be no greater than she chooses.'

'Oh, but—'

'Haven't you got a clinic today, Nadeem?'

'This afternoon.' She glanced at her wristwatch. 'Actually, since I'm here, could I ask you about some new incubators?'

'Tell Partridge what you want. He'll sort it out.'

Nadeem certainly knew how to pick her moments, Rose thought as the dark beauty smiled so that her entire face lit up. 'I thank you. The mothers and babies of Ras al Hajar thank you, Hassan. Now, Miss Fenton—'

'Rose, please.'

'Rose.' For a moment she wore a look that suggested she had not finished. Then she made a very feminine gesture of resignation. 'Is there anything I can bring you? Anything you need?'

'Your brother has made every effort to ensure my comfort. Except for clothes.' She plucked at the nightdress. 'This isn't really my style.'

'No?' For a moment Hassan's eyes lingered on the rise and fall of her breasts beneath the solid cloth. 'No,' he repeated, his voice softer. Then he cleared his throat. 'I'm sorry that my choice didn't meet with your approval, but there's a trunk full of stuff in your size. I'm sure you'll find something you like.'

Rose, whose heart was already pounding with quite unnecessary vigour, lurched uncomfortably as he turned to the trunk lid and reached for the box of tissues. The weight would warn him...

'Go *away*, Hassan,' Nadeem said. 'You've no business in here.'

'Rose Fenton is not one of your wilting virgins, Nadeem. If she wants me to leave, she'll say so.' He glanced at her. There was no apparent change in his expression and yet she knew, deep down, he was smil-

ing. 'I guarantee it. But you're right. If you two are
going to be sorting through clothes, I'd rather be somewhere else. Will you stay and have breakfast, Nadeem?'

'Just some coffee,' she said, waving him away with
an imperious gesture. She waited until he had gone,
then checked the outer room before turning back to
Rose. 'Look, it doesn't matter what Hassan says. If you
don't want to stay here you don't have to. Just say the
word and you can leave with me now.'

No. She'd stay and see it through. She had promised
Hassan as much. The words might have been in her
head, but she knew and so did he.

'No. I'll be fine. Really.'

Nadeem's smile was knowing, and hoping to distract
her, hoping to distract herself, Rose asked, 'What's a
lakh of gold? Some kind of jewellery?'

'A *lakh*?' Nadeem was clearly astonished at her ignorance of something of such importance. 'No. It's a
weight. A hundred thousand grams.' *Of gold?* Rose
tried to imagine how much that was and failed.
Nadeem, however, dismissed it as nothing. 'Don't
worry about it. Whether you stay here or come home
with me Hassan will still have to pay your brother for
carrying you off the way he did.'

'Pay my brother?' She could just imagine Tim's reaction to that. Even Nadeem might learn a thing or two
about indignation. If Hassan offered him money for his
sister's honour it was quite possible that Tim might
break the habit of a lifetime and actually hit him.

But Nadeem was serious. 'Of course he must pay.
He has dishonoured you.' She was thoroughly matter-
of-fact about it. Did she take it for granted that Hassan

had shared her bed? Rose wondered. Or did just being alone with him at his camp count? She thought it wiser not to ask. 'Or maybe your brother will just kill him?' Nadeem suggested.

'Er... I don't think so.' Even indignant, she didn't see Tim offering Hassan much more than a sock on the jaw.

'No?' Nadeem shrugged. 'Of course, he is English. Englishmen are so...phlegmatic. Hassan would certainly kill your brother if the situation were reversed. But if you do not want money or blood there is only one other solution. He will have to marry you. Leave it to me. I will arrange it.'

This was getting further into the realms of fantasy than Rose was prepared to go. 'Surely a man of his age, his wealth...' she was beginning to think like Nadeem, she realised '...must be married already?' And, no matter what his sister said, she wasn't sharing.

'Hassan? Married?' Nadeem laughed. 'He'd have to find someone strong enough to hold onto him first.'

'But if marriages are arranged here...?'

'Hassan is different,' she said. 'Hassan is impossible. With you it would be a matter of honour, so he would have no choice, but he wouldn't consider it under any other circumstances. Believe me, we've tried, but he's travelled too much to accept some good, traditional girl who just wants to stay at home and raise children. It wouldn't be kind to either of them. But then he's too traditional to marry one of those actresses or models he spends time with so publicly when he's in London or Paris or New York. Not that it would last five minutes if he brought her back here.'

'Why?'

'Women need to be born to the life. Our men are possessive and modern women do not care to be possessed. They want what Hassan can give them, but they refuse to give up what they already have.' She smiled. 'I pity them.'

'But you are happy.'

'I work at being happy. I have a kind husband, beautiful children and a worthwhile job in a country I love.' She glanced at Rose. 'Hassan loves it here, too. He couldn't live anywhere else.' Then she sighed. 'He would have been a great Emir,' she said. 'He always had it in him. While Faisal…well, Faisal doesn't understand the sacrifices involved.' She thought about it for a moment. 'Or maybe he does…'

'And Abdullah?'

Nadeem started, as if aware she had been letting her mouth run away with her brain, then she glanced at her watch and gave an unconvincing squeak. 'I don't have a lot of time. Let's look at these clothes. I have the feeling you won't find much to your taste.'

'Well?' Hassan regarded her over the remains of her breakfast. 'What did you find out?'

'Find out?'

'My little sister has a runaway mouth. I'm sure you had no difficulty in prising loose all kinds of information.'

'Nadeem is charming and thoughtful and very helpful.'

'If she made that good an impression she must have been unusually garrulous, even for her.'

'Not at all. She told me very little I didn't already know.'

'It's the "very little" that bothers me.'

'Why? Ensuring that Faisal keeps his throne is hardly something to be ashamed of. I had assumed you were planning on seizing it yourself.' If she'd hoped to provoke a reaction, she failed. 'And I'm not going to be telling anyone what you're doing, am I?' She smiled. Not yet, anyway. 'Actually, her main concern seemed to be that you would have to pay my brother dearly for dishonouring me.'

She was teasing him, Hassan decided. Amusing herself at his expense. Well, that was fine. Whatever kept her happy. 'Whatever you think is appropriate,' he said dismissively. A *lakh* of gold would be cheap enough for her co-operation. And she was co-operating. Or very clever. 'Although having met you I begin to doubt that either you or your brother would take so much as a *tula* of my gold.' That at least was the truth. He would stake his life that she was not in Abdullah's pocket. And his heart rejoiced.

'Maybe not, but that leaves you with a problem.' He waited, content to let her have her fun. It was a long time since anyone had amused him half so much. 'According to Nadeem, the only alternatives to a cash settlement would appear to be death or dishonour, and since Tim would die himself rather than kill anyone...' She paused. 'Even you...' He laughed. 'She's decided that marriage is the only answer.'

Rose watched as his hand, carrying a cup to his lips, paused briefly. 'She may be right,' he said. Then he drank his coffee, returned the cup to the saucer and rose

to his feet. 'I see that you are wearing jodhpurs. Is that
a hint that you would like to ride this morning?'

Well, Rose, she thought. That didn't go quite the way
you planned, girl. Not at all. It would certainly teach
her not to try being clever before lunchtime. And she
discovered she couldn't quite meet the challenge of his
gaze. Not yet. But, confronted at eye-level with the ornate *khanjar* he wore at his waist, she realised that he
was still waiting for her answer.

Did she want to ride with Hassan? Was that why
she'd insisted on wearing the jodhpurs in the face of
Nadeem's protest? She was suddenly very confused. It
was a long time since she'd ridden a horse alongside
the man she loved. A long time since she'd done anything. Even been tempted. But the jodhpurs had seemed
so familiar, so comforting...

Still avoiding his eyes, she stretched out her legs.
'They were the only trousers we could find,' she said
evasively. 'Oddly, I have this aversion to wearing long
silk frocks during the hours of daylight. Even ones with
designer labels.'

The underwear had been something else, though. She
had not the slightest objection to silk next to the skin.
But that was as far as she was prepared to go. Hence
the man's shirt and an old pair of jodhpurs she'd raided
from Hassan's drawer chest, while Nadeem had looked
on, torn between horror and amusement, covering her
face with her exquisitely painted hands to hide her gig-
gles.

The shirt was loose and she'd had to cinch in the
waist of the jodhpurs with a belt, but they were com-

fortable. She rubbed her palms over cloth worn soft with use and finally looked up.

'Were they yours?'

He hesitated. 'Probably. I don't remember.' He looked distinctly uncomfortable with the idea of her wearing his clothes, she thought, although it must have been years since he'd worn them. He'd put on a lot of muscle since the jodhpurs had been made for him. 'I would have provided you with your own clothes, but the inference would have been drawn that you had left of your own choice.'

'You brought my boots.' A pair of stout, cross-laced ankle boots that she'd worn with the long woollen skirt she'd travelled in. She'd had no reason to wear them since she arrived and she wouldn't have noticed if they'd been missing for days.

He shrugged. 'The ground out here is rough.'

'And it would be a touch embarrassing if you had to rush me to hospital with a broken ankle.'

He smiled at her apparent naivety. 'Don't be silly. I'd just say I found you like that. You wouldn't betray me, would you, Rose? You'd think of the story and keep your mouth shut.'

The man was insufferable. Right. But insufferable. She abandoned any hope of bettering him and returned to the subject of her clothes. 'Of course, if Khalil had given you all my clothes he would probably have ended up in jail as a conspirator. I don't imagine Abdullah would be very gentle with him.'

'Khalil?'

'My brother's servant. Someone must have passed on information about what make-up I use. And shampoo.

That's a neat shower, by the way.' A small tank had been filled with water and the early sun had heated it to a pleasant warmth. She finished her coffee. 'And who else would have been able to fix the Range Rover without attracting attention? Khalil washes it as often as his face.'

'So,' he said, neither confirming nor denying her musings. 'Do you want to ride?'

'It's one of the promised attractions.'

'*Can* you ride?'

'Yes,' she said, rising to her feet, increasingly uncomfortable as the focus of Hassan's undiluted attention.

'To stay on one of my horses you'll need more than a passing acquaintance with a mild-mannered pony from some genteel riding school for young ladies.'

'I don't doubt it, but I had a good teacher. You aren't worried that I'll be spotted?' she asked, rapidly changing the subject. 'If they use search helicopters?' She rubbed her hand over her hair. 'I'm pretty hard to miss.'

'You do have a way of making your presence felt,' he agreed, with a wry smile. 'But your hair is not a problem. With the right clothes, you'll be as good as invisible. Wait here.'

He returned a few minutes later with a red and white checked *keffiyeh* which he handed to her. She flicked it out of the fresh folds and draped it over her head, then stopped. It was a lot bigger than she had expected and she was at something of a loss to know quite how to deal with it. She held the ends out and looked at him helplessly.

For a moment they both remembered the scarf she

had been wearing and what he had done with that. Then he took a quick breath. 'Here,' he said. 'Like this.'

He swiftly wrapped it about her head and lower face, folding it, tucking it into place, his fingers skimming her cheeks but never quite making contact. Even so, her stomach clenched at his closeness, at the almost-touch that raised the down on her face, raised gooseflesh everywhere.

'There. All done.'

'Thank you,' she said, her voice little more than a whisper from her dry mouth.

'No, thank *you*, Rose. For understanding about Nadeem. If Abdullah found out…'

'Yeah. Well. I won't get a scoop hiding out in Nadeem's back parlour, will I?'

Again there was the smile that did nothing to the muscles of his face, just lit some place behind his eyes. Then he held out a gold-trimmed camel-hair cloak he'd been carrying over his arm.

She turned quickly and slipped her arms through the wide openings and let it hang about her. It was loose and feather-light and billowed softly about her in the fresh breeze coming off the mountains and into the tent.

'You look almost like a Bedouin,' he said, wrapping his own black headcloth around his face.

Rose stroked her chin over the cloth. 'But for the beard.' She put her head to one side. 'But then you don't wear a beard, do you, Hassan? Why is that?'

'You ask too many questions,' he said, and with his hand at her back he eased her through the opening and into the bright morning sunlight.

'It's what I do. But you're miserly with your answers.'

His response was to direct her to the waiting horses. One was a glorious black stallion, exactly like the one she had taunted him with the previous night. She wondered if it had been chosen deliberately, then decided that her wits were wandering.

The other mount was a smaller, but very beautiful chestnut. 'What's his name?' she asked, as she stroked the animal's neck.

'Iram.'

'Iram indeed is gone with all his Rose…' The line ran through her head and she wondered if he was telling her the truth, or simply testing her to see if she knew more than one line from *The Rubaiyat*. She whispered the name and the horse flicked his ears, lifted his fine head. The truth, then. Or maybe a bit of both. 'How appropriate.'

'I thought so. You know the verse by heart?'

'I was made to learn it at school as a punishment for some misdemeanour… I can't remember what.'

'But you remember the verse.'

'I didn't consider it a punishment. And I never forget anything I love.' She gathered the reins and Hassan linked his hands for her, throwing her up into the saddle before adjusting the stirrups. It was a while since she had been on a horse but, held at the head by the groom, he seemed quiet enough as she continued to stroke his neck.

Hassan mounted, glanced at her, then, apparently satisfied with what he saw, he nodded. The grooms stepped back and the horses leapt forward.

For a moment Rose thought her arms had been yanked out of their sockets and was grateful that Hassan was so far ahead he didn't witness her unseemly struggle with the deceptively docile beast she had been mounted on.

By the time he brought his mount to a halt and turned, rearing, to see what had happened to her, she was in control and flying, sweeping past him in a blur of movement. He thundered after her, passed her and led the way, his black cloak billowing and flying in the wind. It was wonderful, exciting, terrifying all at once, and when he finally came to a halt on the bluff of a hill she was laughing and breathless and trembling from the sheer effort of controlling her mount. Hassan was laughing too.

'You thought he'd be too much for me, didn't you?'

'He very nearly was, but you're an excellent horse-woman.'

She laughed. 'It's just as well. But it's been a while.'

Hassan threw a long leg over the saddle, dismounted, gathered the reins. 'Who taught you?'

'A friend.'

He turned to look at her. 'A man, I think. You ride like a man.'

Rose was keenly aware of his level, penetrating gaze fixed upon her. 'Yes, a man. He bred horses. Beautiful horses.' She stroked the neck of the animal beneath her. The creak, the scent of leather and hot horseflesh brought it all flooding back. 'He was my husband.'

There was a momentary pause while he digested this information. 'Was?' he enquired softly, when she volunteered nothing more. 'You're divorced?'

'No, he died.' There was a moment of silence and she could see him trying to decide whether to ask the question. 'It wasn't a riding accident.' If it had been a riding accident she could never have got on a horse again. 'He had something wrong with his heart. He knew but he didn't tell me.' She hadn't talked about it in more than five years. Had just got on with her life. Tried not to think about it. She took her feet from the stirrups and slid to the ground. 'One day it just stopped. And he died.'

Hassan joined her and, leading the two horses, began to walk them. 'I'm sorry, Rose. I had no idea.'

'It was a long time ago.'

She sensed him glance at her. 'Not that long. You're a young woman.'

'It's been almost six years.' She scarcely saw the landscape that stretched before her. She was seeing the life they might have had. Two children by now, with ponies of their own. Michael had asked her if she wanted children, would have given them to her, but she had resisted the idea. She was young and had wanted all his attention. And there hadn't seemed any urgency.

Her eyes misted and she stumbled against a rock. Hassan caught her, held her, his hand at her waist.

'You are fortunate that you have your career,' he said. 'Something to fill the emptiness.'

'Do you think a job could do that? That any kind of career would compensate for what I lost? I loved him. He loved me.' Unconditionally. As a woman. She hadn't had to compete for his attention, hadn't had to be better, or prove anything. Just be herself.

He looked down at her, deeply thoughtful. 'Tell me,

did you get your reputation for fearlessness because you were hoping to die, too?'

Her immediate response was anger. How dared he think he could psychoanalyse her? She'd had years of her mother doing that. Nodding sagely when she'd married Michael, as if it had confirmed some theory she was working on for her latest feminist tract. But even as she thought the words she knew she was wrong. Hassan's eyes weren't knowing, but smoky soft with a sympathetic grasp of how she'd suffered.

'Maybe,' she whispered, admitting it for the first time. 'Maybe. For a while.'

'Don't be in too much of a hurry, Rose. Allah will come for you in his own good time.'

'I know.' She managed a smile. 'But it's a lot easier to get a reputation than lose it. Of course I've got a busy mouth, and that gets me into all sorts of bother as well.'

And suddenly he was smiling too. 'I've noticed,' he said drily.

He'd noticed, but his voice, although teasing, had a warmth that brought her crashing back into the present. It was now that mattered. Today. And for just a moment, with his hand at her waist, his eyes hotter than the sun beating down on her back, she thought that he was going to kiss her again. But he didn't. She saw the moment when he took the mental step back from the brink a split second before he let his hand drop to his side and moved on.

Well, he wasn't getting off that easily. She had a story to write and it was time to get down to serious research. 'So,' she said, falling in beside him. 'Why *did* you shave off your beard?'

CHAPTER SIX

HASSAN laughed, enjoying the lightning switch from thoughtful introspection to attack. 'Who said I ever had one? It's not compulsory, you know.' She restricted her response to a perfectly judged raising of eyebrows, reminding him wordlessly that she was not some gullible girl he could string along with just any old line. 'You're like a terrier with a bone,' he complained.

'Compliments don't impress me, Hassan, I've heard them all before. Why?' She pressed for an answer, wanting to get under the skin of the man. Find out what really made him tick.

'Maybe I'm just a natural born rebel.'

'Your bog standard black sheep?' Rose didn't think so, and her quick head-to-toe trawl of his figure suggested as much. 'That's a bit obvious, isn't it?'

'I was twenty-one,' he said. 'It's not an age for subtlety. And when something works, why change it?' He led the way to a low flat rock, hitched the horses to a scrubby tree and invited her to sit, offered her a drink from the flask he carried on his saddle.

She pulled the *keffiyeh* loose and swallowed the cold water gratefully. He followed suit, sitting beside her.

Before them the land fell away in a rocky escarpment to the coastal plain, and in the distance Rose could see the flash of sunlight on a sea so blue that it merged with the sky. It was a stark landscape in which the shadows from boulders and the occasional copse of scrubby trees stretched for ever.

Stark, utterly different from the cool greens of home, and yet she could see the attraction. There was something compelling, timeless about it. It was scoured clean and strangely beautiful.

Hassan loved it, Nadeem had said. She could easily believe it was a place that could carve itself into a man's heart. Or a woman's. She glanced at him, still waiting.

He shrugged, rubbed his hand over his clean-shaven chin. 'My grandfather decided that I wouldn't be able to hold the tribes together,' he said. 'It was a difficult time. There was big money pouring in from the oil and he knew that rival families would use the fact that my father was a foreigner to stir up trouble for me.'

'He had no sons of his own to succeed him?'

'No. Half a dozen daughters, but no sons. I was his oldest grandson, but when it came down to it he did what all rulers have to do and put his country before his heart.'

'When he named Faisal his heir?'

'My mother remarried quite soon after my father died. A political match. She had a couple of daughters; Nadeem is one of them. Then she had Faisal. He has the perfect pedigree to rule.'

'He's still very young.'

'I know, but we all have to grow up. It's his time. I only hope he handles it better than me.'

She felt for him. His pain was buried deep, but it was there. 'It must have been hard for you to accept.' And she'd have been hard pressed to say if it was the journalist or the woman who was speaking.

Hassan picked up a stone, squeezed it as if moulding it between his fingers. 'Yes, it was hard. I had nothing but this.' He palmed the stone for a moment and then he tossed it away. 'Then I had nothing.' Rose remained silent. What could she say? He'd been disinherited because of his parentage. No words would ever change that. He glanced at her. 'What made it harder to bear was the fact that he named Abdullah as Regent Emir to keep his enemies quiet.' Then he threw up a hand in a gesture of acceptance. 'He had no choice; I know that. He was protecting me. If I'd been ten years older he might have defied them and I might have held it all together. But he was dying and he was probably right; I was too young to handle that kind of trouble. Now the only trouble we have is Abdullah and his cronies, with their sticky fingers in the coffers while the people yearn for education, medical care, all the advantages of living in the twenty-first century.'

She thought of the luxurious medical centre she had been shown. Everything new. Like the fancy shopping mall crammed with designer boutiques, the fabulous health club where she had been given an instant honorary membership, it had reeked of privilege. She had suspected a downside, had planned to look for it. Apparently she had been right. Rose wrapped her arms about her knees and, with her chin propped on them, she stared out across the empty landscape. 'No one would blame you for taking it badly,' she said.

'No one did. And no one did a thing to stop me. Disinherited, I shaved off my beard, took to wearing black and behaved very badly indeed. He might have taken away my right to the throne, but my grandfather compensated for the loss in other ways. I had too much money and too little sense and set about proving to the world that my grandfather had made the right decision, while Abdullah and his cohorts stood on the sidelines practically cheering me on, hoping I'd self-destruct. I was immature, spoilt and stupid. I know this because my mother, who would do almost anything rather than travel on a plane, flew to London for the sole purpose of telling me so to my face.'

If she was anything like Nadeem, Rose thought, hiding a smile as she did so, he could have been left in no doubt what she thought of him. 'You didn't let your beard grow back, though. Or adopt a slightly more conservative form of dress. Or even moderate your behaviour much.'

'The rebel coming to heel like a whipped dog? Wouldn't Abdullah have enjoyed that. He'd have spread rumours that I was trying to get myself back into favour, planning to make a bid for the throne, the perfect excuse to move against me and Faisal. No, I've made my bed and I'm content to suffer for it until my brother is safely installed in his rightful place.' He glanced down at her. 'And while my least favourite cousin is kept busy scouring the countryside for you, Rose Fenton, there's still time.'

He nodded towards the coast where, below them, a pair of helicopters had appeared and were quartering the ground in a search pattern. He leaned back on an elbow, showing no obvious sign of concern.

'What'll you do if they come to the camp?'

'Shoot the first man who attempts to enter the women's quarters.'

'The women's quarters! Oh, puh-leeze!'

'What is wrong with that?'

He didn't know? 'Well, for a start, there is only me, and I'm not one of your women.'

'You're under my protection. And one woman or a hundred, what difference does it make?'

She stared at him. 'But to kill someone…'

'I didn't say kill. Just shoot. A bullet through the leg of the bravest is usually sufficient to discourage the rest.' He shrugged. 'They would expect nothing less.' Seeing that she still wasn't convinced, he added, 'They'd do the same to me if the situation were reversed.'

She shuddered. 'But that's so…primitive.'

'You think so?' The grey eyes glittered in the bright sunlight. 'Maybe you're right. The primitive is nearer to the surface than most of us are prepared to admit, Rose, as you came close to discovering at first hand last night.'

She felt sure he wasn't referring to her abduction, planned and carried out with such chilling precision. He was talking about that moment when they had both come close to abandoning any pretence at civilised behaviour, to toppling over the edge.

Of course it had just been the tension. Captor and captive bound together in a precarious, supercharged atmosphere, a cauldron of combustible emotions that had, under pressure, reached an almost inevitable flashpoint…

She looked quickly away. The helicopters had moved

further down the coast. 'I think we'd better go back while I can still move. It's weeks since I've had any serious exercise and I'm going to be as stiff as a board after this.'

'Really?' He stood up and offered her his hand. When, after the briefest hesitation, she took it, he pulled her to her feet. For a moment he continued to grasp her fingers against his palm. 'Don't tell me you've been wasting your time down at the health club?'

'If you've been keeping that close an eye on me, Hassan,' she said sharply, 'you'll know exactly what I've been doing.' An early-morning workout with some light weights to get back the muscle tone she'd lost during weeks of enforced idleness. Not much of a preparation for riding one of Hassan's horses.

He neither confirmed nor denied her accusation. 'Just say the word, Rose, and I'll be happy to give you a rub-down with horse liniment.'

For the briefest of moments she allowed her imagination free rein to dwell on the thought of his hands stroking some warming unguent over her shoulders and back, along the tightening muscles of her legs. She didn't doubt he was capable of making her feel a lot better. But she retrieved her hand, pulled a face and managed a laugh.

'Thanks, Hassan, but I think I'd better just suffer. You're in enough trouble already.'

Enough trouble. How much trouble was enough? How far did a man have to go before he had reached the limit of the trouble he could get into and still find a way out at the end?

Always assuming that he wanted a way out.

Hassan paced impatiently, hanging onto the satellite phone, waiting for Simon Partridge to come on the line. Waited and told himself to face reality.

Rose Fenton was a woman with the world about to fall at her feet. In another week the press would be pleading for her story. Hollywood would probably want to make a film of it and her agent would be holding an auction for the book.

Every time he went near her he made it easier for her. She only had to look at him and he wanted to tell her his deepest secrets, innermost longings, longings that seemed to involve a lifetime spent getting to know her.

Instead he'd offered to rub her down. How crass could one man get? Except that it was all too easy to imagine the warm silk of her skin sliding beneath his hand.

His groan was heartfelt. He needed this to be over. Quickly.

'Come on, Partridge! Where the devil are you!'

Silk skin, silk lips. He stopped, closed his eyes, and for a moment allowed himself to drown in the memory of her warm lips parting for him, the sweet taste of her on his tongue.

He'd intended to keep this strictly impersonal. Keep his distance. It should have been easy. She was a journalist, and he disliked journalists on principle. But from the moment he'd answered the phone and her voice had filled his head he'd been hooked.

He stopped pacing, leaned against the trunk of an ancient palm tree. Who was he kidding? From the moment he had stepped aboard Abdullah's plane and been confronted by a pair of frankly assessing brown eyes he had been hooked.

She had something special. The something special that made people turn on the evening news for her report from the latest trouble spot. The something special that made people care about her. And, close up, he'd discovered what it was.

She had a vulnerability beneath the toughness. Laughed more readily than she wept.

Even when she wanted to weep more than anything else.

She'd come close to spilling out her grief today. He'd wanted to hold her, comfort her. He wanted to know what kind of man would bring that look to her eyes... Wanted to be that man.

'Yes...hello...' A groggy voice broke into his thoughts.

'Partridge?' he said sharply.

'Excellency?' There was a fumbling sound, a crash. 'What's happened? What's wrong?'

'Nothing is happening,' he said. 'That's what's wrong.' His irritation iced the distance between them. 'Have you found him yet?'

'Excellency, I'll let you know when I find him. But it's four o'clock in the morning here...'

'So?' he snapped.

'So I didn't get to bed until two,' Partridge snapped right back, fully awake now, his hackles rising fast. 'The best information I have is that Faisal is holed up in some cabin in the Adirondacks with a girl. But no one is saying which girl, or what cabin, and there are a heck of a lot of them. Since they're not all arranged in a neat little row along a paved road, it's taking time to check them out.' He paused. 'And while we're discussing missing persons, how *is* Miss Fenton?' Hassan smiled, if a little grimly, at his aide's edgy sarcasm. If he'd heard about Rose's abduction it went a long way to explaining Partridge's unusually quick temper. 'I assume her disappearance is down to you? It's all over CNN that she's missing.'

Well, that was something. 'And who are they suggesting is responsible?'

'No one seems to have a clue. Or if they do they're not saying. Abdullah's line seems to be that she must have wandered away from Tim's car while he was hunting for the horse and got lost, or that maybe she's fallen into a gully.'

'Rose Fenton? They can't be serious.'

'It's a lot more palatable than admitting that she might have been kidnapped. You said you wouldn't do anything...like that.'

Like what? Just what did Partridge think he was doing to his heroine of the airwaves?

'Did I? I remember the conversation somewhat differently. However, you can rest assured that Miss Fenton is in good health and perfectly happy to remain as my guest.' There was a distinctly un-aide-like noise down the line. 'Your concern is misplaced, believe me. She's more than capable of dealing with the situation. In fact I'd say she's taking full advantage of being in the centre of a breaking story and playing the situation to her own advantage. And I promise you she's in no danger.'

'No?' Partridge was clearly not convinced, but then they both knew he wasn't concerned about physical danger. His reputation might be exaggerated but Hassan was the first to admit that there had been a lot to exaggerate.

'Did you know that she's been married?' he asked, cruelly needing to puncture Partridge's precious image of the woman. Hassan knew he'd assume that she was divorced. The lack of a response suggested that he'd hit a nerve. Then, angry with himself, he said, 'Why don't you call your contacts in London and find out what you can about him?' That he had died, that she grieved, that her place on the pedestal was safe. 'With all the interest in her right now, it shouldn't be difficult.'

'Is that an order or a suggestion?' Only Partridge could bristle long distance.

'I don't make suggestions,' he replied curtly. 'And in the meantime, if you're so worried about Rose Fenton's welfare, I suggest you find Faisal and get him back here without delay. Then you have my permission to come back and tell me to my face exactly what you're thinking right now.'

'I don't need your permission for that,' he said stiffly. 'And when I've told you, you'll have my resignation.'

'You can challenge me a to a duel if it will make you happy, but not until you've found Faisal.'

Rose crossed to the tent and went inside, glad to be out of the sun. She unwound the *keffiyeh*, tossed aside the cloak and pushed her fingers through her hair, lifting it from her neck.

She was hot and dusty, the cloth of her shirt sticking to her back. What she needed was a shower, followed by a dip in the deep, cool water of the sports club pool. The shower was empty and the pool was hours away. All that left was the stream, and she had the feeling that the stream would be off limits unless Hassan gave the word. And Hassan wasn't there to ask.

When they'd arrived back at the encampment, he'd paused only long enough to see her safely dismounted and under cover before wheeling his horse and riding away. Visiting his communications centre, no doubt, to find out how his plans were progressing, she'd thought crossly, and she'd watched him disappear behind the thick fringe of palm trees, a couple of his men falling in behind him.

He could have taken her with him. It hurt that he hadn't; she'd thought he'd begun to accept her as a partner in his plot. More fool her.

Well, she had her own communications centre, and she'd jolly well use it, too. She poured some water into a bowl and washed her hands and face. Then she poured herself a glass of iced tea from a vacuum flask. She'd call her mother first. And she'd check her voice mail.

Gordon would undoubtedly have left a message for her. Several messages, possibly. No one else would have thought of that. No one else knew she had the phone.

She stood for a while beneath the wide awning, sipping her tea, looking out across the oasis. It was so peaceful here. In the quiet heat even the dogs had the wisdom not to waste energy in useless barking.

Don't stand when you can sit; don't sit when you can

lie. In the drugging stillness of midday the philosophy held a certain appeal, and she was tempted into a canvas safari chair left in the shade of the awning.

Hassan's Saluki stretched himself at her feet, while below her the endless desert gave the impression that there was all the time in the world. It was actually rather difficult to get herself worked up about anything beyond the empty horizon. She just wanted to stay here, ride, talk.

Make love.

'A Flask of Wine, a Book of Verse—and Thou Beside me singing in the Wilderness—' Down there beside the stream, she thought. Beneath the palm trees and the pomegranates, where they would be hidden from the world by the thicket of oleanders. He'd have a silk carpet spread for her and soft cushions. Because the 'Thou' was unquestionably Hassan.

Dangerous. Trouble. But he made her blood sing.

Make love.

The words had popped into her head unbidden but now refused to budge.

Make love.

It was a long time since love had appeared on her life's want list. Nearly six long years since she'd found Michael where he'd fallen and died in the paddock. It had been quick, the doctor had told her later. His heart had been a time bomb waiting to go off and even if she'd been with him she could have done nothing to save him.

His children had blamed her for what had happened, though. Not as much as she'd blamed herself. But the doctor had been right. Michael had known the risk and he'd taken it without burdening her, given her what she'd needed. He'd been so gentle. So kind. And she'd made him happy. She had nothing to reproach herself for.

And now Hassan had reminded her that life went on. That she was a young woman with hot blood pumping through her veins. The next time he decided to play the savage, she vowed, he wouldn't get off so lightly. And as she set down her glass she realised that she was smiling.

Hassan cut the connection, tossed the phone to the man holding his horse, mounted and rode hard back towards the oasis, hoping that physical effort would dull the need, cool the seething cauldron of emotions brought to the boil by Rose Fenton.

He'd met women who could turn a man's head at fifty paces. Women who could heat a man's blood with a look. But he'd never met anyone like Rose.

Those other women had looked at him, smiled at him, flirted with him, but they'd never seen beyond the jeweller's case in his pocket. And it hadn't mattered. Yet he couldn't even bear to hear Rose Fenton's name on his aide's lips, knowing that Partridge honoured her with his esteem, while he wanted to keep her hidden away, keep her just for himself like some old-style sultan.

She was right. It was a primitive way to behave. But it was the only way he knew, while Rose Fenton was a modern woman, the daughter of a prominent feminist, a woman in control of her own life, moulded for the twenty-first century.

They came from very different worlds and he was forced to confront the vastness of the gulf that lay between them. It was nothing that wealth or power could surmount. It was fundamental, part of who they were.

It made him angry. Restless. He wanted her so much that his skin felt two sizes too small for his body; worse was his certainty that she knew it. From the look in her eyes it wouldn't take much to tempt her to share the bed with him. But it would be on her terms and not his. In a week or two she would go away, resume her career, get on with her life. She would have marked him for ever, while she would go about her business and he would quickly be forgotten, blurred with a dozen other casual encounters.

He realised that his hands were clenched into fists, the knuckle bones white against his skin, and he took a slow, deep breath, stretched his fingers, forcing himself to let go of the thought. Thinking about it was not a good idea. He refused to think about it. He would stay away from her. He had enough problems demanding his total concentration.

More easily said than done. All he'd wanted was to keep her out of Abdullah's way, create sufficient mayhem while he got Faisal home and produced him for his people with the world's press looking on.

Instead she'd taken possession of every one of his senses, robbed him of the ability to concentrate on his purpose.

He'd touched her and couldn't wash away the scent of her skin. The husky whisper of her voice was a constant echo in his head. He knew, deep down, that for the rest of his life all he would have to do was close his eyes and she would be there. One moment indignant, the next laughing at him and with him, then looking at him with eyes that eclipsed the sun so that he wanted to stop all the pretence and make her his willing prisoner, bind her to his side and keep her there for ever.

He'd been brought up to accept that an arranged marriage, where both parties acknowledged a parity of purpose, had more chance of fulfilment than some chance encounter with a stranger. He had accepted it; he knew it could work. Nadeem was happy. Leila, his younger sister, was content. He knew it and yet had still resisted every attempt by his family to persuade him that this girl, or that, would be the perfect wife for him.

And yet he'd never believed in sentimental love. Never believed in that instant of recognition when a man saw the one woman who had it in her power to make him happy for the rest of his life.

Until now, when the emptiness of a future without Rose Fenton at his side appalled him.

It was crazy. Ridiculous. Impossible.

He opened his eyes and let the precious image go. As he would have to let her go. She belonged to the world, while he belonged here. Maybe Nadeem was right. It was time to take a wife, raise sons, stake his place in the future of his country. Faisal would need someone he could trust at his back.

And in the meantime he'd keep his distance from the lovely Rose Fenton. He'd supposedly come to the desert to hunt. Maybe it was time he took the hawks and the dogs into the desert. Time to put some distance between himself and the woman he might have but could never keep.

It was an appealing idea. Unfortunately life was not that simple. He had brought her here, and, although he knew she would protest the fact, he simply could not leave her without his protection.

Ahead of him lay his encampment, spread around the oasis. His own huge tent set a little way apart. He steered clear of it, walking his horse to the edge of the water with the intention of plunging in to cool his overheated skin, his overheated brain.

A shout distracted him, and as he turned he saw one of his men hurrying towards him.

Rose sighed, glanced at her watch and realised she'd been sitting there longer than she'd realised.

Wool gathering. Her mind had been wandering, wasting precious time. What on earth was the matter with her? She'd quickly stiffened up and groaned as she straightened. She'd forgotten how hard riding was on the muscles after a long break.

The horse liniment seemed more and more appealing. Or maybe it was just the thought of Hassan applying it. She shouldn't have been so quick to turn him down, she thought, wincing as she reached for the tissue box. Then she frowned.

She'd left everything in a muddle last night, but it had been tidied, dusted, polished. Everything put back neatly. She glanced around. Someone had been in there. Someone had folded away her nightdress, taken away the *shalwar kameez*, straightened the bed.

In a sudden panic she grabbed for the box, but even as she thrust her hand inside she knew it was pointless.

'Is this what you're looking for?'

She spun around. Hassan let the curtain fall behind him, advanced on her, the little cellphone gripped between the thumb and forefinger of his hand.

For a moment she couldn't think of a thing to say; he knew the answer and there didn't seem much point in stating the obvious. But since he was clearly expecting some kind of response she lifted her shoulders in the slightest of shrugs and said, 'Oh, bother.' Then, because that didn't appear to satisfy him, 'I hadn't anticipated you'd have a resident Mrs Mopp.'

CHAPTER SEVEN

HASSAN didn't respond with one of those wry smiles
he did so well when he was really making an effort.
Maybe he wasn't in the mood for flippant humour. And
who could blame him?

'Who have you called, Rose?' he asked quietly, with
admirable self-control. 'More importantly, what have
you told them?'

Well, that was easy, although whether he would believe her was another matter entirely. 'No one,' she
said, deciding that this would be a good time to keep
strictly to the point. 'And nothing.'

'You expect me to believe that?'

It would be nice, just once in a while, to be surprised,
she thought. Not that she blamed him for doubting her
probity. She'd have doubted her probity if she'd been
in his shoes. It made her all the more determined to
stick to the truth.

'It wasn't for want of trying,' she assured him. 'I
couldn't get through to my mother last night. Not surprisingly, the line was engaged. It probably still is. And
I didn't want to put my brother in a situation where he
would have to try and hide the truth. He'd do his best
if I asked him to, but the poor lamb couldn't fool a
baby.'

'Why would he have to hide the truth?'

'Well, I couldn't tell him where I was, only who'd abducted me, and that didn't seem like a good idea.'

That earned her an odd look, but he let it go. 'But your news desk? Surely you called them?'

She pulled a face. 'I should have done. Gordon will be livid. But all I could tell them was that you'd abducted me—'

'You're saying you wouldn't?' he demanded. 'Wouldn't tell your news editor? Couldn't tell your brother? Why?'

Looking at it from his perspective, she could see his problem. 'I thought I'd find out why you did it first. Before I brought Abdullah's storm troopers crashing around your ears.'

'Oh, right.' He finally succumbed to deep sarcasm.

Well, Rose didn't blame him for that, either, but it occurred to her that she might be able to prove it. She held out her hand. 'Give me the phone.'

'You're kidding?'

'That's my line. Give me the phone and I'll prove I haven't made any calls.' He didn't seem to think that was a particularly good idea. 'If I've already called for the cavalry, Hassan, it's too late to do anything about it now. Give me the phone.'

He surrendered it with a shrug and she quickly punched in the code for her voice mail. There were three messages from Gordon. The last one, giving a special number that would be manned twenty-four hours a day, was timed at less than an hour earlier. While she'd been sitting sipping iced tea and wool gathering and her phone had been long gone. She held it out for Hassan to listen as the messages were repeated.

'Pretty conclusive, wouldn't you say?'

Hassan didn't answer, simply snapped the cellphone shut, pocketed it, and stared at her as if trying to decide what she was up to. Well, she didn't think he was the kind of man who spent too much time grovelling for forgiveness. It probably wouldn't even occur to him.

'Okay,' she said, 'I'll forgo the apology, but I want my network to have an exclusive on the whole story. That's only fair. And you're going to need some help to get the media coverage you want at just the right moment. I could organise that…'

It was eminently reasonable and, considering what he'd put her through, he should have been on his knees thanking her. Instead he looked like something straight out of a thundercloud. Dark and menacing and given to sudden, intemperate outbursts.

'You know what you are, don't you?' he said flatly, ignoring her offer. She thought she did, but decided that since nothing was going to stop him from telling her she might as well save her breath. 'You're an idiot.'

Close, she thought. There was room for 'complete and utter' in there somewhere, but brevity was good. It was one of the hallmarks of a good journalist.

'I can't believe that you'd be so stupid.' Ah. He hadn't finished. Like all amateurs, he didn't recognise the perfect place to stop. 'So irresponsible. So…so…'

'Dumb?' she offered.

Bad move. He practically exploded. 'You had the means to get yourself out of here but decided, in the best tradition of some girls' own comic book heroine, that you just had to go for the story. Is that it?'

'Hassan—'

'Rose Fenton, Ace Reporter.'

'Oh, puh-leeze!'

'Never misses a deadline. Never misses a scoop.' Actually, Rose thought, that was rather good, but before she could tell him so he continued. 'You don't know me,' he swept on, brushing aside her attempt to interrupt him. 'You could have had no idea what I planned to do with you.'

She opened her mouth to tell him that he didn't look like a white slave trader, but his eyebrows warned her that it had better be good. And, hey, who knew what a white slave trader looked like?

She could, of course, tell him that she'd done her homework on him and she'd been deeply attracted to the idea of writing a feature article on the disinherited prince. She could explain that his abduction had happily short-circuited her unsuccessful efforts to meet him. Or even that seeing him as he boarded the plane to Ras al Hajar, the moment when they had exchanged that brief look, had jarred something loose in her brain so that she had finally remembered she wasn't just a journalist, she was a woman.

Perhaps not.

'What the hell were you thinking, Rose?' *Thinking?* Oh, well, that was different. It didn't take much to work out that she hadn't been doing any serious thinking since she boarded that plane... 'What happens the next time someone grabs you in the dark? Will you glibly tell yourself that there's nothing to worry about because everything was fine last time? Will you think, What the heck? Hassan was a real gentleman and I got a pay rise on the back of the story?' She waited. Silence. 'Well?'

She flinched from the sudden whip-crack of his voice. He'd finally got it all off his chest and now he was impatient for an explanation of her aberrant behaviour.

Unfortunately it was impossible to explain why she'd followed her instincts instead of discretion without revealing more of herself than she cared to, at least not while he was angry with her.

'Actually, you know, I'm not so sure about the gentleman bit,' Rose said. 'Last night you were...' No, forget last night. 'And as for the pay rise.' She shrugged. 'Who knows? I didn't call the news desk when I could have, should have, and you haven't promised me that exclusive yet. If I don't get it you can forget the pay rise; I'll probably be looking for another job.'

A hiss of something like outrage escaped his teeth, and as Hassan grabbed her arms and hauled her up, so that her face was within an inch of his, Rose decided that she'd finally pushed her luck to the limit.

Maybe just a bit beyond.

'All right, all right,' she said quickly. 'I *am* stupid. Very stupid. Famous for it. Ask anyone.' Then, slowly and carefully, 'If you'll just put me down and return my phone, I'll call for a taxi and leave you in peace.'

For a moment he continued to hold her, her toes barely touching the ground as he held her up against him, head to head, face to face, warning her, challenging her. And in the shadowy light of the softly filtered sunlight the mood subtly altered.

His swift flare of anger died back to a dull glow. She felt the heat of it lick over her, bypassing her clothes and going straight for the skin. She felt breathless,

weak, and her mouth softened, parted, wanting more
than anything for him to kiss her. To hold her. To love
her.

If he cared that much, it shouldn't be impossible. If
she could just touch him, touch his face, reach for his
hand, she could make him see that.

But her arms were clamped to her sides, and after a
moment Hassan very carefully lowered her to the
ground, steadied her while she found her balance and
then took his hands from her arms. Only then did he
take a step back.

'Taxis…' His voice was shaking, she realised. Well,
that was okay. She was shaking everywhere, and if he
was going for control this time she wanted to be sure
that he was having a really tough time resisting the
primeval pull of a need that had them both in its grip.

She was wrong about him not being a gentleman. He
was being too much of a gentleman. He'd slipped once
but he wouldn't again. Not without unbearable provo-
cation. Perhaps seeing the intent in her eyes, he took a
further step back.

'Taxis?' she prompted, stepping after him, hoping to
goad him into ignoring the consequences, to see heat
turn his granite eyes to molten lava.

'This isn't Chelsea, Rose. There are no taxis here.'
Almost, she thought. Almost. But it would take more
than words to drive him over the edge and he wouldn't
let her touch him. He wouldn't risk coming that close
again.

'Oh, well,' she said. 'Just a thought.' And when he'd
backed out of the sleeping quarters and the air was no

longer humming with unspoken threats, unspoken desires. She added, 'I guess that means I'll be stopping.'

Then she sat down rather abruptly on the bed. She'd lost her phone but she didn't care. This wasn't about the story any more. All right. So, it was a great story. Any other time she would be chasing it down like a speeding bullet. But if she was patient, and stayed where she was, the story would come to her.

And besides, she was supposed to be on holiday.

What had he said as he made her his captive? A little pleasure, a little romance? Well, right now a little romance was exactly what she wanted.

It was a just a pity that for once in his life the playboy prince had decided to behave himself. In theory, she applauded his decision to reform. In practice, she wasn't too happy about the timing, even if she understood the reason for it.

He'd carried her off without so much as a by-your-leave-ma'am and now he felt responsible for her. So be it.

She lay back against the pillows and smiled. He was responsible for her and it was up to her to make sure that he took his reponsibilities very seriously.

'You can't just kiss and run, Hassan,' she murmured softly into the quiet of the midday heat. 'I won't let you.'

Given a second chance, Hassan wasted no time in cooling himself off. He scooped a pail full of water from the trough pumped up for the horses and poured it over his head.

Such an action would normally have provoked ribald

mockery from men he had grown up with, known all his life. It spoke volumes that not one of them so much as grinned at his discomfort. Not that he had much inclination to congratulate himself.

Rose Fenton provoked agitation simply by breathing. Refused to sit quietly in the shadows and wait. She'd have her story. She knew that. But she was going to make him pay for his impertinence.

He wished he'd never heard of her. Wished she'd never come to Ras al Hajar. Wished, wished, wished...

His men were waiting for his orders. He gave them, and wished he could dispense with his own problems as easily.

Then he realised that he could. Or dispense with one of them. He could call Nadeem, accept her offer to keep Rose safe for a few days, and she could flutter those long lashes from now until kingdom come but he wouldn't change his mind. He took the small cellphone from his pocket and switched it on. He'd do it now.

His sister finally came to the phone, not happy at being called from the clinic she ran in the poorest quarter of the city. 'What is it, Hassan? I'm busy.'

'I know, and I'm sorry, but I want you to...need you to...' Damn it, no, he didn't. Couldn't.

'What's the matter, my brother? Is your lady journalist getting a little too hot for you to handle?' Her soft, knowing laughter held a touch of sympathy that caught him momentarily off balance.

But, while Rose Fenton was searing him down to the bone, he wasn't about to admit it to his little sister. 'No. It's simply that on reflection I think you are right.'

'Well, there has to be a first time for everything. Right about what?'

He hesitated for no more than a heartbeat. 'About marriage. I believe it's time I had a wife.'

'Hassan!' She made no effort to disguise her astonishment or her delight at the news.

'I shall have to stay here once Faisal is back. He'll need someone he can rely on.'

'And you will need someone to keep you warm in that big cold fort you call a home.'

The idea filled him with a chill far deeper than the stone walls of the fort could ever achieve. 'Arrange it, will you?'

'Do you have anyone particular in mind? Or perhaps Miss Fenton wishes to press her claim?'

'Please be serious, Nadeem.'

'I was being perfectly serious. She has a claim on you. I cannot speak to anyone else until that is settled.'

'I'll settle it, Nadeem, but in the meantime will you look for some quiet girl who doesn't answer back?' Nadeem was silent for so long that he was afraid that he had betrayed himself. 'A girl who will be a suitable mother for my sons,' he said abruptly. 'I'm sure you know where to lay your hands upon a list of suitable virgins.'

'Leave it with me, Hassan,' she said, rather more gently. 'I'll see if I can find someone you will like.'

'You've nagged me for long enough. Don't make me wait now.' He snapped the phone shut. A man must marry eventually, and if he couldn't have the woman he wanted then he would learn to want the woman he had. But he didn't want too long to dwell on the difference.

Then, with a sigh, he opened the phone again. He called up the memory and punched in Pam Fenton's number.

Rose washed away the dust from her wild ride, searched the trunk for something loose and cool to wear in the heat of the afternoon and all the time, beyond the drapes, she heard soft movements in the living quarters as the table was prepared for lunch. But Hassan did not return. She had not expected him to.

After a while there was a quiet cough from beyond the curtain. 'You wish to eat, *sitti*?'

Sitti? My lady?

Startled by such courtesy, such honour, Rose quickly got up, draped a long silk chiffon scarf modestly about her head and emerged. The table, as she'd suspected, was laid for one. There was meat. Unleavened bread, freshly baked. A tabbouleh. Thick slices of tomato.

'*Sukran*,' she said, making use of one of the few words of Arabic she had learned. 'Thank you. It looks delicious.' The man bowed. 'But I'd like to eat down there. By the stream.' She didn't wait for his protest, but walked past him as if there was no question but that he would follow her.

'*Sitti*…' He chased after her as she swept out of the tent. She pretended not to hear, concentrating on keeping safe on the rocky path. '*Sitti*,' he implored. 'The food is here.' She kept going. 'Tomorrow,' he offered. 'Tomorrow, *insh'Allah*, I will take the food to the stream for you.'

She stopped, turned to look up at him and his face relaxed. Then she looked back to the stream.

'Just there,' she said, indicating the spot she had chosen for her picnic. And walked on.

Behind her there was a buzz of consternation, and Rose smiled with satisfaction. They could not stop her. She was *sitti*, my lady, their lady, and, by a process of elimination, Hassan's lady. They could not leave her to wander off by herself. She might hurt herself. She might try to run away.

But neither could they restrain her. Only Hassan could do that.

It wasn't her problem; it was theirs. She was sure they'd work something out.

Meantime, she sat on a large flat rock above one of the streams that fed the oasis, pulled off the sandals she had been wearing when she had been carried off and dangled her feet in the water.

It was blissfully cool. She leaned back on her hands, lifted her face to the light breeze blowing from the mountains. Later, she thought, she would bathe.

A man armed with a rifle appeared and stationed himself a little distance away, taking care never to quite look in her direction. She wondered what the gun was for. Were there snakes? Or was he hoping for some small gazelle to wander down to the water and provide him with an easy meal.

After a while two men appeared on the edge of her vision, walking towards a shady spot at the stream's edge. They were bearing a large carpet which they spread over the ground. They kept their eyes averted.

She pretended not to notice, sure that any attention from her would embarrass them.

Cushions were brought.

She swished her feet in the water. It had felt strange, putting on a floor-length gown in the middle of the day, but sitting beside the stream, the featherweight silk of her caftan clinging to her legs, trailing in the water, she felt rather like a fairytale princess.

The food arrived, packed in two carrying boxes. Her heart picked up a beat. Would he come? Or had he left the camp, ridden away into the desert where she couldn't torment him.

Or was she fooling herself? Maybe he'd heard from Faisal...

The sun was shimmering on the slate-blue silk of her dress, lighting her hair through the gauzy film of her scarf. Hassan fought to catch his breath as he watched her from a distance, tried to feel nothing.

Impossible.

Trailing her toes in the water, she looked too much like some exotic princess from the *Arabian Nights*. Scheherazade could not have been more beautiful as she spun her web of stories. They had that in common. And cleverness.

His male-dominated society would jar against the bedrock of her feminist upbringing, but she would happily use its conventions to her advantage.

Life would never be dull with her around to torment him. And there would be endless days like this, with Rose waiting for him.

He let the dream fade. Not endless days. How long

before she was fretting for more, for the life she knew, the freedom?

They would have a few weeks of joy, but he would not be able to keep her. And he would not be able to let her go. They would both be trapped.

A shadow fell across her and Rose looked up. Hassan had dismissed the guard and was holding the rifle, waiting, his expression so distant that they might have been in different worlds. She looked away without acknowledging his presence.

'Is that what you wanted?' he asked finally.

Not quite. But it was a start. She offered him her hand. He had no choice but to take it, wrapping strong fingers around her palm to help her to her feet. But the moment she was standing, he released it.

Different galaxies.

'You're wet,' she said.

'I was hot.'

'Hot.' She repeated the word as if unsure of the meaning.

'And dusty. You had possession of my bathroom so I used a bucket.'

'Fully clothed? I thought that kind of modesty was reserved for your women?' Oh, damn. That was no way to woo a prince. She really would have to concentrate. She picked up her sandals and, with her wet hem trailing in the dust, led the way down to the waiting picnic, where she settled herself somewhat self-consciously among the cushions, tucking her feet out of sight and feeling uncomfortably theatrical, like some mythical *houri*.

But so far, so good. She'd got the picnic and she'd got Hassan. Except that he'd taken himself to a nearby rock, where he was sitting, looking away to the distant mountains, merely waiting for her to eat her lunch and grow bored with the game she was playing.

She opened one of the picnic boxes. 'What's the gun for?' she asked, as she examined the contents.

'Leopards. Panthers.'

She'd heard there were cats in the mountains, but thought it unlikely they would come so close to people. 'You kill them?'

'If they attack the animals.' She glanced up. 'They do, occasionally,' he said, apparently sensing her doubt. 'And if the choice was between you and one of them, then, yes, I would shoot to kill. Despite the temptation to leave you to your fate.' She tutted. 'A warning shot would probably be enough,' he conceded.

'I was commenting on your hospitality, not your wildlife management policies.'

'Is something wrong with the food?' he asked, being deliberately obtuse.

'No. It's delicious, but far too much for one.'

'It's probably my cook's way of suggesting you are too thin.'

'I didn't think he was supposed to notice.'

'You have a way of attracting attention.'

Maybe, but not his, she thought, as he kept his gaze fixed on the middle distance. And twenty feet between them. She rolled onto her back and watched the perfect blue of the sky through the branches of the pomegranates.

'Have you heard from Faisal?' she asked.

'Not yet.'

'Maybe he's already on his way?'

'I wish that were so, but Partridge is still looking for him.'

'And when he finds him? Then what? Will you have a press conference? Now you've got the undivided attention of the press?'

'I thought maybe you would like to introduce the new Emir to the world?'

'It would make a great story.'

'Short of World War III breaking out, I'd imagine that the missing journalist appearing with the youthful Emir in tow would pretty much guarantee the front page.'

'Probably.' But she was tired of the story. She wanted Hassan. 'There's a bird up there,' she said, after a moment. 'I've never seen anything like it. What is it?'

'Describe it.'

He was playing hard to get, but she wasn't going anywhere. 'Did you ever read *The Bluebird of Happiness* when you were a child?' she asked quietly, so as not to disturb the bird. If she'd hoped to draw him nearer, she was disappointed.

'It's a European folk-tale,' he replied dismissively.

He was determined to keep some distance between them, even if it was only cultural. She continued to gaze up into the branches of the tree. 'I thought your Scottish grandmother might have read it to you. You did visit Scotland?'

There was the slightest pause. 'Often. But you already knew that, didn't you?'

And he knew about the bluebird, or he would not have dismissed it in quite that way. But she didn't challenge him on it.

'The bluebird is an allegory for something wonderful that you search for all your life, only to discover that it's right there, under your nose, all the time.' He made no comment. 'It's like that,' she murmured.

'What is?'

He was distracted, which was promising. 'The bird. It's bright blue.' As she spoke, the bird swooped away in a low, looping flight.

'It's a roller. A lilac-breasted roller,' he said, watching the bird's flight from the safe distance of his rock. 'Eat your lunch, Rose.'

She closed her eyes. Bother. Double bother. 'It's too hot to eat. I think I'll bathe.'

'Bathe?' Was it her imagination or did she detect a note of concern in his voice?

'You listed bathing in the stream as one of the attractions. Riding, bathing, lying in the sun.' She ticked them off on her fingers. 'Well, I've ridden, I've lain in the sun, and now I want to swim. Afterwards I'll eat. If you're not hungry, you can sing to me.'

'Not a good idea. I've remembered, it's definitely a crow.'

'I'll be the judge of that. Beauty, after all, is in the ear of the listener.'

She stood up, and the simple, flowing caftan shimmered about her, falling loosely from her shoulders. The neckline was modestly scooped and it was fastened with tiny silk buttons from neck to hem, dozens of them. She began to unfasten them, starting at the top and taking her time. One. Two.

'What on earth do you think you're doing?' he demanded. He was on his feet now and a step closer. He could come close enough to stop her, or her could stand there and watch her strip down to some very sexy underwear and swim. This was wild country, and someone had to keep an eye on her. He'd already made that point.

She slipped another button. Three. 'I'm going to dunk myself in that stream.' She almost felt sorry for him. Four.

'There may be snakes in the water.'

Sneaky. 'What are the odds that one will bite me?' she asked. He didn't answer. More buttons. Five. Six. The dress was beginning to part over her bosom, the sun to bite at her skin. She hadn't thought to put sunblock down so far, but it was too late to worry about that now. 'And if one does bite me, will I die?'

'It would be painful.'

She wasn't practised in seductive disrobing but his face assured her that she was doing just fine. He wanted to look away. He really wanted to. But he couldn't do that, any more than he could lie to her. Not even to save himself from this. Her fingers trembled on the next button. It twisted and she had to look down, untangle it.

He was closer. Without looking, she knew he was closer. The down on her skin prickled with the closeness of him; sweat started on her lip.

She licked it away, struggled with the twisted cord.

His fingers fastened about her wrist, stopping her. 'What do you want, Rose?'

She wanted him. Body, heart and soul.

She wanted to lift her hand to his face, lay her palm against his cheek, rest her head against his chest and hear the slow reassurance of his heartbeat. She wanted him so much that the heat of it licked against her thighs, and she longed to lie on the cushions with him beside her, shaded by the trees for all the long afternoon while they learned all there was to know about each other.

The moment was perfect for it, but he seemed set on refusing to accept the gift of it, of her. The distance he was trying to keep between them, however, suggested he wasn't finding the sacrifice of desire to honourable necessity that easy. Well, she hadn't meant him to.

Ashamed of herself, and with an effort of will that sent a shudder running through her, she smiled. 'I simply wanted your attention, Hassan.'

'You have it,' he assured her. 'Fasten those buttons and you'll keep it.' Rose was tempted to suggest that leaving them the way they were was doing the job just fine. That was the trouble with Hassan. He was infinitely tempting. But she would be good, even if his hand about her wrist was making it impossible to do as he asked. She gestured helplessly with her free hand, but he hadn't finished. 'And when you've done that, maybe you'll tell me what you really want, Rose.'

CHAPTER EIGHT

HASSAN kept asking all the right questions, Rose thought a little desperately, but somehow the answers weren't connecting.

'An interview,' she said, desperately improvising. Since she was clearly hopeless at seduction, maybe it was time to try what she did best. 'You're going to be news in a day or two, and since I'm stuck here at your convenience, and you're stuck with me until Faisal arrives, we might as well take advantage of the situation.'

'We? You seem to be doing just fine all on your own.' His gaze, until then kept firmly upon her face, drifted slowly down, stopping only when confronted with the gaping front of the caftan. What the sun had been doing to her skin was nothing compared to the scorching heat of his eyes. He switched his gaze so quickly that she almost gasped aloud as he looked up, confronting her head on. 'Or maybe you always strip off for interviews?'

Tempted to toss off the smart-alecky response—*it depends who I'm interviewing*—Rose restrained herself. She didn't want Hassan getting the idea she made a habit of it. On the other hand, the *whatever it takes* response sounded positively reckless.

And this wasn't reckless? This dry-mouthed, heart-pounding, hanging-herself-out-to-dry seduction routine wasn't reckless? Well, she had a name to live up to.

'Front-line' Fenton always gets her interview. She had yet to claim the man.

'I had to get your attention somehow,' she managed finally.

A muscle worked in the corner of his mouth. 'Believe me, you've got it.' Or it might just have been the beginnings of a smile... It was there for a second and gone before she could be quite certain. But every journey begins with a single step, and she did have his attention. Now she must make the best use of it she knew how.

'Then let's get down to work.'

'It's all been done before,' he warned her, and there was no almost-smile to show that he didn't care. He cared.

'Not the way I'm going to write it.' She wasn't out to destroy him. 'I'm going to write about you, Hassan al Rashid, so that when Faisal is Emir you can be at his right hand and people will not remember you as a rebel without a cause, kicking over the traces because you didn't get your heart's desire, but as a steadfast brother and friend.'

'You're planning to redeem my shattered reputation single-handed?' She could feel the tension drain from him, the fast hold he had on her wrist loosen as his brow creased in confusion. 'What with?'

'Time, patience. Your co-operation.' Reckless was back, but she couldn't help herself. He did that to her. 'You *will* co-operate?'

'I don't appear to have a choice.' There was a long, dizzying pause when he seemed to hang on the edge of some precipice.

Diamonds. Yellow diamonds to match her tiger eyes. Hassan wanted to strip her naked and then dress her in nothing but precious gems, bind her to him with ropes of pearls, make sweet love to her on a bed of rose petals. For a moment he thought he would faint from his desperate need for this woman. It was as if he had been waiting for her all his life. Was it always to be like this? He could have anything in the world but his heart's desire…

'Hassan?'

The hesitant, slightly anxious note in her voice pulled him back from the brink of madness. It was time to finish it, put a stop to foolish dreams.

'I'm sorry, I was just wondering… Would it help, do you think, if you had pictures of my wedding to go with your article?'

'Your wedding?' She began to laugh. Hassan didn't join in, and he knew the exact moment when Rose recognised that he had not been speaking hypothetically. Her entire body stilled, her skin flushed, the huge black pupils of her eyes seemed rimmed with topaz-gold in the clear, bright air. How could he resist her? The words clamoured in his head. *I love you. I want you with me, always.* It was the 'always' that was the problem. Maybe she saw that in his face, because she seemed almost to shrink away from him. 'Wedding?' She repeated the word uncertainly.

'Nadeem is right,' he said, with a casual lack of interest that he knew would disgust her, that he did not have to fake. 'I will have to stay here now, with Faisal, and a man must have sons. I've asked her to find me a suitable bride. Someone quiet,' he said, and heard the words as if they were spoken at a great distance, by someone else. 'Someone who doesn't answer back.'

There was a long, still moment during which Rose withdrew her wrist from his grasp and pulled her dress tightly about her, fumbling at the buttons, giving up and clutching the edges together. The sunlight shimmered on her skin like gold dust, her hair was like fire, but she looked cold, and as he looked on, helpless to do anything, she shivered.

'Sons?' She repeated the word with contempt. He longed to take her into his arms and hold her, to tell her how much he desired her, wanted her. It took everything that was good in him to hold back. 'And what happens if you just get daughters?' she asked, her boldness undermined by the faintest quiver to her voice. 'Will you trade her in for another model?'

'No, I won't do that. There would be no point, since the sex of the offspring is determined by the man.' What would be the point when one woman who was not Rose would be the same as any other woman?

'I know that. I wasn't sure that you did. Don't most primitive men blame their women for a lack of male children? But then, what sperm would dare defy your wishes?'

Her mockery was savage. If only he could tell her what he'd give to have daughters like her. Each named for a flower like their mother. But he wasn't in the business of making her think of him as late-twentieth-century man. He wasn't. Not in any way that mattered.

'That is in the hands of Allah, Rose.'

'Oh, I see.' Her irony was barbed. 'Well, then, I can see why it doesn't matter who you marry.'

Beneath the careless posture, he flinched at her scorn. Then tossed more fuel on the fire. 'Who says it doesn't matter? Family ties. Land. Dowry. These things matter a great deal.'

'That's positively medieval.'

'If you believe that, you'll find a soulmate in Simon Partridge,' he said, and felt murderously primitive at the thought of her finding a soulmate in any man but himself. 'He assures me that I'm galloping at full speed into the fourteenth century.'

'Then why does he work for you?'

'He doesn't. At least he won't once he's brought Faisal home. He took grave exception to the way I abducted you.'

'Then you're right, Hassan. We'll get along just fine.'

He wanted to take her hand. Hold it between his and tell her that this wasn't the way he wanted it. Try to make her see that this was the way it had to be. And he finally understood how helpless his grandfather must have felt all those years ago, bitterly ashamed that he hadn't been mature enough to accept his decision and make an old man's last few weeks on earth peaceful.

Instead, he gestured for her to sit.

For a moment she defied him, then crumpled onto the cushions as if her legs had suddenly given way. She'd forgotten about the buttons. Her dress gaped slightly to offer a hint of lace, to torment him with the soft swell of her breast.

Maybe he deserved it, but in need of distraction he took some bread, filled it with lamb and tabbouleh and salad and offered it to her. She took it, he suspected, simply because it was too much effort to argue. She took it and held it almost defensively, but made no attempt to eat.

He filled another piece of bread for himself, not because he was hungry, but because without something to occupy his hands he was afraid they would finish what Rose had started.

It wasn't much to constrain a man. A piece of bread and an unknown bride without name or substance to stand between him and everything he desired.

'Tell me about your family.' She'd put down the bread. Maybe she wasn't hungry. Maybe it was too much effort to hold it. Maybe all her strength was being channelled into an effort to keep her voice steady. If he hadn't been able to see her, the voice would have fooled him. 'Did your mother love your father?'

'Rose—'

'I know she didn't choose who she would marry, but did she love him?' She looked up sharply, catching him off guard as he watched her. He turned away, broke off a piece of bread and tossed it to a hopeful starling. 'Did she know him?' Rose persisted.

'No.'

'Not at all? They had never even spoken to each other?'

He saw her considering that, wondering how it would be to be married to a man you were given to as a prize. And he wondered how it would be to hold a woman he did not know, who had been given to him because their families had decided it would make a good match. She would have little say in the matter.

What would she think when she saw him? How

would she feel when he touched her? He'd never thought about it from a woman's viewpoint before.

'My mother told me once that he was the most beautiful man she had ever seen.' He'd had red hair too.

'Oh. She'd seen him, then?'

'Of course. He lived in the palace. The women were much more sheltered then, but there wasn't a thing they didn't know, or see. Ask Nadeem.'

'I will.'

'Is this for your article?'

Article? For a moment she'd forgotten about that. She'd write it because she'd promised him, but this wasn't anything to do with a magazine feature on a man who should have been Emir. She just wanted to know. She wanted to know everything about him. 'I'm filling in the background,' she said. 'Editors look for that kind of detail; the readers enjoy it.'

'I'll bet they do.'

'No... Not like that.' He continued to toss scraps of bread to the birds. 'Really. They are simply fascinated to see a life lived so differently from their own.' And it was different. On an intellectual level she'd always known that, but somehow on a personal one it hadn't seemed to matter. Apparently it did.

'Shouldn't you have a tape recorder? Or a notebook?'

'I usually do, but my bag was left behind when you issued your rather pressing invitation.' She shrugged. 'Don't worry, I'll send you a draft so that you can correct any errors. I wouldn't want to write anything that would embarrass her.'

He glanced back at her. 'Her?'

'Your mother.'

'Oh, yes. Maybe you would like to talk to her your-self? Nadeem will arrange it, if you like.'

'Does Nadeem do everything in your family?'

'My younger sister, Leila, is too busy raising her children, and my mother does charity work, has a busy social life.' He shrugged. 'Nadeem was always differ-ent. She demanded she be sent to school in England, went on to study medicine in the States.'

'And her father let her go?'

'Her mother—our mother—persuaded him. She'd been to Scotland with my father. He insisted and he was refused nothing... She'd seen a different life for women there.'

'One that she would have liked for herself?'

That he couldn't say. 'You'll have to ask her your-self. Of course Nadeem was warned by everyone that no man would want to marry her once she'd left the protection of her home.'

'I doubt she was entirely alone,' Rose remarked, somewhat drily.

He finally managed a smile. 'No. She had a positive entourage of protective females in tow. And her hus-band is a doctor, too, with more liberal ideas than most men. He even allows her to work.'

'Allows her to work? *Allows* her to work?' She tried to imagine her mother's reaction to such a display of chauvinism. 'Well, that *is* liberal.'

'He didn't have much choice. She refused to marry him until he agreed. She runs a women's clinic in town.' He smiled, a little grimly. 'It won't have been included in your tour of the highlights of Ras al Hajar; the needs of ordinary women never featured very high on Abdullah's list of priorities.' He tossed the remainder of his lunch to the birds. 'Tell me about your husband.'

'Michael?' She wanted to ask about Nadeem, the clinic, his own priorities, not talk about herself. 'Why?'

Because. He wanted to know. He knew he shouldn't ask, but he couldn't leave it. 'Just filling in the background,' he said, using her own words back at her. He was interested in the details, a life lived so differently from his own, where a wife was a partner, not a possession. 'We've got all afternoon. You can ask me a question and then it's my turn. That's fair, surely?' He took her silence for assent. 'He raised horses, you said.'

'I'm supposed to be interviewing you, Hassan.'

'Racehorses?'

There was a pause, then she nodded. 'Yes. Racehorses.' Then, 'Did she love him? Your mother?'

That was it? Two words? Maybe he should try it on her, let her see how much background she got that way. Except of course he couldn't. He didn't know what his mother had felt for his father. She had been his wife. That was enough. 'Love is a western emotion. A late-twentieth-century one at that.'

'You think so?'

'It's a fact.'

'Yet literature has always cherished lovers... Abelard and Heloise, Tristan and Isolde, Lancelot and Guinevere.'

'Romeo and Juliet,' he added. 'Maybe I should have said happy endings were a late-twentieth-century development.'

'I'll put that down as a "don't know", shall I?'

'Who ever knows about other people's lives?' He pulled a cushion towards him, tucked it beneath his elbow. She was near enough to touch, curled up on the rug totally unconscious of the soft curve of her breast within the compass of his hand. He was tormenting himself. He should move. But Rose Fenton wasn't that easy to shake off. He'd just have to try and keep his mind focused on higher things. 'Tell me about your husband,' he repeated, failing miserably.

'That's too general,' she protested. The coolly probing journalist, expecting him to bare his soul for her readers, was suddenly in full retreat as he turned the tables on her.

'You answered my last question with one word. This time you'll have to work a little harder, or my attention will begin to wander,' he warned. *As if*.

Rose poured herself a glass of iced tea from the flask. She glanced questioningly at Hassan, he nodded and she poured one for him as well. Putting off the moment. Working out what she would say as she turned the cold glass in her hands, pressed it against her hot cheek.

'I'd just come down from university. I was at a loose end until I started work in the autumn and Tim asked me to help him straighten out a truly terrible house he'd moved into. I went out on a call with him late one night to the stables and I met Michael.' She sipped the tea.

'And?'

She shrugged. 'Instant attraction.' And he hadn't been as difficult about it as Hassan. 'Of course my mother said I was just looking for a father figure.'

'I wondered if he was older than you.'

Rose pulled a face. 'His children were older than me.

Twenty-six and twenty-four, going on eight: a pair of sulky brats more concerned about losing their inheritance than whether Michael was happy.'

'Was he happy?' The question was unforgivable, intrusive. He knew it, but, despite the fact that his life had always been cushioned by privilege, by wealth, he'd found that simple happiness—that feeling on waking each morning that he was glad to be alive—had tended to elude him in adult life.

'I hope so. I was. He was the dearest man, and I must have complicated his life enormously.'

'With his children?'

'With his children, his ex-wife, his friends. None of them approved. With the men it was just plain envy, but their wives...' With their wives it had mostly been panic. If Michael could do it, so could their men. 'He must have known how it would be, but I threw myself at him in the most disgraceful way.' She smiled as she remembered. They were good memories, he could see, and the knowledge cut him to the quick. Then the smile faded. 'The sweet man didn't stand a chance.' Hassan could believe it. 'He was far too much of a gentleman to let me fall. So kind.'

'Kind.' Hassan repeated the word. He hoped the girl Nadeem chose for him would be able to say as much. But when he looked at Rose, choked back the feelings that boiled up in him, he knew that kindness was not enough. For a second their gazes locked, and he saw that she had realised it too. 'Rose...' Her name was like a match to a fuse, and as he moved to bridge the distance between them he knew that, fight it as he might, the explosion had been inevitable since the moment he set eyes on her.

'No...' Rose felt as if the word had been torn from her throat. Desire to be held by him, loved by him, swept through her like a forest fire, and an hour ago she would have gone into his arms without a thought for sense or reason.

But not now. He was to be married. So what if it was to a woman he didn't know, didn't care about? It would still be meaningless, wrong, lust instead of love.

Even as he brushed back the scarf she'd draped so demurely about her head in a gesture that left her feeling utterly naked, even as he bent to press his lips to her breast and she burned for him, she knew that this time she must not give in to her own desperate desire.

'No, Hassan...' The painful words were wrenched from her, and she pushed away his hand as she staggered to her feet, chokingly hot. 'Let me go.' She clutched at her dress. How could she have forgotten to fasten it? Surely he would think it deliberate.

Maybe it was. He'd tried, heaven knew how he'd tried to keep his distance. But she had unbuttoned her dress, tormented him, and even then, when he'd stopped her, she'd sat beside him with it gaping open like the most appalling tease...

Burning with shame, she grabbed the edges and, screwing them together in one hand, she rushed to the stream, wading in until she was waist deep, only then releasing the dress to dip her hands into the water and throw it over face and neck, over her breasts and shoulders, until she was soaked.

It made no difference. And when she turned, she knew why. Hassan was right behind her.

She turned, eyes huge, her hair clinging in wet strands to her face, and Hassan felt the breath knocked from him. The thin silk clung to her, even where it was open to the waist it clung to her, moulding itself to her, defining her as a woman.

She was tall, lithe, stunningly beautiful. She was his equal. His perfect partner. Their sons would be strong, weaned on her courage. The daughters he longed for would mirror her beauty.

But to have them, to have her, he would have to leave his home, live in her world, watch her leave him to cover the latest fast-breaking story in some trouble spot, out of his sight, out of his protection. He could not do it.

He must not do it. He was needed here. But he groaned as he reached for her, gathered her to him and held her.

For a moment she resisted him, her eyes fierce. 'No, Hassan.' Her voice was husky with a need that matched the leaden weight in his loins, but it seemed that at last she, too, had recognised the necessity of fighting the attraction.

He made the kind of soft noises that would gentle a skittish horse. 'I hear you, Rose. It's all right. I understand. But come now. The water is too cold. You'll take a chill.'

Or maybe the water wasn't cold. It was simply the chill that had seized his heart. But she seemed incapable of movement, so he gathered her up, lifted her into his arms and carried her out of the water and along the rocky path to his quarters. The way was empty; his men had found excuses to take themselves out of sight, out of hearing.

Nothing could more plainly have shown that they approved his choice. The older men had been surrogate fathers to him, teaching him as they had taught their sons. And their sons were his boyhood friends.

They had seen in Rose the same qualities that he admired—courage, strength of purpose, an indomitable will—and they had shown their respect by referring to her as *sitti*, their lady, by their eagerness to please her.

For them it was so simple. He desired her, he would make her his own and she would never leave his house. His grandfather wouldn't have had a problem with that. If you want her, take her, he would have said. Take her and keep her. Give her children and she will be content.

Unable, unwilling to do that to her, he suspected that his own status would be severely dented.

Despite the heat steaming their soaking clothes, by the time they were inside Rose was shivering uncontrollably. He set her on her feet, found her a towel. She took it, held it 'Rose, please, you need to get out of that dress,' he prompted, and turned away to search the dresser for the soft pashmina robe that had been his mother's wedding gift to his father and went with him everywhere. When he turned back she was trying desperately to finish what she had started with the buttons, but without success.

'I'm s-s-sorry,' she stammered, through chattering teeth. 'My hands are sh-shaking too much.'

'Hush, don't fret. I'll do it.'

'But—'

'I'll do it.' But the wet loops had tightened over the buttons and it was taking too long. In desperation, he took the edges of the silk, his fingers hot against the chill of her skin, and tore it free, so that it sank with its own soggy weight to the floor.

He'd arranged for the wife of one of his men to go into the new shopping mall to buy clothes, underwear for Rose. Confronted with her choice, he had to admit the woman had spent his money imaginatively.

As he unfastened the scrap of lace that cupped her breasts, eased the matching panties over her hips, he was grateful for his own plunge into the chill water of the stream, grateful for the cold wet cloth that clung to him, keeping the fuse on slow burn.

'Come,' he said, folding her into the comfort of the rich blue robe, feeding her arms into the wide sleeves, wrapping it about her, knowing that she would be warm in moments. He wanted to keep holding her. Instead he took the towel and rubbed at the wet ends of her hair. Then he threw back the covers and lifted her into bed. He would have given everything he had to join her there. Instead he pulled the comforter over her, tucked it around her. 'I'll get you something warm to drink.'

'Hassan...' He waited. 'I'm sorry. So sorry. I think about what I want and I just go for it. I did that to Michael. I needed him and it just didn't occur to me that he might not have needed me—'

He was at her side in a heartbeat. 'Hush...' he whispered, his fingers on her mouth. 'Don't say that. He was the luckiest of men. A man who could die with your name on his lips could regret nothing...' His eagerness to reassure her betrayed him. Even as he snatched back his traitorous fingers she reached out for him, held his hand against her face. 'Whose name will be on your lips, Hassan?'

He could not say. Must not. But it made no difference. She knew. 'You mustn't do it, Hassan.' He refused to help her, refused to ask the question, but she needed no assistance from him. 'You cannot marry some poor girl who will love you...'

'Rose!' Too late he tried to stop her, but she was relentless.

'Some girl who will love you, because she will not be able to help herself, Hassan. She will love you and bear your children and if you do not love her in return, you will break her heart.'

'Hearts do not break,' he lied. 'She will be content.'

'It isn't enough. Not for a lifetime.'

No. It would never be enough. But he retrieved his hand and made a determined effort to restore a semblance of sanity to a situation that was quickly spiralling out of control. 'You would have me spend my nights alone?' he enquired harshly.

'I would have you remember your honour.'

Honour? She was beginning to sound exactly like his sister, with her talk of blood or gold... And he remembered his own utterly idiotic agreement that marriage might be the only way to redeem himself. For a moment the siren call of temptation filled his head, a selfish longing strong enough to taste. But there was no honour to be had walking that slippery path. It was time to put an end to this.

'I remembered my honour, *sitti*,' he said coldly,

standing, determined to walk away, 'when you had quite abandoned yours.'

'Is that right?' She flushed angrily, pushed herself up onto her elbow. 'Well, I hate to disagree with *my lord*, but I'd have said we were about even on the day.'

And as anger heated her from the inside out, something clicked inside her brain. On the day. On this day. On this day they might consider themselves even, but Hassan was still deep in her debt. Nadeem had said so.

Gold, blood or honour. She had the right to choose.

Today she had used Hassan's standards to bring him back to her side. Could she use them to keep him there and put an end to this nonsense about an arranged marriage? She half believed he'd made it up simply to keep her at a distance. Except she knew he would not lie, which was why it had worked so well. Instead of seizing the moment, as she'd planned, she'd rushed into the water to cool herself off.

But just for a moment she believed…oh, it was crazy, but hadn't Nadeem said he would never be happy with a traditional bride? Hadn't she said to leave everything to her, she would arrange a marriage?

Marriage? She had to be crazy. She'd had too much sun. It was too soon to be thinking like that. Yet she'd known with Michael, from the moment he had looked up from his sick horse and anxiety had changed to a smile. She hadn't allowed petty-minded people or her mother's psychological dissection of their relationship to spoil their short time together.

And marriage had to be in Hassan's mind too, or why would he resist her so strenuously? He thought she was wedded to her career, travel, and had made the unilat-

eral decision that she could never be happy with him.
A selfish man would not have cared.

And the anger seeped away from her. 'Stay with me,
Hassan,' she said, in a voice she scarcely recognised.
And she lay back amongst the pillows. 'Stay with me.'

'Rose…please… I cannot.'

She was relentless. '*Sidi*, you must.'

'I need to change, my clothes are soaking…' he said,
clutching at straws.

'Then you'd better take them off or you'll be the one
with a chill.' She waited for a moment, and when he
did not move, she said, 'Can you manage? Or do you
need some help with the buttons?'

'It's not the buttons that are giving me trouble,' he
said. 'It's you.' But he sat on the camel stool and
tugged off his wet boots. Then he crossed to the chest
and tugged at one of the drawers and began searching
for something dry to wear.

Rose watched him for a moment, then she wriggled
out of the soft pashmina gown. 'Try this,' she said.

Hassan turned and let slip one brief, desperate word
as he saw the blue robe she was offering him, warm
from her body. His mouth dried, his heart pounded, the
heavy drag of his need for her became so intense that
even to move would be torture. 'What do you want,
Rose?'

'You keep asking me that, but you already know the
answer.' She was lying back against the pillows, her
damp curls tumbled about her face, her naked shoulders
cream silk against the white linen, her throat begging
to be framed in the lustre of pearls. 'You have to settle

with me before you can even think of marriage, *sidi*. I'm calling in the debt.'

'The debt?' Could he pretend that he didn't understand? He could try, but she wouldn't be convinced.

'You said I could have whatever I wished.'

He felt bruised, beaten, as if he'd been fifteen rounds in the ring with a heavyweight. Round one had been in the plane, when she'd done something incredible with those eyes, shaking his faith in his invincibility. Then, in the back of the Land Rover she'd touched his face and he'd gone down briefly. As for last night—well, last night he'd kissed her and she'd nearly had him out for the count. He'd only just made it, and twice today she'd had him on his knees. He was on them now, and going down…

'I meant it. Name your price. Your heart's desire.'

'I want—'

Let it be diamonds. Or her weight in gold…

She let the robe drop, held out her hand to him, murmured his name like an imperceptible caress.

'Hassan.'

Almost nothing, the merest breath across the skin. The down feather from a duck would make more impression. And yet…and yet…the sound of his name filled his head, echoed there until his skin shivered with the impact of it. It called to something deep within him, all the longings, the need…

She'd looked into his soul, seen the emptiness, and the siren call of his name upon her lips promised that within her arms he need never be alone again.

Their fingertips touched, entwined, held fast.

CHAPTER NINE

HASSAN, his head propped upon his hand, lay on his side and watched the gentle rise and fall of her breast. Rose slept like a child, flat on her back, completely defenceless, as if certain that nothing in the world could hurt her.

There was a sweet artlessness in the pleasure she took in her own body, and from his, that suggested no one ever had, and he prayed that it would always be so.

Her lashes stirred against her cheek and she sighed, stretched, smiled at her dreams. For a man inured to the idea of love, the last few days had been a revelation, an awakening, and this was a moment to rend his heartstrings. Forcing himself away from her warmth, away from her love, he thought it was as well that heartstrings made no sound.

Everything had changed and yet nothing had changed. They were entirely different people and yet remained locked into their own cultures, their own expectations.

She would still leave, because her life, her real life, happened somewhere else. He would still remain in Ras al Hajar, because despite everything it was his home.

The memories they had made during the last few days and nights would have to be enough to last a lifetime, because there was no solution to their situation, only an inevitable heartache for an impossible dream.

Outside it was bright, clear, cold enough to fog his breath. Below him the oasis was still, the only sound that of the whickering of a restless animal in the stone corral.

'Hassan?'

He turned, reluctantly. Rose, tousled from sleep, wrapped in the blue robe, her hair kissed by starlight, was all a man could desire. 'I'm sorry, I hoped not to disturb you.'

'It's too late for sorry,' she said, laughing softly, 'you disturbed me the minute I set eyes on you.' Her eyes were liquid as she lifted her hand to his cheek, rubbing the backs of her fingers gently against the bone.

It was an invitation a man would have to be heartless to resist, and if he had learned anything in the blissful hours, days they had spent together, outside of the world, it was that he had a heart. All the hard work of putting some space between them was undone in that moment as he succumbed to temptation and was rewarded with the tug of her teeth against his lower lip, followed by the teasing caress of her tongue.

But maybe she could sense the distance he strived for, because after a moment she eased back, looked up into his face. 'You've found Faisal, haven't you?' she said.

Straight to the point, no messing. Already she could read him better than a book. She would be a hard woman to deceive. He'd tried it with his brave talk of an arranged wedding; she'd seen straight through him.

'Yes. He's on his way home.' He could not keep

himself from looking at her, seeing the effect on her at his admission that their idyll was at an end.

Her hand rubbed softly at his sleeve in a gesture of comfort. 'That must be such a relief for you.'

'Yes.' And no. He'd begun to suffer from the crazy delusion that they could stay where they were for ever. Crazy. Even if Faisal had remained on the loose, he would have had to take Rose home. Her mother had arrived with the news crew from her network and she was not hanging around patiently while Abdullah wrung his hands and said his men were doing everything possible. According to Nadeem, Ms Pam Fenton was giving His Highness a seriously hard time. Having come to know her daughter so well, he would have expected nothing less.

'What about the girl he was with?' Rose asked.

'The girl?' He hadn't thought to ask, and Simon Partridge, in a hurry, hadn't mentioned her. 'I'm sure Partridge will make arrangements to ensure that she gets home safely...' He paused, then added, 'With adequate compensation for her interrupted vacation.'

Rose suspected that this throw-away line was some kind of attempt to provoke her, remind her that he wasn't one of her 'English gentlemen'. She already knew him too well to be deceived.

'Yes, I'm sure he will.' And she wondered what compensation might be considered adequate for her own interrupted holiday. Blood, gold or honour. Blood would be unthinkable. Gold, insulting. There was no contest, really. She stepped away from Hassan, stepped from beneath the wide awning and into the darkness.

He reached out for her, his hand staying her. 'Where are you going?'

'Up there.' She pointed to the rise above the camp. 'Come with me. I want to stand up there with you and look at the sky.' She looked up at him, lifted his hand from her shoulder and kept it in hers. 'It seems so close out here in the desert, as if one might touch the stars.'

'You want to touch the stars?'

'The moon,' she said, taking in the thin silver sickle of the rising moon in a wide sweep of the heavens. 'The stars…'

'That's all? Why not a couple of planets while you're about it?'

'Why not?' She challenged his flippancy. 'With you to lift me I know I can do anything.'

His smile faded. 'There's something about you, Rose, that almost makes me believe you could.'

Just hold on to that thought, Hassan, she thought, as they walked together to the top of the high ground above the camp, where the heavens were a huge, star-filled dome above them. *Just hold on to that thought.*

Rose stopped as, away to the west, a meteorite streaked across the sky in a shower of falling stars.

'Look—look at that!' she whispered. 'It's so beautiful. Did you make a wish?'

His hand tightened imperceptibly over hers. 'Our destiny is written, Rose.' Then, glancing down at her, 'Did you?'

'I think it was my destiny to be standing here with you tonight at just the moment that star fell. It was my destiny to make a wish.' He waited, not asking, knowing that she would tell him. 'It was nothing dramatic,' she said, after a moment. 'Wishbones, wishing wells, falling stars—I always make the same one. That the people I love will be happy and safe.'

She thought he sighed at that. 'Nothing for yourself?'

He expected her to say that she wished to stay here always? Did he hope for it, just a little? 'That *was* for me. If they are happy and safe nothing else matters.' Then she smiled. 'Besides, the little things, like destiny, I can handle myself. I got myself here at just the right moment, didn't I?'

'You are so...so...' The words erupted from him. He wasn't exactly angry, Rose thought, he was simply at a loss to understand her head-on attitude to life, a determination to bend events to her will.

'So...what?' she asked. She really shouldn't tease him, she thought, he wasn't used to it. 'Assertive, perhaps?' She offered him the word, quite unable to resist the temptation. Getting no immediate agreement, she sighed dramatically. 'No, I thought not. You just think I'm wilful, don't you? Wilful and obdurate and bloody-minded—'

His fingers stopped her mouth. 'Resolute,' he countered softly. 'Uncompromising.' His hand strayed to a wayward curl and he tucked it behind her ear. 'Blessed with fire and spirit.'

'Same thing,' Rose said, a little huskily.

'Not quite.' Not at all. The one was infuriating, the other enchanting, and there was no doubt in his mind which of those words applied to Rose Fenton. She was enchanting, and he was undoubtedly bewitched because inside his head other words crowded forward, pushing their claim to be recognised. Words like…*unexpected, rare, lovely*…like a rose in the desert. And in that moment he knew which of all his possessions he would give her. An unspoken declaration of his love, something that, whenever she looked at it, touched it, would bring back this moment.

'Have you ever seen a desert rose?' he asked.

'A desert rose? Is it like a rock rose?' She glanced around, as if expecting to see one growing at her feet. 'My mother has a yellow one growing in a sink garden—'

'No, it's not a flower, not a plant of any kind. It's a crystal formation. Selenite.' *Unexpected, rare, lovely.* 'They're pink sometimes, and the crystals look like petals. You find them, if you know where to look, in the desert.'

'And?'

And what? His mind was playing games with him; he was too close to betraying his heart to this woman. 'And nothing, except the coincidence of your name. It just occurred to me that I found you in the desert, that's all.'

'Like a desert Rose.' He thought she might have smiled, but instead she just gave a little sigh. 'We'll have to leave tomorrow, go back into town, won't we? Back to the real world.'

Straight to the heart of the thing, his desert Rose. 'I wish things could be different, but we don't have a choice. We both knew that this couldn't last.'

He had decided it couldn't last; Rose preferred to make her own decisions. There were always choices, but it took a special kind of courage to cut through difficulties that appeared insurmountable, courage and trust and a belief that nothing could destroy you except your own self-doubt. Her mother had taught her that. Her mother hadn't wanted her to marry Michael, but she'd given her the strength to withstand the prejudice of petty-minded people who had tutted ominously over the age difference, declared it would all end in tears.

She could do it again.

She would give a little, he would give a little, and their small sacrifices would be rewarded a thousandfold. She knew that. Hassan, she suspected, was going to take some convincing.

Hassan was right about tomorrow, though. Nothing could stop real life intruding, but they still had what was left of the night, a few hours of magic before the world crowded in on them.

'Tomorrow will take care of itself, my love,' she said, lifting his hand to her lips, touching his cold knuckles to her cheek. Then she looked up into his face. 'Right now we should be making the most of the little time we have left.'

They had made the most of their time, the tenderness of their lovemaking bringing him almost to tears. But even though it would break his heart to leave her, he would end it here. This would always be their special place, and the memories they had made would remain untarnished by the inevitable slide into discord when their worlds clashed.

He left the tent early, and this time, exhausted, she did not stir, even when he brushed a strand of hair from

her cheek. Kissed her softly. Whispered goodbye.
Placed his small gift on the pillow beside her.

It was nothing precious. He would have showered
her with precious jewels, anything her heart desired, but
he knew she would be insulted, offended by such
things. If he'd learned anything from Rose Fenton, it
was that a gift from the heart was worth more than gold.
And knowing that she had a part of him with her would
be a comfort in the lonely years ahead.

Rose stirred, woke, and knew instantly that she was
alone. That he had gone. She was not surprised. Last
night he had been so tender, and when he had kissed
her she had seen a shimmer of tears silvering the steely
grey of his eyes. But he had still gone.

And people said *she* was obstinate.

What would it take to convince him? Maybe she
should insist, make Tim demand that he marry her, then
he'd have no choice. But the thought of Tim forced to
confront Hassan with his duty just made her smile and
this was serious.

Besides, he had to make the decision himself. She
reached for his pillow, hoping to draw inspiration from
its closeness. Instead her hand closed over something
rough, hard. She knew instantly what it was. A desert
rose. He'd left her a desert rose. And a note.

This is a part of me to take home with you, small
return for the memories you leave behind.

Hassan.

She picked up the rose. It sat in her palm, small,
exquisitely formed, but so different from the rosebuds

that Abdullah had deluged her with. There was nothing soft about it, nothing to wither and die. It was fixed, immutable, unchanging.

Did he understand the message it conveyed? That this was an unconscious betrayal of his feelings? Rose thought not and she held onto the crystal for a long time, suddenly afraid that nothing she could do would ever move him to change his mind. Afraid that his will was like the rock and about as easy to soften. Afraid that he would make it impossible for her to get close enough to try.

'Miss Fenton?' The figure standing at the foot of her bed swam before her eyes. Tears? What use were tears? They never solved anything. 'Rose?' Rose blinked and a tall, slender woman, her dark hair streaked with silver, came into focus. 'Hassan asked me to come and take you home.'

'Home?' London, cold and bleak? No, this was home. Here with Hassan. 'I don't understand.' Then she did. He couldn't wait to get her out of the country...

'Your mother is waiting for you.'

Her mother? Then she realised who this was. 'You're Hassan's mother, aren't you? And Nadeem's. I can see the likeness.'

'Hassan said you wanted to talk to me.'

'It was kind of him to remember... I'm sorry, I don't know what to call you...'

The woman smiled, came closer, sat beside her on the bed. 'Aisha. My name is Aisha.'

'Aisha.' It didn't seem quite enough for this regal woman. 'Hassan must have more important things to worry about. And so must you, with Faisal coming home.'

'I've already spoken to Faisal… He called me from London. What have you there?'

Rose opened her hand for Aisha to see. 'It's a gift, from Hassan.'

'Well.' The older woman reached out, but stopped her fingers before they quite touched the rose. 'It's a long time since I've seen that.' She looked up, catching Rose unawares. Her eyes were dark, but they had the same powerful impact as Hassan's.

'He's had it a long time?'

'All his life.' Aisha's smile came not from her lips, but from somewhere deep inside. 'His father gave it to me, oh, so long ago. Before we were married, even—'

'Before?' Hassan's mother raised a finger to lips that curved in a smile that told its own story. It was a smile that knew all about love. 'And you gave it to Hassan…when you married your second husband.'

'I gave all of Alistair's things to Hassan. His clothes. This robe.' Her hand gently brushed against the soft blue pashmina gown that lay over the foot of the bed. 'All the things I had given him, all the things he had given me. One cannot take souvenirs from one love into another man's house. You have been married before, I am told, so you will understand.' Her words were softly inflected into something that was almost a question. Almost as if Aisha were testing her.

'Yes, I understand.' After she'd buried Michael she'd left his house and all that was in it for his squabbling family to pick over, taken off the rings he'd put on her finger and restarted her life from the point where she had left it on the day she had met him. She had married the man, not his possessions. Then she realised what Aisha had just said. 'How did you know that I'd been married?'

'Your mother told me when I had lunch with her yesterday. A most interesting woman—'

'She's here!'

'She arrived two days ago. Did you know that Hassan sent her a message? She did not know it was from him, of course, and I did not tell her. Just that someone had called to say that you were safe and well. He asked her not to tell anyone and she didn't.'

'My mother!' Rose made a move to get up, realised that she was naked and, blushing, stopped.

Aisha picked up the blue robe and held it for a moment, then handed it to her. 'Take your time, Rose. I'll walk for a while. It's too long since I was in the desert.'

The minute Aisha left, Rose scrambled from bed; she didn't have time to waste. Her mother was here? Her mother had heard from Hassan? Why hadn't he told her? Because he didn't want her know that he cared. The thoughts tumbled into her brain too quickly. She needed to think. She needed to slow down, take her time. Consider all the possibilities.

There had been a finality about the desert rose, the note. He had certainly meant them to be read as goodbye. She hadn't been able to convince the man. Could she convince the women in his life? His mother, his sisters. Would they help her?

She towelled her hair dry, then, unlike the Rose Fenton who would have grabbed the nearest pair of jeans and gone racing after the story, she sat at the mirror and carefully applied her make-up. Her *shalwar kameez* had been washed and returned to her and it lay neatly folded on the chest of drawers. She put it on and draped the long scarf over her hair.

By the time she was ready Aisha had returned from her walk and was relaxed upon the divan, drinking coffee. She turned, looked up at her and smiled. 'How charming you look, Rose. Would you like some coffee?'

'Coffee would be wonderful. And, if we have time, a little advice.'

As the plane taxied towards the airport terminal the Emiri standard was unfurled on the nose and fluttered its uncompromising statement. Hassan, standing second in line to greet the returning Emir, glanced at his cousin. Abdullah's jaw was set rigid, but in the face of the massed ranks of international newsmen he could do little other than wait to greet his youthful successor.

Behind him Hassan was conscious of Rose, standing out from the press of newsmen, not in the combat fatigues she usually wore in the dangerous places she reported from, but looking like a princess in silk and chiffon. Looking totally in control. Even the most hardened media men seemed to stand back slightly, give her space. One glance had been all that he permitted himself; one glance was all it had taken to know that it would never be enough.

The plane stopped, the steps were wheeled into place, the door swung open and Faisal appeared to a barrage of flashlights. Faisal, wearing jeans and a T-shirt that declared his support for his favourite American football team. Hassan was silently enraged. How could he? How could he take the moment so lightly? How could Simon Partridge allow this? They both knew how important this moment would be.

Then behind Faisal the slender figure of a young woman appeared. A California-girl blonde with a smile as wide as the Pacific. She was followed by Simon Partridge, his expression a mute plea for understanding.

Faisal loped, long-legged and agile, down the steps and crossed to Abdullah, bent over his hands in a gesture of respect. For a moment Abdullah looked triumphant. For a moment Hassan thought that he had thrown it all away. But then Faisal, with all the confidence of youth, extended his own hands and waited for Abdullah to return the honour, acknowledge him first as equal, then as lord.

For a moment Abdullah resisted, and Hassan held his breath, but Faisal did not move a muscle, simply waited, and after a moment that seemed to stretch time the Regent finally conceded to his King.

Faisal then coolly moved on to Hassan, extended his hands, this time with a wry smile, as if aware that he was in for a tongue-lashing. Hassan's bow disguised a stony expression, one that hid a considerable degree of respect. The boy had become a man. And even without the trappings of a prince to lend him dignity, he had forced Abdullah to back down.

Rose watched this performance from a little distance, reporting the characters in the drama as a voice-over to the pictures being beamed by satellite to her news network. She noted, without comment, that the young woman was whisked away into a waiting limousine while Faisal went through the motions of the ceremonial arrival.

Then, as he crossed to the car, Hassan at his side, she called out. 'Are you glad to be home, Your Highness?'

'Very glad, Miss Fenton.' He stopped, crossed to her microphone. Hassan, clearly torn between a desire to leave a safe distance between them and keeping his young protégé on a tight rein, finally followed him, but remained a clear six feet away from her, his gaze fixed somewhere above her head. 'Although as you can see my journey was at rather short notice, hence the somewhat casual attire. We have all been most concerned about you.' He made it sound as if her disappearance had provoked his sudden return.

'I'm sorry to have been such a nuisance.' She had explained away her disappearance as the result of a sudden relapse of her illness, conveniently remembering nothing until waking in the kindly nursing of some wandering tribesmen who spoke no English but who had finally arrived at a distant village with a telephone.

Her mother might look knowing, and Tim was giving a fair impression of a pressure cooker about to blow, but she hadn't wavered in the telling and no one was indiscreet enough to ask any awkward questions.

Faisal's smile was warm. 'I'm glad to see that you are none the worse for your recent adventure.'

'On the contrary. The desert is an awe-inspiring place, sir, and the hospitality of your people boundless.'

'Then we must ensure that you see more of both. Hassan will arrange a feast; we have much to celebrate.'

'I look forward to it.' But she didn't quite have the

nerve to meet Hassan's gaze. And she didn't ask about the pretty blonde. She didn't have to. She'd already had that story from Aisha.

Hassan watched Faisal's car drive away from the airport, then he headed towards his own waiting car. 'What in heaven's name were you thinking of, Partridge? I know I'm not in your good books, but did you have to do that to me?'

'I didn't—'

'Surely you could have found him a suit to wear? And as for bringing his girlfriend along for the ride. Eyes were popping faster than flashguns when she stepped out of the aircraft behind him. If she had to come surely you could have managed it with a little discretion—' He bit back the words. With the scent of his love on his skin he had no business lecturing anyone on discretion. 'Who is she?'

'Her name is Bonnie Hart. It seems that Faisal married her two weeks ago.'

'Married!'

'You…we…interrupted their honeymoon.'

'They were on their honeymoon? With the world to choose from, he picked a cabin in the Catskills?'

'The Adirondacks.'

'It doesn't matter where…'

'I rather got that impression. And they didn't go far because Bonnie has to be back in college next week.'

'College! Please, give me strength. What planet is Faisal on?'

'I'd say he has his feet very firmly on this one. She's a lovely girl, very bright. She's an agronomist—'

'I don't care what she is. Faisal had no business marrying her.' He was supposed to marry some girl who had been carefully chosen for him. Someone with all the right political connections, who would bring honour to his house. 'Please,' he begged, 'please, Simon, tell me that this is some kind of elaborate wind-up.'

'Why on earth would I do that to you?'

Because of Rose… Hassan dragged his hands over his face. 'No reason. I was just clutching at straws. What on earth are we going to do with her?'

'Give her a large patch of desert to play with?' he suggested. 'She's got some tremendous ideas. Apparently Faisal met her when he went to visit that hydroponics station you asked him to look at.'

'You mean this is all my fault?'

'No, sir. Faisal isn't a boy any more. He's a man. And he has some very firm ideas about what he wants. I suggested the jeans would not meet with your approval. He told me, very politely, to mind my own business.'

CHAPTER TEN

FAISAL and his bride had been taken to the fort and were both waiting for Hassan in his private drawing room. That alone broke all the rules of social etiquette, but Faisal was completely unfazed. 'Bonnie, this is my big brother, Hassan. He growls, but he doesn't bite. At least not unless seriously provoked.'

'Then, honey, you'd better get out the Band-Aid, because I'd say you've just done a gold medal job of provoking him.' Bonnie, showered and changed from her jeans into a pair of even more disreputable cut-offs, grinned amiably and offered him her hand. 'I'm Bonnie Hart. I'm sorry to confront you with a *fait accompli*, but Faisal said if I wanted him I'd better make up my mind fast, because once you got him home and tucked up in your palace it would be too late.'

Hassan knew when to accept that something was beyond mending and smiled graciously. 'My brother was teasing you. As Emir, as he well knows, he can do whatever he wishes. You are most welcome to Ras al Hajar, Your Highness.'

'Your Highness? Please! I'm an American. We had a revolution to put a stop to that kind of stuff—'

'Bonnie, sweetheart, why don't you take a nap while I catch up on things with Hassan? You'll want to look your best when company comes calling.'

'And it will come calling,' Hassan assured her. 'When Princess Aisha hears the news—'

'Aisha? We spoke on the phone from London,' Bonnie said, 'and I can't wait to meet her. And Nadeem and Leila. Gorgeous names.'

Was he the only one not in on this particular secret? Was he such a monster that his entire family had conspired to keep this from him? Did they think he wouldn't understand? Five days ago they might have been right. 'If you like their names so much, perhaps you'd like them to help you choose something as your own official name before you're introduced to your people.'

She glanced at Faisal. 'Er, I don't know about that—'

'Not now, honey. Hassan is busting his breeches to give me hell, but he can't do that with a lady present.'

She laughed. 'Sure. I know when I'm not wanted. Simon, why don't you show me around?'

'Would you mind, Simon?' Faisal asked.

'For heaven's sake, Faisal, she's your wife,' Hassan protested as their laughter echoed down the hall. 'She can't go running around with her legs on show to the world like that.'

'You think it'll give the old boys heart failure?'

'Not just the old ones.'

'Aren't they great, though? Tell me, Hassan, how were Miss Fenton's legs? You didn't waste much time getting them all covered up, I notice.'

Hassan gritted his teeth. 'Rose Fenton wears whatever she chooses, but she has a fine grasp of what is acceptable. And now I really have to insist that you change into something more suitable for the *majlis*. It will be crowded this evening.' Every man of substance in Ras al Hajar would be coming to give respect to their new ruler. No one would want to be seen as wavering.

'I want you to take the *majlis* in my place this evening, Hassan.'

'The hand-over is a dangerous time, Faisal. It's not a good idea to confuse people.'

'I'm not confusing anyone. You are going to take the *majlis* because I am going to make a television broadcast.'

'Are you? When did you arrange that?'

'During the lay-over in London. I spoke to Nadeem and she said she'd set up a network link with Miss Fenton.'

Hassan refused to acknowledge yet another mention of Rose Fenton, certain that it was nothing but a ploy to distract him. Actually, it was doing a fair job, but he persisted.

'I see. And what do you intend to say?'

'Maybe you'd like to give me some help with that. How do you see the country moving forward, Hassan? What would you like to change?'

Hassan was surprised. He'd scarcely dared to hope that Faisal would be so swift to grasp the reins. 'You really want to know?'

'Of course. I want to know what you all think. I know what Nadeem wants, and Bonnie has some great ideas, too. I want to tell the people, Hassan, I want the people to know that they have a Head of State who cares about them more than himself.'

'Actually, that's not a bad idea. Once they've seen

you on television no one will have any doubt about who's Emir.'

'That's my intention.'

And once that was settled, Hassan decided, he would get Nadeem to sort out the bare-legged revolutionary princess, put her right about palace etiquette. It was the least she could do, having kept Faisal's marriage from him. 'I did begin to wonder if you were having doubts about this, Faisal. You've stayed away longer than you should. It gave Abdullah ideas—'

'Why would I have any doubts, big brother?' Faisal grinned. 'Now I'm Emir I don't have to put up with you giving me a hard time about a thing. Not even my choice of wife.'

'Your wife is your problem. As for the rest, don't count on it.'

Hassan paced the palace audience room, running over the radical plans they had made, wondering whether it would cause outrage or rejoicing.

Nadeem and her husband had been full of ideas for improving medical services, particularly for women and children. Leila had been unexpectedly forthright on the subject of compulsory education for girls. A study to consider the development of hydroponic farming had been Bonnie's contribution. Well, there was no shortage of water from the mountains; it made sense, although what people would make of a princess who farmed on water was anyone's guess.

How he'd wished Rose could have been there. She had so much to offer... He checked himself. There was nothing to be gained from dwelling on something that could never be, and he picked up the remote and turned up the sound on the television.

Faisal was wearing traditional robes, yet he still managed to look like an American football player. In the last year he'd put on muscle, mental as well as physical. He'd become a man and Hassan was proud of him.

Faisal began as they had planned, by thanking his cousin Abdullah for his careful stewardship of the country. He then promised that he would always put the good of the country first. This was followed by his plans for Ras al Hajar, his strategy for making it into an outward-looking country in which women would play their full part.

'I have tonight,' he concluded, 'signed the statutes for a new government department so that there is no delay in setting these plans in motion. You will hear more about this in the coming days and weeks, but I will tell you now that this department will be run for women, by a woman.'

Hassan frowned. Statute? They'd discussed the idea of a department for women's affairs, but hadn't settled anything, let alone who would run it. This wasn't in the final draft of the address they had agreed.

He turned as Simon Partridge joined him. 'What is this?' he demanded. 'What's Faisal doing?'

Rose, standing to one side of the studio watching the subtitles as Faisal's words were translated into English, was approached by a royal messenger who handed her a thick envelope with the royal seal.

She continued to watch the monitor as she broke the

seal, pulled out the thick document. Then she glanced away to read the short letter that accompanied it.

Dear Miss Fenton,
My mother and sister both believe you will be a shining addition to our country. Hassan will need you. Please stay.

Faisal.

Gordon was standing beside her. 'What's that?' he whispered, when she opened the accompanying document.

She opened her mouth, then closed it and shook her head, tucking the letter and contract away as quickly as her shaking hands would let her. 'I'll tell you later. What's happening?'

'He's winding up. Are you ready for the close to London?'

'Many years ago, when he knew he was dying, my grandfather chose me as his successor.' Rose watched the words scrolling, then glanced at the envelope in her hand and had a flash of premonition.

'Oh…'

'What?'

She pressed her fingers to her mouth and shook her head.

'I knew, everyone knew, that I was not his first choice. Political necessity is, however, a hard task master.

'I have been Emir for one day, and in that day, with the help of my family, I have taken enormous pleasure in moving this country forward into a new era. I will continue to do that throughout my life, not as your Emir, however, but as his most faithful servant and subject...'

Hassan stared at his aide. 'You knew he was going to do this?'

'He swore me to silence.'

'You are my aide.'

'Yes, Excellency. But Faisal is Emir, or he is until midnight.'

'I won't let him do this, Simon.'

'Well, I'm sure Abdullah would be more than happy to resume his place, if you allow it.' Simon Partridge turned to the television as Faisal concluded his address.

'From midnight tonight I freely and gladly surrender all my claims to the throne of Ras al Hajar and pass that heavy burden to my grandfather's rightful heir and successor, his first grandson, my brother, Hassan.

'At the summit there is only room for one. It is a lonely place, and it gives me much pleasure to tell you that my last act as Emir will be to sign a contract of marriage for Prince Hassan. I wish every happiness to him and his chosen princess, along with my vow and pledge to support and honour him as Emir of Ras al Hajar.'

He was trapped. The *majlis* was mobbed. Apparently there wasn't a man in the country who didn't want to make his obeisance to his new lord.

Faisal had been so clever. Arriving in jeans and T-shirt and trailing a foreign wife. Even the waverers were glad to cleave to the tradition that Hassan had always honoured.

What would they do if they knew that while he was sitting there, acknowledging his friends and his enemies alike, forcing himself to put names to dimly remembered faces, he was acknowledging that his young brother had more courage in his little finger than he had shown? That all he wanted to do was find Rose and tell her...tell her...that he loved her and beg her to stay.

It was after one o'clock before it was over, but he headed straight for the phone. 'Tim Fenton.' The voice sounded heavy with sleep. 'Is it the foal?'

'No. It's Hassan. I have to speak to Rose. Now.'

'Well, you can't.' Fenton sounded thoroughly smug about that. 'She's not here.'

'Where is she? She can't have left already—'

'I don't think her whereabouts is any of your business, Your Highness. And by the way, I resign.' He hung up.

An hour earlier his fortress had been thronged with people; suddenly it was empty but for servants, guards. Faisal had taken Bonnie to stay with Aisha before the broadcast. Now he understood why.

Nadeem...well, he'd told his sister to arrange a wedding and waste no time doing it. No doubt tomorrow she would make a formal call to tell him who she had chosen as his bride, inform him of the settlements, the wedding arrangements. Tomorrow would be soon enough. He was in no particular hurry to find out.

Rose spent a day with the kind of pampering she had only ever dreamed of. A top-to-toe grooming, a massage with essential oils, her hands painted with exquisite arabesques, first in orange henna, then in black, which Nadeem told her lasted much longer.

Pam Fenton was in her element too, watching, taking notes. 'Darling, you really are the most wonderful daughter. An absolute inspiration. First you marry a man old enough to be your father and give me enough material for a book. Now this.'

Rose, watching the progress of the delicate hand painting, didn't even turn her head. 'What is it about *this* that particularly pleases you?'

'Modern woman with a have-it-all career gives it all up to live in a harem.'

'Write a book that portrays me like that and I'll sue you.'

'Really? That'll be so good for sales.'

'It's not true, Mother. Nadeem lives a full and active professional life, as you well know. And I am going to be running a new government department set up to improve the lot of women; Abdullah never did anything for them. Why don't you stick around and study that? Help out, even?'

'Oh, please, darling. You don't even speak the language. And you'll be knee-deep in babies before you're much older.'

'I already speak French, German and Spanish, and my Arabic is coming along in leaps and bounds.'

'And babies?'

'They never slowed you down.'

'That's true. Actually, that would make an even better book...'

*   *   *

'*Rose Fenton!* Rose Fenton is going to run the new government department?' Hassan's heart was threatening to explode.

'Can you think of anyone more suitable?' Not in a million years. But that wasn't the point; surely the boy could see that? When he didn't immediately answer, Faisal shrugged. 'Of course you can't. She's the perfect choice, Hassan. She understands the media, knows how to communicate with people. I'm amazed at how quickly she's picking up the language.' He hesitated. 'Well, maybe not that amazed. When you have one-to-one tuition… You think it will be awkward for you, is that it?'

Awkward? What rubbish was the boy talking? He loved her. To see her, know she was near, that he could never touch her, never hold her. Awkward he could handle. This wasn't awkward; this was his worst nightmare.

'How long is her contract?'

'A year. I thought she would need that long to get the department up and running, sort out the priorities. After that, well, maybe she won't want to stay. Unless you can think of some way to persuade her?'

'Faisal—'

'Yes, Your Highness?' His innocent tone cut no ice with Hassan.

'I think perhaps you'd better go. Take your pretty wife and disappear for a year or two. By then I might have got over this compelling desire I have to wring your neck.'

'I give you a crown, a bride and a media queen all

in one day and this is all the thanks I get,' he retorted in disgust. 'Some people are impossible to please.'

'Go!'

Faisal raised his hands in surrender. 'I'm out of here,' he said, backing to the door. 'I'll, um, see you at the wedding.'

Hassan rose to his feet. 'There will be no wedding…' The words erupted from somewhere deep within him. 'There will be no wedding.' Whatever it took, he would stop it. If he could not have Rose, he would have no one. No one.

Nadeem stood back and smiled. 'Stunning. You look absolutely stunning. Don't you think so, Pam?'

'I wouldn't know. I can't see her.'

'Well, it wouldn't be right for Hassan to see her before they're betrothed. The clothing and jewels are enough to indicate that the girl beneath them is a suitable bride for an Emir.' She turned away as she heard a movement beyond the hangings that divided the room. 'He's arrived,' she whispered. 'Quickly, slip out this way, Pam.'

Hassan waited impatiently for his sister. He'd come to put a stop to this nonsense, whatever it cost. How on earth could the pair of them have plotted and planned and then landed him in a situation where to reject the bride they had chosen would cause more offence and bad feeling—?

'Nadeem.' He turned and crossed swiftly to his sister as she slipped through the heavy drapes.

'Hassan.' She took his hands. 'I'm glad to see you so eager. We're ready for you.'

'No. I'm sorry, but I came to tell you that I can't do this. There is no way I can go through with this marriage.'

'I don't understand. You asked me to arrange it without delay.' She looked deeply shocked. 'The contracts are signed.'

'Faisal overstepped himself.'

'He was thinking of you, Hassan. During this last week we have all been thinking of you.'

'I know.' He could not look her in the face. 'I know. This is my mistake, and mine alone, but I have a prior call on my honour. One that can never be expunged other than by marriage.'

'Rose?' she asked. 'You mean Rose?'

'Of course I mean Rose. Who else could there be?'

'But you assured me that you would deal with that—'

'I thought I could. I thought I had. I was mistaken.'

'Hassan, I have seen enough of Rose to be sure she would not bind you in any way that was disagreeable to you. Would you like me to speak to her?'

'*No.*' Then, more gently, 'No. It would make no difference. Whatever her answer, I will never be free. You see, I find that I cannot live without her.'

'You are in love with her, then?'

'She is…' He clenched his fist, laid it against his heart. 'Inside of me.'

Nadeem's smile was gentle as she took his hand and held it between hers. 'I understand, Hassan. And so will the girl who is waiting for you. You must explain your feelings, open your heart—'

'Nadeem, please—'

'She will understand; I promise you.'

'But—'

'Trust me.' Then, with the sweetest of smiles, 'I'm a doctor.' And, still holding his hand, she drew back the curtain for him. Behind it, in the centre of the room, stood a tall, slender young woman in a floor-length gown of vivid red silk thickly embroidered in gold thread. About her waist was a belt made from heavy gold mesh. Over her head was a veil so dense that he could see nothing of her features, or her expression.

He realised, too late, that he did not even know her name, and he half turned, but behind him the curtain had closed.

From beneath the veil, Rose watched him. She had not been happy about Nadeem's plan. There was no way she could marry Hassan without him knowing who she was. There was no way she would marry a man who would contemplate such a match.

But she need not have worried. Nadeem understood her brother better than he understood himself. She had known that he could never go through with such a marriage. And now he stood before her with instructions to open his heart, confess his love for another woman.

But his pain was heart-rending. She could put him through no more of it. She had heard enough, and she extended her hand to him. *'Sidi,'* she said softly.

Her hands were painted; she was dressed as his bride. How could he possibly begin to explain…?

'Lord,' she said again, in English, and something jarred deep inside him.

He took a step towards her. 'Who are you?'

'You know me, lord.'

'Rose…' He couldn't believe, didn't believe it. But her hand came into his like a sweet memory. 'You once said that if a man was fortunate enough to have you, you would make it your life's work to ensure that he wanted no other—'

'I meant it.'

'It didn't take a lifetime…' He lifted the veil. 'I love you. You are my life. Stay with me, Rose. Always. Live with me, bear my children, be my wife and my princess.'

Had he changed? Could he change? 'You want me to stay at home and raise your sons, Hassan?'

His hands went for her waist and he pulled her closer, his expression deadly serious. 'That sounds good to me.' She stiffened in his arms, but he was learning to tease a little. 'Do you think you could fit that in with your busy new career running a new government department?'

'You know about that?'

'Faisal confessed what he'd done about half an hour ago.'

'And you wouldn't mind?'

He minded. He didn't want her out of his sight for a minute. But if that was the price of keeping her, he would learn to live with it. 'You've got a contract signed by the Emir of Ras al Hajar. Who am I to argue with that?'

'And if I have to travel abroad, go to conferences—?'

'I'll hate it,' he admitted. 'But I love you, Rose…

I'll have you or no one. On any terms. The question is, my love, will you have me?'

'You have a contract signed by the Emir of Ras al Hajar,' Rose replied, lifting her hand to his face, touching her lips to his. 'Our destiny is written, Hassan, and who am I to argue with destiny?'

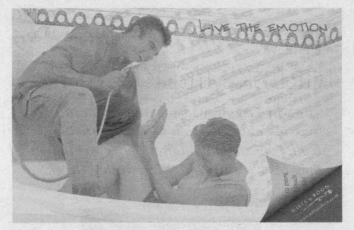

Modern Romance™
...international affairs – seduction and passion guaranteed

Medical Romance™
...pulse-raising romance – heart-racing medical drama

Tender Romance™
...sparkling, emotional, feel-good romance

Sensual Romance™
...teasing, tempting, provocatively playful

Historical Romance™
...rich, vivid and passionate

Blaze Romance™
...scorching hot sexy reads

27 new titles every month.

Live the emotion

MILLS & BOON®

Next month don't miss –

GREEK MILLIONAIRES

Be whisked away to a country of luxury, passion and seduction with three striking Mediterranean millionaires! They're tanned, they're rich and they're irresistibly Greek!

On sale 2nd July 2004

Available at most branches of WHSmith, Tesco, Martins, Borders, Eason, Sainsbury's and all good paperback bookshops.

0604/05

MILLS & BOON

Red-hot AUSTRALIANS

Sizzlingly sexy, seriously rich – these men are the best lovers in Sydney!

miranda Lee

On sale 2nd July 2004

Available at most branches of WHSmith, Tesco, Martins, Borders, Eason, Sainsbury's and all good paperback bookshops.